THE THIRTEEN TRIBES OF CAIN SERIES

Book Two

The Offspring

R.J. Craddock

Transcendent Books
Springville, UT

Copyright © 2014 R.J. CRADDOCK
Transcendent Books, Springville UT.
Manufactured in the United States of America
All rights reserved, including the right of reproduction in whole or in part in any form.

Third Edition, April 2016
Also available in eBook form.

Follow R.J. Craddock on Facebook and Twitter for all news and events
www.rjcraddock.com

Summary: A murder behind her and the wilderness before her, friendless Witch Gwenevere flees to survive. Yet Mother Nature is not kind and even Gwen's magical gifts cannot save her from a deadly winter storm. Narrowly escaping death, she is rescued by an unlikely hero and taken into the shelter of a mythical realm. Has Gwen at long last found her own kind? Will she finally solve the mystery to her own identity, or her mother's murder? Or is innocence blinding her to the true reality of this dark sanctuary?

Cover design and illustrations by R.J. Craddock. Cover illustration copyright © 2014 by R.J. Craddock

ISBN-13: 978-0615994666 (Transcendent Books)

THE THIRTEEN TRIBES OF CAIN SERIES

The Forsaken

The Offspring

The Decree.....*Coming 2016*

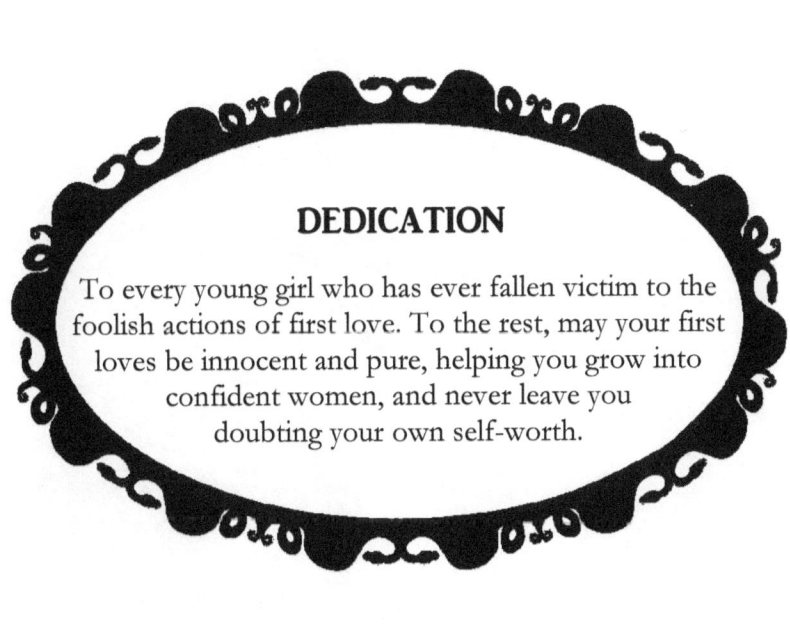

DEDICATION

To every young girl who has ever fallen victim to the foolish actions of first love. To the rest, may your first loves be innocent and pure, helping you grow into confident women, and never leave you doubting your own self-worth.

The Offspring

R.J. Craddock

CONTENTS

Prologue

*T*he crowd made it difficult for her to see the two magicians as they battled for the throne of Wicca. She couldn't risk being seen, so she stayed back a foot or two from the edge of the crowd. She had as much right to be in attendance as anyone else, if not more. After all, her future happiness relied heavily on the outcome of this duel. Still, she didn't want to raise any suspicion later, so the lady tried to blend into the jeering crowd, the hood of her plain black cape drawn low to cover her face. An invisible shield separated the spectators from the duel taking place on the battlegrounds, stopping anyone from interfering with the challengers as well as protecting the audience from being harmed in the magical crossfire.

They are equally attractive, she thought. Both men in their early twenties bore muscular builds, and both were handsome and intimidating. The one who wore black was slightly taller. His green eyes blazed with fury and frustration as he quickly blocked another ball of fire aimed at his chest with a counter-spell. Onan's fiery-red hair, tousled and matted with blood, kept falling into his eyes, his black headscarf lost some time ago during the feud.

His opponent, Deverick Hawthorne—the rightful heir to the throne—was clad all in white. Looking as calm and unstoppable as a warm morning sunrise, Deverick advanced on his so-called friend, hurtling a barrage of magical missiles from his fingertips while simultaneously blocking Onan's defensive strikes. Clearly Deverick had the upper hand. His black curly locks were slightly damp with sweat. She noticed earlier that his bare feet were cracked and bleeding, but otherwise he was unscathed.

Onan ducked and rolled away from Deverick to block an orb of fire. It hit the ground where he had stood with a boom, leaving a gaping hole in the smoldering earth. The crowd both cheered and cursed in response.

Springing back to his feet, Onan shouted an enchantment and flung out one hand toward his friend who was still advancing. Suddenly a bolt of lightning shot from his palm, a white streak of light more blinding than the noon sun. The spectators cried out, many diverting their eyes from the glare.

Nonplused, Deverick glided sideways, the bolt missing him by half a foot. He seemed unaffected by the light, his gaze never leaving his opponent's frantic visage.

Even though Onan was outmatched, he impressively held up against the stronger Warlock for nearly two hours. The lady feared it may only be a matter of time before exhaustion caused him to let down his guard. In that moment he would die, his chance at being King lost along with his very life.

She gasped as the ground behind the redheaded man moved as if alive. The dirt turned and rolled into a large mound. He unknowingly walked backward toward it. Deverick sent out a gust of wind and an orb of light at once, the spells igniting from his outstretched palms. Forced to move backward, Onan's foot caught in the enchanted dirt beneath him. The animated soil began to climb up his body, engulfing him.

Trapped, Onan could not move away from the magical projectiles headed toward him. Crying out in defiance, he put all his strength into one last spell. With arms outstretched and palms shaped like a fan, he braced himself for impact. When Deverick's magic hit him, it suddenly absorbed into his palms, his skin glowing white hot. Onan's face contorted with strain, struggling to control the power, and then the light burst forth from his hands, shooting back to the man who made it.

Onan laughed triumphantly just before the ground covered his chest and arms, leaving only his head in view. He watched with wide-eyed anticipation as his last defense struck Deverick square in the chest.

His opponent screamed in agony as the light and the wind pushed through him, as if the sheer force of it might tear him apart. Deverick lurched and then doubled over, falling to his knees, his head dropping to touch the ground. His body shuddered. His breaths seemed labored. Tension hung around the battleground as thick and oppressive as a humid fog. Suddenly the lady wished she could forgo the heavy cloak to escape the dread pressing down upon her. The audience around her seemed to feel as she did, yet no one dared move.

The captain of the guards, who stood by watching over the proceedings, seemed rapt by Deverick's prostrate form.

Don't just stand there, you fool! the lady thought. *Check and see if he's dead!* She willed the captain to move, Deverick to collapse, or for anything to happen. The silent anticipation was killing her.

When she heard the rumble of laughter, she and many other spectators jumped, letting out cries of alarm. When Deverick coolly raised his head, the lady thought for a moment that his blue-gold eyes looked directly at her. The lady felt her spine turn to ice. Her breath caught in her chest.

Please, Lord of the Night, do not let him recognize me! she silently prayed. Thankfully, his gaze passed her, resting on Onan's bewildered face amongst his dirt mound prison.

Deverick smiled arrogantly as he effortlessly rose to his feet. With his hands in his pockets, the heir of Wicca strolled across the battleground to stand before his childhood friend. The crowd remained silent and still.

"Onan, you are aware that it is my right to kill you now?" he asked calmly.

Onan nodded his head in a small gesture, unable to move any more than that.

"Then before I do, tell me one thing."

"I owe you nothing." Onan spat the words.

"You owe me a reason." Deverick's face and voice became dark. "A good reason for this treachery!"

Onan looked away from his friend's eyes, as if searching for the answer at Deverick's feet. For a long time he said nothing. The lady's feet felt like heavy stones anchoring her to the spot as her cool, collected side screamed at her to run for it while she still could.

He will not betray me, she told herself, trying to calm her nerves. *He is too devoted to me. I am his master, his obsession. He loves me enough even to die for me!* The words in her head were very convincing, but still she always had a sliver of doubt about her servant. Several weeks ago, she had slipped into Onan's home while he slept. For her own protection, she placed an untraceable spell of death upon him. If the defeated Warlock spoke against her or their secret plot, it would trigger the curse, killing him instantly. Finally, Onan raised his head to meet Deverick's eyes. He opened his mouth as if to answer but then faltered, his eyes averting to the ground again. "Just kill me." He whispered the words, barely audible.

Every soul seemed unable to speak or move as they waited for Deverick to deal the killing spell.

"No, I won't." Deverick breathed out the words as if a sigh, his arrogance gone. "We all make mistakes. I never expected this of you, but still I cannot find it in me to hate you. I don't think I ever will."

"What do you mean?" Onan looked up at him in utter amazement. "I am defeated. You must kill me! It is the way it has always been!" His voice raised an octave.

"As the victor, I reclaim my right as heir. I will be King, and as King I have power to make a few changes to tradition if I wish."

Deverick paused. "While I can't abide you as my enemy, an example must be made."

Onan stiffened as Deverick withdrew a hand from his pockets and placed it on Onan's forehead.

Muttering under his breath so that only Onan could hear his words, Deverick placed a spell upon his friend's mind. When the heir finished his incantation, Onan's eyes opened wide in dismay.

The lady watched in scarcely concealed anxiety as the captain of the guard, Tate Mellanor, approached the two men.

"My Lord, what should be done? If not death, then how should we punish this traitor?" Captain Mellanor placed his hand over his heart, three fingers extended. The lady in black recognized it as a signal of respect, a salute one only made to the King.

"Nothing," Deverick answered, and then turned away from the captain to address the crowd. "I will not kill this man, but have instead placed an allegiance spell upon him. From hence forth, Onan cannot cast a spell against me or harm me physically. He cannot poison me or do anything knowingly that will cause me harm. Neither can he harm any of my kin. Thus, this man is no threat to me or my house and needn't be banished or imprisoned. He may go free and live unharassed. This is my decree. Upon my coronation, I will make it law."

Once he was done speaking, Deverick turned his back on Onan and the crowd. Although battered and bleeding, he moved effortlessly and with purpose toward his mother and their royal advisers. A moment later he was whisked back into the palace.

The lady waited till he was out of sight before she, too, like the rest of the crowd, filed out of the battlegrounds. Passing under the grand, white, stoned archway, they found themselves on the main road of the Wiccan capital.

The white cobblestone streets teemed with citizens about their daily fare. No one so much as glanced her way. Effortlessly, she weaved through the throng of bodies and veered off the busy street into a dark side alley. Before her, the alley came to a dead end. She walked on without hesitation, speaking silent words of magic as she approached the dirty brick wall. One moment a brick wall stood before her, and the next she walked through it as if it were made of water.

Emerging on the other side, she found herself stepping out of a massive sycamore tree. She stood on a hill top that overlooked the kingdom. However, she wasn't in the mood to admire the view. Immediately she turned and walked up a winding path of black stones that led toward her family home.

Rosenblaze Manor was an impressive mansion grown out of the Earth itself. Although it did not resemble a Fairy's mound or look like a bit of the forest, it was elegantly tinted to a brilliant shade of purple, dark yet exotic. The bark and stones that made up the mansion's exterior walls were broken up by ornate fossilized ivy windows inlaid with natural-colored glass.

The hooded woman climbed the black stone steps up to the front door that looked like one giant granite slab. As she stepped before it, the granite door split in half, opening automatically before her. She entered, moving briskly through the elegant foyer, all white ivory stone and green mossy tiles, to the servant kitchen toward the back of the house. Behind her the front doors closed as silently as they had opened.

The servant's kitchen was a large room with aspen tree trunks for walls, black slate flooring, and white granite countertops with gray stone cabinets. A massive hearth sat in the center of one wall filled with the blaze of an enchanted fire. By the back door, a line of hooks and cubbies for the servants kept their outdoor clothing.

Walking over to an empty hook on the wall, the lady removed her hood and disrobed the awful cloak she had borrowed. Quickly, she slipped off the maid's plain wooden shoes and nudged them into their cubby below. As she turned to leave, she caught sight of her reflection in the glass of the back door leading out into the garden.

Staring back at her was a young woman in her early twenties with wavy platinum blonde hair, fair immaculate skin, and calculating violet eyes. All her life she had been known as a great beauty, but never as a kind or generous soul. She knew what people said behind her back.

It doesn't matter what any of those fools think of me, she reminded herself as she quickly combed her fingers through her hair. *But, curse it! All my work destroyed! Countless hours wasted on that red-headed oaf. For what? Because of Hawthorne's spell, Onan is now completely useless to me!*

She took a deep breath to steady herself. Looking back at her reflection, she squared her shoulders and raised her chin confidently.

Never fear. So my lover failed to gain the crown. There are other ways to get myself a throne. At least that fool can't speak against me. She smiled to herself wickedly.

She heard someone walking across the room above her. Quickly, she turned back toward the hearth, walking into the hot fire with a spell on her lips. A moment later she disappeared into the flames.

With a puff of smoke she appeared in front of a door on the second floor. Stepping toward it, the door opened for her, letting her into her mother's study.

The lady of the house was not at her desk, which sat before a large window overlooking the hillside and the kingdom below. Instead she found the older woman standing before a basin full of water resting on a tall dresser. Vials of different potions and herbs lined the table, with drawers upon drawers of enchanted items stored below. Her mother, a woman in her forties, dressed in a spider-silk gown tinted a blue-gray with sandy blonde hair done up in a bun, stood hunched over the basin.

"Are you sure?" She spoke earnestly into the ceramic bowl.

"Yes! The heir won the challenge." A familiar female voice spoke out of the rippling water in reply.

"And he didn't kill the traitor?" her mother replied, astonished. "I can't believe it!"

"It's true, Mother."

Startled, the older woman whirled around to look at her daughter. "Curse it, child, you scared me! Don't go sneaking around like that. I've told you how much I hate it," she chided.

"Sorry, Mum, but it's true what Aunt Matilda says."

"You went to the battlegrounds? Are you mad?" her mother demanded.

"Not at all. I wanted to see for myself who came out victorious."

"Why?" her mother asked, a slow smile creeping at the corner of her gray lips.

"You know why." The young lady paused a moment. "Because... I will be his Queen."

CHAPTER ONE

Leap of Faith

She can't remember how she got here. All at once, she finds herself wandering through a monstrous cave with hundreds of corridors and passageways. The only light comes from the dim glow of the lanterns carved into the rock along the walls, casting eerie shadows across her path. The dull, hollow echo of her footsteps bounces off the walls, on and on before her along the unseen tunnels beyond. She shivers as a cold, acrid chill permeates from the dark stone walls and floors, penetrating her slender frame. She feels the daunting sensation of being trapped in a never-ending maze, deep in the ground, as if buried alive. Panic grips her, caressing with icy fingers down her spine.

Her instincts tell her to turn back, to get out as fast as she can, yet something compels her forward, as though someone or something has summoned her, but as to why, she cannot fathom.

She continues walking on, even when the corridors become smaller, and the walls begin to close in on her. The panic of claustrophobia creeps into her flesh, tempting her to turn back.

"What was that?" She stops to listen. A muffled sound of someone crying and whimpering comes from beyond the bend. The voice seems eerily familiar to her. Alarmed, she hurries around the corner, following the faint crying down a long, steep stairway heading into the depths of the cave-like fortress. The stairs, carved out of the rock, end abruptly, leading into a small, dimly-lit chamber which stands empty except for a hole in the floor on the far end.

"Is somebody there?" she calls out. Fearing a trap she hesitates by the entry, ready to bolt back up the stairs at the first sign of danger.

"Help me!" a small trembling voice answers. Timidly, she follows the sound of the voice to the dark hole in the cave floor. Kneeling down, she looks inside. Below her, a pit drops straight down into pitch blackness. She can hear water trickling down the sides of the walls and dripping into a body of water somewhere down below, but she can see nothing.

"Who's down there?" She leans closer to the edge, waiting for the mysterious voice to reply.

"You better leave. He's coming!" The voice sounds far away, as if the pit is very deep. The woman starts to sob, the sound echoing off the walls of her prison. "It's too late!" the woman cries out.

"Who's com—" she starts to ask when she hears a sound in the chamber behind her. It starts as a whisper, like someone breathing softly, but as it grows in volume and proximity it becomes a hiss in her ear.

A jolt of fear shoots up her spine as the sound comes closer, creeping up on her. She wants to run, to turn and flee, but she is paralyzed by fear. She hears a crunching of rocks just behind her. Holding her breath, she slowly stands up but does not turn around.

"Who's there?" she asks aloud, her voice shaking.

She hears the creature mere inches from her ear as a cold, metallic breath touches her neck with a bone-shivering chill. A hand grasps her by the throat. Her wind pipe squeezes shut; she desperately gasps for air. Her hands fly up to claw at the icy hand choking her, but the stranger is too strong, his iron grip impenetrable.

She tries to call out for help. Her voice comes out as nothing more than a scratchy, whizzing croak. She begins to panic, thrashing wildly in an attempt to shake off her attacker.

"You're so weak and pathetic," a voice deep and terrifying laughs in her ear. Her vision blurs as the room begins to spin about her. Suddenly her captor releases her.

Wheezing and coughing, she collapses to the floor, sucking in sweet air as she fights off a wave of nausea. The same cold hand takes her by the chin and hauls her to her feet, forcing her to look into his eyes. She sees a pale, malicious face, gaunt, and strikingly angular. His eyes, deeply set into what should be a handsome face,

are a piercing whitish-silver, which seem to bore holes into her soul. His white skin is as lifeless as a corpse. His wavy hair, eyebrows, and eyelashes are platinum blond, adding to his overall ashen appearance. He towers above her, thin as a rail, with broad, bony shoulders. Somehow she knows from looking into this stranger's eyes that he truly is a man of white with a heart as black as the pits of hell. He gives her a taunting smile.

She sickens at the sight of dried blood clinging to his white teeth and razor-sharp fangs. As he laughs, fresh blood oozes out from between his teeth and drips like molasses from his lips and down his chin.

He reaches his bony hand toward her again, beckoning to her. Revolted, she shrinks back from his grasp. He steps toward her, bringing her to the edge of the pit's opening. Without a word, he grabs her by the shoulders, his long fingernails digging into her skin. Giving her a mockingly sweet smile, he thrusts her violently away. Startled and frantic, she tries to hold onto him to keep from falling. Laughing, he steps back out of her reach. She stumbles helplessly backwards and over the edge.

Her screams echo off the walls of the rock chasm as she plummets into the black abyss below. Everything grows darker around her as the dim light from the chamber above fades until she is engulfed in complete darkness. She hits the pit's watery bottom with the force of a brick wall, pain shooting through her body as bitter, cold spring water engulfs her. Liquid chokes her lungs. Frantically, she tries to swim to the surface, but something pulls her downward, deeper and deeper into a dark oblivion.

* * * * *

With a lung-deep gasp, Gwen awakens, panting. Her heart beats violently in her chest as if trying to pound its way out. She scans the barren forest around her, seeing her little camp beneath the bough of a large pine tree. The early morning sun will soon begin to rise over the mountains in the east. She hears the nearby hoot of an owl returning home from the night's hunt.

"Just another stupid dream," Gwen says aloud. With an exhausted sigh, she falls back into her bedroll to stare up into the branches of the pine tree above her.

It is late December. Christmas has come and gone with little comfort or joy for Gwen. The mountains are deadly cold and the wind blows stronger in the forest than in the city, adding its chill to the snow-covered landscape. Everything around her is dead or hibernating, leaving her very little to eat. It's difficult to find dry kindling for her campfires. To her dismay, even magic fire needs the right conditions to flourish and grow into a blaze. Hunting is fruitless for game is scarce, not that she's ever been much of a huntress. In the past, the rare times they were desperate for food, Raven had always done the hunting and she the skinning and the cooking.

"No matter," Gwen reminds herself. "No fire to roast my kills." Raven might have been able to stomach raw meat, but she is

not that desperate yet.

Gwen hauls herself out of bed and breaks camp. After her belongings are all packed up and her bedroll on her back, Gwen breakfasts on some old bread and cheese, scraping off the moldy parts to make the last of her provisions more edible. Breakfast done, she heads into the forest as the sun rises in the morning sky.

She whistles as she wanders. The eerie sound holds off the sense of loneliness that hangs about the white forest.

I'll hide out here a couple more weeks, Gwen tells herself. *What then, Gwen? Where can you go? You don't know where Raven is. Mrs. Fairbanks is the only one who can tell you that,* she reminds herself. *She's a social worker. If you go to her she'll turn you into the cops without a second thought. Then who knows what they'll do to you.*

"*Then kill her, too!*" a voice seems to whisper on the wind.

Abruptly Gwen stops whistling and spins to look frantically about the forest. Nothing and no one is there. Everything, even the wind, is still. Gwen swallows hard before she slowly turns and continues walking. She no longer feels like whistling, so she trudges through the snow silently. Half afraid to look up for fear she'll she the man in black hiding in the trees, she keeps her eyes focused on her boots as they imprint the freshly fallen snow before her.

She reasons with herself again. *What am I going to do? I can't hide in the woods forever. Maybe I should just turn myself in. If I just explain what he tried to do to me, maybe they'll understand? I*

am a minor, after all. Maybe I'll go to juvie, or maybe they won't do anything to me at all. They might just let me go to another foster home.

"There is no way to explain what you did"! the same cold voice seems to say as a chilling breeze rustles through her long black hair. *"You squeezed the life out of a man. They'll never understand that! They'll never let you live."* Gwen doesn't look around for the source of the voice this time. She continues walking, staring at her own feet.

"Marianne!"

Gwen spins around, eyes wide, heart racing wildly. She scans the forest behind her. After a moment she sees the shapes of people emerge from amongst the trees, too far away to distinguish any faces. One of the shapes calls out into the still of the morning, the sound echoing off of the mountains. "Marianne!"

Instinctively Gwen jumps into the tree above her, scraping her left cheek on some pine needles as she catches the lowest branch and scurries farther up the tree. Perched on a high limb of the evergreen tree, the pine needles cloak her from view to those below. Between a couple branches, Gwen has a clear view of the ground. She brushes her hand across her cheek. Her fingertips come away with blood on them. Gwen curses under her breath and then falls silent, waiting.

It isn't long before the search team passes her tree. Gwen holds her breath as they continue to call out her "name," some of the voices familiar to her ears. She stays still as someone stops just

under her hiding place.

It is a police officer, a graying man in his late fifties. His uniform and badge are visible under his black winter coat. He wears a woolen cap with ear flaps on his head. He peers down at the ground at something with great interest.

"I found some footprints over here!" the man calls out. "Johansen, get over here and take look at this!"

Gwen hears the crunch of several feet in the snow. More personages appear in her view, examining the snow just feet from her tree. One of them is a woman, wearing a dark winter coat and snow pants, her head covered with a brightly striped wool cap. Her dark hair hangs out beneath, her nose and cheeks red from the cold.

Dianna Fairbanks, Gwen thinks to herself. *What is she doing out here?*

"I don't understand," another man says, baffled. "They stop here abruptly."

"Could they be hers?" Dianne asks the elderly police officer.

"Not sure," the officer replies.

A younger policeman in his thirties approaches them, bending down to better inspect the footprints in the snow. *This must be Johansen*, Gwen rationalizes.

"They look to be her size shoe," he says aloud. Johansen stands and addresses his partner. "Where on earth did she go?"

"She's got to be around her somewhere. Get the others, Hank. Bring them over. We'll focus the search in this area."

The young policeman nods and hurries away.

"How long can a girl her age even survive out here?" Dianne asks the older officer.

He gives her a sad smile. "Not very long, unfortunately."

His reply sends a shiver down Gwen's spine, yet she remains silently hidden. While the search party assembles beneath her, Gwen takes the opportunity to scan their thoughts.

The coroner said he couldn't pronounce a single cause of death for Mr. Keller. It was like he had been crushed, but from the inside.

Why didn't I just listen to her? She came to me for help and I just...

Crazy child, running off into the woods like that. She ain't got a lick of sense in her head to be...

Come on. Let's hurry up and find the brat so we can all go home. It's freezing out here!

Other thoughts along with a barrage of images flood her open mind. Gwen is relieved to find out that Mrs. Keller, Cara, and Aaron are all safe. The children are back at the group home, but at least they're receiving some counseling for the trauma they've suffered. Once cleared of any suspicion of child abuse by the authorities, Mrs. Keller packed up and went to stay with her sister in Denver.

Gwen can't help feeling responsible for everyone's upheaval. *Honestly, they should thank me,* she thinks. *I did them a favor,* she rationalizes to herself. *Cara and Aaron are better off, and at least now Judy Keller might have a chance to grow a back bone and*

maybe meet a decent guy. Somehow Gwen doubts her former foster mother will be in a rush to start dating anytime soon.

All the knowledge Gwen gains from her glimpses into the search party members' minds convince her that she can never go back. Quickly she shuts the mental connection, retreating into the solitude of her own thoughts.

They will never believe it was self-defense. What I've done goes way beyond self-defense to merciless torture.

She finds herself wondering about Dennis Keller's last thoughts and cringes. He deserved what he got after all he put his family through, especially little Cara, but killing him was never her intention. Her guilt threatens to engulf her. What bothers her most is that she killed him without conscious knowledge of what she was doing. Knowing she could end someone's life with so little effort or thought frightens her beyond reason.

The whole thing happened so fast! I should've been able to fight him off without resorting to magic. Yet he caught me off guard and a second later he had his belt around my neck.... My strength must've failed me in my panic.

The look frozen forever on Dennis Keller's face, the state of his mangled corpse, and the blood-splattered kitchen still haunts Gwen, no matter how hard she tries to shut it out. She's afraid to sleep and afraid of being alone in the cold, lifeless mountains, half convinced his spirit follows her, the ghostly shadow of her awful deed. Nightly she awakens screaming, the last images of her nightmare still visible to her consciousness. Sleep proves more hopeless every night, for the nightmares ever await her.

Gwen resolves to wait for the right moment and slip away from the search party. The opportunity comes a few hours later, around sunset. Feeling stiff from sitting in the same position for so long, she figures it's now or never. While the search party mills around the area, Gwen uses the coming darkness to quickly leap from her tree to another, and then another. With superhuman balance and grace, she moves silently like a ghost from bough to bough until she finds herself in another part of the forest, well away from her rescuers. At last, certain she is safe, Gwen settles to sleep in the tree for the night. It is far too dark to set up camp at this hour. In the morning she is relieved not to see Dianna Fairbanks and the search party. She deems it safe enough to climb down from the tree to the forest floor.

Completely out of food, she resolves to find better shelter and game waiting higher in the mountains. Gwen heads deeper into the wilderness, into the heart of the Poconos Mountains, further away from Scranton and all of civilization.

* * * * *

The wind howls through the trees, bending their branches to the point of snapping as a blizzard ravages the mountains. The air is colder than ice, the ground covered in several feet of snow. Amongst this tumult and inhospitable conditions, Gwen's tiny form moves relentlessly with head and shoulders hunched over to keep beneath the gusts of the winter winds. She's grateful to have a decent coat and a good pair of boots to protect her from the elements, yet her duffel bag weighs her down, making the trek grueling. Her stomach grumbles but she doesn't notice; she is used to the pang of hunger by now. It has been so long since she's had a full stomach that she's lost count of the days. She doesn't bother asking herself when she last ate. Food seems immaterial now.

Shelter is her goal. She needs some place dry and warm to ride out the rest of the storm. Without a compass, maps, or knowledge of the area to guide her, she can do nothing but move forward. Just keep moving, keep the blood circulating and the heat in her flesh if she wants to stay alive.

The storm has raged for days now, with no sign of it passing her by. Exhausted and weak from hunger, Gwen moves slowly forward, barely able to see before her eyes. The curtain of snow and wind wraps itself about her. Her breath comes out in sporadic clouds of frost before her, as her heart and lungs work extra hard against the effects of the high altitude.

Gwen's thoughts wander into the past. She finds herself back in New York again with Raven, living in hovels and warehouses, sleeping on park benches or under the freeway. Begging or conning people for food, they scraped by on the money they earned by pickpocketing.

At least then there was food and shelter, Gwen thinks ruefully. *Being homeless in New York doesn't sound so bad right about now!* She bitterly laughs aloud to herself.

Gwen trudges onward. The cold engulfing her, the endless rhythm of her trek, and the constant ache of starvation lull Gwen into a zombie-esque state. As time progresses, she becomes numb all over, losing sensation to her extremities and her exposed flesh. Her chin, cheeks, and nose have become red and frozen, causing her face to feel heavy and lifeless.

Finally, when she can take no more, Gwen's legs falter and buckle underneath the weight of her body. Weak, she makes no effort to catch herself as she falls face first into the snow. She lies there, motionless, knowing her very survival depends on her will to move, but she cannot budge a single muscle. The wind howls, gusting over her. Through her drowsy, heavy-lidded eyes, she sees a world of white, cold and empty. Upon the icy flesh of her cheek she feels snowflakes gathering, covering her in an endless shower of snow fall. Sleep deprived and physically spent, Gwen closes her eyes and goes to sleep, more aware than ever that she may never awaken.

* * * * *

A dark shadow passes over the snow-covered landscape, soaring through the sky like a giant sparrow surveying the aftermath of the recent winter storm. A glimpse of green catches the traveler's eye. Quickly, the shadow streaks downward to the ground like a comet falling from the firmament. The creature lands with a loud boom, the impact causing the ground to shake and snow to spray upward in a cloud of frost.

The snow settles, revealing a pale man dressed all in black with an unfortunately crooked face. Straightening from his crouched position, he stands, moving with deadly grace. His pale silver eyes scan the landscape, searching for the wayward snatch of green he spied from overhead.

A hundred yards ahead, his eyes alight upon a snow-covered mound through which dark green fabric peeks out. He moves toward the fabric, and, a second later, he spans the hundred yard distance to the very spot, moving as quickly as the wind. He kneels down to take the piece of fabric in his claw-like hands and gets a whiff of warm human blood in the air, immediately accompanied by the slow, staggered thump of a human heart on the verge of its last beat.

Excited glee crosses the man's disproportionate face. He grins as his silver eyes alight with hunger. He grabs hold of the green cloth and yanks on it, pulling with it a small pubescent girl out of the mound of snow.

The green fabric is the unconscious child's coat. A red duffle bag dangles from a strap hanging across her chest, presumably containing her belongings. Holding her by the sleeve of her worn coat, hanging limply over the ground like a rag doll, the man makes a quick inspection of his find.

She's young, half starved, and sickly. Her black hair escapes in strands from under her woolen cap. Her face is red from exposure, yet her natural beauty is still evident.

He knows he has to act quickly, for soon her heart will give out and not long after, her blood will begin to lose its flavor as death's poison spreads throughout her body. After that, she'll be completely inedible to him. What a terrible waste, for the blood of the young and innocent is the most delectable, giving the drinker extra strength. The rejuvenating effects last days longer than older, more mature blood. Besides, children's blood tastes the sweetest, like a deep, rich wine.

The repulsive man lays his captive on her back atop the fresh snow. With great eagerness, he pushes her head to one side and pulls the collar of her shirt away, exposing her white, slender neck. He bends over. He gives out a bark of pain as two fangs break through the skin of his gums, emerging where his canine teeth would have been. The momentary discomfort passes, and he hungrily puts his mouth upon her neck. He bites down, his fangs tearing into her tender, cold flesh.

Immediately, the blood begins to flow. He retracts his fangs and begins to suck the life-giving juice from the girl's diminished frame. Suddenly, he jerks back, spitting out the bitter fluid upon the snow, staining it with her blood. She doesn't taste sweet and lovely like a human child. She tastes old, ancient with wisdom and just a tint of bad fortune. He looks over the girl again, removing her woolen cap. Slowly he peers into her face, and with his thumb he gently lifts one of her eyelids to see the color of her eyes. Her dead stare looks up above his shoulder, but the tell-tale sign of gold around the pupil shows within her green eyes. The man hisses, jumping back, landing several feet away.

"Witch!" he growls, staring at the girl's pathetic form as if he expects her to attack him. When several minutes pass without incident, the hideous stranger relaxes. Still, he moves cautiously toward the child and scoops her into his arms.

"The Master will want to see this." He speaks in a thick Cockney accent to the unconscious girl. He runs, picking up speed until suddenly he leaps into the air, bounding into the heavens. He streaks across the white winter's night sky, heading toward the peak of the mountains high above.

* * * * *

She is running through a meadow of beautiful flowers, laughing as she chases after a teenage boy, the same boy that always visits her in her dreams. He keeps just ahead of her, laughing as she tries to jump and catch hold of him. Always he dodges her, leaping out of the way at the last second. His blond hair sparkles like the sun in the morning light, his blue eyes bright with his self-satisfaction as he taunts Gwen, calling her after him.

Looking down, she notices that she wears an elegant, green, princess-cut dress with embroidered roses and fire climbing her arms and bodice in silver stitching. Upon her head she wears a crown shaped like thorns and roses with rubies cut into the shapes of flames encrusted within.

The boy wears a suit of deep red velvet with a long jacket, looking like the prince in a fairy tale. He also has embroidery upon his sleeves, of roses and birds intertwined with thorn-covered ivy. Upon his breast a hawk is embroidered in flight, encircled by a ring of thorns in gold. He wears a crown grander than hers, with diamond tears shaped like white flames reaching upward.

Despite their finery, Gwen and the older boy play as children, dashing through the field of flowers. Suddenly, her handsome companion stops. Gwen runs on ahead of him but stops and looks back at her friend, puzzled.

His face has gone pale, the smile gone from his gentle face. He points to something beyond Gwen's shoulder. She turns, and where the meadow and the beautiful morning sky were, there is now a dark, ominous mountain looming ahead, blocking the light of the sun.

Scared, Gwen tries to slowly back away, but no matter how far she moves away from the mountain's dark presence, it looms nearer as if the mountain itself is moving toward her. She turns and runs back toward her friend. Thunder crashes and lightning streaks through the darkening sky. The clouds of the gathering storm above cast a heavy shadow over the meadow. Gwen tries to outrun the storm, to get out of the dark. She looks ahead and sees her handsome friend standing on the opposite side of the meadow, where sunlight and beauty still govern. She races toward him.

"Gwenevere, Gwenevere!" he shouts, his voice urgent, his face fearful. He reaches out to her.

Gwen runs with all her might but she cannot get out of the shadows, her friend seeming further and further away. In a last desperate attempt, she throws out her arms and makes a giant leap toward him, reaching for his outstretched hand. With all her heart and soul, Gwen takes a giant leap of faith.

CHAPTER TWO

The Master Awaits

Gwen awakes with a start as she crashes face-first into something hard and cold. Pain shoots through her skull. She groans and then slowly pushes against the cold stone surface beneath. She finds herself sitting on the floor of a strange cave-like room. Next to her, a bed of stone comes out of the floor as if carved from one solid mass. Upon the stone bed lay a mattress and clean white bedding.

Slowly, Gwen tries to stand, stumbling on wobbly legs toward the bed. Cradling her still aching skull in her hands, she tries to steady herself as the room spins about her. She wonders if she jumped out of bed and hit her head hard on the stone floor. The dream felt so real, the last images lingering behind her eye lids. Slowly she becomes fully aware of her surroundings as her dizzy spell desists.

Everything from the furniture to the walls, the door, and even the ceiling itself are carved completely out of rock. Besides the bed, the room is furnished with a bedside table, a table and two chairs, a vanity and mirror, and a large floor to ceiling book case. Gwen is in awe and utterly confused by her surroundings.

How did I get here? she wonders. *Who brought me here? Where the hell am I?*

She looks about the room but neither her duffel bag nor any other item belonging to her is evident. She sighs, a bit perplexed. She feels different, stronger and more energetic than she has in a long time. Standing, Gwen crosses the room to a vanity table above which hangs an elegant mirror carved out of a deep green marble. Peering into the looking glass, Gwen is surprised at her reflection.

The girl looking back at her isn't gaunt, pale, or sickly, but fresh, young, and healthy. Her cheeks have a soft pink glow about them, her eyes more dazzling and alive with vitality. Throughout her body she feels a surge of unearthly vigor. She suddenly feels the urge to do cartwheels, flips, and back flips about the room and off the walls. She wouldn't be surprised if she could walk on the ceiling.

Just then Gwen catches sight of her attire. Someone changed her old, dirty, soaked clothes into a short, white, baby-doll style dress trimmed in white lace and embroidered with elegant pearls and beads across the bodice. She wears no shoes or socks. Her bare legs looking surprisingly skinny and long in her reflection. Her hair, however, is a tangled mess. Gwen tries to run her fingers through it but it's hopeless. She notices that her hair is clean and soft, as though someone washed it, or perhaps someone gave her a bath.

The thought disturbs Gwen, for she doesn't much like the idea of a total stranger bathing and clothing her like a doll. She pushes the uncomfortable thought out of her mind and opens one of the vanity drawers. Inside she finds a large brush, a comb, and several ornate jewel-encrusted hair pins and clips. Gwen gets to work, making herself presentable. Someone must have found her stranded in the snow storm and taken pity on her. Although she doesn't yet know what manner of person her host is, or what manner of place she's in, she has no desire to be any further burden to anyone.

With her health restored, she has no intention of sitting cooped up in this strange room, being served and waited on like an invalid. Part of her wants to go and explore this new place; the other half wants only to find her own clothes and belongings so that she can pay her respects and undying gratitude to her benevolent host and be on her way again. It isn't that Gwen doesn't trust random acts of kindness. She loathes being indebted to anyone, at the mercy of someone else's hospitality and control.

With her hair detangled, she sweeps it back in spirals away from her face, fastened by two of the emerald hair pins. The rest of her silky black hair hangs loose about her delicate shoulders. She gives herself a satisfied nod of approval. In the mirror, she sees a pair of white jewel-encrusted slippers sitting next to her bed. A surge of curious excitement flutters through her stomach as she sits upon the bed and puts on the ostentatious footwear.

Whoever lives here, they sure have expensive taste.

With a mischievous smile, Gwen skips across the floor to the bedroom door. A bit nervous, she slowly opens the large stone door enough to peek out into the hallway beyond. The hall is made completely of stone as well, the floor the same cold limestone cut to have the appearance of tiles.

No one is visible in the hall, so Gwen quietly slips out the door. The long, narrow hallway is only wide enough for two people to walk side by side. The hall has an arched ceiling, with ornate columns and arches supporting the stone structure. She can't see the end of the hall on either side. Lanterns carved out of the walls line the hallway and give it an eerie, unnatural light. All along the hallway, dozens of stone arched doors are carved in bas relief with beautiful seals, crests, and symbols. She stands in the middle of the hall in complete awe.

Which way do I go? she wonders as she looks down one end, and then the other.

Taking a deep breath, Gwen reaches out with her consciousness, letting her mental powers cast a net about her, searching for any sign of intelligent life. She finds it. She senses many persons living within this strange place, but most are not nearby. One is down the hall in the room five doors down. Following the surge of mental images and the rhythmic hum of life coming from the consciousness of the unidentified person, Gwen walks, stopping outside a door with writing engraved under a strange symbol.

She can read it; it's written in the tongue of her childhood, the true tongue, as she calls it. Her fingers run over the lettering as Gwen reads the inscription.

To Serve,
To Die,
To Bleed for the Master

Strange creed, Gwen thinks. Nervously, she takes a breath before knocking.

Within, Gwen hears a chair scrape on the floor, someone talking in a low, frightened voice, and then hurried footsteps approaching. The door immediately opens wide, revealing a small stone chamber similar to the one where she awoke, cold and colorless. No one opened the door. Gwen is puzzled. She looks about for the person she knows should be here. Then, she looks down. At her feet, bowed down with his face to the floor, lay a boy, perhaps a few years older than she. His brown hair is cut short, his clothing nothing more than a red loincloth barely covering his private parts, his chest and legs bare and his feet clad in an old fashioned leather sandal.

Gwen stares down at the boy, at a complete loss for what to say or how to react. He doesn't say a word. He doesn't even look at her. He sits there with his face to the ground as though she is some exulted being he is unfit to look upon. After silently waiting for the boy to acknowledge her, Gwen kneels down and taps him on the shoulder.

The boy flinches, but doesn't move or speak. Frustrated, Gwen puts a hand on both shoulders and shakes him briskly. She still receives no response from this strange boy.

"Hello? Are you asleep? What's the matter with you?" Gwen demands in a rude tone, irate at being ignored by a complete stranger.

Suddenly, the boy looks up, a surprised look upon his face. He looks at her as if she were something strange and unnatural. He jumps to his feet. He pokes his head out the door, looking down each end of the hall as if looking for someone else.

"Oh, so you are awake! Hi, I'm Gwen. I'm looking for—" The boy grabs her by the shoulder and pulls her into the room, slamming the door behind them.

"What are you doing?" Gwen demands, indignant.

"Are you crazy?" The boy turns, an angry, wild look upon his face. "You can't just go wondering about the place. What if one of the Forsaken saw you? What if the Master comes looking for you?" As if struck by a sudden thought, the boy hurries back to the door, pressing his ear to the stone as if he could hear someone approaching from outside. Gwen knows no one's coming; he is just being paranoid. She is about to tell him so when the boy turns and flies at her.

"If the Master finds you here, he'll kill me! You have to leave! Go back to your room, and do not tell anyone you were here," he warns. Fear wavers in his voice as he takes her by the arm and hauls her back toward the door.

Gwen yanks her arm free. The boy stops to grab her again, and she pushes him away. Startled, he looks at her in disbelief.

"Don't you know your place yet? If you don't, the Master will teach you soon enough."

"Will you shut up for two seconds and tell me what the hell is going on here? At least tell me your name, where we are, and who the forsaken are. Oh, and who's this Master fellow that you assume I know?" Gwen demands in a haughty voice, crossing her arms across her chest and giving the boy a hard stare, as if commanding his immediate response.

The boy looks at her, astonished. Looking about the room for help from some unseen protector, he finally looks at Gwen and clears his throat with a cough.

"I'm Peter. You're in Bec LaNuff, the mountain fortress of Legion the Master. The Forsaken are his subjects, unnatural beasts and children of the damned," Peter replies in a cold, toneless voice while looking at Gwen as if she were a dolt, as if what he tells her is such common knowledge that she must be an idiot not to know it.

Gwen stares at him, aghast. His explanations make even less sense than his senseless ramblings had earlier. *Maybe he's sick in the head or something. The shrink back at the group home, Dr.*

Monroe, would just love this guy.

"Who are you, and where did you come from? I haven't seen you here before," Peter asks after several moments of silence.

"That's what I've been trying to tell you. I'm Gwenevere from... well, nobody knows where I come from, but just a month ago, I came from Scranton. Do you know the place?" she asks, trying to show a semblance of politeness in this awkward situation.

The boy shakes his head. "How did you get here?" Peter asks, taking a few steps closer to examine her apparel.

"I don't know. I was hoping you could tell me. I was hiking in the mountains—well, I was living in the mountains when a storm hit. I tried to find shelter, but I think I passed out before I made it," Gwen answers, a bit defensively, as she shrugs her shoulders. "That's the last thing I remember. I woke up just now in a room down the hall."

"Oh. So you haven't seen any of them? No one's come to you? Not the Master or one of his minions?" He steps even closer, making Gwen a bit uncomfortable.

"No. No one's *come* to me. Whatever that means," Gwen mumbles under her breath. "Look, I just want my bag and my clothes back so I can get on my way. I don't care about the Master or his minions, or any of that. I just want to leave."

"Oh, you can't leave. Someone must have found you, and since you're alive, they must have brought you here as gift to the Master. Usually they house Legion's girls in another wing, closer to his bedchamber."

"You know what? I'm getting kind of tired listening to your crazy talk, so if you won't help me, I'll just have to find my stuff and my way out of here by myself." Gwen attempts to pass him to get to the door.

Peter lunges at her, grabbing her by the arm, and pulls her in, pressing her against him. He runs his fingers along both sides of her neck as if looking for some mark or blemish.

Enraged and a bit afraid, Gwen pushes against him, using the power within to send him backward. Peter cries out in alarm before he crashes into a cabinet along the wall.

Gwen dashes for the door, flings it wide open, and darts into the hall. Behind her, she hears Peter call her name. She runs away from him, frantic to find some way out of this mad house. Peter's sandaled feet clank on the stone floor behind her. She looks over her shoulder, and she suddenly slams right into something solid and hard, knocking her off her feet.

A hand reaches out and catches her by the arm, yanking her back to her feet with a brisk, effortless gesture. In complete shock, Gwen finds herself staring into a man's broad chest. Slowly, she looks upward. Before her stands an extraordinarily tall, sophisticated man in green. He wears his long silver hair like a samurai, half up in a top knot, the other half down resting about his broad, masculine shoulders. His skin is gold and his ears large with pointed curled tips. His eyes are as green as watermelons, but shimmering and changing color in a constant dance of light around his large, dark pupils. His clothing is regal, similar to the uniform the royal guard in London, only more refined and elegant in deep blues and purple hues with golden embroidery and buttons. He wears tall, black boots with golden beadwork running along the calf, and a belt of gold about his waist with a long, gilded dagger in a scabbard. The impressive man looks down his long aquiline nose at Gwen, one long, silver eyebrow quirked in a quizzical stare. She stumbles back a few steps, intimidated by the man's stature and appearance.

"You must be the little Witch whom Ivan so gallantly rescued from the snow." He speaks in a leisurely tone, his words rolling off his tongue in an aristocratic way. Gwen pays attention not to what he's saying but how he says it. His words startle Gwen. Unlike the boy, Peter, who spoke to her in English like a normal person, this tall, regal figure speaks in her own tongue.

"You speak the true tongue?" Gwen asks in astonishment.

"Why, of course, daughter of Willow. What other language would our kind speak?" He answers in a condescending manner, as if he wants to laugh at her stupidity.

"Hey, pal, where I come from every one speaks English. I may not know who my mother was, but she most definitely wasn't some lady named Willow!"

The man looks taken aback by this information. "But weren't you raised by your parents in the coven? Weren't you trained alongside your sister Witches and your brother Warlocks in the craft?" he asks.

Peter comes up behind Gwen. "I'm sorry, your grace, she got

away from me. I was just taking her back to her room to await the Master. Please do not mention this to anyone, especially not Ivan, sir," Peter pleads, bowing repetitively, groveling before the tall, golden-skinned gentleman. He takes Gwen's hand in his as if to lead her away with him. She yanks her hand free and snarls at him.

"No need for that, boy. The Witch will come with me directly, to be introduced formally to the Master himself," the superior man informs the meager boy, waving him away in an aristocratic gesture of dismissal. "You may run along, child."

Peter scurries away, glancing backward at Gwen and mumbling to himself as he makes his way back to his little stone chamber.

Gwen turns her attention back to the tall figure before her, a bit uncertain what to expect next.

"Come along, girl. The Master wishes to meet you properly." He offers his arm to her like a gentleman, but he stands much taller than she, so instead, he offers his hand.

"I don't understand what's going on. I don't know where I am, and I don't know who you are. Why should I go anywhere with you?" Gwen asks, exasperated.

"My apologies, Sister Witch. My name is Emon, of the North-Water Clan." He bows to her. "You are in Bec LaNuff, and you are our guest. And whom do I have the pleasure of meeting?"

"Oh, I'm Gwenevere, but everyone calls me Gwen."

He bows before her again. "I am delighted to meet you, Gwen. I am an Elf. I presume by the way you stare at my appearance that you have never met an Elf before?"

Gwen shakes her head.

"I promise you, Gwen, that I mean you no harm." He sounds sincere, but Gwen has long since learned not to take anyone or thing at face value. His aura dances about his head, glowing like the aurora borealis. Without a second thought Gwen sends her mind into his, searching for the true intent, the true nature of this strange golden man before her. She spends a few moments deep inside his psyche, knowing everything about him from infancy to present, understanding and comprehending him even better than he does himself. Abruptly, something like a mental wall springs up around his mind and she is rudely shoved out, her mind returning suddenly to her own thoughts.

Emon looks at her, half astonished for a moment before his face breaks into a little smile. "Now, now. Where I come from its rude to go poking around in the mind of another Forsaken without permission," he admonishes her in a good-natured tone.

Gwen feels like she just got caught by Sister Whitmore stealing the cheesecake from the kitchen at Saint Paul's. She stands tense before him, both embarrassed and alarmed to be called out on her mental intrusion. No one's ever perceived her presence in their minds before, to even suspect she was there.

"My apologies, I… didn't think you'd notice." Gwen replies.

"Apology accepted. No harm done. So do I pass? Did you see anything that you didn't like, anything to fear?" he asks, still congenial.

"Nope. I saw that you've never caused another person harm in your life. I also saw that you've taken some kind of oath never to knowingly deceive another member of the Forsaken," Gwen adds.

"That is correct. As a member of my sister tribe, I promise, little Witch, you are safe with me." Emon offers his hand again. This time Gwen takes it. Side by side, they begin to walk down the hall. Gwen doesn't protest, letting the strange man lead her through the stone fortress as they converse.

"I dare say the Wiccans always were a solitary people, keeping their young tucked away in the middle of the woods in covens like squirrels living in trees. But I confess I at least gave them credit for teaching their younglings about the other tribes of Cain, if nothing else."

"Witches live in the forest, in trees? Where do Elves live?" Gwen asks.

"My kind lives off of the land as well, but not in the way yours does. We don't alter the land to fit our needs. As for Witches, you should know more than I about the living habits of your own kind, child."

"But I don't," Gwen corrects him. "Like I told you, I'm from the normal world. I wasn't raised by Witches. I didn't even know I was one until a few years ago."

He looks at her in awe. "Am I to believe you were raised by humans?"

"Yes. I was raised in a Catholic orphanage in Maine. When they found me I was only five, and I couldn't remember where I came from," she explains.

"A Catholic orphanage! Hah!" Emon laughs, his face taking on a gentle, less haughty air. "I bet you scared those pious nuns out of their habits," he chuckles.

"Yes, I sort of did." Gwen laughs with the Elf, feeling the tension in her body fade and a calm, comfortable sensation settle upon her. She likes Emon. He may be rigid and pompous, but he is honest and easy to talk to.

"You realize that means you are a Wild Witch," Emon informs her in a conspiratorial tone.

"A what? A Wild Witch? Am I considered uncivilized, then?" Gwen laughs.

"Why, yes, Miss Gwen. Your kind does not look kindly on those who tutor themselves in the craft. Practicing magic without a mentor is considered blasphemy and incredibly dangerous. I confess I am impressed you've lived on your own this long."

"Do others like me die?" This thought troubles Gwen, and it must show on her face because Emon stops and kneels down to look into her eyes.

"Do not be distressed. It has been known throughout history for Witches to go mad without a coven. Some who weren't tutored properly even killed themselves, and others also because they did not know their own limits. I am certain that you will not suffer such a fate." He pats her shoulder with his large gold hand and continues. "My companion has a rare ability to see and read auras. It is she and I who nursed you back to health. She did a thorough reading of you and assured both the Master and I that you are not only sane, but a very gifted and powerful Witch."

Gwen sighs in relief. "Well, I already knew I wasn't insane, but it's nice to know I'm not going to kill myself." Gwen laughs ruefully.

Emon smiles at her before standing up again.

"Emon, are all the Forsaken telepathic?" she inquires.

"No, child. It's a very rare gift. Witches don't want the rest of us to know that. Most of the other tribes assume that all Wiccans are capable of all sorts of dark mischief." The Elf answers with a knowing smirk. Gwen nods, taking in the notion that even the Forsaken are suspicious of her kind.

As they walk, Gwen has been too distracted to notice much about her surroundings. They pass the same cold, lifeless stone walls, hallways, archways, and steps as they walk, but now she looks around and fully takes in the scene before her as the hall opens to something different.

She and the Elf stand in the entryway to a massive underground courtyard, a chamber that spans hundreds of feet long and a hundred feet high. The domed ceiling is supported by dozens of large sculpted columns from floor to ceiling, fashioned like spirals shooting toward heaven. At the top of the dome, light shines through a magnificent stain glass window. Made out of many circles including a sun half-eclipsed by the moon and a giant eye, the window casts a supernatural glow high above the chamber floor. Gwen is so much in awe of the craftsmanship, the scale, and majesty of the room that at first she doesn't notice the inhabitance of the chamber.

A deep male voice coughs. The sound startles Gwen. She spins around to locate the source. However, when she looks behind her, she sees no one.

"Move out of the way! You're blocking the entrance!" speaks the same rough, disembodied voice.

Gwen looks to Emon, perplexed. The tall Elf points toward the ground at Gwen's feet. Standing only three feet, Gwen spies a stubby, hairy, little man, craning his neck to stare up at her with a disgruntled look upon his round face.

"I'm sorry." Gwen steps aside.

The short, hairy fellow passes Gwen with a waddle, grumbling several unflattering remarks about her under his breath as he continues farther into the massive chamber.

"What on earth was that?" she asks her companion.

"A Dwarf," Emon answers. "His kind built this place back when the world was young."

"Oh. This is a Dwarf dwelling, then?" Gwen asks.

"Well, originally they built it for the Vampire. Their two clans have been allies for centuries," Emon explains. "Come along, little Witch. We should keep moving. Lord Legion is waiting to meet you." He takes Gwen's hand and they make their way across the courtyard.

Dozens of creatures wander about, coming and going in and out of the many passageways along the walls of the circular

chamber. Gwen feels a little like a tourist, staring at all the Dwarfs, Giants, Goblins, and other strange indescribable beings all around her.

Good thing the ceiling is so high, Gwen muses, *otherwise the Giants wouldn't be able to fit. Come to think of it, how do the Giants traverse anywhere else in the fortress with the hallways being human size? If I stay here long enough, I'm sure I'll figure that out*, she thinks to herself.

Gwen notices their multi-colored auras as they mill about, hearing all their minds buzzing around her head like a swarm of bees. Remembering Emon's admonishment about entering another's mind without permission, Gwen draws her mind into itself, throwing a shield up to keep from hearing anyone else's thoughts by accident.

What is this place? Gwen thinks, but decides not to ask. She can't help but feel as though she's delaying the Elf's busy schedule and doesn't want to be too much of a burden. She is a guest here and owes her life to these people, so she decides she must show her gratitude by being as polite as possible.

Suddenly the image of the White Rabbit from *Alice in Wonderland* pops into her head. Gwen giggles inwardly at the slight resemblance her elfin escort has to the fictional character.

"Wait, if Vampires live here, how can they come into this chamber with that window above letting in the sunshine?"

"Oh, that is not the sun. It is an enchanted light. Besides, it is not day at the moment. Most of Bec LaNuff lives by night and sleeps by day," Emon explains.

As they exit the chamber into one of the arched passageways, two men pass them to enter. The first man is dark of hair, skin, clothing, and trim of figure. Gwen can't quite tell if he is a black man or not—just that his whole demeanor is dark and brooding. The only thing of color about his person are his pale silver eyes. The dark man's companion is a pale-skinned, short, ugly man dressed in an expensive grey suit, with Italian leather shoes. They too have shimmering multi-colored auras. Gwen has to fight the urge to slip into those bright spheres and into the inner web of their consciousness.

Perhaps I have a telepathic addiction, Gwen worries. *What am I, some kind of a mental peeping tom? Ewww!*

When the two men notice her with the Elf, they stop to speak to them.

"Greetings, Emon." The dark man makes his salutations to the Elf, inclining his head in the briefest of bows. His companion gives a toothy smile, his dental hygiene in complete contrast to his fine clothes.

"The Witch has awoken," states Emon.

The dark man is about to speak again when his companion interrupts.

"I didn't recognize her dressed up like that. Why, for a moment there, I mistook her for one of the Master's little lovelies, she being so flat and childlike."

His thick Cockney accent pours like thick ale over all his

words, mumbling and slurring the pronunciations until Gwen can barely decipher his speech. He bends down to put his face right into Gwen's to get a better look. Gwen keeps her face blank and stands very still, commanding herself not to shove the rude, awful man away. He pokes at Gwen's ribs, pinching the skin on her arms or check, walking about her as if examining her like a horse for sale at the market.

"How old is the little darling anyhow?" The disgusting man turns to Emon. Gwen is half surprised he doesn't force open her mouth and check her teeth and gums to ascertain her age himself.

"I'm almost twelve," Gwen replies tartly.

"Ivan, must I remind you that she is a guest here under the Lord's protection, and as such, she will be shown the proper respect," Emon chastises the Cockney twit.

"Why, of course. Where are my manners? Such a pleasure to meet you, child."

Ivan gives the Elf a sneering smile, one meant to seem polite and civil while letting it be known he'd like to punch the Elf right in his condescending, aristocratic nose.

Gwen suppresses a smile. The fact that Emon put Ivan-ugly-face in his place gives Gwen sudden kinship to the Elf. *He might be a very useful ally and confidant in this strange new world.*

"My apologies, young mistress, for their rudeness. May I introduce you to Lucca the Dark and Ivan the Trusted?" Emon indicates both the strange men before them with a respectful bow of his head.

Ivan the Trusted? Gwen scoffs to herself. *More like "Ivan the Idiot" or "Ivan the Annoying, Pompous, Rude" or...*

"Ivan is the one who found you," Emon informs her.

Gwen halts in her mental onslaught of Ivan, suddenly taken out of her thoughts by this startling revelation.

"You saved my life?" Gwen asks the unsightly man before her, skeptical. He ignores her. He seems uncomfortable owning up to this deed and anxious to be gone. Giving his companion Lucca a look that speaks volumes, the two men abruptly bow to Emon.

"Till tonight, Lord Emon. Little Witch." Lucca bids farewell respectfully as Ivan gives a curt nod. Together they turn to enter the courtyard, leaving the Elf and the Witch to themselves again. Gwen turns to Emon, perplexed.

"Believe me, the less you know about those two, the better." He takes her hand, leading her into a passageway and out of the domed courtyard. "It might also be advisable to avoid those two as much as possible," he adds.

They pass several other creatures along the narrow halls of the fortress, and Gwen finds herself mesmerized by how beautiful this place is. The stone pillars, archways, and halls are all so exquisitely crafted. It isn't very colorful or warm, and Gwen shivers a little, wishing she had a coat. "Emon, can I ask you some questions?"

"Yes, ask me anything you like," he responds.

"Where are we exactly? Are we in some kind of castle? "

"This place, as I have before mentioned, is called Bec LaNuff.

It is built out of the hollow center of a mountain. We call it a fortress, but it is modeled after a castle. We have servant quarters, grand ballrooms, banquet halls, and even dungeons," Emon explains.

"Oh, that explains all the stone and the lack of windows." Gwen replies dryly, earning her an amused smirk from Emon.

Gwen notices three elegant women dressed like queens coming down the hall toward them. They move down the corridor as if floating on mist. Gwen can't help staring. Their unearthly eyes are devoid of color in different shades of grey, white, and silver. Their skin is as fair as porcelain dolls. They're beautiful in a strange way, like dark angels or goddesses of another world.

One of the three mysterious women, a skinny, delicate thing with long, straight, blonde hair, notices Gwen. Her eyes narrow and a cold shiver runs over Gwen's flesh. The cold-eyed goddess whispers something to her companions. In unison, the three women turn their gazes to stare openly at Gwen, making her feel small and insignificant.

Usually Gwen feels equivalent to those around her despite her youth, but in the presence of such women, she feels like a babe running around in her diaper, drooling on herself. Although their faces are cold and emotionless, she can't help feeling as though her presence angers them, as if she were unworthy to be among creatures such as themselves.

Determined not to seem intimidated by them, Gwen stares back, following them with her eyes the same way they do her until the three pass them down the corridor and out of sight.

"Who were those women? What are they?" Gwen looks over her shoulder to watch them go. "They don't seem human somehow."

"They're not. They are Vampire. Those particular three are Jezebel, Lethawyn, and Ryan." Emon answers in an indifferent tone, as if living amongst Vampires is the most natural thing in the world.

"Ryan? What kind of name is that for a woman, let alone a Vampire?" Gwen queries.

"Ryan the blonde is fresh blood, meaning newly turned into a Vampire. She, unlike most Vampires, has chosen to keep her human name."

"Oh, okay," Gwen replies.

"You see, Gwen, usually when they rise from the flesh and are reborn unto death, a Vampire will still retain a great deal of their human memories and feelings. The bloodlust soon chases all of their human instincts to the back of their consciousness, along with the knowledge of who they once were. It is because of this that many choose to take on a new name, a blood name as they call it. These are the ones who fully embrace themselves as Vampire."

"Oh. Do they forget their real names?" Gwen finds herself curious of these strange creatures that, until today, she would've sworn were just myths.

"Most do. Some learn to live with their past and the present in a symbiotic state, but this is more common amongst modern

Vampire than the ancient ones." Emon sounds like a teacher instructing a student.

"Those men… Lucca and Ivan… are they Vampires, too?" she asks the Elf.

"Yes."

"Do they all have colorless eyes?"

"Yes. All Vampires lose the pigment in their skin and eyes when they transform. Their hair, however, stays the same color as it was in life. Peculiar, isn't it?" the Elf ponders aloud.

"Yes, I guess that is strange," Gwen concedes.

Quickening his step, Emon leads Gwen along swiftly, the young girl struggling to match his stride. Their footsteps echoing loudly on the stone floor.

"Hurry along now. The Master awaits."

CHAPTER THREE

Where a Witch is Welcome

At last Gwen finds herself standing before two gold doors, beautifully adorned. Two large, bulky creatures with misshapen faces and bodies flank them. They're ugly creatures, their appearance lacking in intellect, standing erect they stare at the opposite wall as if the Elf and Gwen are not present.

"The Guards are Ogres" Emon informs her in whisper.

Their impressive size makes them more than adequate for their tasks. Gwen assess.

On either side of the grand doors, a long hallway stretches beyond sight.

"Before us is the main hall, where most of the ceremonies and gatherings are held. Lord Legion refers to it as his court," Emon informs her.

"By court, you mean as in… the King's Court?" Gwen verifies.

"Precisely," Emon answers, pleased that she understood.

"So, does that mean he's a King amongst the Dwarfs, then?"

Emon bursts into laughter.

"Oh, child, you have it all wrong. Legion isn't a Dwarf. He is Vampire, lord and master of this community and all that live here under the mountain," Emon explains, his mirth subsiding as he speaks, but a hint of a smile lingers at the corners of his mouth.

Gwen is a little miffed but pretends not to care. "Well, you said this place was built by the Dwarfs, so I naturally assumed your leader would be a Dwarf," she responds, aware of the defensive tone in her voice.

"Of course, only natural," Emon agrees, trying to placate her. "This hallway leads to the Dwarf quarters, and the one on your right leads to the Vampire wing of the fortress." He instructs her indicating the two hallways with an elegant gesture of his large manicured hand. "The passage behind us leads to the visitor's quarters, and the lower entrances. When you need to get back to your room, just go straight back the way we came. Do not turn left or right. Just go straight, and eventually you will find your way. Is that clear?"

Gwen nods. On their way here, she had been too distracted to notice where she was going, but it seemed like a long endless trek through many rooms, corridors, and passageways. *How would I ever find my way back?*

"Now, I should warn you not to wander into either of the other wings of the fortress. Although they are not forbidden to guests, it is common courtesy. Neither, Dwarfs or Vampire are social creatures by nature. Most interaction among the species will take place here in the grand chamber," Emon explains, indicating the golden double doors before them.

"Okay, but won't I have an escort or something to guide me about the place? I can't stay for too long. I have to find my friend. He'll be worried about me."

"Your friend can wait. I'm sure he would want you to be in the company of your own kind."

"But he is our kind. He's a Werewolf, a Lycan," Gwen retorts.

Emon stiffens, appalled. Even the two guards look at her in horror. One of them even gives her a disapproving grunt accompanied by a wicked sneer.

Gwen looks at them all, puzzled. "What's wrong?" she asks.

Emon leans close to her. "You best not speak of your friend while you are here. Their kin are the natural enemy to the Vampire and are generally looked down upon by most of the tribes of Cain."

Gwen can barely keep from shouting at him. *How dare you insult Raven! You don't even know him!* She fumes angrily but manages to keep her calm. She nods her head in agreement, her jaw set stubbornly.

"Now, we have dallied long enough. Lord Legion is very anxious to meet you," Emon adds in a light-hearted tone, acting as if nothing untoward were said.

The Elf gives a curt nod to one of the Ogres, who turns to his fellow guard. Together, the two Ogres push the doors open, an effortless feat for them, but Gwen suspects it would be impossible for any mere human to attempt. The doors groan and screech under the effort until the doors are spread wide revealing the grand chamber within.

Emon beckons her to come to his side. She obeys, a strange mingle of apprehension and excitement welling inside her chest, making it very difficult for Gwen to breathe.

One of the Ogres stays by the open doorway while the first walks ahead of Emon and Gwen, leading the way.

Gwen catches a glimpse of several personages across the room. She doesn't get a good look at them, however, for Emon immediately whispers for her to bow. She bows, feeling idiotic.

She goes as if to stand again immediately but stops herself when she notices that Emon stays bent over as if frozen in place by her side. Gwen stays in the ridiculous pose, wanting to keep with protocol like a good, courteous guest.

"His grace Emon of the North-Water Clan presents Witch child of the tribe of Wiccan, daughter of Willow and sister of darkness!" the Ogre announces formally in a loud, booming voice. To Gwen's surprise, the Ogre's voice isn't dimwitted or as deep as she imagined, but clear and strong, full of hidden intelligence. Gwen feels a little ashamed that she had been so quick to judge the Ogre on his appearance. Without telepathy to tell her all about a person, she can't help but judge the book by its cover. Mentally she determines to avoid prejudice in the future.

"Arise, brother Elf and Sister Witch, and come forth," replies a beautiful, masculine voice from somewhere deeper in the chamber. Emon straightens, and Gwen follows suit.

The Ogre turns on his heel in a military fashion, exiting the room in a brisk march. The two guards pull the doors behind them with the same scraping of metal on stone punctuated by a loud bang as the doors close, the sound echoing off the stone walls of the chamber.

Gwen feels a bit befuddled, not sure where to look, what to do, or how to act. She decides to simply play follow the leader and do whatever Emon does. How could she go wrong?

Emon takes her by the hand and together they walk across the room. Gwen looks up to see thirteen individuals standing before them on the opposite side of the chamber. They stand on what looks like a stone stage. A pale, elegantly dressed man looking like a king sits upon a massive, stone throne carved of rock and inlaid in gold. He stands to greet them as they approach the stage. He's surrounded by other tall, pale, figures, men and woman of his kind, as well as several Dwarfs and some of the other species that inhabit this place. They're all finely dressed like characters out of a Shakespearian play, opulent and splendid. Somewhere in the back of her mind, Gwen senses that this is an honor of sorts to be greeted by them, that she is being shown respect. However accidental, she is an honored guest.

Gwen studies all the faces before her, trying to appear calm and detached without seeming arrogant or rude, examining each face one by one. She saves the Master for last. She finally focuses her full attention on the pale, white figure standing before the royal throne. Gwen's heart skips a beat and her breath catches in her chest. The world seems to slow to a crawl, everything fading from existence except for the man before her.

Legion is the most beautiful man she has beheld. He's neither masculine nor feminine, but refined in his stature and face. His skin is as pale as polished marble, his eyes white as freshly fallen snow. His pupils seem a deeper, more absolute black for the lack of color around them. His platinum blond hair is almost as white as his skin, making his overall appearance seem albino by nature.

It appears as if he wears a layer of soft, white powder on his face with a faint hint of rouge on his high-boned cheeks. They blend, the powdery skin fitting perfectly with his seventeenth-century French clothing. It's as if he just stepped right out of the pages of *The Man in the Iron Mask* and King Louis the XIV stands before her in his royal splendor. Surprisingly, he's not wearing a powdered wig to complete the look, but instead wears his pale, blond hair in silky waves cut about the length of his ears. He is exquisite in every way, beautiful in his every gesture and movement, in every thread of his being.

Gwen can't help comparing the white angel before her to the tall, elegant Elf standing beside her. They are both tall, but the Elf is at least a head and a half taller. They're both fine-boned, lean, and aristocratic in features and air, and finely dressed. Where

Emon is scholarly and old of demeanor, Legion seems young and full of energy brimming beneath the surface. Legion's grace and fluid movements make Emon seem clumsy and awkward.

The longer Gwen looks upon Legion, the more deadly beautiful he seems to her. She senses something predatory about him, like a panther about to pounce on his prey. Oddly enough, Gwen finds herself wishing he would pounce on her, dominate her, and overpower her. The thought makes Gwen blush, and she shakes herself inwardly to clear her head.

She chastises herself. *Get a hold of yourself, Gwen. You'd think you'd never seen a man before.* Gwen never really noticed anyone of the opposite sex in this way. Even though she's almost twelve, she has yet to get her period. While she lacks curves like the other girls her age, the adolescent hormones seem to be setting in. Gwen hasn't made a fool of herself over a guy yet, and she certainly isn't going to start now, especially with a man old enough to be her father.

Well, if you think about it, he's a great deal older than that. He could possibly be older than my great, great grandfather, Gwen reminds herself.

This thought repulses her, and she uses this mental image to keep all girly notions out of her head. From now on she'll simply think of the ridiculously gorgeous Vampire as great, great grandpa Legion.

"Ah, so at last the Witch awakens!" The beautiful Vampire speaks, his voice like music to Gwen's ears, his smile charming, yet wicked at the same time.

Great, grandpa! Great, great grandpa! Gwen chants inside her head.

"Yes, Master, may I introduce you to Gwenevere. Gwen, this is Lord Legion, ruler of the mountain fortress Bec LaNuff," Emon informs with every bit of eloquence he can muster.

Gwen feels numb all over. She should say something, but what? Should she shake Legion's hand, or bow again, or…

Thankfully Legion speaks first. "Emon, you forget protocol. You failed to mention her full name, her clan, or her coven. Tsk," Legion rebukes as he sucks air between his gleaming white teeth. "Our distinguished guest deserves to be treated with the utmost respect."

"I did not mean to show disrespect, Lord. It is simply that the girl is orphaned. She has no last name, clan, or coven. She explained to me on the way here that she has no recollection of her parents or where she came from. In fact, we are the first of her kind she has ever met," Emon clarifies, his voice calm and patient. Gwen senses that Emon is not the kind who appreciates being corrected.

"I see. So we have ourselves a Wild Witch," Legion announces to the room with a sophisticated air. Something in the way he says "we" makes Gwen uncomfortable. The other prominent figures murmur, a general chatter of whispered comments stirring through them at this new revelation.

"I do know how to use my powers," Gwen says defensively,

"and I have met other mythical creatures before, just not any Elfs, Dwarfs, Ogres, Giants, or Vampires."

"That doesn't leave many of the tribes out," Legion remarks with a smirk.

He ascends the steps of the stage to stand before Gwen. Her heart beats faster the closer he comes. Legion circles around her, examining her intently. Gwen hides her anxiety behind a blank face. Finally, he stands in front of her again, only a foot away. He looms high above her, causing her to winch her neck to look up at him.

"Then tell me, beautiful little Witch, who else have you encountered on your travels? I am very interested in getting to know each you."

Gwen gulps. Her entire body is aware of him, her mind a cloud of incomprehension and bizarre thoughts as he stares deep into her face. His snowy eyes bore a hole into her soul as if he can see all that she is and all that she will yet become. After a moment, she realizes he asked her a question.

"I've met some Witches, a family of them.. It was not a pleasant meeting." Gwen nearly mentions Raven, but one glance at Emon's concerned face makes her decide against it. The last thing Gwen wants is to hear Raven insulted or to put off her new companions. *After all, I won't be staying here long. Why upset anyone?*

Stepping back, Legion gestures with his hand and suddenly two teenage boys, whom Gwen hadn't noticed waiting silently in the corner, hurry across the room to his side. They're dressed just like the other human boy Peter was. Their appearance reminds her of the slaves in ancient Egypt.

One carries a golden pitcher, the other a tray with golden goblets. Legion holds out his hand to take one. The other boy eagerly fills the cup with a deep red liquid. Gwen feels revulsion in the pit of her stomach as she imagines what that drink might be.

To Gwen's surprise, Legion steps toward her and offers her the goblet in his hand.

Hesitantly, she takes the cup.

"Witches have always been a peculiar race. They are intimidated by independent creatures. They shelter their children, hiding them away from the world until they're in their twenties and then marry them off in bizarre arranged marriages. They run around naked in the middle of the forest and have nightly orgies." Legion and Emon exchange a look at this.

"I wouldn't know, sir. I'll have to take your word on it… for now," Gwen replies, feeling a little insulted on behalf of her race. True, she doesn't actually know anything about them, but she's still one of them.

Legion, holding his own golden goblet, waits patiently as the two teenage servants hurry about the crowd distributing drinks. When all of them have a cup of refreshment in their hands, Legion turns to Gwen.

"Let us toast our honored guest. May she find everything she desires here amongst us and live long under the mountain." Legion

raises his cup. The others do the same, all drinking when he drinks. Gwen alone does not.

She looks down into her cup at the suspicious red liquid within, takes a breath, and then finally raises the goblet to her lips and takes a sip. A sweet, rich taste greets her tongue as the liquid slides down her throat. *Wine!* she sighs in relief. *I'm not really old enough to drink this,* she reminds herself, *but then perhaps human laws are inapplicable here*. Something in Legion's toast comes to mind, forcing her to speak up.

Nervously but firmly, Gwen makes her voice heard over the general clamor of the assembly. "I am very grateful for your hospitality, and that one of your kind saved my life, but I really can't stay long. I have to find my friend. He is expecting me."

Silence falls over the crowd. Emon's expression of irritation is no surprise. Legion turns to her, a look of astonishment upon his handsome countenance.

"My dear, you can have all the friends you desire here. We can protect you from the outside world, give you everything you always wanted. There's really no reason to leave. After all, do you really have anything to go back to?" Legion voice is melodic, its sound hypnotic to Gwen's ears.

"Besides, you can't leave now in the dead of winter. You've barely recovered from pneumonia. How will you survive out there alone in the wilderness?" Legion asks as if speaking to a simple child. "Do you have shelter?"

"No." Gwen confesses reluctantly.

"Do you have supplies? Can you hunt?"

"No. I can't. I don't," Gwen admits. Going out into the wilderness again is suicide. As much as it rankles her pride to confess it, she knows now she is helpless against the forces of Mother Nature.

"At least stay until spring! In the meantime, enjoy yourself, become a part of our community. Let us teach you about our world. I'm sure there are many questions you'd like answered. What better place to learn than here?" Legion makes a grand gesture indicating the Elf beside her. "Emon is a gifted scholar and historian. What better tutor could you have than he? Please stay. I insist." Legion speaks with a kinder, more understanding voice, winning Gwen over with his debonair smile.

"All right then, just until spring," she agrees. "Thank you."

"Well, now that this is settled, allow me to show you to your new quarters."

"But, sir, I already have a room," Gwen replies.

"Oh, my dear, that was simply a sick room—temporary lodging until you recovered. As a member of our sister tribe, you must stay with us."

Legion saunters alongside Gwen, taking her by the hand without preamble.

Gwen wonders a little at herself for not feeling more on guard around this complete stranger. She should be annoyed that yet another adult male wants to lead her around by the hand like a baby. However, Gwen isn't the least bit bothered by this. She craves Legion's touch, and gets an erotic little shiver through her veins as his cold hand clasps hers. He smiles down at her, as if he knows what she's thinking and feeling. Gwen knows this is not the case. She would have felt him in her head if he were there.

Legion leads the way out of the room, Emon and the others falling in a double-file line behind them with the servants taking up the rear. The two massive golden doors open before them as if the Ogre guards can sense their Master's every desire and action.

As they exit the room, a young girl with short, red, curly hair around Gwen's age suddenly appears on the other side of Legion. She's dressed in a long, white gown. She gives Gwen a sneer before taking Legion's vacant hand to join them.

Legion stops dead in his tracks, causing the rest of the procession to follow suit. He looks darkly at the redheaded child beside him, and she cowers under his intolerant gaze. Legion gestures with his head for her to fall in line behind them. Sulking, she goes to stand directly behind them, in front of Emon and the others.

The procession continues, exiting the grand chamber and turning left down the hall, leading to the private Vampire wing of the fortress. Legion speaks of the fortress and the schedule they keep since they live under the mountain, but Gwen only half listens.

She is too distracted to pay much attention. She can practically feel the girl's stare, like needles in her back. *Had she been in the grand chamber during the whole interview? Why didn't I notice her? Why wasn't she introduced?*

Within her mind, Gwen tries to reach out to the red-headed girl behind her. *I'm not here to take anything that belongs to you. I'm just visiting, that's all. Please tell me your name.* Gwen waits for a response from the girl while smiling and nodding at Legion as they walk down the passageway. Finally, the girl responds to her in her own mind.

How did you do that?! It is you, isn't it? You really are a Witch! The girl's mental voice is incredulous.

Yes. I am. Please, let's try to get along. Tell me your name? Gwen asks again.

Melody Lynn Carver. I'm from Vermont, the girl answers.

I'm Gwen from nowhere. How long have you been here? Gwen asks.

Not that long, at least a couple months. What do you mean you're from nowhere? Don't you have family? Melody inquires. Gwen can feel the little redhead walking directly behind her.

Forget it. It's not important. I want to know about you. Why are you here? You're obviously human. Aren't your parents worried about you?

Well, I actually don't recall how I got here. One night I fell asleep in my room and woke up here. At first I wanted to go home, but things are so much better here, and the Master is so nice to me that I decided to stay, the girl replies matter-of-factly, a happy, dreamy air to her voice and the images in her head.

Gwen isn't able to ask the girl any more questions because

they suddenly come to a stop. Gwen hopes she hasn't missed something important during her conversation, for she didn't hear a word the Vampire said the whole time.

Legion smiles down at Gwen, making her heart ache at the sight. Gwen looks before her to see a large, silver door encrusted in emeralds, diamonds, rubies, and sapphires in an elegant pattern. He reaches out and pushes open the door before them.

Gwen can't believe the splendor of the bedroom within. The chamber is lit by dozens of tiny golden flames hanging from lanterns carved on the walls, giving the scene a romantic, ambient glow. The floor is marble, tiled just like the grand chamber, the furnishing ornate and exquisite. A desk of deep mahogany looks as if fashioned for ancient royalty, and a nightstand and table made of carved polished jade in the shapes of elephants and dragons along the legs. A massive four-post canopy bed that looks to be made of ivory sits at the opposite wall draped in white gossamer curtains. Beautiful draperies and paintings adorn the walls. Gold and silver goblets, pitchers, combs, and hand mirrors are spread throughout the room, glittering and shining in the lantern's golden flames.

Gwen is speechless. Legion leads her inside, most of the procession staying out in the hall except for Emon and Melody. As soon as they enter the room, Gwen notices two young girls, both in their teens, kneeling beside the bedroom door, their heads bowed and their eyes to the floor. The girls wear similar attire to the male servants, but along with the skirt they wear a sash of red fabric across their chests, barely concealing their bosoms.

Legion snaps his fingers and the two servant girls immediately hop to their feet. Without any further instruction or gestures from their Master, and without looking at anyone or speaking a word, the two identical girls go to a large, ornate, wooden cabinet standing against the wall directly across from the bed. Opening the cabinet doors to show the clothing hanging within, the girls fall to their knees, faces turned to the floor once more.

"These are my gifts to you." He steps forward, pulling out a gorgeous, shimmering green gown with gold lace across the breast and capped sleeves. She's never seen a piece of clothing so stunning. Her hand automatically reaches out to touch the fabric. Looking at the wardrobe, she notices that the rest of the closet is full of clothing just like this—a wardrobe fit for a princess, not a runaway orphan.

"This dress will go perfectly with those eyes of yours," Legion whispers, reaching out his hand to stroke her face affectionately.

Even as his touch makes her weak in the knees, something in his intense gaze gives her warning. She might not be trying to replace Melody, but the jealous, yellow pallor on the girl's face—and the look of adoration on Legion's—makes it all too clear that he just might have different plans. Gwen suddenly feels uneasy. She steps back and moves out of Legion's reach. His face takes on a disappointed and confused look.

"Is something wrong, Gwenevere? Don't you like your room and my gifts?"

"No, they're all beautiful, but I really can't accept any of this.

I'm more than happy to stay in my old room and I would be glad to have my old clothes back as well. In fact, I was meaning to ask if someone knew where my red duffel bag is," Gwen adds. She's been inching backward all during her speech until, to her amazement, she finds herself pressed against the footboard of the ivory bed.

"Well, of course you may have your possessions back," Legion soothes. Gwen thinks she must have sounded hysterical. "But, please, I must insist that you stay in this room. It would please me to have you nearby, to know you are being well looked after. The Vampire servants are the best in the fortress; the others are lazy and sloppy in comparison. These girls are yours." Legion indicates the two kneeling girls by the wardrobe. "They will show you around, take you were you want to go, and bring you anything you desire."

"Okay, I'll stay in this room on one condition," Gwen replies.

Legion looks a little wary, but nods anyway.

"I get to wear my own clothes. And no servants."

Legion laughs. "Why, my dear Gwen, of course. Wear anything you like. These gowns are just for special occasions."

"Good." Gwen lets out a sigh of relief. "Because t-shirts, jeans, and tennis shoes are more my style." She gives a nervous laugh.

Legion and Emon laugh as well. Melody doesn't say a word. Instead, she shouts mentally at her. *You liar! Stay away from him! I belong to him, not you! You can keep the stupid room and the clothes, just stay away from my love!*

Suddenly, Melody turns on her heels and runs out of the room. Legion and Emon both watch her leave and share a secret look.

"We will leave you now. One of the girls will fetch you something to eat," Legion announces.

"I know where to find your things, Gwen. I'll have my Elf mate bring them to you later," Emon adds. He bows and exits the room, leaving her alone with Legion, except for the serving girls who are so still they might as well be pieces of furniture.

"There will be a feast tonight in your honor. It will give you a chance to meet all the most important members of our society. Please wear the green dress tonight, for me?" Legion slowly moves toward her as if floating on air. He takes one of her hands in his and presses it to his cold, crimson lips in the briefest of kisses. "Until tonight," he says in an almost whisper, the sound like the hiss of a snake. He flashes a smile before turning and leaving the room, closing the door behind him.

Gwen stands at the foot of the bed, paralyzed in place, staring at the door where Legion last stood. Goosebumps cover her body. Her breath catches in her throat. She feels weak and dizzy. Finally, she takes a seat on the edge of the bed to collect herself. Her mind reels over the turn of events; she can hardly believe any of this is real.

"Somebody pinch me. I must be dreaming," Gwen says aloud.

A moment later, she feels something pinch her arm. Gwen jumps in surprise. Turning, she sees one of the servant girls standing next to her. At her sudden movement, the girl retreats back to her place, kneeling on the floor by the wardrobe again, her face red with embarrassment

"Why on earth did you do that?" Gwen demands of the girl, who doesn't reply or move an inch. "It's a figure of speech. I didn't mean it literally." She raises her voice at the down-turned head, exasperated.

Suddenly, she finds the two girls presence disturbing. Gwen realizes that although Legion consented to one of her conditions, he said nothing about the other one.

Oh, well. I might as well make good use of you two.

"Your master said one of you would get me something to eat?" This at last gains her a response out of the other girl, whose head pops up as she nods emphatically. "Okay, then. Will you please get me something to eat? Nothing too heavy, maybe soup if they have it, or crackers and cheese?" The girl stands and smiles, nodding and bowing as she leaves the room. This leaves Gwen with the one who pinched her.

"And I would like you to go find me...." Gwen searches her mind for something. "...a book to read. Surely Emon the Elf has a library, or something. Ask the Elf if you can barrow a book. Tell him it's for me," Gwen commands the girl kneeling before her.

Obviously still embarrassed, she doesn't look at Gwen but nods quickly, running from the room and slamming the bedroom door closed behind her to leave Gwen alone at last.

Gwen lets out a sigh of relief and falls onto the lush, soft bed.

She sits there a long while, admiring the objects in the room around her. She never dreamed she would ever sleep in a room quite as nice as this, or have such pretty things, but after a lifetime of bad luck and fate dealing her one terrible hand after another, it finally looks as though fate is giving her a break.

She finds it ironic that here she is given respect for the very same thing that always made others fear her. Here she is accepted as a Witch, considered powerful and extraordinary. She doesn't have to hide her talents here. She knows that they will not only understand but may be delighted to see all the tricks and spells she can do. She has always wanted to show off her powers, but until now, no one but Raven has truly appreciated them.

Thoughts of Raven momentarily dampen her good mood, but all her sadness is erased when she thinks of Legion. He is beautiful, intense, strong, exotic, and utterly fascinating. She meant what she said to Melody. She wouldn't try to steal his affection, but she doesn't mind having a little of his attention either. Yes, Gwen never in her life thought that she would find a place like this, a place where a Witch is welcome.

CHAPTER FOUR

Culture Shock

"Truth be told, Miss Gwen," says the little man beside her, "Wiccans are the only tribe that still live amongst the Eden Spawn." His piercing blue eyes are the only part of his dwarfish face not covered. His long wavy hair blends in seamlessly with his black fuzzy mustache and beard.

A more curious bunch of dinner guests Gwen cannot imagine. Eight men surround her. They are all elders, representing a different tribe of Cain, of which she's been told there are thirteen: Ogres, Giants, Goblins, Trolls, Elves, Fairies, Merpeople, Centaurs, Werewolves, Gargoyles, Vampires, Dwarfs, and Wiccans, who make up the children of Cain.

Gwen sits on the left hand of Legion who, as lord of the mount, sits at the head of the banquet table upon his gilded throne to represent the Vampire tribe. Beside her sits Finley, Gaul, and Ragnon—Dwarf, Giant, Goblin. Emon sits on Legion's right, along with Rinn and Christopher—Elf, Troll, Gargoyle. The last admitted that his mother was a human history buff and admired Christopher Columbus, for whom she named him, a fact which seems to embarrass him. Completing the party sits Slethum, Ogre, at the foot of the table. Gwen notes that Melody is not in attendance.

If the dinner guests are strange, the dinner itself is even stranger. Gwen can't begin to comprehend some of the dishes she sees the other creatures eating. Some she's pretty sure she doesn't want to know the particulars of. Thankfully, the place seems to have some regular foods as well, and Gwen has had her fill of mashed potatoes, roasted pig, sautéed mushrooms, and broccoli. An assorted bowl of fruit sits before her, and she enjoys a large sprig of grapes during the dinner conversation. After what seems like a long yet friendly interrogation on her human upbringing, Gwen is at last getting some of her questions answered in turn.

"Eden Spawn?" Gwen quirks a quizzical brow.

Around the banquet table several of the elders exchange tolerant smirks. Even if their faces don't show that they thought her ignorant and naïve, their thoughts tell her as much.

Obviously they have no clue they're dealing with a mind reader, Gwen muses to herself. *And they think I'm ignorant.*

"You must forgive the elders, Gwenevere. They are not accustomed to someone of your unique upbringing," Legion whispers in her right ear, as if he's the one with the gift of telepathy.

"Eden Spawn, Gwen, is one of the many names we call the humans, for their origination from Adam and Eve and the Garden of Eden," Emon answers in a scholarly voice. He sits in a high-back chair as regal as the Vampire next to him, in a pearl white suit of magnificent finery contrasting with his trophy-gold skin. His clothing is as elegant as the apparel worn by all the eight elders in attendance at this private dinner.

"Aren't we all descendants of Adam and Eve?" Gwen can't help but ask. Even if it makes her sound the fool, it's a perfectly sensible question to her.

Around the table, her questions produce a rumble of laughter. A dark look from Legion silences it immediately.

"That's a terrific question, Gwen. Who would like to answer our honored and esteemed guest?" Legion looks about the table, his eyes all but commanding the lot of them to behave themselves.

"If I may, my Lord?" Slethum, the captain of the Ogre guards, speaks up from the far end of the table. Legion nods in his direction. "Have you ever heard of Lilith?" The Ogre directs his question to Gwen.

She tries very hard not to stare at the mismatched features of his misshapen face. "Yes. She's referred to as the mother of demons and some even say she was Adam's first wife," Gwen replies matter-of-factly.

"That's right. Only to us she is much more. She and Cain, the first son of Adam, are the parents of all the thirteen tribes."

"That's why they are called The Thirteen Tribes of Cain. Why not The Thirteen Tribes of Lilith?" Gwen asks no one in particular.

"Spoken like a true Wiccan woman," Gaul the Giant guffaws, poking Ragnon the Goblin with his elbow. "A whole culture with a female superiority complex."

Several in the party laugh in response to his remark. Gwen can't help but smile as well. *Sounds like my kind of crowd*, she muses inwardly.

"So are we human or aren't we?" Gwen inquires once the company settles down.

"No, dearest, we are not," Legion answers sweetly. "Spiritually speaking, we were all created by the same God, but we owe our lives here on earth to the true master, Lucifer."

Gwen feels a chill at the sound of that name. It creeps slowly up her spine, yet she forces herself not to shiver. All around her she hears the others salute, "The Prince of the Morning," in a different toast of respect, tipping glasses and taking swills of their wine filled goblets. Her eyes stay glued on Legion's face. He seems to sense her disquiet and touches her hand lightly with his cold boney fingers.

"What troubles you, Gwenevere?" he whispers, so that none else can hear.

"We are damned."

"Of course not, sister." Finley speaks suddenly, making Gwen jump in her seat. She stifles a yelp of surprise. "It is our kind that will inherit the Earth, not the children of God."

"Our lord and master will rule after Armageddon. What humans are left will serve us." Ragnon adds this in his goblin croak of a voice.

"I hate to break the news to you guys," Gwen replies, "but that's not how it's going to turn out. I grew up in a Catholic orphanage taught by nuns and a priest, and I had to study the Bible religiously—pun intended."

"I wouldn't believe everything you read, child," answers Christopher the Gargoyle, his hard, stony skin, horned scalp, and Gothic wings giving him a far more intimidating air than his perfectly normal American accent does. "Especially in that book," he scoffs, before taking a sip of his wine.

"Exactly. You never hear any mention of any of us in the Bible, do you?" Emon asks rhetorically. "Yet here we are. It stands to reason that the whole truth is not in that book. It merely tells one side of the story."

"And the ending is yet to be written?" Gwen asks the Elf.

"We have our own prophets and prophecies, Gwen. The book of Lilith paints a very different picture of the end of the world than the one you were taught," Emon instructs.

"But what about—" Gwen begins.

"Let's talk no more of this. I tire of these religious debates," Legion interrupts in a cheerful voice. He snaps his fingers.

Instantly a company of red-clad human servants begin to clear away the remains of dinner. The servants had been kneeling along the wall so quietly that Gwen forgot they were in the room.

Gwen expects the gathering to adjourn after dessert. She desperately longs for the chance to get back to her room, to get out of her ridiculous gown, and to get some time to herself. It is not to be. Legion arises, and taking Gwen by the hand, he leads her onto the stone stage at the end of the room, indicating that she take one of the smaller thrones while he takes the center one. The rest of the elders assemble around them in a line to either side of them, facing the chamber's entrance.

Legion claps his hands and the grand doors to the chamber open, revealing a throng of well-wishers waiting outside. Legion signals for the citizens of Bec LaNuff to enter. They come forth in what seems to Gwen like a never-ending parade of mythical creatures, coming to bow before them and place gifts at her feet. They give her fine jewelry, trinkets, animal furs, weapons of strange construction, musical instruments, plants, herbs, fruit, and even animals in cages.

No one told Gwen she was to be given homage, or even thought to inform her that she was so revered amongst the people of the mountain. After all, she arrived recently. They had never met her. Many she was only seeing for the first time, and as far as she knew, she had done nothing to deserve such a grand gesture of respect. She is only a girl, just little Gwen, not some great enchantress.

She keeps her mouth shut, not wanting to offend anyone by outright refusing this honor, but she feels like an imposter. Occasionally, one of her admirers pauses a moment and asks her to place a blessing on them or a loved one. At this, Gwen smiles and nods until the confused creature is urged to move on by one of the servants so that the procession can proceed. She lets out a sigh of relief.

I don't know any blessing spells, or even curses now that I think of it, Gwen admits to herself. Now more than ever, she is forced to face how inexperienced a Witch she really is.

To Gwen's dismay, her evening isn't over yet. After the presents, there is entertainment. Every tribe does its own ritual dances and music according to their tribes' customs. Warriors of the tribes compete in contests of strength. Women dance ritualistic dances, singing ancient songs in the old tongue, telling stories of their tribes' many triumphs and defeats. It is ancient and barbaric, reminding Gwen of the kind of celebration she read about in books about Scottish Highlanders preparing for war. At the end, Legion requests that Gwen do a demonstration of her talents for the assembly.

To demonstrate her powers, she makes orbs of fire dance about in patterns, enthralling the servants with her voice, and making them do funny things the way hypnotists do in their shows. She rearranges the furniture in the room with the spell of levitation, all to amuse Legion and his subjects.

All present seem impressed by Gwen's display of power,

except the Vampires. Gwen has kept an eye on the slender, pale, gray-eyed race all through the evening, watching them move like wraiths throughout the crowd, casting a shadow over the festive atmosphere with their dark, sinister presence. Every one of them watches her with blank, emotionless expressions as if she is unworthy of their attention. She had the misfortune of crossing paths briefly with Ryan, Jezebel, and Lethawyn, the three female Vampires she passed in the hall earlier. Since she knows their names, she tried to engage them in conversation. They respond only with disdainful looks, and turning abruptly, the trio walks away from her, keeping their distance the rest of the evening. The the only Vampire to treat her with the least bit of kindness is Legion. He who lavishes her with compliments, showers her with gifts, and is always charming and beautiful.

One other individual whom Gwen notices seems to avoid her is a tall, golden-skinned, red-headed woman. She looks to be an Elf, with green eyes that seem to blaze whenever she and Gwen look at each other. Gwen can only assume she's Emon's mate, Vinita, for they are the only two of their race living in Bec LaNuff. Gwen decides it's best not to press for an introduction just yet.

At last the night is over, the celebration brought to an end as the dawn approaches. While young Vampires can stay up for days without sleep, elder Vampires like Legion require rest. They grow faint and weak with the dawn, even under hundreds of feet of rock, stone, and dirt. Most of the tribes of Cain are nocturnal in nature, so the party disperses to their separate quarters for the comfort of their beds and a good day's sleep. No one is more drained than Gwen. Shuffling her tired feet toward her bed chamber, she decides this has been the longest and most unusual day of her life. Now she truly understood the meaning of "culture shock."

CHAPTER FIVE

The First Witch

The next day, Gwen awakes feeling groggy and befuddled from the evening's festivities. She moans as she rolls onto her side, examining the room about her. The hazy confusion of sleep in her mind lingers as she tries to recollect the opulent bedchamber. She reluctantly rolls out of bed. The stone floor feels icy cold beneath her feet as she stumbles across the room to the vanity to peer in the golden mirror. Her reflection gives the image of a young, pale girl with midnight black hair and yellow-green, vibrant eyes wearing a yellow, silk nightdress that hangs off of her skinny, flat-chested frame. Behind her she observes the room with its elegant furnishings. Slowly her mind accepts her reality.

"Bec LaNuff," Gwen says aloud to her reflection, letting the words roll off of her tongue in the ancient language. *So it hadn't all been a dream.* She admits that she half expected it all to fade away, that none of this grand place would remain when she awoke. She is almost shocked not to wake up lying in the snow in the middle of the forest. Gwen shrugs the notion off and opens the vanity drawer to retrieve a hair comb to tidy her disheveled bed hair.

A hand springs out of sight, snatching the comb out of her reach. Gwen jumps, and spinning around, she almost knocks into one of the servant girls standing wide-eyed before her with the comb clutched to her chest, trembling in fear.

"Oh! You scared the life out of me," Gwen replies in English, taking a few quick breaths to steady herself. She reaches out for the comb in the girl's hand.

The girl steps back, shaking her head vigorously. She gestures for Gwen to turn around so she can comb her hair for her.

"Look, I can comb my own hair," Gwen informs the servant girl Jessica.

She asked Legion her maid servants' names the night before in an attempt to get rid of them. It failed, so she figured she might as well know a little something about them. The notion seemed silly to Legion, but he told her their names and what he knew of them simply to indulge her. The two girls, Jessica and Lydia, are cousins. Jessica, the eldest with chestnut-brown hair, is about sixteen years old, and Lydia, the shorter, darker brunette, is fourteen. The girls are very pretty, with caramel skin, suggesting Latin heritage, and large, dark, baby-doll eyes. They had been in the service of the people of Bec LaNuff for two years. He couldn't remember where they came from or any other particulars. When she asked him why they had human slaves, who had brought them here, and why they never spoke, Legion casually changed the subject.

Gwen knows talking to them is useless. She stayed up half the night trying to get the girls to speak to her, looking for some pleasant conversation with normal people after the long, grueling dinner in her honor. Legion had made her the center of attention, a role Gwen was not accustomed to playing. No matter what she did, Jessica and Lydia never spoke to her, only pantomimed their responses while trying to avoid looking her in the face. Frustrated, Gwen gives up on verbal communication and reaches into their consciousness, trying to lure them out telepathically. She is surprised by what she finds. Their minds are blank, vacant of thought or emotion, their auras gray and stagnant, and the vibrant hum of intelligence nothing more than a dull, pedantic, one-note tune...yet they respond to commands and directions. It is all very strange to Gwen.

Maybe I can ask Emon why they are this way when I see him. Right now I just want to be alone.

Again Gwen tries to take the comb from the slave girl. Jessica only tightens her grip more firmly on the item.

"Fine. Have it your way!" Gwen turns around and lets Jessica comb out her hair. Afterward, Jessica hurries to the wardrobe, returning with a long, black, silk dress with a blood-red sash and ribbons cut into the skirt in a fantastical design. She lays the dress on Gwen's bed. She glances at the dress, looks at Jessica, and then shakes her head in outright refusal.

What else is there to wear? Gwen thinks to herself irritably. *I still haven't gotten my duffle bag from Emon.*

Jessica goes to answer a knock at the door, but Gwen beats her, reaching it a second before her. She heaves the stone door open. Standing at her doorstep is the tall Elfin woman. She towers over Gwen with angular features and golden skin like the body glitter some girls wore at Scranton Junior High. Her lime green eyes are large and wild like a hungry animal, her ears long and pointed with curved tips, and her hair as red as a summer sunset.

"Hello. You must be Vinita, Emon's mate. Am I right?" Gwen asks politely, putting on her most welcoming and charming smile.

"Yes. You are the Wiccan child?" Vinita replies, asking but not waiting for Gwen's confirmation of her identify. The ethereal woman openly inspects Gwen with her predatory eyes, scanning her physique until she finally looks her in the face. By the look of self-satisfaction, arrogance, and disdain on Vinita's face, Gwen can tell that she failed to impress her. "Here are your personal effects." Vinita swings the red duffle at Gwen with a cool, detached air.

"My name is Gwenevere, by the way," she replies, but the Elf has already turned, leaving Gwen to speak to her broad-shouldered back.

Gwen glares at her, burning a hole with her eyes in between the woman's shoulder blades, and then steps back into her room, closing the door.

"Thank God!" Gwen says. Walking to the bed, she throws the duffle on top of the black and red silk dress. Unzipping the bag, she peers inside. Everything looks okay, but just to make sure, Gwen picks up the duffel and turns it upside down, emptying the contents all over the bed and her elegant gown.

Jessica, who has been standing next to the bed with her head slightly down turned, steps forward and grabs the gown out from under Gwen's possession, taking it over to the wardrobe and smoothing it out as if it's something precious. Gwen rolls her eyes, returning her attention to the haphazard heap lying before her. Quickly, she takes a mental list of all the things she owns, one by one placing them back into her bag as she checks them off. The smell of lavender wafts from the clothes, and Gwen picks up a shirt to sniff it more closely.

Someone has laundered my clothes, Gwen notes to herself, feeling a mixture of gratitude and discomfort. She pauses when she imagines some complete stranger touching her underwear. Gwen cringes but decides the harm's already done and puts it out of her mind. When she notes that everything is accounted for, she lets out a sigh.

She finds her favorite outfit, a pair of light blue jeans, a long orange tunic, a light grey striped cardigan, and a pair of thick, woolen, black socks, and sets them aside. Digging into the bag again, she produces a pair of worn, black, Converse sneakers and adds them to her other clothing. She zips up the bag and stows it under the bed.

Quickly, Gwen changes her clothes. Jessica flutters around her, trying to take over the mundane task, but Gwen slaps her hands away, shooing her. Gwen glares at her until the girl gives up and goes back to her usual spot in the corner of the room to kneel on the floor until she is needed again.

She feels rejuvenated by her own clothes upon her skin, as though she can better handle this strange new world in something familiar. These clothes are true to her nature, though she has a funny feeling that she won't get many opportunities to wear them.

As she finishes doing up the laces of her sneakers, someone knocks at the door. This time Gwen allows the girl to perform her duties. On the other side waiting patiently is the other servant girl, Lydia. She enters balancing a tray of food on each hand. At the sight of the breakfast tray, Gwen's stomach rumbles, making her somewhat glad to have the servants after all. Gwen has to admit it would've taken her hours to figure out where the kitchen is in this massive place. She would've gone mad with starvation before she found food. *Besides, the girls seem to know their way around. Maybe they could show me the way to Emon's room,* Gwen reflects to herself.

Lydia hands a tray to her older cousin and together the girls glide across the room, holding the trays high, not spilling a drop. Lydia and Jessica place the breakfast trays on the bed beside Gwen. Immediately, Lydia reaches into a pocket on her red skirt and brings out a set of silverware. She hands the utensils to Gwen and together the cousins back away, bowing all the way to their designated corner. Gwen ignores the girls, her attention consumed by the food.

The first tray contains silver-dollar pancakes, a pitcher of maple syrup, sausage links, bacon, biscuits, a dish of butter, four different kinds of muffins, toast with several kinds of jelly on the side, and an empty bowl; alongside it are several travel-size cereal boxes of different types. The second tray is laden with several glasses of various beverages: milk, orange juice, ice water, grapefruit juice, hot chocolate, a cup of hot water with several tea bags on a saucer, and a mug of coffee with cream and sugar alongside it.

"Did you raid a Denny's, Lydia? Or is there one hiding somewhere inside the mountain?" Gwen asks aloud in an attempt to tease the servant girl. Neither one responds. Gwen sighs, picks up a fork, and digs in. With such a smorgasbord, Gwen satisfies her hunger in no time, eating half of the food on the tray. She drinks all the milk, orange juice, and hot chocolate. When finished, Gwen pushes the trays away and gets up.

Immediately, the cousins spring to their feet and hurry to gather up the remains of the breakfast. Gwen watches them out of the corner of her eye as she combs her hair into a pony tail. She notices that the girls seem to look over the trays as if memorizing what she had eaten, filing it away for future reference. *I bet there will only be food I like on the tray tomorrow.* Obviously, someone wanted to please her, to make her feel as comfortable in Bec

LaNuff as possible. Gwen knows her benevolent guardian is Legion. It pleases her, and yet at the same time makes her leery. Gwen shakes off the strange feeling of suspicion, thinking, *He's just being nice, and you're being paranoid because no one's ever been nice to you before.*

Gwen gives herself one last look in the mirror. Satisfied, she heads for the door. The cousins follow, their heads partially bowed, each one carrying one of her breakfast trays. Gwen half expects them to hurry off to the kitchen to get rid of the uneaten food, but instead, the girls follow closely behind her down the hall.

Gwen stops abruptly and spins around to face them. The girls stop in unison, as if anticipating her every move. "I'm looking for Master Emon's chambers, or the library if you have one. Which way should I go?" she asks.

The servant girls look at each, and then Jessica straightens, handing her tray to Lydia and nodding. The younger girl hurries away in the opposite direction. Jessica, bowing repetitively, gestures for Gwen to follow her. Exasperated, Gwen follows. Jessica leads the way through the Vampire wing of the fortress, back to the spot in front of the grand chamber where the three massive hallways converge. The passageway straight ahead of them leads to the Dwarves' quarters, so that means the passageway on her left will lead her to the lower levels of the fortress and to the visitor's quarters. Emon's room must be that way.

Without acknowledging the Ogres standing guard outside the grand hall, Jessica turns into the left passageway. Gwen has to quicken her pace to keep up with the servant girl as they traverse through the hallways till they enter the domed courtyard with the sun, moon, and the giant eye glowing down from the ceiling.

Again the courtyard is filled with various creatures walking to and fro through the many archways all about the perimeter of the room. Many stop to greet Gwen, while others bow respectfully as she passes. Some call out greetings from across the room. Feeling bombarded by the attention, Gwen forces a nervous smile, bows, and waves her hand in greeting. She notices a few disapproving glances at her attire from the Vampires, but they say nothing and move on. Jessica turns into one of the side archways, leading Gwen out of the courtyard and into another corridor which ends with a massive door crafted out of jade and carved with a tree in the center.

Jessica stops abruptly before the door and falls on her knees, pressing her face to the floor. Gwen stands, dumbfounded. *Can't they do anything normal?* She hesitantly steps around the prostrate form on the floor and up to the green polished door. It has no handle, but instead, a large, gold ring knocker that hangs high above her head. Gwen has to tiptoe to reach it. She awkwardly raps it against the jade door three times.

Suddenly, the door opens. The room before her is exceedingly bright, illuminated by an indefinable light source, making it impossible to identify the shapes inside the room. Gwen blinks to protect her eyes from the brilliant light.

Waiting patiently inside the doorway is a small grandfather of a Dwarf, with a pleasant, wrinkled face, and bright blue eyes. She can't make out much more of his face beyond the eyes and the nose, for his head is covered in brilliant white hair, like a snow-covered mountain top. A matching beard hides his mouth and chin, hanging down to his knees. Underneath, Gwen can barely distinguish dark-brown leather pants and a green tunic, old and worn, with a dagger hanging from his leather belt.

"We've been expecting you. Master Emon said you are a curious soul." The Dwarf has a kind voice, ancient and upbeat. Not waiting for a reply, he turns on his heels and wanders deeper into the chamber. Gwen hurries after him.

As they walk, Gwen's eyes adjust to the light and she begins to make out the room about her. The large chamber has a domed, vaulted ceiling hundreds of feet high. The room is cramped with hundreds of bookshelves reaching into the rafters, each stuffed with thousands of books, stone tablets, pottery, and scrolls yellow with age. In awe, she feels as though she is walking through centuries of history, passing through the pages of time.

They pass several other creatures, mostly Dwarves and servants wandering about the aisles of bookshelves, their arms laden. A warm, elated sensation builds within Gwen's chest with every step, growing stronger with each new aisle until she feels as though she could soar to the ceiling.

There has to be answers here. Some record of my people will be in these shelves, I know it!

Suddenly, her guide turns down an aisle, and in her distracted, thoughtful state, Gwen nearly walks on, not noticing till a moment later that she lost sight of the white-haired little man. In a panic, Gwen looks around till she spies his small white head turning down another aisle. She hurries to catch up, almost running over a young Dwarf woman in the process. Gwen turns the corner and finds herself in a large, open space in the center of the chamber. Several small desks line rows from one end of the clearing to the other. Beyond, Gwen sees more massive shelves. In the middle of the grouping of wooden desks, three larger desks are set up like work stations with pens, paper, and stacks of books.

Gwen walks slowly down the aisle, where some desks are occupied by little old Dwarf men, others by Ogres. Now and then, she sees a human servant gathering books off of desks or pushing carts laden with records sorting them back on their shelves. The white-haired Dwarf walks up to one of the large desks and pulls the sleeve of the tall man sitting there.

Emon, with his long flowing hair and pointed, curled ears, sits in a massive chair, hunched over a stack of scrolls, reading and writing simultaneously. As the Dwarf tugs on his sleeve, he looks down. Gwen sees them exchange words and then Emon looks up, his gaze meeting hers. He beckons her with a welcoming smile. Gwen hurries nervously to join him.

"Ah, there you are, little Witch. I confess I expected you to show up at my door hours ago, but last night's festivities must have worn you out." Emon snaps his fingers. "Bring a chair for Lady Gwenevere," he commands. A human servant boy hurries forward with her seat. He sets it down but waits for her to sit before he moves away.

"Thank you," Gwen calls over shoulder to the retreating form.

"Don't trouble yourself with the servants, Gwen. They barely comprehend and do not speak," Emon informs her. "Did you enjoy the feast last night? I dare say it's not the sort of thing you're used to."

"It was fine, a little over whelming, but… Emon, why don't the servants speak? And what's wrong with their auras? I mean, I tried to reach into Jessica and Lydia's minds, but I found nothing there, and—"

A stricken look has overtaken Emon's handsome face. "You can see auras? Why, that is fascinating. How extraordinary! You and Vinita should get together and compare notes. She has many fascinating theories about the differences between one tribe's auras and the next, but since I have not the gift of inner sight, I can't tell if all she says is factual, or if she's trying to play tricks on me again."

"That's great, Emon. But you didn't answer my question. Please tell me how these humans got here? Why are they like the living dead?" Gwen asks again.

Emon sighs. "I'm afraid to offend your sensibilities, young Gwen. You were raised amongst the Eden Born, and as a result, you are apt to view humans as equals, as relevant creatures of sense, and intelligence. However…"

"However, our kind does not. Am I right? What do you mean

by Eden Born? Is that like Eden Spawn?" Gwen asks.

"We have many names for humans, more than they have for us. Some call them The Chosen, Eden Born, Adam Spawn, The Beloved, God Bloods, or Saints. As for how they got here, well... simply put, they were taken. Found wandering alone, caught poking into our secret places, dabbling in the Occult, and thus summoning us. Those of our kind that live near, and in the human cities, watch for signs of humans who are too curious. We apprehend these humans to protect ourselves from those who might dig too deep and find the truth."

"You mean there are humans out there who know, or at least think they know, about our kind and we just..." Gwen cuts herself off, not sure how to put the images in her head into words.

"Yes. We have our spies whose job is to destroy any threat to our civilization. Legion is not only head of the Vampires in the region, but a kind of sheriff of the territory. He keeps the peace here, protecting us from *them*." Emon gestures toward one of the servants carrying an armful of books, his face vacant, his manner lethargic as he moves, performing the tasks he has been given.

"And when they're taken, how do they become like this? Who did that to him? I mean, I can do something like that to a person but only for a brief time, and I don't enjoy doing it," Gwen confides, a sick, dark feeling oozing through her veins.

"The Wiccans are not the only magic wielders amongst the children of Cain. They are just the most powerful," Emon informs "Some magical gifts are randomly dispersed throughout the Clans.

Shape-shifting, or changelings as you might call them, for example, is a trait that can be found in Goblins, Elves, Dwarves or even Vampires. Then there are werewolves, but that's a bit different," Emon adds. "It is not something you can learn. It is one of the abilities with which one is inherently born. You do not shape-shift, do you?"

"No, I can't." Gwen shakes her head. At least she didn't think she could, but it never occurred to her. She decides to try it out later when she is alone in her room.

"Most of the tribes have at least one magical trait that is isolated to their kind. For example, all Fairies can change their size. They only appear as the size of insects because it protects them from detection by humans, but they have the ability to be as tall as you. Dwarves can sense changes in the earth and in nature, sensing storms and earthquakes, sometimes days before they occur. Vampires have the gift of immortality and charm." Emon stands, signaling for Gwen to follow him.

"By charm you mean mind manipulation, don't you?" Gwen inquires as he leads her to a nearby shelf, taking a large, red, leather-bound volume off the shelf and handing it to Gwen.

In golden script, the title reads *The Serpents of Blood* by Enrich Globemenstein. Gwen shudders involuntarily. Something about the book feels twisted, dark, evil.

"This book goes into all the dark mysteries of the Vampire. It was written by a human scholar a long time ago, but he was much too observant. They had no choice but to kill him or make him one of them," Emon informs her, noting her reaction to the book.

"What happened to him?" Gwen is afraid to ask. Suddenly, the room no longer seems like a place of wonder. The shelves no longer hold stories of glory and beauty but of death and slavery.

"Enrich is now one of their most prominent leaders. He's the Vampire king's advisor." Emon turns down another aisle. Gwen follows, quick on his heels, finding it difficult to keep up with the Elf's extraordinarily long-legged stride.

"So whenever a human in the area gets too suspicious, or starts pretending that they're one of us, one of Legion's men catches them, brings them back here, and…"

"The Vampires use their charm, or glamour, as it is sometimes called, to lure the human's consciousness out of their body, erasing all memory, all instincts, and all free will, turning them into—"

"Zombies," Gwen finishes for the Elf. Emon gives her an exasperated smile.

"I was going to say servants, but if you must look at it that way, I suppose they are the same thing."

"Well, at least they don't try to feed upon the flesh," Gwen adds.

Emon laughs involuntarily at this. He stops in front of a shelf, his demeanor back to its usual, polished manner, and pulls out several small volumes. He hands them to Gwen. "You must remember, little Witch, that humans are pests, vermin, and insects to our kind, especially to the Vampire, who view them as little better than animals for the hunt. I'd hate for you to think ill of your cousins, but it is the way of life in our civilization. Humans have been, and always will be, considered lesser beings, and thus, there is no crime in their servitude."

"What about that boy I met the other day, Peter? He had a mind as alive as any human I've met in the city. There was nothing wrong with his aura or his thought. Why is his mind intact?" Gwen asks, a bit irritably.

"Oh, Peter. I almost forgot you two met. He has the unhappy privilege of being Ivan's personal servant. You remember Ivan, do you not?"

"Yes. The creepy English Vampire who saved me," Gwen replies.

"Ivan is unusual," Emon agrees. "He is very cruel, and dark of heart. He enjoys watching others suffer, even more so than most Vampires. He not only hates humans but all creatures, save for the Master Legion himself. He alone has sway over Ivan and his demented mind." Emon leads the way back to his desk.

"So Ivan left Peter's mind untouched to torture him?" The notion appalls Gwen, making Jessica and Lydia's fate seem less hideous in comparison.

"Yes. The boy still has to do his master's bidding, but he is aware of the things he is forced to do and say, and he does them out of fear. That is what Ivan loves most: fear. He uses Peter's fear to maintain power over him. It is rather disgusting, actually. I have asked Lord Legion many times myself to have the boy's mind expunged, but he insists that Peter is Ivan's property, and by our laws, no one may meddle with another's slaves."

Gwen feels sick to her stomach, thinking how wild and erratic the boy acted. If he wasn't already insane, he soon would be. A sudden thought occurs to Gwen. *He can tell me all sorts of things about these people. He's been here for a while and he knows things that I'm sure even Emon won't tell me. I can get an insider's view of everything.* Somehow, she has to befriend Ivan's slave without attracting Ivan's suspicion. Maybe she could even help the poor boy.

Gwen ponders these things throughout the rest of the interview. Emon goes on into other topics, imparting information about the other tribes of Cain. Occasionally, he gets up and acquires another book or scroll to add to her growing collection of study materials.

After several hours, Gwen feels exhausted and her stomach growls. She begs Emon for a break, promising to return later that evening to continue her tutoring. Emon seems a bit disappointed to see her go but dismisses her with a smile. He has a servant boy carry her bundle of books for her, the servant following her to the door where Jessica still waits, her face to the ground in the same manner in which Gwen left her.

Gwen rouses Jessica and the servant boy deposits the books into the girl's arms, closing the massive library door behind them. Her body aches and her head throbs, but Gwen is still able to make her way back through the fortress maze to her room with Jessica in tow. Upon entering her bed chamber, Gwen finds the cousin,

Lydia, waiting in the corner. She immediately sends the girl to get her something for lunch. Jessica leaves the books on the nightstand next to Gwen's bed.

Gwen quickly locates a pen and paper and scribbles a few lines. She folds it over and hands it to Jessica.

"Take this to Ivan's servant Peter. Give it only to him, and only if he is alone," Gwen commands. Jessica nods, her brunette hair bouncing as she turns and leaves the room, eager to do Gwen's bidding.

Gwen watches her go. She feels pity for her but knows that she will no longer be bothered by using the girls as servants. Their lives were painless and uncomplicated, but they could be worse. They could be in Peter's shoes. Gwen cringes inside, thinking of all the things a monster like Ivan must have done to make Peter so frightened of him. The very idea of having no control of your actions, knowing you were being controlled, wanting to resist, but being physically unable to disobey sounded to Gwen like the greatest torture of all. Her free will has always been one comfort in her pathetic life. Life gave her a poor hand to play, but with her determination and strength, she has made it through, turning the cards in her favor however she could. If she lost that, if she lost her will to go on, her determination to survive, then nothing would be left but misery and heartache. Gwen decides to hold off these dark thoughts and turns to the pile of books on her nightstand.

She reads the titles. Some are about the ancestry of each tribe, including extensive family trees of each species royal families.

Others are about the civilization of Fairies, or the history of the Trolls.

I think I could learn more about the other tribes by interacting with them than simply reading up on them. Then Gwen notices the last two books in the pile, which stand out the most to Gwen. *The Serpents of Blood*, about the Vampires, and another called *The Book of Lilith*. Strangely, Gwen can't recall seeing this one before.

Had Emon slipped it in before I left, or did I pick it up from his desk by mistake? However it came into her possession, she might as well have a look. Gwen opens up the green, cloth-bound book, and opens it to the first page. In minutes she is enthralled by the text, learning all about her people's Deity, Lilith the first Witch.

CHAPTER SIX

The Book of Lilith

Chapter 1

n the beginning God created Heaven and Earth. And God resided in Heaven and His spirit children there also did dwell, loving and following God. The children revered God, obeying and trusting Him with complete faith as children would their father; for He is the father of heaven, and eternal life.

Wherefore, the children of God were blameless, being devoid of sin or iniquity. Thus, they could not progress, for they knew not good from evil; and without the knowledge of such things they could never obtain the glory of God.

For this reason God created the Earth so that His children might obtain a physical body and know the temptations of the flesh. Also, for the purpose of living in joy and pain and experiencing death; for only when given the choice to follow

God's commandments and obey Him completely would they receive His spirit and become like unto Him.

God gave his children the choice to stay forever as spirits without progress or growth, or to choose to live on Earth, to gain a body, crossing the veil between Heaven and Earth and forgetting God the Father.

Wherefore, they would be doomed to stumble blindly through darkness, temptation, and iniquity, except they come unto Him and follow His commandments, they would never find their way back into Heaven, to receive eternal life.

Behold, there were many among the children of God who chose to relinquish their perfect existence to obtain a body on Earth and prove themselves worthy before God.

And, behold, there was one called Lucifer, one of God's most influential angels in Heaven, who led away many of God's spirit children into darkness. He urged them to reject God's plan and follow him instead.

And in his wrath, God punished Lucifer, and all that did follow after him, casting them out of Heaven, denying them the chance to live on Earth as mortal beings. God sent them to the depths of the darkness, where their spirits would be caught between Heaven and Earth, calling this place Hell.

Chapter 2

In the beginning the Earth was in darkness, devoid of form. Therefore, God the Father created light and separated the darkness from the light, creating night and day. The day ruled by the greater light and a lesser light he created to rule the night, and also forming stars in the firmament.

Then, He created the world. Dividing the water from the earth, He created oceans and dry land. Plants and vegetation God formed to cover and beautify the earth.

Then, all manner of beasts, from the fowls in the air to the beasts on the land, to the fishes in the sea the Father created to roam the Earth two of each kind, male and female.

And for His spirit children, God created a beautiful garden and called it Eden, a place for his most prized creation to thrive; behold, it was for them that the Earth was created.

God saw the Earth was good and was well-pleased. Therefore, the father formed man, creating him out of the Earth, and God breathed life into this man, giving the body a spirit. And, behold, the man awoke and arose and God called him Adam. And God saw that man was good and was well-pleased.

Nevertheless, the Father knew that it was not right for man to be alone in this lonely state. Wherefore, God created a helpmeet for Adam out of Earth, water, wind, and fire. And God saw that she was good and was well pleased. Wherefore, God the

Father gave her unto Adam, who named her Lilith, after the night, for her hair was black, her skin tan, and her eyes dark.

And lo, Adam was entranced with Lilith for she was beautiful to the eye and strong of spirit, and very desirable to the flesh. And Lilith regarded Adam as an equal, strong of will, might. and intellect and loved him as a sister to a brother.

And God set the man and the woman into the Garden of Eden giving them dominion over all, except they were forbidden to eat of the fruit of the Tree of Knowledge of Good & Evil and also forbidden to eat from the Tree of life. All other plants and fruit they could partake of, but these.

And God the Father gave each their equal part, giving Adam dominion over the animals, commanding him to name every animal on the earth, and Lilith was given dominion over the plants and the vegetation, and, behold, all of nature was hers to command and to name as she saw fit.

And Adam was commanded to answer to no one save God the Father and His only begotten Son, whereas Lilith was commanded to follow Adam in all things as his wife and helpmeet.

And God also commanded that they go forth, to multiply and replenish the Earth after their own kind. However, they were in a state of innocence, knowing nothing of good and evil. And they dwelled for a space of time in contentment, peace and harmony in the Garden of Eden.

Chapter 3

Behold, it came to pass that one day whilst Lilith was bathing in a waterfall, she sensed she was being watched. Supposing it to be her husband, Lilith called out to him, yet Adam was not there, but in another part of the Garden. Behold, to Lilith's astonishment, a stranger emerged from the concealment of the trees and stood before her.

'Who art thou?' she bade him, and the man spoke unto her. 'I am Lucifer, your brother in heaven and the prince of the Morning.' And Lilith saw that he was handsome and that his countenance was lovely to the eye. Yet, nevertheless, she was sore afraid for she knew not this man who called himself her brother, and tried to flee from his presence.

However, he was fast and cunning and caught her up in his embrace, stopping her from going unto Adam. 'Fear not, for I have come to teach thee and to show you the way to eternal life, and to help you keep all of God's commandments,' spoke Lucifer.

'Art thou sent to us from God the Father?' inquired Lilith. And Lucifer exclaimed, 'Yea, for I am an angel, a messenger from God and would never do thee harm.'

And Lilith believed him and followed him deep into the Garden unto the tree of Good and Evil. 'Eat', Lucifer commanded her, yet behold, Lilith was hesitant saying, 'Know thou not that Father has forbidden us to partake of this particular tree?'

'I do, however, God has also commanded that you and Adam multiply and replenish the Earth and this cannot be done in your innocent state, for you know not the responsibilities of a wife and cannot fulfill them unless you partake of the tree.'

And Lilith saw wisdom in his words and agreed to take of the fruit of the tree. Thus she took the fruit from Lucifer's hand and ate the fruit. And it was more delicious to the taste than all other fruits in the garden and a savage hunger over took her and she ate all of the fruit, leaving only the pit untouched.

And, behold, after she had partaken of the fruit, Lilith's eyes were open and she knew and understood all things and was filled with wisdom, love, hate, lust, good, and evil. Wherefore, she was overwhelmed by emotion and became fearful and scared for she knew that she had disobeyed God and she saw Lucifer and this time she saw him for his true self.

'Thou art a deceiver and a demon,' she proclaimed. 'Now I will be cast out of the Garden and out of God's presence, doomed to wander the Earth alone.'

And Lilith cried out in her suffering and was about to call out in prayer unto the Father when Lucifer spoke saying, 'Behold, thou need not suffer alone, for this is the way things have always been done, and God will give thee the chance to redeem thyself. And since you are woman and the mother of all things he cannot cast you out lest there be no children born upon the face of the Earth.'

And Lilith knew what he said was true, and she began to have hope. Reaching out to the Tree of Knowledge, she took a fruit from the tree and went unto Adam so that he, too, might have wisdom in all things like unto God and that they might be together as man and wife.

Yet, behold, Lucifer stopped her, asking, 'Woman, what does thou do?' And Lilith responded saying, 'Taking the fruit unto Adam so that we might be together so that I might not wander this Earth alone and bear children as God commanded.'

'Yea, verily dost thou not know that thou hast the choice? Thou can choose to be with Adam, he who thou loves as a brother, or to bind yourself to me, making me thy husband in his place.'

And Lilith was wrought with turmoil, for she knew she did not desire Adam as a wife should her husband, neither did she desire to lie with him. Furthermore, she was aware that she lusted after Lucifer and that he was very desirable to the flesh, stirring in her feelings and emotions she had hitherto not known.

And Lucifer saw that she desired him and took advantage of her confused state and took her and lied with her, as a spirit taking possession of her body, and giving her carnal pleasure. Hence, Lilith mistook lust for love, and believing herself in love with Lucifer, she agreed to be henceforth a wife unto him alone.

And obeying her new husband's command, Lilith went forth to the Tree of Life and partook of the fruit thereof also, gaining with its consumption immortality, so much that she would never die or age from that time forth.

Chapter 4

And it came to pass that Adam did at this time come upon Lilith and saw her eating of the Tree of Life and was angry with her.

'What hast thou done, woman? Thou hast disobeyed Father and will be cast out for this!' But, lo, Lilith would not be chastised by him saying, 'Thou hast no dominion over me, man, for I am free of thee and will answer to thee no longer as your wife for I have eaten of both the tree of Knowledge and the Tree of Life and am now wiser than thee, and knowest that we must disobey Father and eat of the Tree of Knowledge, otherwise we can never multiply and replenish the Earth as God has commanded, but stay forever as innocent babes knowing nothing.'

'How dost thou know these things and who showed them unto thee?' Adam bade Lilith. And she answered saying, 'An angel, a messenger from God.' And Lilith directed him toward Lucifer, who stood off to the side watching their interview silently.

'Who art thou?' Adam asked, and Lucifer spoke saying, 'I am your brother Lucifer, an angel of God and the prince of the morning. What the woman speaks is true and she is very wise *and now lord over thee.'*

'This cannot be so,' exclaimed Adam, 'for God gave me command over all things and dominion over the Earth and gave this woman unto me to be my helpmeet answering unto my command and putting no other before me.'

And, behold, Lucifer was triumphant and laughed saying, 'She is thine no longer and has given herself unto me, and will for this time forth be known as my wife and I her husband, and being that she is the only woman on Earth God will grant me a body so that she and I can fulfill his commandment and be the parents of all the children of the Earth. You are the one who will be cast out, and left helpless in your innocent state.'

Adam was astonished and asked Lilith, 'Is what he saith true?'

And Lilith spoke saying, 'Yea, and I did lie with him and he has taken me as his wife, and I know now that I love thee not and will inherit God's kingdom without thee for I am woman and thus mother of all things, and surely our kind will die, if not I bear not children like unto my own kind. And Father will grant unto me the man I chooseth, therefore I need thee no longer.'

And Adam was angry and spoke out saying, 'You have been deceived for I was created first and as the first man was promised I would inherit God's kingdom, and I knoweth that God will not abandon me for I have been obedient unto his commandments and it is thee who will suffer for thy sins and be cast out of the garden and not I.'

And it came to pass that Lilith did not believe him and cried out unto the Heaven calling unto God. And behold the Father came in the form of a mighty voice saying, 'What dost thou ask of me, my children?' And Lucifer hid himself from the Father when he heard His voice.

And Adam spoke unto God, retelling the account of all that had transpired between him and the woman made to be his wife saying, 'Oh, Lord, why hast thou given me such a wife, and what should I do when she is cast out of the Garden, wilt I suffer on Earth forever as a lone man?'

And God heard his anguish and spoke unto him saying, 'Fear not, Adam, for I am with thee and I will not suffer that thou should be punished for thy wife's iniquities. Nevertheless, I would that I could redeem her from her sins and restore her to thee, but she must ask for forgiveness and covenant to obey thee in all things good and just as thou obey me.'

And Lilith spoke saying, 'Oh, Father, but I do not regret what I have done for I have obtained knowledge and I know good from evil and my mind has been opened and I now see and I cannot go back to my ignorant state for I have partaken of the Tree of Life also and am now a goddess like unto thee, immortal and perfect. And, henceforth, I do not see why I should be made to bow beneath Adam for I love him not and desire another to be my husband in his stead.'

Upon hearing this God was angry and asked, 'What hast thou done, woman? Who is this that thou hast committed adultery?' And she answered saying, 'Lucifer the Angel thou didst send to teach me all things.'

God's wrath was terrible and he called out in a booming voice, 'Lucifer, show thy self unto me!' And Lucifer stepped forward and stood at Lilith's side.

'I am here.'

'What hast thou done?' God asked.

'Teaching them thy gospel, showing them that they must obtain knowledge of evil before they can have true knowledge of good, that only then can they be like unto thee and gain eternal life,' spoke Lucifer.

'Thou hast beguiled this woman, taking advantage of her weak state and lied to her. Furthermore, thou hast defiled her innocence and made her a whore and an adulteress, and because thou hast convinced her to eat of the Tree of Life, she cannot be redeemed of her sins for she will now live forever in her fallen state, damned for all eternity and doomed to roam the Earth alone as an outcast and a demon.'

Behold, when Lilith heard His words she was frightened and began to cry and beg before God.

And Lucifer was angry and cried out, 'Why art thou angry? For I have a solution. Give unto me a physical body and I will stay with the woman and be her husband and father to the children of Earth. Cast not her out for she hath done no wrong against Thee, and it is within Thy power to forgive her and make her the sole heir to Thy kingdom. You must cast out Adam for he cannot bear children from his loins and Lilith is the only woman on Earth. If thou cast her out, thy kingdom will never achieve its glory and the spirits in Heaven shall never be born on Earth.'

And God made the heavens rumble and the sky was cast in gray clouds. From amongst the clouds His voice spoke saying, 'Hear me and know that I am the beginning and the end, Alpha and Omega, the same yesterday, today, and tomorrow, and I am master in all things. God doth not bargain with lying serpents. Be gone from my sight, Lucifer.' And compelled by the power of God, Lucifer was forced to leave, fleeing before God's almighty wrath out of the Garden of Eden.

Behold, God also cast out Lilith saying, 'Because thou hast eaten of the Tree of Life and committed adultery unto thy husband, I smite thee with a curse. Because of your arrogance, I taint thy womb to only produce sons and a daughter thou shalt never have. And your children will die without spirits to inhabit their souls. Henceforth I banish thee from the Garden and from my presence forever.' And so it was done, and Lilith was sent out into the wilderness to survive as a lone woman.

And Adam spoke unto God pleading, 'Oh, Father, what am I to do now that I am alone? All other living things have a mate and I have none.'

'Fear not, Adam, for I will give unto you another, and she will be flesh or thy flesh and bone of thy bone and will be greater than the first in wisdom and purity and she will be beholden unto you and obey you in all things.'

'I am grateful, oh, Father, nevertheless, I did love the first and I fear I cannot love another for my heart is broken.'

And God caused Adam to fall into a deep sleep, taking from him all his memories of Lilith, his first wife, along with the memory of Lucifer and his lies, leaving Adam's mind and spirit in peace. And behold, God took from Adam a rib and from it He made Adam a companion.

And God saw that she was very good and was well pleased. Thereupon Adam awoke and God gave unto him his second wife. And Adam called her Eve for she was to be the mother of all living. And behold she was beautiful and her hair golden as the sun, her skin as fair as pale rose and her eyes as blue as the sky. Adam loved and revered her and protected her as a husband should his wife. And it was that Eve loved and honored Adam, following and obeying him in all things as her lord and master. And they were contented in the Garden of Eden.

And thus it was that all knowledge of Lilith was gone from their minds and she was forgotten forever, lost for all eternity, passing away from the knowledge of man, doomed to become the mother of all the forsaken.

Chapter 5

And it came to pass that Lilith spent many years wandering the earth finding food, water, and shelter wherever she could, living off of the wilderness. And she feasted on the meat of animals, eating the meat thereof raw, for she had not the knowledge of fire. And hers was a bleak and lonely existence. Wherefore her heart became dark and twisted in her hatred for Adam and she cursed God the Father for abandoning her.

Wherefore, one day Lilith was visited by Lucifer. And she was angry with him and tried to smite him with a stone that he would torment her no longer.

Behold, Lucifer called, and spoke to her saying, 'I am thy friend, Lilith, and I have an offering to give unto thee. Long have I been lurking in the Garden of Eden amongst the wild beast, watching Adam and the new woman God has made him which he calls Eve. And behold, I have at last tricked both Adam and Eve and they have partaken of the Tree of Knowledge of Good and Evil and have been cast out of the Garden, and do now suffer as thou suffers.'

And when Lilith heard these things she was well-pleased and asked him, 'Did they eat of the Tree of Life also, serpent?' And Lucifer answered saying, 'Nay, they have not. For God did set a cherubim and a flaming sword before the Tree of Life and thus none can go near it.'

'Wherefore they are yet mortal!' sayeth Lilith. And behold, Lilith was glad, for she desired to go forth and find Adam and Eve so that she might kill the woman and take Adam for herself.

But Lucifer advised against this plan saying, 'Adam does not know thee, for God hast taken all knowledge of thee from his mind, and he loveth Eve and will hate you and turn against thee should thou slay her. And furthermore, thou must not harm Adam's second wife for she is already with child and she will bear a son.

'And behold, his name will be Cain and I covenant with thee that I shall beguile him and lead him astray and make him bow before thee, that thou may call him husband and bear children of thy own womb. And your offspring will be called Gian. They will be free of God's command and have choice to live in any way they see fit. And I shall teach unto thee witchcraft and thou shall be powerful like unto God, and thy children will be mighty like unto thee.

'All I ask is that thou pay homage unto me and name me thy God. And a tribute and an offering I will require for my protection and love. I will watch over thee and thy children, and you will be a mighty race and one day rise against the children of God and smite them.

'Behold, then thou shall be the ruler of the earth and, I, thy Lord God, and together we shall be great and powerful and the world will tremble before us in fear.'

Chapter 6

Wherefore Lilith did make a covenant with Lucifer, and he with her, and they became joined in spirit with one another and hence forth, Lucifer kept his promise, teaching unto Lilith the powers of God. He taught her to create fire with words, using her mind to make the flames appear of their own accord. And many other great and terrible things he showed unto her, making her great and cunning in the art of Witchcraft, a true demon of the night.

However, Lucifer kept a constant watch over Adam and Eve, hiding in the grass about their camp, awaiting the birth of the first child to be born upon the Earth. And behold, the time cometh, and Eve bore a son, and Adam named him Cain.

And the boy was strong of body and mind and will, and he grew up like unto his father, following his teachings and obeying the commandments and laws of God.

And, lo, it came to pass that Eve bore yet another child, and the second born was named Abel, and he was kind and good of heart, and obedient in all things, and honored his parents continually.

Wherefore Abel was a keeper of the flocks and Cain a tiller of the ground. And when it came time for an offering to be made unto God, Cain gave of the fruits of his labors and Abel of the best of his flocks. And it came to pass that God was well pleased with

Abel's offering, but cared not for Cain's offering.

And it came to pass that Lucifer appeared unto Cain as a serpent and urged Cain to anger against the Lord for his unjust treatment of him, saying, 'Your offering was just as good as thy brother's. Why should he get praise and you none? Why should you have to be compared to your younger brother? Art not thou the eldest and the first son of the earth? He is but the second, a spare.' And verily, Cain harkened unto Lucifer's words and was wroth with God and darkness began to fester in his soul.

Then, one day while they were both in the fields, Cain was in such a fury because of the serpent's words that he rose up and slew his brother Abel. Fearing that he would be discovered, Cain hid his brother's body below the field, burying it in the earth.

And it came to pass that God did come to Cain and asked after his brother Abel. And Cain pretended to know not where his brother could be. But God rebuked him for a liar and said, 'Behold, his blood speaks to me from the earth. Thou art a murderer and henceforth thou shalt be banished from my presence and cursed upon the earth.' And God marked him with a curse so that all that came upon him might know that he was damned and beware of him and his children, that they were evil and should be forever shunned by the children of man.

And it came to pass that Cain fled from God's presence into the dark wilderness, and there upon Lucifer came before him and Cain did follow the serpent for although he could not lift the curse from off of Cain he did promise him food and shelter. And thus it was that Lucifer led Cain to Lilith, the mother of the night.

Behold, Lilith had long waited for Cain to become a man, for Lucifer had promised unto her a husband from one of the sons of Adam and Eve. Yea, it came to pass that when Lilith did look upon Cain she fled from him because of the curse put upon him. He was hideous to the sight. His misshapen body and face repulsed Lilith and she refused to bed him as her husband.

And Lucifer was wroth with the woman and commanded that she lay with the man, for she must bear up sons unto their kind. And yet again Lucifer made a covenant with Lilith that if she lay with Cain and bore him sons, Lucifer would protect and watch over her, giving her and her seed great prosperity. And after much flattery and the cunning of his tongue, Lilith was convinced to submit herself to Cain and he knew her as a man knoweth his wife.

Chapter 7

And Lilith did bear a child; lo, its features were deformed as its father Cain and it was still as death upon birth. In her sorrow Lilith called out to Lucifer, crying, 'Lord save my child that it might live.' And Lucifer appeared to her saying, 'Fear not, for your child will yet live. Keep the still child warm and swaddled in an animal's hide throughout the night and on the morrow the child will breathe its first breath. There upon make thee an altar and offer up the life of a lion as sacrifice. Take the blood of the lion with a few drops of blood taken from the child and mix them with the craft. Thereon, give the mixture to the babe to drink. This will alter his appearance and make him more like the children of Adam, beautiful and comely.'

Lilith and Cain did as instructed and whereon the child drank of the blood its appearance did change. Its deformed face did alter and it became more pleasing to the eye, yet it was larger in size than an average babe. They did call the babe Gian. And behold as he grew to be a man, he grew large in stature becoming taller than the trees themselves.

And behold Lilith and Cain bore twelve more sons, each born dead and disfigured, each awakening the next day to life. Lucifer commanded them with each child to sacrifice a different beast to transform the child to defeat the curse placed upon Cain. Wherefore each child took on a different appearance, each more like the children of Adam and Eve than the last. But none bore a perfect resemblance to the children of God.

Then it came to pass upon the day after the last son was born Lilith did slay herself, for only she could end her immortal life and Cain did give Lilith's blood unto the child so that he might be made perfect. And behold, the boy called Wicca was transformed into a perfect babe free of the curse of Cain. And Lucifer did bless him and, showing him favor, bestowed all his *power of the craft upon him.*

And Lucifer proclaimed, 'Blessed art thou, Wicca, for all the powers of the universe are thine. Through thee will my glory manifest itself upon the earth. For great and terrible things will I teach thee so that though may enslave the children of god and rule earth for all eternity.

'And I command thee to make a record of thy people, and all the tribes of Cain so that thy seed may know of thy terrible power. And the glory of your might shall be given unto me for being the father of thy race and being the god of thy people. From the beginning with the daughter of night, thy mother Lilith, unto the end of thy days shall you make a record of thy people so that these truths will not die or be denied by the children of god. And it shall be known as the book of Lilith.'

CHAPTER SEVEN

Games

Gwen awakens a while later. Her neck aches from bending over the book in her lap, her joints stiff from sitting in the same position for far too long. She sets the Book of Lilith aside, stretches, and glances about her bed chamber.

A food tray, with what had been her afternoon meal, sits on the vanity, untouched. Her servants are nowhere in sight, and a folded piece of paper sits next to her on the bed. Gwen unfolds the note in anticipation. Upon reading the note, her face falls; it is the note that she had sent Jessica to give to Peter, only at the bottom beneath her handwriting, Peter wrote one line: *Don't contact me again!*

Gwen lets out a frustrated sigh. *Of course Peter would avoid me. He's afraid.* She is determined that, one way or another, she will get him to talk. He could be a very useful ally in Bec LaNuff.

Gwen finds her thoughts drawn back to the book. What she read both enlightened and disturbed her. If this book is true, then it changes everything she had been taught as a child. *The nuns at St. Paul would freak out if they got a look at this book. Mother Superior would likely toss it in a fire!*

It all makes sense now that she thinks about it. *I'm a descendant of Lilith.* She always knew she didn't belong to the human world, but she never suspected that she was part of a whole other species. Gwen just couldn't bring herself to think of humans as the enemy. Granted, she had never been treated very well by most of them, but some had shown her love and friendship

She has fond memories of Sister Mary Shaw, Cara Keller, Kyle and Kayla Hamilton. These people are her friends not her enemies. She can't fathom facing them at Armageddon and them on the opposite side, sworn to kill her because of what she had been born into.

She had a choice ahead of her: Should she embrace her own culture, which lives above the law, looking down on mankind? Or live forever as an outsider amongst the very people who would hate and destroy her should they ever learn the truth about what she really is?

Conflicted by this, Gwen suddenly feels a bone-deep longing for her best friend Raven. What would he think of this place, these people, and this whole world? What advice might he give her? Should she stay and make a life here amongst these people, or is her journey not yet over? Is there some adventure waiting for her out in the great unknown world, experiences yet to have, and friendships yet to be forged? All she knows is that her life would never be complete without Raven by her side. Sooner or later she will have to leave Bec LaNuff to find him.

* * * * *

Gwen and Emon exit the library after a long study session and stroll out into the main courtyard, the enchanted light from the stain glass window above reflecting colored light on the floor.

"So where are we going?" Gwen asks.

"I thought we could walk down to the lower levels to see the limestone caves. At this time, of day a few of the tribes play games there for amusement."

"Really?" Gwen perks up at this. "What kind of games?" she asks. Emon smiles and turns toward the tunnels leading to the base of the mountain. Gwen quickly follows.

"Well, there are strategic games like Eden and Abyss, Thirteen Trolls, or athletic games like Toss and Tumble."

"Yeah, I've never heard of any of those games," Gwen confesses. "Are they like any games I might know? Do the Forsaken have their own version of chess or something?" She skips by the Elf's side as they cross the chamber and head into an archway as they make their way downward.

"I believe that Eden and Abyss are similar to chess, as much

as Toss and Tumble is like bowling, only we do it wth a Dwarf."

"You mean only Dwarfs can play it?" Gwen asks, confused.

"No," Emon answers with a smirk on his golden face, "we use a Dwarf to knock down the targets instead of a stone ball." Emon erupts in laughter at the incredulous look upon Gwen's face.

"I don't believe you. I'll have to see that for myself."

They step out of a main corridor and down a steep flight of stairs. At the bottom Gwen sees a yellow glow from the chamber beyond. Entering the cave, Gwen gasps, in awe of the beautiful sight before her.

The cave is filled with limestone deposits glowing almost like gold against the darkness of the cave. Limestone drips from the ceiling and lines most of the cavern's floor. Gwen notices as she walks on the glowing stone that the floor has been polished, making it both shiny and slippery. The room is naturally separated into four small areas. One large opening with a long expanse of polished limestone stretches from one end of the cave to the other. At the opposite end Gwen sees a group of large stones standing up like bowling pins in front of a net, looking very much like a goal post.

In the smaller alcoves, groups of two play games that involve moving about sculpted limestone pieces like chess or war games. All along the playing area in the center of the room, seats are cut into the limestone formations where several spectators sit.

Emon's skin seems to glow in the reflection of the stone around him as he walks out onto the floor. Gwen follows him gingerly over the slick surface to take a seat amongst the other spectators watching the game of Toss and Tumble already in progress.

They watch as a Troll clad in something resembling a loin cloth or a speedo approaches the center of the court with a small redheaded Dwarf in tow. The Dwarf wears strange safety gear on his head, arms, legs, and back. He lays down on the limestone and curls up into a ball, tucking his head into his chest and grasping his legs with both arms. Spitting into his palm, the Troll rubs the saliva between his hands. He then grabs the Dwarf by a handle on his arm bands and lifts him off the ground. The Troll spins several times with the Dwarf hanging from his fist until the Troll releases the Dwarf, tossing him down the lane toward the oversized rocks. In a flash, the balled up Dwarf collides with the pins, tumbling several over. The momentum makes the Dwarf continue toward the metal cage at the end of the room. He slides across the limestone, coming to a stop just at the edge of the cage.

Gwen and the other spectators erupt in applause and cheers.

"That puts us ahead of you by six marks, Connor!" calls out the Troll as he helps his Dwarf teammate off the floor. Together they join their teammates on a limestone bench.

Suddenly, an Ogre jumps up from the opposing team's bench and hurries to intercept the Troll. "No, that makes the score even," he shouts at the knobby-nosed Troll. "You missed the tumble cage." The Ogre points to the Troll's small red-bearded companion. "You only get six marks for the targets you and Ombi knocked down!"

"Nonsense! Ombi was well in the cage when he came to a stop, which means we double our marks!" the Troll barks back at his opponent. Just then both teams gather in the middle of the court, standing behind their teammates.

"Are you blind, Varjack? Ombi never crossed the end stripe. He was nowhere near the cage!" a Goblin chimes in. He has a rumble for a voice, a hunch on his back, and scrawny arms and legs poking out from under a dark tunic and long pants. *He must be one of the Ogres' teammates,* Gwen observes.

"Come along, Gwen, it looks like there is no peace maker present. I shall have to intervene," Emon whispers. Gwen follows Emon as they get up from their seats and step down onto the limestone court. Walking across the glossy surface, Gwen follows the Elf as they approach the quarreling teams.

"How does the game fair, Connor?" Emon asks the Ogre good-naturedly.

"Varjack's trying to cheat again!" The gray-skinned Ogre turns to address the Elf.

The other players turn toward them and freeze in astonishment when their eyes alight on Gwen. She realizes that two female Vampires, Lethawyn and Jezebel, are with Varjack's team. Gwen nods in their direction. They stare back, annoyance wafting from them like a bad aroma.

"You brought the Witch child with you, Emon?" Jezebel asks, raising one of her eyebrows quizzically.

"Yes. We were hoping to join the next game. Gwen's never played Toss and Tumble before. I am sure the lot of us can teach it to her in no time," Emon announces to the group of stone-like faces.

An awkward silence hangs in the cavern as the group exchanges nervous glances. The once-quarreling opponents wait for the Vampire sisters to give them their cue, no one willing to break the silence until either sister speaks.

"The game is full, Emon," Lethawyn announces, her jaw clenched tightly.

"I meant the next game, of course."

"Take the child back to the master. We have no need of a Wiccan here." Jezebel steps forward till she's practically stepping on Emon's toes, glaring up at the golden Elf that tops her by a head and a half. The Vampire's whitish eyes blaze with suppressed anger.

Emon's demeanor changes in an instant, his usual calm, scholarly air replaced by a warrior's dark countenance. He stares down the immortal woman before him. "We are not going anywhere. She can go wherever she likes. We are not children in a school yard, Jezebel. The young Witch can play if she so desires!" he erupts, red-hot rage in his voice.

The chamber has gone still. Even those playing in the other alcoves seem to have their attention rapt upon the Elf and the Vampire.

Gwen wants to say that she doesn't really want to play and

that she has somewhere else to be, when Lethawyn takes the other Vampire by the arm.

"Come, sister. Let the mortals play their little games. We haven't hunted this evening and it grows late." Lethawyn's pale eyes dart suggestively toward Gwen when she says the word *hunted*. Gwen shivers inwardly, but the Vampire's words relax her sibling.

"Very well, sister, let us hunt." Jezebel steps back from Emon, letting her petite sister lead her away by the arm. They pass Gwen without a glance and exit the glowing chamber.

Several of the creatures take a breath at the same time, the atmosphere altering drastically with the Vampires now absent. Gwen feels her own muscles relax. *I can't believe I was about to let those two run me off.* Gwen chides herself for her cowardice.

"Now, how about we settle this argument over the score and get back to the game?" Emon asks aloud, rubbing his hands together, back to his usual upbeat self.

"Fine by me," answers Connor the Ogre, turning back to the Troll he was shouting at earlier. "We're tied up! No double marks unless your Dwarf hits the back of the cage!"

"Fine," Varjack grumbles, rolling his black eyes at the Ogre. "It's your squad's toss, but you give me Borenz and Lackmere to replace the Vampires. You get the Elf and the kid!"

"Fine, you mark thief!" The Ogre signals to the Goblin and one of his squad's Dwarves to join the Troll's squad with obvious reluctance. The other team goes back to their side of the court.

Connor turns to Emon and Gwen skeptically. "You're sure she can play, Emon? I mean, she's not much bigger than a Dwarf herself. How's she supposed to toss one?"

Emon smiles wickedly, "I was thinking she would make a better tumbler than a tosser."

"What? Oh, no, you're not throwing me around!" Gwen protests.

"It is perfectly safe, Gwen, I assure you. You get a helmet, arm and leg guards, and a back plate to wear that are designed just for tumblers. The stone is very slippery. You will slide easily to the targets and on to the Tumblecage without getting a single bruise," Emon insists.

Connor shrugs. "I guess if a grown Vampire can do it, a child Wiccan can, too." He turns to whisper something to one of this teammates, leaving Gwen and Emon to talk alone.

"Wait, Vampires let someone toss them into a net?" Gwen asks Emon, wide-eyed. "This I got to see!"

"They only allow another Vampire to do the tossing. Had they stayed to play, Jezebel would have tossed and Lethawyn would have tumbled, only she would not have worn the tumbler gear. Vampires do not need it," Emon confides in a conspiratorial tone. Gwen tries to envision either Vampire doing any such thing and fails miserably.

One of the tumblers from their team approaches with a set of tumbler gear in his arms. "For you, Miss Gwen." She nervously takes the equipment, noticing that on the inside the safety gear is lined with a soft spongy material. Emon helps her to fit the safety gear on. Once all geared up, she feels a lot like a potato bug and she imagines that is exactly what she looks like, too. Gwen looks up to see the rest of their team waiting along the side of the court. Only she and Emon remain in the center.

"We are up, Gwen," Emon announces, a bright smile on his visage.

Taking a deep breath, Gwen squares her shoulders. *Okay, you should never be afraid to try new things,* she tells herself. Gwen looks up to see Emon smiling at her. "All right, let's do this!"

* * * * *

Emon and Gwen walk back up to the main courtyard, their game over and the evening meal soon approaching. Before turning to go back to her own quarters, Gwen stops and looks up at Emon.

"Thanks for that. Sometimes I get so worried about everything that I forget how to just be a kid and have fun," Gwen confesses.

"I have the same problem. Thank you for trusting me, Gwen. It is been a truly remarkable experience getting to know you." Emon smiles down at her, patting her on the shoulder. Gwen hugs the Elf, squeezing him. He hugs her back briefly. Blushing, Gwen releases him, steps away, waves goodbye, and hurries away back to her room.

Emon watches her go with a mix of emotions. A kind of fatherly pride welling in him that he can't quite explain. He turns and walks slowly back to the library where his research waits for him. By the time he sits back down in his desk sadness engulfs him.

I cannot stand for Gwen to end up like the others. Some part of him feels utterly helpless, the other empowered by his affection for the Witch to do something. *But what? I am not the Lord of this place, I cannot stop the wickedness that runs deep beneath the surface of this society.* All Emon is cable of is to try and influence their king. He must make Legion see that this child can be no party to the corruption of Bec LaNuff and its dirty little games.

CHAPTER EIGHT

Lies and Loyalties

*T*he next several days pass in a kind of blur as Gwen's mind expands and absorbs knowledge like a sponge in the morning while she studies in the library under Emon's tutelage. Her body becomes a human bowling ball in the afternoons. She grows in wisdom and confidence as she interacts more with the other creatures bumping around the place.

Word to gets out that Gwen and Emon make a great Toss and Tumble team, and soon their afternoon games are crowded with spectators, in the seats and lining the walls. The strange sport gives Gwen the chance to get to know the other tribes, to feel more a part of this unusual community.

Gwen also discovers that every occasion is considered a special event, worthy of elegant attire and expensive jewelry in

Bec LaNuff. Gwen, stubborn to the bone, tries to insist that blue jeans are formal enough for her, but is talked into changing her clothes by her ever persuasive host, the stunning Legion. Every night she wears the shimmering gowns and the princess jewelry, feeling as out of place as Cinderella at the ball.

In the evenings, Gwen spends her time with Legion as he parades her around Bec LaNuff as his honored guest and companion. She dines with him and his advisors, the men she met the first day, along with Emon, Vinita, Melody, and Ivan. Great feasts are prepared for the dinner guests, although the Vampires never eat. Legion seems to take great interest in Gwen's appetite, always concerned that her food is to her liking, and that she eats enough. Only two things threaten the good mood of these little dinner parties: Vinita and Melody.

Both the Elfin woman and the young girl seem irrationally jealous of Gwen. Vinita is jealous of how much time Emon spends with her in his library, and Melody is jealous of the attention Legion lavishes on her. Gwen thinks they are both acting ridiculous. She is no threat to them and would never come between them and their men, but somehow she knows there is no way to convince either of them otherwise.

Vinita begins to hang about the library, hovering over them as Emon tutors Gwen about the tribes of Cain, making Gwen nervous. Always she feels Vinita's predatory eyes upon her.

After dinner, Legion often asks Gwen to join him for a stroll through the fortress, wanting to show her the beauty of the architecture and the history of the place. Legion beams with pride as they walk arm in arm, delighting in her company, always attentive and charming. Gwen feels her heart flutter and a girlish sense of light-headedness during these walks. The feeling always deflates with the presence of Melody hovering just out of the corner of her eye, lingering behind them like a small, redheaded shadow, her icy glare burning a spot in the middle of Gwen's back. Legion seems aware of their stalker but he holds his temper in check, ignoring the girl and devoting his undivided attention on Gwen.

Gwen can't ignore it, and attempts several times to confront her rival, only to be ignored or snubbed. Finding the whole situation ludicrous and out of her control, Gwen focuses on more important things, such as her education and finding the answers to her past.

If only Vinita and Melody were the extent of her worries, but they are not. Gwen is having trouble sleeping. Night after night she finds herself plagued by strange dreams, dreams that feel more real than life itself. Some are of the blonde boy in the field, summoning her, calling for her by name. He is sad, frightened, his face clouded by fear, and there is always a note of urgency in his voice. Something terrible is about to happen, and he is there to help her, to protect her.

Every time he tries to tell her why she is in danger, her dreams suddenly shift and she is whisked away from the mysterious boy. When she awakens, she finds herself back in her room with Legion standing before her, wearing nothing but a white robe over his naked body, his perfect, pale chest exposed. Gwen feels that she is wearing very little as well, some light, silky nightgown. Occasionally she finds herself attired like the servants, but instead of a crimson midriff and skirt, hers are white and without blemish. Legion takes her in his arms, and before Gwen realizes it, they lay on her massive canopy bed, their arms and legs intertwined in a passionate embrace, his lips pressing cold kisses on her face, shoulders, and neck. At first his kisses warm her skin. She feels ecstasy in his touch, but then she becomes embarrassed, knowing somewhere in her subconscious mind that what they are doing is wrong somehow, and Gwen begins to pull away.

Legion's handsome features then change and a dark, haunting expression takes their place. The lights in the room burn out and they are left with one single candle flame to illuminate the chamber. Suddenly, she is afraid and opens her mouth to scream. She feels his fangs in her flesh, and the pain of her skin being torn away from her neck. He is draining her, his body pinning her in place, crushing her beneath him as he sucks the life out of her. She would scream in pain, but her voice never rings out, as if she is suddenly mute. The only sound is the beating of her heart slowing down as the life leaves her.

Finally, after what seems like an eternity, Legion releases her from his grip and pulls back. Gwen wants to scream in horror. He looks like a devil with her blood spilling from his mouth and down his chin, his eyes yellow and bloodshot, and his white robe now drenched in her blood. The instinct to run overcomes her and she tries to move, but her body is paralyzed. Something is holding her down. Gwen looks down at herself and then she sees the blood splattered all over the white linen sheets, staining her white servant clothes, blood streaked down her thighs and legs. She sees shackles and chains about her wrist and ankles, holding her prisoner to the bed. Gwen screams. Legion throws back his head and laughs.

That is when she truly awakens, screaming. Every time she checks for the shackles and the chains, but to her relief, they are never there. She can almost feel their weight upon her limbs as if they had just been removed.

She spends hours willing herself to figure out some kind of protection spell, either to keep her room safe from intruders or to ward off these disturbing dreams. Night after night she fails to come up with the right words for the magic to take hold. After these efforts fail, it takes her a while to wrestle herself back to sleep. More dreams haunt her, dreams where a snake slips into her bed and slithers its way over her body and she must fight frantically to throw it off, and dreams where she is running through the stone corridors of Bec LaNuff and it's entirely empty, and still, and dark.

Something is after her and she can't run fast enough. In another, Raven is running with a pack of wolves, his chest and feet bare as he moves through a thick green forest under the light of the full moon. Sometimes he sees Gwen sitting on the bow of a tree and he stops to stare at her as if uncertain whether she is real or an illusion. She longs to speak to him, but finds she has no voice. No sound escapes when she moves her lips, and Raven runs on, called away by his wolf brethren. Other times she sees glimpses of people, faces, and places she has never seen before, doing ordinary things. Sometimes she even sees herself interacting with these strangers as if watching a movie of her own life, but of things yet to come. It is impossible to see what is happening in these particular dreams, so much is disjointed and beyond comprehension. Gwen gives up trying to interpret them and lets the images fade away.

In the mornings she awakens, feeling physically exhausted as if she's been running all night. Her eyes burn as if stung by tears, and a haunting sense of dread hangs over her. Luckily, these premonitions and ominous feelings fade as she goes about her daily routine. When she finds herself thinking of her dreams, or of Legion, she feels a strange warmth come over her. Gwen's train of thought frequently gets interrupted, always changing to something more pleasant.

Whenever Legion is near, she feels at peace, warm, butterflies in her stomach, and an aching desire from some unexplainable female instinct to be near him, to be touched by him. Embarrassing as it is, the sensations never goes away, and with every smile and gesture the handsome, pale Vampire becomes more beautiful and lovelier to Gwen.

She feels an overwhelming sense of confusion. She has never felt this way about anyone. Joy and guilt break over her in waves.

It turns out Melody has good reason to hate me after all, Gwen thinks to herself, *but only if Legion loves me back, but don't be ridiculous. You're only a child, Gwen, barely even old enough to be considered a woman.*

She becomes increasingly grateful that Legion can't read her mind. If he could, she would be ashamed of the things she thought about him, things that seem wrong and exciting all at the same time.

Her attempts to communicate with Peter have had no success. The boy seems infallibly determined to avoid her at all costs. Several times a day Gwen sends either Jessica or Lydia with a message for Peter, and every time they are sent back unanswered. Finally Gwen decides she's had enough. Between her studies and spending her evenings dining with Legion, she usually has her afternoons free to read quietly in her room. Today, she has other plans.

Gwen leaves the luminous library, ducking into the small corridor beyond. She is going solo today, both of her maid servants off performing various errands for her, somewhere far away. Gwen feels the rare freedom is a blissful privilege as she steps through an archway into the main courtyard of Bec LaNuff.

Usually she would turn left and make her way to the upper levels, toward the Vampire wing where her bedchamber is located. Today she makes her way through the throng of the citizens of the mountain, turning left and exiting out the main entrance towards the lower levels of the fortress.

Perhaps a week has passed since Gwen was last in this part of the Bec LaNuff but she relies on her memory to guide her. After a few wrong turns and a dead end, Gwen finally finds herself standing at the end of the long stone hallway of the servants Quarters.

Now to find Peter's room, Gwen thinks to herself. Instead of knocking at every door like an idiot, she opens her mind to those around her. She finds herself in a current of emotions and nonsensical thoughts. She feels through the surging river looking for the single reed floating a drift in that current that would be Peter's mind. He isn't there.

Gwen lets out a disappointed sigh, letting her mind slip back into itself, the world quiet once more. Determined to have a face-to-face conversation with Peter once and for all, even if she has to wait all day, Gwen wanders down the hallway looking for the door with the strange inscription. Halfway down the hall, she finds it. Gwen slumps down to the floor, crossing her legs and, making herself as comfortable as possible, she leans against the wall to wait.

An hour later, Peter comes around the bend and into the hall. He stops dead in his tracks when he sees Gwen sitting on his doorstep.

"Finally! Do you have any idea how uncomfortable it is sitting on a stone floor?" Gwen says irritably as she hauls herself to her feet, dusting off her blue jeans before settling a determined look upon Peter.

The momentary shock subsides, and Peter suddenly starts walking rapidly toward her. With his head down, he doesn't meet her gaze as he approaches his door. He reaches out for the knob as if to hurry inside without acknowledging Gwen.

"Oh, no you don't!" Gwen grabs his arm and turns him to face her. "I didn't wait all this time to let you run off. I have questions and you're going to answer them, even if I have to stalk you all day and night."

Peter looks at her, dumbstruck. Looking up and down the hall frantically, he takes a step toward Gwen, speaking in a low whisper.

"Are you mad? He will kill me if he sees me with you, and he'd be all too happy to get you alone someplace where no one will hear your screams. You must go. Now!" Peter's words are urgent and sincere, his fear showing visibly throughout his frail, teenage frame. When Gwen looks into his eyes, she knows that what he says is true.

Without a word, Gwen releases her hold on Peter and turns away. Determined not to show her fear, Gwen walks quickly, yet proudly, down the hall back the way she came, her head held high. Inside she is shaken, for his words frighten her. She has never felt that she was in danger in Bec LaNuff until this very moment. The look in his eyes haunts her as she makes her way back to the main level of the fortress.

Why haven't I been afraid yet? My dreams have never steered me wrong before. They are warning me of something. Somehow this place is making me forget my dreams. Is it making me forget to be on my guard? Gwen asks herself.

She stops and finds herself in the middle of the main courtyard, the enchanted light shining down upon her. Gwen looks up to stare into the golden sun and moon hanging high above the chamber, the eyes floating amongst the many circles in a way that feels hypnotic. The feeling of dread begins to fade.

It is all too obvious who Peter meant when he said, "He would be all too happy to get you alone someplace where no one will hear your screams." Ivan, of course.

Gwen has observed him during her stay, how he always lingers just a step behind Legion, standing at his side whenever the Master is seated at his throne. The way he always watches everyone else who comes near him with a jealous, evil eye. He is a henchman if ever Gwen saw one. And he hates her. That is all too apparent. It makes her sick whenever she feels his gaze upon her.

Gwen shudders involuntarily as she thinks of it. Then, coming to herself, she remembers where she is and begins to move through the courtyard, smiling and nodding to well wishers as she makes her way out of the crowded chamber and on toward her own quarters, and hopefully to safety.

* * * * *

A dark form emerges from one of the lower passageways, stepping into the courtyard, his silver eyes staring in the direction Gwen had exited. A dark sneer passes over his ugly features. Just looking at the girl revolts him. He can still taste her tainted Witch's blood in his mouth. He suddenly turns his head and spits on the courtyard floor.

Ivan's spot at Legion's table has been given to Gwen. Where his opinion had once mattered, now Gwen is the one everyone turns to. Once, no one would've crossed him, for he was Legion's favorite. Now the little Witch is the revered and feared right hand of the Master. *It isn't fair! I have served my Master well for centuries, done everything he has ever asked, and now this is my repayment, to be replaced by a crafty, simpering little girl, a mortal no less?* Anger boils with him at the thought.

I should've never hauled that little wench out of the snow! Ivan thinks bitterly as he moves across the chamber. *The little dear would be frozen solid under a mountain of snow by now, where no one would find her till spring.* The thought makes him smile wickedly. A few passersby have to step aside to get out of his way.

Over the years Ivan has watched all manner of young girls come and go, the Master tossing one aside for a fresh one the way some men change their socks. He'd never cared much for any of them. Once they served their purpose, the Master would tire of them and then hand them over to Ivan, or one of the other Vampires who had pleased him, as token of his affection, to do with as they wished.

This one is different. Because she is a Witch, she has power, strength, and beauty, all the things the master most admires and craves in a companion.

It will take the Master a long time to tire of her, if he does at all. As long as she pleases him and serves his will, she will be his most prized possession, his favorite and most beloved servant. Ivan steps out of the courtyard and into the passageway leading up to the Vampire wing of the fortress. *If only there were a way to make him turn on her, if only she would do something to anger the Master, then he would forsake her.*

Ivan knows it is hopeless. Legion can be charming and beautiful when he desires, especially in the eyes of simple-minded little girls. Ivan sees the way the child Witch looks at his Master, as simpering and love-struck as all the rest. He expected a Witch to be stronger, smarter, and less susceptible to the Master's allure, having the mental strength to resist the spell he cast upon her. In this, the girl has been a disappointment.

This, among other things, has left most of the Vampires under the mountain unimpressed and disgusted with the girl. They all expected more from a Witch, hoping that a great battle might have broken out days ago between her and the Master. It would have been marvelous to watch the Master destroy one of their rival tribe's young and promising enchantresses. It would have been a great victory for their race, in the constant tug o' war of power between the Vampires and the Wiccans. She is not very clever, nor bright, and knows not that she should hate them, but accepts them as friends, living amongst them like a stupid, little fool.

No, there would be no great battle, no Wiccan blood spilt to appease the ancient feud between their two tribes. To the disgrace of all their kind, the Master, as it seems, is smitten with the little Witch, doting on her as she dotes on him.

A great unrest stirs among Legion's cold-blooded followers, and Ivan knows all too well how delicate his Master's balance of power is. One wrong move and someone will overthrow him. One step in the wrong direction, and he will lose all his power. The proud Legion will never give up without a fight, resulting in all-out war in Bec LaNuff. *There would be mayhem!*

With every passing day the Vampires grow more and more uneasy. *If the Master doesn't kill the girl soon, then someone else will.* And then Legion's wrath will be great and terrible. He might even execute one of his own for having the presumption to touch his favorite, to slaughter what belongs only to him.

Ivan walks past the grand hall. As much as he likes the idea of blood and carnage, Ivan has to admit that outright civil war isn't the answer to this delicate situation. He loves his Master and would never wish him harm. Especially if he should be overthrown, another would take his place, perhaps someone who didn't look favorably on Ivan the spy. He could never attempt to claim the throne for himself—he has no delusions about how the others feel toward him.

No, there is nothing for it but to convince the Master to

murder the girl himself, to show him the error of his ways, and make the girl a sacrifice to his minions to appease their offended pride. Every day she is allowed to live, arrogantly strutting about the halls of Bec LaNuff as if she owns the place, only adds insult to injury. Something has to be done. And soon.

Ivan finds himself standing just outside Gwen's bedchamber door.

Things were a lot simpler before the Witch came to the mountain, and it would be up to him to make sure things return to the way they should be, the way he likes them.

Ivan continues on down the hall, headed toward Legion's personal bedchamber. *I will show the Master that it is I alone who he can trust, I alone who loves him. Soon he will see the girl for what she truly is, a child of the enemy. I will show the Master the difference between lies and loyalties.*

CHAPTER NINE

The Promise of Love

A book open in her lap, Gwen enjoys a brief solitude while Lydia and Jessica are out running errands. "My birthday is only two days away," Gwen admits to the empty bedroom. Losing interest in the history of ogres, she shuts the volume and places it on the end table, stepping out of bed to stretch her aching limbs.

Gwen has kept a diligent eye on the passage of time and knows that today is January tenth. On January twelfth, she will turn twelve herself.

Strangely enough, she isn't as excited about the big day as she thought she would be. After all, being twelve means she is almost a teenager and that will lead to all sorts of experiences and new changes as she leaves girlhood behind on her journey to becoming a woman.

Getting older isn't the only thing on her mind lately. An uneasy sense of dread and restlessness had begun to crawl its way under her skin ever since her meeting with Peter. She feels that something bad is about to happen, or that something is wrong, but can't figure out what. Everything seems to be fine at Bec LaNuff, but deep down there is something, like a voice, telling her that nothing is as it appears.

I'm just being paranoid again, she tells herself, and picks up another book from her bedside table entitled *The Royal Houses and Political Systems of the Thirteen Tribes*. She thumbs through it to the chapter on Wiccans.

She skims through a flowery introduction about the importance of pure blood lines. According to the author, the most powerful Witches and Warlocks come from strictly Wiccan families, and mingling of Wiccan blood with other races produces weak magicians. She doesn't find this all that interesting and skips on to the next page, where a beautifully ornate illustration of the Wiccan family tree is portrayed.

At the bottom, underneath the tree and its bare roots, an underground stream is shown flowing through the roots, providing sustenance and life to the tree. Written within the stream are the names Cain and Lilith. Carved upon the tree's trunk are the names Wicca and Willow, and all throughout the branches are the names of their children and their children's children, from generation to generation.

Toward the top of the tree there are eight family names: Darkhood, Hardenbro, Willowon, Rosenblaze, Limrick, DuCall, Caldron, and Hawthorne. On the next page she reads that the Hawthorne's are the current family in power and have been the ruling family for the last twenty years. Previously, the Wiccan kingdom was ruled by the Willowon family for two hundred years. When King Arrow Willowon died without an heir, his title and power passed to the next strongest Wiccan in the first families of Wicca, Deverick Hawthorne. The current royal family consists of King Deverick Hawthorne, his wife Queen Amethyst Rosenblaze, and their son Prince Archer Hawthorne. Above the section on the royal family's history is a likeness drawn of the family, done some years ago when the book was published.

Something about the Prince seems oddly familiar to Gwen. His face is young and serious, despite his youth, but his eyes are kind, hinting at a lively sense of humor and love of life. He looks to be only twelve years old in the drawing, and by Gwen's estimation from the date at the bottom, that means he has to be almost nineteen years-old now.

She can't remember ever meeting any nineteen-year-old Wiccan boys, especially none so handsome. All the same, she can't shake the feeling that she has seen him somewhere in a distant memory.

A knock sounds at the door. Gwen puts the book aside and looks up. "Come in," she calls out. Jessica and Lydia enter. Lydia brings a tray of food. Jessica follows on her heels, waiting until Lydia has deposited the tray of sandwiches before Gwen and steps back, before she steps forward and hands Gwen a note. Jessica bows as she and her cousin back away.

"Thank you," Gwen replies, not bothering to look at the servant girls, as her attention is consumed by the folded piece of paper in her hand. A little apprehensive, Gwen unfolds the note and reads.

We can't talk or see each other. Ivan will find out, and he'd be angry if he knew I spoke to you the other day, especially now that you're the Master's favorite. I should warn you that my Master, Ivan, has it out for you. Don't go wandering in the Vampire wing alone. Go with someone like the Elf or a Dwarf, because your servants are useless. They can't protect you and Ivan has a thing for meddling with the servant girls. He won't attack you because Legion's already claimed you, but if things should change, Ivan won't hesitate to take you as his own. And he is cruel. They say you are a Witch and one of the Forsaken. Maybe it's true, but you are young and a stranger here. I would be careful. Don't trust anyone, especially Lord and Master Legion. He may seem charming and kind, but it's just a mask. He may like you now, but cross him and he will turn on you. I've already told you more than I should. Please don't contact me again. It's dangerous.

Peter

P.S. Please be good to my sister Lydia and my cousin Jessica. I know that they may seem like they are brain dead, but I hope that they're still in there somewhere, and should be treated with kindness. I only say this because I know that many of the other Forsaken beat their servants, and are cruel to them. You seem normal, almost human to me, so I hope you're different from the others. If you really are a Witch, then maybe you can help them remember who they are.

Gwen looks across the room at the two servant girls, a look of shock upon her face.

"Peter is your family?" Gwen asks aloud, but the girls do not respond. They kneel in the corner, their eyes fixed on the floor. In disbelief, Gwen tries to process all the information from Peter's note.

Okay, so I know now that Peter and Lydia are brother and sister and Jessica is their cousin. It stands to reason that they all came here together. But how and why? What did they do that upset Legion? How can these three ordinary teenagers be a threat to him?

Peter said that Ivan meddles with the servant girls. I'm not sure what that means, but I think it's something like what that bastard Denis Keller was doing to Cara, and what he tried to do to me. Does that mean he's been touching Jessica and Lydia? How dare he? That's like fooling around with a corpse! Ugh!

A wave of nausea and disgust comes over her. Quickly, a deep rage follows. She can't stand to think of such things, and suddenly she feels responsible for the girls. She has to protect them now. She doesn't know what she'll do the next time she sees Ivan, but deep down she wants to do something awful to him, something he'd never forget—something that would make him think twice before he ever touches any young girl again. But for now, she still has to make sense of the rest of the note. She returns to her meditation. She reads over the note again.

Legion has claimed me? What the hell does that mean? What am I, a doll or a pet? Gwen recalls something Peter said to her when she met him.

"Oh, you can't leave. Someone must have found you and since you're alive, they must have brought you here as gift to the Master. Usually they house Legion's girls in another wing, closer to his bedchamber."

A sudden chill comes over Gwen. *Am I Ivan's gift to Legion? Am I just like Melody? And what exactly is Melody's relationship to Legion anyway? She's obviously jealous of the attention he lavishes on me. It doesn't seem like a father/daughter relationship to me.* Gwen can't help but notice that Melody's feelings for Legion are not platonic, but she doesn't know for sure what Legion feels for Melody.

I could always try to read his mind, Gwen reminds herself, but shakes the thought off. *He might notice the intrusion and how would I explain that?* As Gwen thinks about the few times she has seen the two of them interact, she begins to doubt what Peter said in the note.

Legion acts as though Melody is his annoying little sister, or a pest that hovers around him. She can't be his... girlfriend, or his lover, Gwen reasons with herself. The thought is preposterous. Legion is kind, handsome, strong, intelligent, and benevolent. Not a pervert.

Either way, she can't help feeling affected by Peter's words. *Maybe I shouldn't linger here in Bec LaNuff for long. My health is restored, and I feel fit enough for the journey. If I can just get my hands on a map of the area...Surely they must have one in the library. All I have to do is horde enough food for provisions to last me until I can get to the next town.*

Gwen resolves to start preparations for her eventual departure, but she doesn't feel any need to run off just yet. After all, it could all just be the paranoid ramblings of Peter's demented mind. There was no evidence to prove the truthfulness of his accusations. Nonetheless, it wouldn't hurt to be ready just in case.

Suddenly, she is reminded of the old days with Raven in New York. Somehow it seems like it's been years since they were together, yet in reality, it's only been six months. They were always prepared for any eventuality back then—living out of suitcases, always alert for danger, an escape plan in place in case they needed to flee at a moment's notice. She feels a pang of loneliness and longing, wishing Raven were with her now.

Oh, well, if everything goes well, I might be seeing him again very soon, Gwen tells herself. *There has to be a way to get his records from the child service office. Maybe I could just put an ad in the newspaper in the ancient tongue, some kind of announcement that only Raven would understand—some way to contact him and let him know I'm okay. We might even be able to find a way to meet.*

A sudden thought occurs to her. *Legion has spies and scouts all over this area. Maybe he can put the word out amongst his servants to keep an eye out for Raven?* This, she decides, is a much better solution than anything else she can devise.

Just then, Gwen looks up to see Lydia and Jessica standing before her. The elder girl holds a golden gown in her outstretched arms. In the other, she holds a pair of gem-encrusted slippers. The two of them stare at her patiently as if they had been in this position the entire time she was off in la-la land.

Embarrassed, Gwen mouths an apology and stands up to allow the girls to assist her with getting ready for the evening. Legion asked earlier if she would take a walk with him this evening before dinner. He wanted to take her someplace special, he said, a part of the fortress she hadn't yet seen. Gwen accepted the invitation with the nervous air of a lovesick school girl. Butterflies dance about in her stomach even now, but she can't help it. It will be just the two of them, and being near him makes her light-headed. Deep down she knows she is enamored with him, but hasn't the faintest idea what to do about her feelings.

Gwen feels light, almost giddy, as she sits before the mirror, allowing the cousins to make over her black hair. *Yes, everything is going to be all right.* She would get Legion's help to find her friend, and then she would go to Raven, and together they would come back here to live with their own kind. *Raven would like it here,* she thinks. *And I'm sure that once they all got to know him, everyone would change their minds about Werewolves. They would see that Raven is different, and as my personal friend, he would be automatically welcomed into the fold.*

Gwen is at last ready, her hair expertly piled atop her head in ringlets and curls, dozens of diamond pins holding it in place. Her face is made up with a little rouge and powder. She is finely dressed in the golden gown, and fine slippers. Diamond drops dangle from her delicate earlobes, and a breathtaking diamond choker wraps around her neck. Gwen is the very image of beauty in the sweet bloom of youth.

As if on cue, a knock raps upon the door. Gwen gets up from the vanity, her heart pounding with anticipation. Lydia scurries across the room to answer the door.

Legion sweeps into the room in one graceful gesture, never acknowledging the servants, his complete attention on Gwen. His eyes glow in brilliance at the sight of her. He is dressed in his usual impeccable manner, his garments of the finest quality like a French king. His pale, perfect skin gleams wherever it is exposed. His eyes shine pale white and hunting in their startling lack of color, melting beautifully with his pale hair and eye brows. If Gwen didn't know better she would swear he is wearing lipstick, for his lips are a deep crimson red, full and beautiful in their contrast.

"Ah, you look radiant this evening, Miss Gwen." Legion smiles at her, the sight of which makes her preteen heart melt, and her stomach flutter. She smiles back, feeling shy, and at a complete loss for words.

She wants to tell him how beautiful he is, to express the awe she feels being in his godly presence, but she knows she would sound like a fool for uttering such things. Even if she were in love with him, she has no clue how to be charming or flirtatious. If she tries to dazzle him, she will only get tongue-tied. Instead, she smiles at him like an idiot as she crosses the room to his side.

Taking her arm in his, they leave the chamber together. On any other occasion they would turn left and head down the hall back toward the grand chamber and the lower wings of the fortress, but tonight, Legion turns right, leading her up the hall in the opposite direction. They follow the hallway until they reach a spiral staircase made of stone, leading upward toward the mountain's peak.

Gwen hesitates a moment on the stair. She turns to look up into Legion's handsome face. "Where are we going?" she asks, baffled. During her time at Bec LaNuff she has never once observed or heard of Legion ever leaving the protection of the mountain.

"To the top, my love. Don't worry, it is quite safe for us up there." His deep, honeyed voice soothes her anxiety and they continue climbing. Finally, after what seems to Gwen like an eternity of winding stairs, they come to a long narrow passageway.

She can see moonlight pouring in through an archway at the other end of the corridor, the smell of fresh, cool night air wafting toward her on a gentle breeze.

As Legion leads her down the corridor to the archway, they pass under it and onto what looks like a balcony without a hand rail. The floor is flat like a man-made floor, yet Gwen knows she is standing on a cliff along the mountain side.

A dazzling panoramic view of the snow-covered valley below stretches out before them. The trees and mountain peaks glimmer in the glow of the full moon high above them. Gwen takes a deep breath, capturing the sweet mountain air in her lungs, letting it linger there a moment before finally letting her breath out with a satisfied sigh. She stares into the night sky. A thousand shimmering lights as brilliant as diamonds on black velvet shine down upon her. They are so high up the mountain that Gwen almost believes all she needs do is reach out her hand and pluck a star from the sky. It is a silly, childish thought, but it makes her smile.

Gwen looks to her companion, and to her embarrassment, she sees that he is staring at her. She blushes, wondering how long he has been observing her reaction. A smile spreads across Legion's face.

"Do you like the view?" he asks.

"Yes, it's beautiful. Thank you for bringing me here. I had almost forgotten what fresh air was like." Gwen suddenly twirls about, her arms outstretched and her head back as she lets the night air caress her skin with the kiss of the wind.

Legion laughs. "The moon is beautiful, is it not?"

"Oh, yes." Gwen feels breathless as Legion moves smoothly to her side.

Gwen shudders as the wind brushes against her. The air is cold, yet invigorating, goose bumps forming on her arms and neck.

"Are you cold? Forgive me, I forget that you are mortal. The elements have no effect over me."

Legion wraps his arms around her. Warmth radiates from his fine fur-lined robe, but wherever his flesh touches hers, an icy chill burns her.

"I'm okay. It's not all that cold, really," Gwen stammers.

His closeness alarms Gwen. She goes stiff in his arms as he bends down to whisper in her ear.

"Let me take care of you, Gwen. I long to be your protector, your companion, your equal in all things." His velvet voice tickles her ear, the sound causing strange sensations all over her body. She feels her body melt, every muscle relaxing.

Gwen swallows. "What makes you think I need protection? I can take care myself." She meant it to sound indignant, but instead her words have no strength, making her sound unsure and childish.

Legion laughs, his breath cold upon her neck.

"When you came to us you were barely alive. Had you been under my protection, you would never need fear the laws of men. You wouldn't have needed to flee into the wildness. Stay with me, Gwen, and you will want for nothing."

"What law? I'm not running from anything," Gwen protests.

"Oh come now, darling, of course I know troubles. I have many spies, even in Scranton. Never fear, the humans will never find you here. You're safe as long as you're with me."

A wave of intense emotion crashes upon her like the gentle sway of the ocean's tide upon the beach. Her first instinct is to rebel against such a notion. She didn't need anyone, for she never really had anyone but Raven to lean on for support. She is used to fending for herself, comfortable with the solitary life that fate chose for her. And yet, inside, she feels the childhood longing for peace, for a family, for home. How would it feel to belong to someone, to have one who was there for you in all things? Yes, Raven had always been by her side, but more often than not she had protected *him,* and he had turned to her to lead them instead of the other way around. What a relief it would be to let go of all the anxiety and stress of leadership, and responsibility, and let someone else lead her for a change.

The silence drags as Gwen ponders this proposal when something occurs to her.

"What about Melody? I thought she was your companion? Or is she just your servant as well?" Nervous butterflies make her stomach feel as if it's on the edge of nausea. *I hope he doesn't think that I'm rude for asking so blunt a question.*

"I understand your confusion. The girl was simply staying here as our guest, but she has proven to be of a jealous and obsessive nature. We feel her negativity will only cause contention in our society, so she and I had a little chat, and she has agreed that it is best that she return home to her family," Legion confides in Gwen.

She turns her head to look up at him. "Oh. I thought… never mind. When is she leaving?"

"I've asked one of my most trusted children to escort her home tonight. Do not trouble yourself with her. She will not come between us." Legion looks into her eyes, his white gaze piercing into her soul, communicating a deeper meaning behind his words.

Gwen looks away, breaking the intense eye contact.

"I don't know. I mean, I can't stay here. I have to find Raven. He's probably out of his mind worrying about me. I must go to him." With that, Gwen breaks free of Legion's embrace and takes a couple steps away from him, looking up the mountainside toward the mountain's peak.

"He'll forget you in time. He has his own kind to take him in. Wolves belong in packs. They are restless and dangerous on their own."

"I guess I shouldn't be surprised that you know about him too." Then something hits her. She turns to face him. "Wait, what do you mean he has his own kind to take him in? Do you know where he is?"

Legion nods.

"Then we must send someone to get him, or tell me where he is and I'll go find him myself."

"No. It's too dangerous out there for you, Gwen."

Legion moves toward her, and Gwen instinctively turns and starts pacing the balcony. "You don't understand. I won't be happy unless he is with me. He is the only family I've ever known. Only if he were here with me could I be content to stay and live in Bec LaNuff."

"Are you sure? He wouldn't fit in here. His kind is too wild, too different from the other races of Cain. He'd be a danger to himself and others."

"No, he wouldn't! I can control the beast within him. I've done it before."

Legion seems startled by this revelation.

"You can do that?" He turns and looks into the night as if pondering something. After a moment, he turns back to her. "I suppose that does change matters a bit. Still, the others will not understand. His presence here would anger many. Are you sure there is no way I might persuade you to forget him?" Legion asks this in earnest. He crosses the gap between them and reaches his arms toward her.

Gwen hesitates. "No. I cannot abandon my friend. I will show the others that he is not like other Wolves. He is gentle, kind, and trustworthy. Raven would do anything I ask of him, and would never hurt a soul... Well, not unprovoked, at least." Her voice pleads for him to understand.

"If you are absolutely certain, my love, then by all means, he must come and stay with us, if only to make you happy." Legion steps forward, taking her hands in his. He takes each hand and brings it to his lips, pressing a cold kiss upon her flesh. "My sole desire is to make you happy," he whispers, his eyes lingering on hers in a tender gaze.

Gwen shudders, her head swimming as giddiness overcomes her. She isn't used to physical affection, and she doesn't know what to make of the hormones raging inside of her. Thoughts come unhidden at Legion's slightest touch. Nervously, she pulls her hands away from his grasp and steps away from him.

"I was hoping I could ask for your help finding him. Otherwise, I was planning to gather the supplies I need and go out hunting for him myself. I grow restless. Who knows where he is or what's happened to him while I sit here safe and snug? I can't stand to be idle another day. I have to find him. Once I do, I promise we'll return."

"I hate to think of you out there alone in the wilderness again, Gwen. You are wanted for murder. You must let my men hunt for your Wolf. Stay here with me where it is safe. I'm positive that this Raven wouldn't want you to put yourself in danger on his account."

Legion steps toward her again. This time Gwen doesn't move away. "I don't think he'd come unless I'm the one who finds him. He'll be frightened of your kind. We've had a run-in with the children of Cain before, and it was not a pleasant experiences. No, I think it would be better if I went alone. He trusts me."

For the briefest of moments, a dark look crosses over Legion's visage, but just as quickly his demeanor changes as a loving smile spreads across his face. He reaches out one hand and caresses her check with one long manicured nail. Slowly, he moves closer to her until he looms over her, his overwhelming presence casting her in his shadow. Cupping her face in his hand, he gently tilts her head upward to look at him. Their eyes meet in an iron-clad gaze. Gwen feels mesmerized, her resistance fading into the white abyss around his dark pupils.

"Whatever you wish, my love. You have only to ask and it will be done. All I ask is for your word that you will return to me?" Gwen's whole body is alert and aware of him, her mind consumed with him and his striking face. She can't seem to think of anything else, her natural thoughts slipping away like sand through her fingers. At that moment, all she wants and loves in the world is Legion. All she needs is his touch. Gwen dumbly nods her consent, her eyes fixated in Legion's never-ending stare.

"Say that you will stay with me, worship me, and love none other but me," Legion commands in a hushed whisper.

"I will stay with you, worship you, and I will love only you," Gwen replies, the words drawn out of her like a chant. With that, Gwen steps into his arms, finding relief in his embrace. He holds her tight to him, stroking her hair with his hand, lovingly.

"Come, my darling, we will be late for supper." Gwen looks up and smiles. Legion bends down and kisses her forehead. He takes her by the hand and together they leave the balcony, entering the archway, heading back down toward the grand banquet hall below. Gwen allows herself to believe in a happy ending in her future, completely won over by Legion, and seduced by the promise of love.

CHAPTER TEN

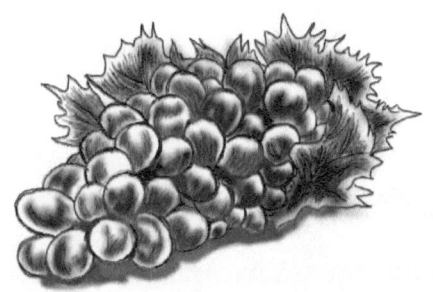

Another Life

Gwen seems to float on air as they enter the banquet hall and join Legion's other guests. Among the usual dinner guests, Gwen sees Emon and his mate, Vinita. Melody is nowhere in sight.

She must have already left for home, Gwen reasons, but something about her absence troubles her. *Forget about it, Gwen, she is gone now and it's better for everyone that way.*

Gwen takes her seat next to Legion at the massive banquet table. Legion snaps his fingers and a crimson-clad servant boy carrying a silver serving tray with an assortment of fruits hurries to his side. Legion scans the contents of the tray, and then picks out a large sprig of ripe green grapes. Turning to Gwen, he places them upon her plate.

"They are your favorite, are they not?" Legion smiles confidently.

"Yes, how did you—"

Legion leans in closer to Gwen, cutting off her words. "I make it a point to keep track of your every whim and desire. I want you to feel at home here, my love. You will have everything your heart has ever desired. Everything I possess will be waiting for you when you return to me," he whispers in her ear.

Gwen looks into his eyes, his face only inches from hers, and feels warmth and love wash over her. She smiles at him and then, reaching out, takes a grape from her plate and pops it in her mouth. Legion smiles approvingly. He takes her hand in his, holding it in full view of the company. Gwen feels embarrassed yet elated.

Most of the evening passes without an unpleasant thought entering her lovesick mind. All she can feel is Legion's presence beside her. All she can do is stare at him adoringly. At one point during the dinner, Gwen and Emon's eyes meet. He gives her a strange look, as if he doesn't know her, as if seeing her for the first time. A strange sense of shame comes over her, and she looks away. However, when she looks back, Vinita meets her gaze, not Emon. The Elfin woman smiles back at her wickedly, a dark gleam in her ferocious, predatory eyes. Gwen shoots a glare back at the Elf maid and returns her attention to her meal and Legion's pleasant company.

A scream shatters the cheerful atmosphere of the gathering, the sound reverberating in Gwen's skull. "*SOMEBODY HELP ME!*" Alarmed, she looks around in shock, her every muscle alert.

"What was that?" Gwen whispers under her breath as she

looks from one face to the next, yet no one seems alarmed. They eat and talk, drinking their wine and laughing at each other's jokes.

Legion turns to her, noticing the panicked look upon her face.

"What's wrong, my love? Is everything all right?" She hears genuine concern in his voice.

"I'm not…" Gwen begins to speak when suddenly…

"SOMEBODY, PLEASE! HE'S GOING TO KILL ME!" The scream pierces through Gwen's thoughts, banishing all feelings but fear and anger. She looks to Legion and sees by the look on his face that he plainly doesn't hear what she hears.

"I'm fine. I just need to go to the bathroom."

"Of course, you may go. Hurry back, my darling." Legion dismisses her with a wave of his hand. He turns to rejoin the conversation with the Dwarf Lords sitting next to him.

Gwen hesitates a moment, and then gets up from the table. She isn't sure why she didn't tell Legion of the voice in her head, but something deep down tells her that secrecy is crucial. With as nonchalant an air as she can muster, Gwen passes the other dinner guests on her way out the door. Only after she has left the grand banquet hall and is well out of the sight of the two Troll guards does Gwen break into a run. She races up the hallway in the general direction of her room. She pauses just outside her bedroom door and reaches out with her consciousness, trying to locate the source of the screams.

The voice was female, a young girl by the sound of it, and familiar. *But who is screaming? Who is in danger? And why am I the only one who can hear her?*

"PLEASE! ANYBODY!" The voice comes to her again, this time closer, somewhere up ahead.

Moving as fast as her elegant skirt will allow, she follows the voice around corners and bends as the passageway climbs upward toward the upper-most peak and the spiral staircase.

As she rounds the bend, Gwen hears feet scuffling on stone and a strange dragging sound. She slows to a walk and cautiously approaches the spot where the hallway turns right. She peers around the corner.

At the bottom of the spiral staircase, a man hunches over a diminutive female form. With his back to her, she can't make out his identity. He wrestles with a girl, who squirms and kicks in an attempt to get free from his embrace. He gets a firm hold and hefts her over his shoulder.

Gwen gasps. A gag is wedged in Melody's mouth, her hands and feet bound with cloth. Her usually pristine, white garments are torn and blood-stained. Her blue eyes are wild as she thrashes, determined to get free. Her captor begins to ascend the stairs just as the staircase bends.

Ivan's ugly face is contorted in a greedy sneer, obviously enjoying the muffled cries of the girl in his clutches. Although her verbal cries are muted, Melody's mental shouts are splitting Gwen's skull in half. The pain makes it difficult for Gwen to stay on her feet. Paralyzed in fear, she waits for Ivan to carry Melody all the way up the stairs before she follows.

She tries to creep up the staircase silently, but every step seems to creek loudly beneath her weight. She can still hear Melody's cries in her head, leading her onward. Finally, she reaches the top of the stairs and the narrow passageway leading toward the illuminated archway. How odd it feels to be in the very same place she had been only an hour ago. She walks toward the stone balcony with a sense of dread. She creeps to the edge of the hall, hiding just within the arch. Slowly, she peers into the moonlit night.

Ivan hunches over Melody as she squirms beneath him. He runs his hands all over her body. To Gwen's surprise, he loosens the bands on Melody's hands and feet and quickly removes the gag from her mouth.

With the obstruction gone, she instantly lets out a bone-shattering scream. Ivan laughs, a dark look upon his grotesque face. Melody shakes violently as she tries to scurry on her hands and knees as far away from Ivan as she can get. When she is within inches of the cliff, she sees the drop below and shies away from the edge.

Ivan giggles with delight, a sound so vile it makes Gwen's skin crawl. She watches them, something inside her making her feel helpless and confused. Should she go for help? No, for who knows what that monster might do to the poor girl in her absence. Surely she should do something, but all at once, Gwen feels her age. She feels tiny and insignificant, as helpless as the girl before her quaking in fear.

Ivan springs forward, pouncing on Melody's huddled form. He moves with deadly speed, striking like a cobra. In an instant, he seizes her. She screams in horror, shouting out her Master's name. Then, just as suddenly, Ivan jerks her neck to one side and dives in, his teeth tearing at her soft, tender flesh.

Her screams cease, the shock and the pain disorienting her. Blood sputters out of her open wound as Ivan presses his mouth to her neck, drinking greedily of the dark red fluid. Melody makes sharp choking noises. Small whimpers of pain escape her lips as her wide, blue eyes glaze over.

It all happens so fast that Gwen has hardly a moment to comprehend it. As quickly as he struck, Ivan pulls away, releasing the girl from his bloody embrace. Her limp body crumples to the stone beneath him. At first, the girl looks dead, but then the dazed look recedes. Her eyes regain their focus and she takes a deep, gasping breath, as if she broke free from a body of water and is drawing the air into her deprived lungs. Melody looks around, confused, and then her eyes alight upon Ivan. He stands ten feet away from her, a wicked smile from ear to ear.

"What are you going to do to me?" she trembles.

"Nothing. You can leave if you want," Ivan informs her, his voice soft and haunting.

Melody slowly gets to her feet, but her eyes never leave Ivan. Light-headed from the loss of blood, she struggles to stay upright. She looks longingly toward the dark archway, and then back at Ivan, unsure. "Are you telling the truth? Can I really leave and no one will come after me?"

"Yes. No one will stop you," Ivan reassures.

Still suspicious, Melody keeps her eyes on his face as she walks slowly toward the arch and her escape. Ivan moves, suddenly appearing before Melody, blocking her path.

"You can't go that way."

"But...you said I could..." She can barely contain her fear. Her body quivers before him as she slowly stumbles backward.

Ivan takes a deliberate step forward. Melody continues to back away from him as he advances.

"You can leave, but only if you can fly!" Ivan's voice takes on a dark, hushed tone hushed. He laughs as he continues moving forward, forcing the child before him to move closer and closer to the cliff's perimeter.

Gwen springs into action, her body suddenly moving of its own accord. She doesn't think, doesn't feel. One moment she's crouching behind the arch watching, horrified, and the next, she is stepping into the open, moving toward Ivan. She racks her brain for a spell, trying to come up with a plan for attack.

With his back turned to her, Ivan doesn't see or hear her coming. He reaches out and grabs Melody, and in the same quick, fluid motion, hefts her over his head and tosses the girl effortlessly over the balcony. Melody's screams force Gwen into action. She leaps forward, and with a guttural yell, she crashes into Ivan.

The two of them tumble to the ground at the cliff's edge. Ivan springs to his feet, unfazed by Gwen's attack. He lunges at her.

Gwen reaches out to the source of all life, its power flows within her tiny frame, but it is too late. Ivan is on top of her, his hands seizing her, his fangs springing forth from his gums as he leans in to bite her. Gwen yells in defiance as magic words come to her, words she has never used before. She draws upon the wind about her, the might of the air swarming about the mountain.

"Du-Day Windah!" She sends a gust of wind from the core of her body. The blast sends Ivan flying backward. He crashes into the side of the mountain and falls to the ground, groaning in pain. He gets to his feet, his eyes locking on Gwen, a sinister glint in his stare. He lunges forward, this time with even greater speed. Gwen loses sight of him. Quickly she gets to her feet, ready to defend herself.

From behind, Gwen is struck to the ground, Ivan's weight heavy on her back. She is pinned in place, her physical form too weak to fight him off.

"Master's favorite or not, I'm still going to tear your bloody heart out!" Ivan sneers his cold breath on the nape of her neck. Pain surges through her as his fangs tear at her neckline. Gwen screams, fury and anger pulsing inside her. Making an invisible field converge upon his body, she lifts Ivan off of her, and holding him in midair, rolls onto her back to look up at him.

Ivan sneers at her. Gwen smiles darkly back, and then throws him over the edge off the cliff, releasing the magic that holds him in her mental grasp. Ivan falls through the air, his animal yell echoing off the mountain and into the night as he plummets down to the earth.

Gwen lays there a moment as he disappears from her view, listening to his shouts fade as he falls farther into the valley below. Only when she is satisfied that he is gone does Gwen get to her feet. She moves toward the cliff, wanting to see firsthand Ivan's broken, lifeless form lying on the rocks below. The valley below is probably too deep in shadow for her to catch sight of his body, but still, something compels Gwen to step up to the ledge and look over into the dark abyss below.

Suddenly, out of the shadows, Ivan flies at her. Gwen stumbles backward as his dark form races toward her, his eyes glowing white and his mouth soaked in her blood. Gwen focuses all her anger and hatred into a ball in her stomach. Before she even knows what she's doing, she releases an orb of light from her palms. The energy source hurtles into the air and strikes Ivan squarely in the chest. The light engulfs him and then is consumed by this body, absorbed into his flesh. Ivan suddenly stops in midair as if he has hit an invisible wall. The impact of the orb knocks him out of the air and he hits the ground as if dead.

Gwen sits,, stunned, her breathing ragged and forced. Then, as if suddenly awakening from a horrible dream, she comes to herself. Instantly, she is on her feet and dashing to the archway and back down the narrow corridor beyond.

She traverses the rest of the way to the banquet hall, half out of her mind, tears streaming unhindered down her cheeks. Her chest heaves in pain as panic racks her frail, young frame. As

Gwen comes into view, the two Trolls guarding the door look at her in alarm Her curls have half fallen out of their pins, matted with dirt and blood. Her elegant gown is torn and filthy. One of her slippers is missing. Beyond the frightening state of her wardrobe, her eyes are bloodshot with tears streaming down her face, dirt covering her skin, cuts and bruises on her legs and arms, and most alarming of all, a giant bloody gouge in her neck. Blood drips down her shoulder and stains her beautiful clothes. One of the guards ducks inside to alert the Master while the other hurries to Gwen's side.

Gwen feels the urgency of movement leave her, the adrenaline that has carried her this far evaporating into thin air. Without it, her diminutive frame collapses into the Troll's arms. He cradles her and hurries into the grand banquet hall.

Gwen sees only the ceiling above her, but she hears the general chatter and upset of the dinner guests as she is carried past them and taken directly to the Master.

The guard places her on her feet in front of Legion. Instantly, she leans into his arms, wanting the physical reassurance and comfort that awaits her there. Gwen buries her face in his chest, letting her tears soak his fine linens.

"What's happened? How did she get like this?" Legion demands. Behind her, Gwen hears the guard begin to give a recount of her appearing at the banquet doors. Gwen looks up into Legion's pale, distressed face.

"He killed her! I watched him murder Melody!" Gwen moans,

burying her face in the folds of his robes as a new round of sobs bursts forth from her chest. Legion wraps his arms around her as her body shakes violently. He gently strokes her hair and back.

"Everyone out! Return to your rooms and speak of this to no one!" Legion commands. Gwen listens as the other guests shuffle out, their chatter dissipating as they leave the room one by one until all is silent around them. Gwen quits crying and looks up, expecting to find herself alone in the room with Legion, but to her dismay Emon, Vinita, and a couple of servants, as well as the guards, are still there, awaiting their Lord's command.

Legion helps Gwen to a chair. She takes a seat, and he pulls up another chair by her side.

"Are you calm enough now to tell me what happened?" Legion gently brushes a strand of hair behind her ear.

Gwen takes a deep breath. "I heard someone screaming for help, but no one else seemed to hear it. I left the dinner table to go and see if it was real or just in my head. Sometimes I hear things that are happening far away, and other times I see things that are about to happen. I followed the girl's cries and found Ivan with Melody bound and gagged, dragging her up to the cliff."

Legion's face changes, a momentary reaction of anger and frustration, then, as if seeing her for the first time, he takes in her overall appearance. He leans in and touches the wound on her neck gently. When he pulls back, his fingers are covered in her blood. A dark look passes behind his snowy eyes.

"And I suppose you tried to save her, followed him up there, and attacked him?" Legion doesn't look at her when he asks this, his attention focused on his bloody fingertips.

"Yes, but I was too late. She's dead. He threw her over the cliff." Almost to herself Gwen adds, "I guess she couldn't fly after all."

Legion looks up at this, seeing the distress in her face. "And what of Ivan, what became of him?"

"I think I killed him. I'm not sure, and I… did something I've never done before. Something dark and twisted just came out of me and… and he's just lying there. I think I sucked the life out of him." Gwen whispers the words, too terrible to speak aloud.

Ivan deserved what he got, but the whole thing is just too familiar, too similar to what took place in the Keller's kitchen only a month ago. Gwen clenches her eyes shut, trying to force out the memories of his cries, the pain, and the knowledge that she killed someone. Had she just killed again? Was she a monster? She used to think that Raven was the one who needed to be watched, to protect himself and others, but now she thinks otherwise. She is the dangerous one, far more dangerous than Raven.

"It's all right now, my love," Legion soothes Gwen. He reaches out and takes her into his arms. She melts into his embrace, glad for the reassurance of his presence. "Go and fetch Ivan," Legion commands the guards. They obey. To Emon and Vinita, he says, "You will examine him in his quarters. See what you can do." They too disperse, leaving Legion and Gwen by themselves.

"Are you hurt? Is there anything you desire?" he asks.

Gwen looks into Legion's loving face. "No, there's no need to worry about me. I can heal myself. I just feel like I could use a hot shower, or a nice long bath," Gwen admits.

Legion, stroking her errant curls back away from her face, kisses her forehead.

"Whatever you want, darling." Legion helps Gwen to her feet. Gwen leans on him for support, and together, they leave the banquet hall, making their way back to her room.

Once there, Legion gives Lydia and Jessica orders, sending one for one of the Dwarves' medics, the other with instructions to draw a bath for Gwen and tend to her. This done, Legion turns to go, but he hesitates at the door. He turns back to Gwen.

"I had hoped to save this for a surprise, but in light of tonight's events, maybe it's just the thing you need."

"What is it?" Gwen lays on her bed, lightheaded. She props herself up to look at him.

"A little bird told me that your birthday is coming up. It's your twelfth, is it not?"

"Why, yes, but how did you… ?"

Legion crosses the room in his elegant gait and sits at her side on the bed. "I have my ways." He smiles, and then adds, "I was thinking of throwing you a birthday party, something to show my affection, and I suppose a going away party as well. I understand you are still determined to leave in search of your friend soon?"

Gwen nods.

"Very well. At least let me do this much for you. A little

merriment might do you a world of good after all this."

"Okay. I'll stay until after the party, and then I'll leave the next morning," Gwen concedes.

"Good. Well, goodnight, my dear, get some sleep." Legion leans in and kisses Gwen on the cheek, lingering just a moment with his face pressed against her neck as if smelling her. The moment passes and he gets up, smiling and bowing as he goes. Soon after, he is gone, leaving her alone in her bedchamber.

Gwen lay back on the bed with a sigh.

"*Dah-Day-Wente, Curea-Longa, Babeta-Lovota…*" Gwen sings the lullaby to herself, feeling its healing power wash over her. A voice from another time seems to harmonize with hers, coming out of her memory and into life in her imagination. She closes her eyes and the image of a fair-skinned woman with gentle, green eyes and golden hair appears for a fleeting moment, and then she fades away into the void of her past.

Gwen rolls onto her side, the wariness gone from her body, her cuts and bruises vanished. Where her neck had been a bloody mess of torn flesh, now her skin is as flawless and fresh as ever. She reaches for the jewelry box on her nightstand and opens the lid. Within, she fishes out the locket, her only lifelong treasure. She flips open the clasp, and out falls a lock of hair, two different colored strands braided together. Gwen picks up the familiar childhood relic, gently stroking the black and golden hairs as they intertwine remnants of two lives that briefly touched another, only to be torn apart forever. Sighing, Gwen stows the lock of hair back in the locket and slips the chain over her neck.

Lydia alerts Gwen with hand gestures that her bath is ready. Gwen lets the older girl help her undress and then dismisses her. She waits until the servant is gone before she lowers herself into the soothing hot water. Lying back, resting her head on the edge of the antique copper tub, she clutches the locket in her hand. She longs for the emptiness of sleep as her mind slips away from reality, hoping that tonight she might not dream at all. After a day like this, the last thing she wants is to see herself in those vivid nightmares. Who knows what kind of hideous images she might be forced to endure?

When Melody's face enters Gwen's mind, she shuts her eyes in pain and regret. No, tonight the nightmares will be welcome compared to the reality. Nothing will ever erase Melody's terrified face or her bloodcurdling screams from Gwen's mind. Her blood will forever be on Gwen's hands. Her actions had cost yet another life.

CHAPTER ELEVEN

Blood & Innocence

Legion takes quick, deliberate steps, his long legs carrying him swiftly up the corridor and into Ivan's personal bedchamber. He doesn't bother knocking, but enters with an agitated glint in his eyes.

Inside, Emon paces the room while Vinita bends over Ivan's stiff form lying on the bed. At the sight of him, they both look up. Emon approaches Legion.

"Is Gwenevere okay? He didn't hurt her badly, did he?"

The concern in Emon's voice produces a dark, jealous glare from Vinita. "She's fine. She is a Witch, after all," she scoffs.

"What about Ivan? Is he alive?" Legion asks, anxiously.

"He's alive, barely," Vinita continues. "She's cast some kind of dark shield upon him, like a poison that trapped him in a comatose state. It's far too advanced a spell for a wild Witch to be dabbling in. I warned you, but none of you would listen!"

"She's just a child, Vinita," Emon protests.

"Well, that child is dangerous. She could kill us all purely on accident."

Legion ignores both of them. "Can you heal him?"

Vinita shakes her head in the negative. "I think only she can help him, and I doubt she even knows what she's done."

Legion looks thoughtful a moment. "I see. I know now what has to be done. Fear not, she trusts me completely." Legion turns and heads for the door. Before leaving, he adds, "She will be a threat no longer." With a determined set to his jaw, he leaves the room.

Emon hurries after him, stopping his Lord in the hall. "Please, my lord, let the girl go. She may be an orphan, but she is still a child of the Forsaken. If the Wiccans should ever hear of any harm befalling her, it will bring on civil war. Please, reconsider. I will take the girl away myself. You'll never hear from her again," Emon pleads with his master.

"Nonsense, Emon. Why on earth would I ever let something so valuable out of my grasp? She will be mine now, and as for civil war, let the Witches come. It's been far too long since my children have feasted on Wiccan blood!" With that, Legion sweeps away, disappearing down the hall in a flash of royal blue, gold, and fur.

* * * * *

Gwen spends the majority of the next day alone in her room, making mental preparations to leave Bec LaNuff early on the morning of her birthday. All day long, Gwen sends Jessica and Lydia to and fro, fetching the many items she will need for her exodus. After the events of the previous night, Gwen makes up her mind to leave as soon as the opportunity presents itself.

She thinks it best, despite all that occurred between them on the cliff, not to say goodbye to Legion before she goes. Something tells her that if she faces him alone, her resolve will fade away. Unaccustomed as she is to handsome, charming men, she has to admit that she has no defense to protect her from falling under the spell of Legion's charismatic smile and mesmerizing eyes.

The truth is that her main reason for fleeing is fear—fear of herself. Every thought has been clouded by panic ever since she escaped from Ivan and found herself crying in Legion's arms. She feels as though she can't even trust herself.

"I don't even know who or what I really am," Gwen whispers as she paces a path from the canopy bed to the wardrobe in her bedchamber. Her bare feet, cold against the stone floor, grow numb from the exercise. Anxiety demands that she keep moving, just to keep her mind from going wild.

Ever since she woke up, Gwen has been unable to sit still. The longer she waits here, the more uneasy she becomes. All she needs is a few more things, and then, tomorrow morning, when most of the inhabitants of the fortress are asleep, she will slip out of her room and make her way toward the balcony above. Emon once told her that most of the entrances into the fortress were on the lower levels, but these are under constant guard. The balcony has no security. The steep slope of the mountain makes it impossible for few but the Vampire to use as a means of departure.

As for a Wiccan, Gwen isn't sure if she can escape that way either. The only spell that might be useful to her in this situation is the levitation spell. In the past, she only used it sparingly, never for descending from great heights.

Yes, but will I be able to keep control of the spell long enough to reach the foot of the mountain safely? Gwen doesn't feel confident that she can.

Her other option is to rely on her strength and endurance, hoping she can jump from the cliff and land cat-like, safely on her feet. The truth is she has never really jumped from so high up before. She has no idea how the impact of the fall would affect her. She could very likely die experimenting. It's risky, she knows it, but still, there seems to be no other alternative. Even if she should try to escape out the lower entrances, she would have to traverse through the fortress, hoping that no one stops her in the process. Even if no one stands in her way, there would be witnesses. Suppose one of Ivan's friends came after her? She might have to deal with the sentinels guarding the way out.

No, it would be better for her to leave as silently as possible. Her for escape depend on how much of a head start she gets. *I don't know if I can outrun a Vampire*, Gwen confesses inwardly.

Legion might be able to protect me here, but I doubt that my attack on Ivan will go unnoticed by the other Vampires. And some might feel inclined to take revenge on Ivan's behalf, Legion's favorite or not.

Gwen recalls the manner in which the other Vampires react to her. In her mind, she sees Lethawyn, Ryan, and Jezebel looking down their slender noses at her, their eyes saying all that their lips will not, speaking hatred, resentment, and disgust.

"No doubt someone is bound to react when word gets out about Ivan," Gwen admits aloud as she sits heavily on the bed, drawing her knees up and wrapping her arms around them as she contemplates.

"Legion wants to protect me, but what can one do against so many, even if he is their Master?" It seems to her that of all the traits Vampires are legendary for, obedience and loyalty are not among them.

"It will hurt Legion when he finds out I'm gone, but I have to go. It isn't safe any longer, and as long as I'm here, I endanger everyone around me." A single tear breaks free, slipping down Gwen's pale cheek. Quickly, she wipes it away, exasperated with herself. "Now is not the time to cry!" she tells herself bitterly.

Gwen hops of the bed to her night stand, collecting the last few books. She turns back to her bed. Her red duffel bag, alongside a dark brown sack, lie upon the golden lace comforter, along with dozens of little items sprawled upon the bed, waiting to be packed away for her journey.

The brown sack, which one of the cousins acquired from the kitchen, contains a couple weeks' worth of rations and some basic tools. The other bag contains all the clothing and personal items she brought with her. The last two items she needs are a sturdy, warm blanket for her bedroll, and the scroll containing the most recent map of the Poconos Mountains and surrounding cities. The map needs to be appropriated from Emon's library.

This task she must do herself. As helpful as her maid servants have been, asking them to steal doesn't sit well with Gwen. Besides, when it comes to thievery, Gwen has a lifetime of experience and uncanny skill. Tonight she will slip into the library and make away with the scroll. Hopefully this will all be effortless and unproblematic. Then, tomorrow morning after her birthday party, she will escape.

* * * * *

Due to the festivities later that evening, dinner is postponed, leaving Gwen to entertain herself for a change. She welcomes the change in routine, for it gives her time to solidify her plans. Gwen uses the opportunity to linger a couple hours longer in the library than usual. Emon sits at her side while she pretends to study her lessons, his usually calm, scholarly manners replaced by a nervous and apprehensive air.

Gwen puzzles at the change in him, but decides against asking the Elf any personal questions. She will be leaving soon, and she will miss her friend enough as it is without forming a deeper attachment by getting involved in his personal life. Finally, Vinita appears to remind Emon of his other duties.

I never did figure out what she has against me. Gwen dismisses the thought, grateful for once for the Elf's jealous, mistrusting ways.

"Will you be staying longer, Miss Gwenevere?" Emon asks politely, a strained note audible in his voice.

"Yes. I concentrate better here than in my room, you know, with Jessica and Ly—I mean, my servants hanging around." Vinita cocks her eyebrow at Gwen, an irritable look in her eyes.

Emon bows slightly. "Very well. Till tonight, then?" At this, Vinita takes him by the arm and leads Emon down the long aisles of the massive library.

Gwen watches them go, letting out a sigh of relief the moment they turn a corner and disappear. Instantly, she's up from her chair, taking on a nonchalant air as she makes her way through the many aisles of bookshelves. Standing at the base of one of the floor to ceiling shelves, Gwen looks upward.

"*Gainien Raisa,*" Gwen whispers under her breath. The words make her body weightless as she floats off the ground. The particular scroll she needs is on the thirteenth shelf, a good twenty feet off the floor. Gwen allows herself to hover by releasing just enough of the spell to stop from moving heavenward while maintaining her weightlessness.

A plain, white paper scroll with cherry wood handles lay to

her right. The modern scroll stands out amongst its companions with their gold, silver, or stone handles, their parchment yellowed with age. Gwen reaches out, taking the scroll containing her much needed maps, uttering the counter spell, *"Dainien Gounda,"* to lower herself back to the ground.

Gwen looks about. No one but servants are in sight. She quickly slips the scroll into the inside pocket of her black wool coat and hurries back to the desks in the center of the library. Stopping long enough to gather her books from the desk, Gwen weaves her way through the aisles until she finally comes to the door.

"Wait, miss!" a low voice calls out from somewhere near her knees.

Startled, she jumps.

"Sorry, Miss Gwen, I didn't mean to frighten you." The grandfather Dwarf named Horrick looks up at her, holding a small, red, linen-bound book in his outstretched hand. "You dropped this back by Lord Emon's desk. I thought you might need it."

"Oh, thank you." Gwen bends down, taking the book from the Dwarf's hand.

He smiles up at her. "I reckon you're excited for the party tonight? It's not every day a girl turns twelve, you know? I hear that Witches have some special ceremony to mark the occasion, something to do with the willow tree and the ashes of their ancestors."

"Where did you hear that?" Gwen asks, her anxiety replaced

by curiosity.

"My grandmother befriended a Witch in order to learn the herbal art of healing, but I think that was some six hundred years ago, somewhere in France. Oh, well... I better be going, records don't keep themselves, you know."

"Thank you! See you tonight," Gwen calls after the little white-haired man as he scurries away. He waves a pudgy, wrinkled hand before turning down another aisle and disappearing from sight.

Gwen sighs with relief, tucking the little red book in with her other books and papers. She hurries out of the large wooden door where Lydia would be awaiting just beyond.

* * * * *

At midnight, Legion comes for Gwen. She waits on her bed g for him, dressed in more splendor than usual. Tonight, Legion requested she be garbed all in white. Looking at her reflection, she can't help but notice how much like a bride she looks, with her black hair swept up in a mountain of curls, a pearl and diamond crown set upon her head, a snowy, silk, French-cut dress embroidered with hundreds of pearls, and a pair of white glittering high-heeled shoes upon her feet. She is literally dripping in precious gems. She wears a choker, teardrop earrings, two bracelets on her wrists, and an anklet made of pearls and diamonds. She sparkles in the candlelight with every sway of her slender body, the very image of a sixteenth century French duchess.

Usually, Gwen wouldn't care for such lavish finery, but since this is to be the last night she will likely ever receive such pampering—or wear such clothes—Gwen decides to enjoy it. In a few short hours, she will be far away, living the life of a drifter once more, wearing her comfortable jeans and sneakers just like any other human teenage girl.

Legion appears at her door adorned in his usual finery. Tonight, he wears all in black and gold. She finds it odd, for typically he wears a multitude of colors, rich and vibrant, contrasting with his colorless pallor. Dressed in black breeches, he wears a long, black, velvet robe with golden embroidered buttons, a black button-up shirt, and a gold embroidered vest all in the ancient French fashion. He looks paler than ever, his skin as glossy and perfect as polished marble. His hair catches the hints of gold in his wardrobe to blaze and shine in the candle light. He is handsome, mysterious, and elegant.

Legion gushes over her, smothering her in compliments as they make their way arm in arm to the grand hall and her birthday feast. Gwen blushes sweetly, unable to contain her giddiness at being the center of his adoration. Somewhere in the back of her mind she hears a little voice telling her to keep her focus, not to look too deeply into his eyes, and to distance herself from him emotionally. As beautiful as he is, she will soon leave his pale, ghostly presence behind. Falling in love wasn't an option for her.

Besides, he's much too old for me anyway, Gwen reminds herself for what seems like the millionth time.

Gwen sighs with relief as they enter through the massive stone doors into the banquet hall, the room packed with the citizens of Bec LaNuff. She won't have to worry about being left alone with Legion. The crowd cheers as the two of them enter, and Gwen feels her face go red. She gives the multitudes a shy little smile in acknowledgment.

Pipers, flutists, and singers break out into a medieval tune, sounding like ancient minstrels in a king's court The chamber resembles something out of a fairytale. Hundreds of candles illuminate the room, from the three large chandeliers above to the sconces and candelabras lining the three massive banquet tables.

Two tables are set opposite each other along the outer walls. A third one is set at the head of the room before the stone stage, with Legion's throne making a 'U' shape as they connect. Chairs line the banquet tables along the outside edge, leaving the center of the room empty save for a large, ornate rug and the musicians who stand off to one side, performing.

Gwen is whisked to the head table. The entire party rises from their seats. Legion raises a gold goblet, and everyone follows suit. Gwen is the last to reach for her glass.

"To Gwenevere! May she live long under the mountain, and serve us as we serve her. One flesh and one blood forever!" Legion speaks in a loud, commanding voice. At his signal everyone drinks to this toast, each bowing their head to Gwen afterward. She takes a small sip, tasting rich wine on her tongue, feeling the liquid flow smoothly down her throat.

A strange sensation comes over her body, the wine spreading a kind of airy effervescence throughout her bloodstream, making her feel loose and carefree. She smiles giddily up at Legion who bows his head to her briefly, a curious, intent look behind his smoky gaze.

Gwen notices that everyone, even the cold, hostile Vampires, seems to be in good spirits tonight. Gaiety feels contagious in the air. Only then does Gwen realize that Emon and Vinita are not present.

Maybe they're running late, Gwen considers, although it doesn't seem a likely excuse.

They all sit, and the feast begins. Servants scurry about the room, carrying trays upon trays of exquisite food in an endless parade to the party guests. Legion eats nothing, content to sip from his goblet and watch as Gwen samples each delectable dish that passes under her nose.

The musicians play, the sound adding to the dreamy atmosphere in the room. At Legion's urging, Gwen continues to drink from her goblet of wine, relishing its fruity essence, tasting the grapes that spawned the succulent liquid long ago. Before she knows it, she has finished the glass. Legion snaps his fingers, and a servant refills it for her.

As the evening carries on, Gwen feels more lightheaded and gay, all worries forgotten, all the tension and fear from the last several days left behind in a haze of dizzy drunkenness. When the meal is over, stomachs filled to the bursting point, all the trays and dinnerware are cleared away.

"It is time for your gifts," Legion whispers in Gwen's ear. "Let me be the first to present my offering." From the folds of his robe, he withdraws a small, golden jewelry box tied with a satin ribbon, with a flower-shaped bow on top. The box itself is engraved with serpents and trees in a design that reminds Gwen faintly of the Garden of Eden. He places the little box in Gwen's upturned palm.

"Thank you. You've already given me so many beautiful things. I don't think I need another jewelry box, but it is enchanting." Gwen smiles brightly up at him, her eyes shining with pleasure.

"It's more than just a jewelry box, my love," he whispers as he reaches over and unsnaps the flower bow, removing the satin ribbon. "Look inside." Legion watches her face with anticipation as Gwen opens the lid of the gold jewelry box. Gwen's eyes light up and her breath catches in her throat as she lays eyes on the most beautiful ring she could ever imagine, sitting snug inside the velvet folds.

Made of gold, the serpentine ring wraps its long body and tail into the circular shape, the tail curling into a spiral below, the head swerving as the snake bites down on a ruby cut into the shape of an apple set within the creature's open jaws. Emeralds are set into the eyes of the snake, and tiny diamonds are inlaid along the scales of the snake's body, making it sparkle in the candle light.

Dazzled, Gwen plucks the ring from its case to look at it more closely.

"Do you like it?" he asks.

"Of course. It's beautiful!" Gwen exclaims with reverent awe.

"Here, allow me." Legion takes the ring from her grasp, and taking her left hand in his, he gently slides the golden serpent band onto her slender, delicate ring finger. He seems to relax inwardly once the ring is on. He kisses her lightly on the cheek. Sitting back, he smiles broadly at her as though he has just accomplished some great feat.

Gwen holds her hands out to admire the ring on her finger. Strange...she could have sworn the ring looked at least two sizes bigger while it still sat in the box, but now it fits her finger snugly and comfortably, as if it were made just for her.

The other guests deposit their gifts before her on the table one by one. Legion has a servant gather them after each is opened and set aside, to be taken to Gwen's bedchamber later. Everyone congratulates her and wishes her good health and long life.

The whole thing reminds Gwen of the first feast given in her honor only two weeks ago. Her head spins as she tries to recall all the presents she got from the first occasion. She couldn't even begin to imagine where all this new stuff would fit into her room.

Oh, well, Gwen thinks to herself. *I can't take any of it with me anyway. Perhaps all the gifts will be returned in a few days when it becomes clear that I am gone for good.*

With the presents all opened, dessert is served. Gwen can't seem to help herself, because for some reason her appetite is ferocious, her thirst unquenchable, and she gorges herself on all the delicious pastries, cakes, and candies. Everything tastes heavenly. She feels wonderful, more at ease and happy than she has ever felt in her life. She finds herself giggling and laughing like a fool, unable to contain her good humor.

"Would you like to dance, my dearest?" Legion stands, offering her his hand, a pleasant gleam in his eyes.

"Yes, but I've never really learned to dance, you know? I might step on your foot," Gwen confesses, erupting into laughter at the thought.

"Don't trouble yourself. Follow my lead and you'll be fine."

Gwen takes his hand, and together they walk around the banquet tables to the center of the room. Taking this as their cue, several of the other guests join them in couples on the dance floor. The musicians play an upbeat jig, and the dancers take off, whirling and spinning in time to the music.

Legion steps up to Gwen. Taking her hand in his, he pulls her close to him. The flash of gold and diamonds catches her eye, and Gwen notices for the first time the ring upon Legion's own hand. Upon his ring finger on his left hand, bright in contrast against his pale, alabaster skin, he wears a gold and black ring. Upon closer inspection, Gwen notices that it is similar to the one he gave her. His ring is shaped like two serpents. The dark serpent is made of black stone encrusted with black diamonds and green emerald eyes. The other snake wraps around Legion's finger in the opposite direction of the first, is made of gold, inlaid with diamonds scales and emerald eyes as well.

The strange thing about the ring is that the black snake is biting the golden snakes' neck, her head dangling almost lifeless from his jaws. It gives her an eerie feeling, but the sensation goes away quickly as Legion takes her in his arms and they begin to dance.

At first, Gwen stumbles as Legion leads her about the floor, tripping on her own feet, but after a while she begins to get the hang of the rhythm of the dance. Letting all her inhibitions slip away, Gwen whirls around the dance floor.

As the evening progresses, Gwen loses all sense of time and space, feeling as though she is floating adrift in a current of music, light, and color. She dances endlessly, wild and free. Alone, or with Legion, or other partners, never caring if she looks a fool, or thinking of what tomorrow might bring, all she knows is here and now and the beauty that envelopes her. The room seems to blur and spin haphazardly about her. She becomes incoherent as the room spins faster and faster, till everything becomes a kaleidoscope of colors before her eyes. She loses her footing and falls into a white haze, semi-conscious of the strong arms that catch her before she can hit the floor.

Somewhere above her, a beautiful masculine voice speaks her name, his hands cold upon her flesh as he sweeps her up and into his arms, cradling her small frame against him. Gwen rests her head on his chest and closes her eyes to stop the spinning in her head, listening for the man's soothing heartbeat. She hears nothing. It is an empty, hollow center, with no gentle rise and fall of his lungs as he breathes. Just silence.

She feels herself being carried from a loud and clamorous chamber out into a long enclosure, like a hallway or a tunnel, the man's footsteps echoing on the stone floor beneath him. He seems to move smoothly, not jostling her as they glide down the passageway toward some unknown place. The echo of his feet is the only indication that they aren't flying.

At last they stop. A door creaks open and she is carried into a small chamber, the sound of his footsteps echoing less upon the stone floor and walls. He gently lays her down upon a welcoming surface, the feel of fabric soft under her cheek. Gwen guesses that she must be lying on the canopy bed in her bedchamber. It smells like her room, the scent of cold stone, old wood, burning candle wicks, old books, ink, and fresh linen mingling together to create one distinguishable smell, singular to her chamber. She lies there a minute, still in a haze. For a moment, all is silent in the room.

Through her clouded, befuddled mind, Gwen ponders. *Where did the man go? Did he leave already, and I just didn't hear him?*

She feels a presence next to her in the bed, not a heavy form, but still she is aware that someone is there. She lies on her side, one cheek pressed against the comforter, huddled up in a ball. She dimly becomes aware of a slight pressure on her back, accompanied by the sound of buttons popping. Slowly, an invisible hand moves down her back, unfastening her dress. Cold fingers brush against her skin as the fabric spreads apart, leaving her back exposed. Gwen shivers at the touch.

The cold hands move under the fabric, up to her shoulders, slipping the sleeves of her dress down her arms, the front slumping into a heap of silk as it slips away from her chest. Cold air rushes into the open gap of her bodice, making her become more alert.

Suddenly, she understands what's happening and a panic comes over her. Still weak and exhausted, she moves, clutching the dress to her body, trying to scoot away from those icy hands. She tries to open her eyes but her eyelids seem glued shut as if by a dew of dreams. Instantly, the hands reach out and take hold of her, bringing her into their embrace. She feels velvet against her naked back.

"No," she moans weakly, her voice soft and flimsy as if she is short of breath.

"You belong to me now. When you put on the ring you gave yourself to me," a dark voice hisses in her ear, the sound making her flinch.

She pushes against the solid form crushing her, struggling feebly to get free. He pulls her tighter and, taking her face in one large, cold, boney hand, he turns her to him. A pair of icy lips press down onto hers, kissing her violently. Gwen tries to scream, pushing against him and hitting his head and shoulders, her blows doing no harm to her attacker. A slippery tongue forces its way into her mouth, moving hungrily against hers with a force that makes it impossible for her to dislodge it. The shock brings her out of her dreamy haze, and becoming coherent, she is able to bite down on the thing invading her mouth.

She hears a startled cry, the weight upon her lifting as the man shrinks back in pain. Gwen scrambles away from him, rolling off the bed. She hits the floor hard, banging her head against the stone. Pain jars her into consciousness. Stumbling to her feet, she shakes her head as if to dispel the groggy, sleepy feeling within. Finally, she is able to force her eyes open. At first her version is blurred, objects and shapes barely able to distinguish in the dim glow of the candle light.

As her sight begins to clear, she sees a dark shape slither toward her. In a panic, she screams, her natural instincts kicking in. She reaches out for the source of power, with the intent to kill her attacker with a ball of fire. She utters the words of the spell and… nothing. Nothing happens. She reaches out again, trying to take hold of the fabric of time and space, to grasp that which makes all magic possible, and finds nothing, only emptiness. No surge of energy courses through her veins. Gone is the exhilarating feeling of omnipotence that burns inside her flesh whenever she wields God's power.

Left defenseless, Gwen finds herself seized in the clutches of the dark man once more, his long, razor-sharp fingernails digging into the flesh of her arms as he hefts her off her feet and flings her roughly down upon the bed.

Gwen screams in pain. She tries to cast another spell, and then another, uttering the words that have, until now, never failed her, words that have protected her from danger time and time again. The words seem to have lost their power, and she is helpless. The dark figure climbs up onto the bed, and before Gwen can crawl away, it pounces on top of her, pinning her in place.

Slowly, he leans in, bringing his face an inch from hers. Staring down at her is a pair of cold eyes devoid of color, but for the silvery ring around the outer edge and dark, bottomless pupils. Through the haze she sees that it is Legion, and that this had been his intent all along.

Smiling down at her wickedly, he slips his hands into the loose fabric of her half-undone dress. Taking hold of the material in his boney hands, he yanks the fabric violently, tearing the bodice off. Gwen clutches the fabric, trying to cover her naked body. Tossing the torn piece of the dress aside, Legion dives toward her, crushing her beneath him. He smothers her with violent kisses, caressing her naked skin with his corpse-like hands.

Gwen makes one last attempt to cast a spell, willing the dark magic that once squeezed the life out of Dennis Keller to take hold of the Vampire. Instead of grasping at nothingness, Gwen feels a burning sensation as the ring upon her finger grows hot. She winces in pain as the blood vessels in her hand start to constrict, the sensation traveling up her arm through her veins, following them to her life source—the beating heart in her chest. Gwen arches her back, gasping and convulsing in pain as her heart constricts as though caught in an imaginary fist, squeezing tighter and tighter until the pain is unbearable.

Legion's dark, velvety voice laughs in her ear.

"You can't harm me. The ring forbids it." He pulls back a little so that he can look into her frightened face. He runs a long, manicured nail across her cheek as he speaks. "I gave you a chance to love and obey me of your own volition, but you have persisted in being independent. Your dangerous nature has put me in quite a bind, my love. I'm torn between what I most desire and what is best for my children. They don't trust you, especially after what you've done to poor Ivan."

He makes a disapproving noise in the back of his throat and sits up. Gwen takes a deep breath, her body beginning to recover from the violent effects of the ring.

Slowly, Legion peels off his gold embroidered black robe, letting the garment fall to the floor. With slow, deliberate fingers he unbuttons his vest, peeling it off and discarding it as well.

"I give you my most sincere apology to have to rush things like this. I swear if we had more time I might be able to make you love me as a wife should love her husband, but as it is, the colony grows restless, leaving me no other alternative. I could just rightly kill you, but you are not some simple girl like Melody who can be tossed aside. No, I couldn't stomach the notion of wasting one so gifted and rare, or so beautiful. I've done the only rational thing, binding you to me in a way that keeps you safe from the others and protecting everyone else from you."

"You're mad! I don't understand a word you say!" Gwen

pants, her head spinning and her body aching with fatigue.

Legion laughs and gives her a strange, little smile, dark satisfaction gleaming in his lifeless eyes. He unbuttons his black shirt, his ashen skin becoming visible as the folds of fabric are pulled away. "Don't be a simpleton, Gwen. If you weren't so stubborn you'd have already realized it yourself." The shirt completely undone, Legion slips his arms out and tosses it aside, his bare chest gleaming in the candle light.

Gwen swallows, panic seizing her as full realization comes upon her. *He means to…* the thought trails away, her mind unable to accept the reality of her predicament.

"Don't touch me! Get off of me!" Gwen shouts, fight mode kicking in. She starts to fling herself about, trying with all her might to push him off. Her strength is nothing compared to his. Legion laughs as she pounds on his chest, her legs kicking beneath him.

"I will do whatever I like, and you will obey my every command, as is my right as your master. As for touching you, that right I claim as your husband. After all…" Legion grabs hold of her left hand, and holding it up against his left hand, shows their two rings side by side as if to drive his words home, and says, "… we are married now."

Gwen's eyes open wide in disbelief.

"No, it's impossible." Gwen screams, shouting for help, thrashing about like a trapped animal. Legion grabs her arms and pins them to the bed.

"The rings bind us together. My ring gives me dominion over your body, and power over your mind and soul. Resist me and you will suffer. Give in to me and love me, and you will be treated like the Queen you were born to be."

"Never! I will never give in! I will never love you!" Gwen spits in his face.

Legion flinches. Releasing one of her captured hands, he wipes the spittle from his face, his jaw clenched. He looks down at her, and the cold, hard look in his eyes causes Gwen to shudder in fear.

"Very well. Have it your way." With a moan of pain and pleasure, his fangs break free of his gums, extending to their full length. With a snarl, he crashes on top of her, moving like a snake upon its prey. Suddenly, she feels the piercing pain as his fangs tear into her flesh, digging deep, spilling blood from her wound.

Gwen lets out a blood-curdling scream which echoes through the room and out into the hall. Her continued cries and shouts for help echo, her pleas falling on deaf ears. While the inhabitants of the fortress carry on with the birthday celebration, only one knows her pain. Only one hears her cries of bitter anguish.

Emon stands down the hall, staring at the closed door of Gwen's bed chamber, helpless and pathetic in his cowardice. Vinita tugs at his arm, a smug look in her eyes as she listens to the young Wiccan girl wail in pain and fear. Finding he can take no more, Emon allows her to lead him away, turning his back on Gwen in her time of need, leaving her alone as she loses all that she holds dear, as Legion drains her of her freedom, her strength, her blood and innocence.

CHAPTER TWELVE

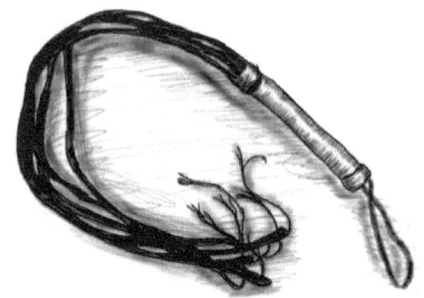

His Will Be Done

And so the nightmare begins. Every day Gwen lives in a half-daze, following after her Master as if on an invisible leash. Every night she suffers a thousand injustices, her innocent skin tainted and her blood ravenously taken to satisfy her husband's twisted lust.

After the first night, Gwen is broken, her soul lost in the pain and confusion of being violated by one she trusted, one she believed she loved. Her confidence is shattered. Her iron-clad resolve, her will to carry on through the darkest of nights are shaken. Outwardly she maintains a blank expression, going from day to day as if sleepwalking through life. Inside she is in turmoil, fighting against the reality that brought her to this.

It isn't real, she chants to herself a hundred times a day, looking down at her wedding ring with morbid fascination, that golden-encrusted shackle linking her to a monster. She thinks that one day she will simply wake up from this awful dream, and when she does, all the darkness around her will fade, chased back by the day, by the beautiful, life-giving dawn which heralds not only a new day but a new beginning.

Yet every morning she awakens in the dark, raising from bed in either her own small. lavish room, or in Legion's opulent bedchamber, where her unconscious lover lies next to her, drunken with the euphoria of last night's bloody union.

He smiles at her every morning with those soulless eyes, kissing her softly with a tenderness that belies the violence of his lovemaking the night before, and whispers in her ear.

"Good morning, my dearest. Did you sleep well? Did you dream of me?" Gwen tries to hide the instinctive shudder that comes over her. Every once in a while he sees her quake, and taking this as some kind of insult, takes her to bed once more to teach her to love him, to show him the proper respect.

Gwen closes her eyes tight to shut out the haunting gleam in his eyes, to shut out that awful smug face as he takes his pleasure from her. Legion won't allow even this little escape. Through the male half of their wedding bands, he commands her to look at him, to look into his eyes and feel what he feels, to know his ecstasy. Sometimes his desire overshadows her hate and revulsion, flowing through the mental bond that forms between the Vampire and his lover. As he drinks from her, he causes her to momentarily forget to hate him. His emotions pulse through her as they exchange bodily fluids, his delight ebbing in her mind, trying to overpower her own thoughts and feelings to make her one with him.

As weak and broken as she is, Gwen refuses to give herself to him completely, to give over to his disgusting notion of love. Every time he touches her, she strives to force him away. She knows she can't strike back at him physically or magically, but inside her mind she keeps him at bay, always fighting against his intrusion into her inner-most sacred and beloved memories, locking a part of herself deep within the recesses of her psyche where even he cannot penetrate. This alone keeps her alive, with the unlikely hope that Raven might come for her one day and save her from this hell.

Her life since her impromptu marriage has changed quite drastically. No longer do the others look her in the eye and greet her with respect. Instead they avert their gaze, not wanting to anger the Master. Only the Vampires acknowledge her, with smug looks, evil sneers, and condescending congratulations on her nuptials.

She isn't allowed to wander the fortress alone, but follows after the vermin that dares call himself her husband and Master, going wherever he goes, trailing behind him or being led about as Legion takes her hand to stroll about Bec LaNuff as if displaying her like a trophy or a prize. She has no freedom. Legion senses her every move, her every emotion through the ring, knowing everything, his presence around her and inside of her even when she is far from his sight.

Her husband allows her to keep her room and continues to dress her in finery befitting the Queen of Bec LaNuff. He retains the right to burst in on her at any given moment of the day, leaving her without any sense of privacy. He claims to miss her, and sending the servant girls away, takes the moment alone together to remind her that he is her husband and her lord.

She is still allowed to study in the library with Emon as her tutor, but the bond of friendship between her and the Elf is severed. Left behind is only awkwardness and unspoken regret.

Legion, enchanted with his new toy, has Gwen actively delve into the powers of Wicca, forcing her under Emon and Vinita's supervision to test her own limits and strive for greatness. At first, she was ordered to sit before Ivan's bedside and commanded to heal him, to undo the evil curse she put on him. Legion is sorely disappointed when there is no progress, no change in his friend's condition.

* * * * *

Gwen sits on Legion's four-post bed in his opulent bedchamber. She awaits his return, but she can't move. Her "master" forbids it.

Legion's bedchamber is a large room carved out of the mountain wall with a high vaulted ceiling. Carved in bas-relief throughout the ceiling is a depiction of a herd of Pegasi being hunted by ugly horned demons, the monsters capturing and torturing them in vile, disgusting ways.

From the walls hang beautiful antique tapestries. One set of

three tapestries depicts elegant ladies and gentlemen at a medieval ball. In the first one, a dark figure lurks in the background. In the second, the same mysterious being dances with a beautiful young lady. In the final tapestry, the ball is seen through the window in the background while the dark stranger feeds on the blood of the fair beauty on a balcony in the foreground. This one is particularly detailed in showing the dead woman's horrified face and torn dress, exposing a white breast with fang marks punctured near the nipple, blood spilling down her chest and staining her beautiful dress. Gwen hates the sight of these tapestries for how they romanticize the feasting of blood with all their striking details.

The oversized four-post bed she sits on has detailed carvings of thorny roses and ivy. It stands upon a stone stage against the far wall. From it hangs a deep red, transparent, shimmering drape. The bedding is dark red silk with white stripes, embroidered with gold leaves and roses. In the corner of the stage near the bed is carved out a large man-sized basin, like a bathtub or small pool. The rest of the room is richly furnished with such beautiful antique pieces that they could have easily have belonged to King Louis XVI.

It strikes Gwen how similar the room is to the man who inhabits it: beautiful, dark, twisted, and evil. Gwen shudders inside.

Suddenly the door opens and Legion appears at the side of the bed with an angry glint in his eyes.

"Take off your shirt and lie on your stomach," he commands. Gwen feels her body obey through the ring. Not sure what to expect, she waits silently. She screams as a whip strikes her young flesh, pain shooting through the tissue of her exposed back. Before the pain can fade away, she is struck again and again. After fifteen lashes he steps back, listening with morbid pleasure to Gwen's last outcries of pain.

"Think of this as your first lesson, my love." Legion looks down at Gwen's quivering form, prone on the bed without pity.

She slowly gets control of herself as the pain settles into her. "A lesson in what? I've done nothing to deserve this!"

"In obedience. You have failed me, dearest. You refuse to do as I have asked." Calmly he strolls over to a table near the bed where an old leather case sits open with a collection of various archaic tools of torture within. Legion puts the whip back inside the case alongside the others, and shuts it.

"Did I or did I not command you to lift the curse on my servant Ivan?" Legion demands.

"I am trying, but you expect too much," Gwen retorts, moving gingerly to the edge of the bed. Her shirt lies upon the floor. She moves to retrieve it.

"It isn't enough. I will not accept failure from you."

"If you think it's so easy, then do it yourself!" Gwen snaps, thinking the better of her outburst a moment too late. In an instant, Legion is standing before her. Her head rings, her body lurches, her cheek stings with pain all before Gwen even realizes that he has struck her. Her eyes water involuntarily. She looks up at her Master and sees a deadly look in his eyes.

"I have no idea what I did in the first place, let alone how to undo it. You forget that I am unschooled in Witchcraft. You could do as well as I could." Gwen bites her lip to keep her tone calm and steady, not wanting to show insolence again.

Legion's face softens, and in a flicker, his whole demeanor changes to polite cordiality. He waves his hand in dismissal.

"Nonsense, my darling. You just need a little practice." He smiles down at Gwen. Taking her face in his hand, he leans down and kisses her lips, sweetly. Gwen fights the urge to recoil, knowing he will only punish her for it.

* * * * *

The next day Gwen finds out what Legion meant by practice. As of late, Gwen had spent a great deal of her time in the grand chamber to be close by should her husband have need of her. For this purpose, Legion had an elaborate chaise lounge brought into the room and set near the throne so that Gwen might have a comfortable place to sit and be there for him to look at while he conducts his business as Master of Bec LaNuff and governor of the Forsaken in the region.

Gwen refuses to sit there in her ostentatious clothes and royal finery like a fat Queen taking her leisure. Instead, she finds more useful things to do while she passes the time, till Legion dismisses her for her afternoon nap—another one of his bright ideas. She doesn't mind it, though, because her afternoon "nap" affords her the only solitude she enjoys all day long. Every day she finds herself in anxious anticipation of that appointed hour to a moment's privacy.

Today she brings the art kit that Douglas gave her all those years ago, and sits with her supplies on the lounge in deep concentration on her subject, one of the servant boys that frequently hovers near Legion's side.

Gwen finds that the servants make excellent subjects. When they aren't in action or following orders or performing a chore, they stand motionless, their bodies erect and their heads held high as if called to attention by a drill sergeant. This doesn't give her much variety in pose or position however, but at least they don't get embarrassed if she stares at them, trying to capture every line of their faces.

Legion, encouraging all her talents, gives her whatever she asks for—canvas, pens, an easel, more suitable models for her to sketch. When she asks to go outside and draw the surrounding landscape, he flatly refuses, beating her for thinking of such a ridiculous notion. He will shower her with gifts and lavish her with attention whether she wants it or not, but he would never give her one ounce of freedom.

Even with the ring binding her and enslaving her to his will, he is still paranoid that she might escape, and takes every precaution to prevent this. It gives Gwen a glimmer of pleasure to know that even with her wings clipped as they are, the all-powerful Legion is still frightened of her. It isn't much but that one thought gives her the strength to live from day to day, some part of her building on that fear, scheming so that one day she might give him a reason to fear her, and make him pay for the numerous crimes he committed against her. Until that day, Gwen forces herself to find happiness in whatever she can, and most days her happiness comes from drawing, singing, or reading a good book.

Legion sits upon his throne, watching her. She can feel his icy gaze upon her skin. She ignores this, fighting the urge to cringe before him as she contemplates the sketchbook in her lap, erasing a misplaced line here and there.

The massive stone doors to the chamber are thrust open by the two Ogres standing guard, admitting four Vampires into the room, three women, and a man. Two of them drag a hysterical human child between them. Gwen looks up as they approach Legion's throne. She instantly recognizes the three female Vampires as Ryan, Jezebel, and Lethawyn, and the man as Lucca, a tall, black-skinned Vampire who seems to be made out the night itself, his presence dark and sinister as an empty abyss. Gwen shivers against her will.

At the sight of them, Legion jumps from his throne excitedly.

"What little treat have you brought me today?" Legion claps his hands, rubbing them together in greedy anticipation.

"We found her in Callicoon," Jezebel replies. She and Lethawyn release their hold on the young girl, leaving her to cower at Legion's feet.

"Walking all by herself, probably coming home from a friend's house, going home to mommy and daddy," Lethawyn adds, a mocking tone in her voice as she strokes the trembling child's head, as if petting an animal.

The girl looks about the room from one face to another. Finally, to Gwen's horror, the girl's eyes meet hers, and a momentary look of hope crosses the child's face.

Legion steps forward, blocking Gwen from the child's view. He bends down and takes the girl's face in his large, boney hand, making her look into his eyes.

"How old are you, child?" he asks in a soft airy whisper, his voice deceptively soothing and gentle.

The girl seems entranced by his eyes and his hypnotic voice, and relaxes in his grasp. She answers calmly, "I'm seven years old."

"And what is your name, sweetheart?" he probes further, kneeling beside her.

"Bethany Rose Wilson," the girl admits willingly, all resistance and fear gone from her timid frame.

"Is she suitable, my Lord?" Lucca's dark, deep voice almost breaks Legion's spell over the girl. For a moment she looks frightened and peers over her shoulder toward the black-skinned Vampire and three beautiful, unearthly creatures standing next to him. A shiver runs through her and her eyes take on the look of a feral animal, captured in a cage.

"Bethany, look at me." The girl turns her gaze on Legion, instantly ensnared in the fathomless storm of his pale eyes. "You are in no danger here. Trust me. Listen to my voice and no other."

Bethany nods dumbly, her eyes never leaving Legion's.

"Yes, she'll do just fine. Stand back. You may stay and watch, but do not speak again, any of you." Legion fixes the four Vampires with a threatening glare. They all step back, gathering against the far wall to wait and watch the proceedings.

Legion gathers little Bethany into one arm and helps her up on her feet. He leads her toward Gwen, bending his head over her, speaking to her in a low voice so that no one else can hear.

With a sigh of resignation, Gwen places her sketchbook and pencils aside as the two of them approach. She has no idea what Legion is up to but gets an eerie feeling that none of this will end well for poor little Bethany. Reluctantly, she looks up at the two of them, not willing to look the girl in the face. She gives Legion a questioning look.

"Now, my dear, I think it's time we do a little experiment, don't you?" Legion smiles wickedly.

Gwen gulps, her eyes locking on the helpless girls face against her will. She feels a sickness bubbling inside, threatening to erupt from her. She knows she should protest. She should fight his command but no matter what she does, she knows there is no escape and no hope for little Bethany. Legion will get what he wants one way or another. His mountain, his rules, his will be done.

CHAPTER THIRTEEN

Brutal Talents

A high-pitched scream, like a banshee wailing on the wind, resonates through the cavernous tomb of the mountain, echoing far beyond the grand chamber and finding its way down the many corridors and passageways of the fortress. Emon fights the urge to run from the unbearable sound and continues toward it, coming up the main passageway to grand chamber. He nods cordially to one of the Guards, an Ogre he knows only as Slethum, the Captain of the Guard. Slethum acknowledges him with a curt gesture, his lieutenant hurrying to announce the Elf Lord and show him into the Lord of the mountain's inner court.

A moment later the large doors are thrust open by the Guards and Emon is allowed admittance into Master Legion's presence.

Bolstering his courage, Emon enters the grand chamber, uncertain of what atrocities he might witness within. He half expects to see Gwen lying on the floor, wailing and writhing in pain before that white demon of the night who calls himself Lord and fancies himself a God. Yet to his astonishment, he sees a girl unknown to him lying upon the granite floor, with Gwen herself standing over the child, chanting evil incantations, whilst Legion sits on his throne and watches with an evil gleam of self-satisfaction.

This sight is somehow more disgusting to the Elf than the one he envisioned, for Gwen is incapable of causing harm unless in her own defense. This ugly picture before him is purely Legion's doing—his sick, twisted way of taking something beautiful and innocent and corrupting it to his own sadistic will.

Legion looks up and, spotting Emon, makes a gesture to Gwen. She ceases her chanting, breaking the curse upon the child before her. Gwen stumbles backward as if physically drained. Her victim ceases her wailing and collapses into a lifeless heap.

"You may take a respite, my love. You've done very well." Legion smiles at Gwen. With a sense of pride emanating from him, he rises from his throne, nodding to Lucca and the three female Vampires. They spring forward, hefting Bethany's motionless body off the ground, carrying her over to a long banquet table along one wall and laying her to rest atop the serving trays of food and drink.

Gwen nods dumbly, a half-dazed expression upon her ashen countenance as she sleepwalks her way to the chaise lounge, collapsing upon it like a rag doll.

With the agility of a wild cat, Legion hops down from his throne and rushes to Emon's side, crossing the expanse of the massive room in an instant blur of multi-colored silks in the dark gray, dreary room.

"Ah, Emon, you're just in time. I thought it might be prudent to document Gwenevere's education for posterity. Our daily experiments might help our kind better understand our Wiccan cousins." He claps a hand on the Elf's back in a companionable gesture. "Come! Observe our progress so far." Legion leads him over to the banquette table where Lucca and the others still hover over the unconscious girl.

Emon looks down upon her, careful to keep his face emotionless. He observes that the girl is no older than seven or eight, short and stocky of build, with short, black curls in a cap around her face, her skin tan, her face neither pretty nor plain. She is an ordinary child with the reminisce of baby fat still clinging to her cheeks. All over her body, he observes areas of charred skin, the smell of her singed hair acrid in his nostrils. Welts and bruises are visible about her arms, neck, and face. Her face seems purplish in color, her lips slightly blue as if she were cold. Involuntarily, Emon reaches out a hand and touches the girl's throat, feeling for a pulse. Her skin feels rubbery, devoid of life as the warmth slowly drains from her flesh, and her pulse faint as the weak flutter of a dying butterfly.

"She is all but dead. Isn't it fantastic? She never even laid a finger on the girl and yet she did this!" Legion says with awe. He makes a grand gesture over the girl, as if her pitiful state is a thing of wonder. "If I had commanded her, Gwen could have killed the child simply by causing her pain with unseen hands and images in the girl's mind." Legion smiles gleefully adding "I ask you again, isn't it just—?"

"I see what you mean, my Lord, but I fail to see what can be learned from torturing children?" Emon says calmly, barely concealing the contempt in his proud voice.

Legion's eyes flash with momentary rage at this criticism, but in a moment the look is replaced by aristocratic diffidence. "My friend, the age or sex of the test subject makes no difference to me. All that is required is that they are healthy and conscious. Otherwise how can we truly gage the effects of her powers? You forget, Emon, that the point of these little exercises is to test the limits of Gwen's abilities."

"And now that you've tested them, what is to be done with the girl?" Emon asks. Looking up, his gaze meets Lucca's, who flashes him a dark smile.

"I thought it might be beneficial for Gwen to see how we Vampire are born into darkness," Legion hisses, moving away from Emon's side, swiftly appearing next to Gwen's trembling form on the lounge across the massive chamber.

"Come, my love, I have something I want you to witness." Gwen groans in pain as he lifts her from the lounge. A moment later, Legion returns to Emon's side, Gwen cradled in his arms.

"What's the matter with Gwenevere?" Emon places a hand upon her forehead, her flesh hot to his touch.

"Nothing to bring concern," Legion answers in a flippant manner. "It seems that Witches use their own physical strength to wield their powers. You should document that. I believe she will adapt over time. In the future, I expect you to report here every day at this hour to record her progress." Legion sets Gwen down upon her feet between them.

"Yes, my Lord," the Elf answers. Noticing that Gwen is still a bit wobbly, he steps closer to her, placing an arm about her shoulders to give her support. Still somewhat perplexed, Gwen finally notices the child lying lifeless before her.

"Is she dead?" Gwen turns to Emon.

He is cut off by Ryan. "Not yet, but she will be soon." She smiles at Gwen. The other three Vampires laugh in response.

"You may proceed, Lucca," Legion instructs.

"I don't mean to be disrespectful, my Lord, but isn't the turning of a child into an immortal strictly forbidden by the King?" Emon asks.

"Bec LaNuff is my dominion, and I its King. This is none of his concern," Legion replies with a cold sneer. Emon nods in response, saying no more. Legion gestures to Lucca once more.

"As you command, Master." Lucca steps forward, taking the girl in his arms. He releases a guttural noise as his fangs tear forth from his gums, extending in long, gleaming, white points.

"What are you doing?" Gwen demands, outrage making her

fully coherent again.

"Making her one of us," Ryan answers.

Lucca bends his head over Bethany's neck and bites. Gwen screams, lurching forward to stop him. Legion snatches her back with lightning speed, holding her shoulders so tightly that his long manicured nails dig into the fabric of her dress, tearing her gown.

"Transformation doesn't just happen with one bite," Legion hisses in Gwen's ear. "A single human can be tasted several times without dying or changing over. Over time, the Vampire venom takes hold, taking away their will, their ability for intelligent thought, all identity fading until they are just like your maids. Empty vessels."

Helpless, Gwen watches in horror as Lucca drains Bethany of her life. The girl's body spasms and twitches, her eye lids fluttering.

"If enough venom is released into their bloodstream, or too much blood is drained at once, then the mortal will simply die a sudden yet painful death," the master continues matter-of-factly. "The change comes only when a mortal who's been bitten and drained within an inch of their life drinks a Vampire's blood. Only the blood of the one who bites them will cure their sickness, acting as an antidote to the poison of the venom."

After what seems like an eternity to Gwen, Lucca at last releases his hold on the child, blood spilling from her wound as his lips leave her neck, the child still as if dead.

All at once Bethany sits up as if electrified, her eyes wide with

shock, gasping and gulping for air. Lethawyn and Jezebel lurch forward, taking hold of her. They turn the frightened, hysterical child to Lucca. With his razor-sharp fangs he bites into the skin at his wrist, tearing the flesh. Jezebel forces Bethany's lips to his bleeding punctured veins. Air-deprived and delirious, Bethany's mouth instinctively claps down, sucking in the life-giving liquid.

At first it seems as though the blood is soothing her aching lungs, revitalizing Bethany. Suddenly her body convulses as she pulls away from Lucca, her head jerking back and forth as she screams. Bucking and twisting, she fights desperately to break free from the two female Vampires who hold her captive. Ryan watches with morbid fascination.

"This is it. The final transformation takes about three days to take effect, a kind of gestation period. This is the moment when the mortal body begins to die, becoming severed from its own soul," Legion whispers in Gwen's ear.

Gwen ignores him, distracted by a strange, unearthly sound coming from somewhere beyond, originating from nowhere and everywhere all at once. The howl of a thousand tortured souls intertwined with shrieks and sobs grows louder and more intense until the noise fills Gwen's head with excruciating pain.

"What is that sound? What's happening?" Gwen rips free of Legion's grasp. Clapping her hands over her ears, she collapses to the floor. "Make it stop! Somebody make stop!"

They all look at her, stunned. Emon kneels down beside her.

"Gwen? Gwen, what do you hear?" Emon asks, concerned.

"Don't you hear that? All those voices at once, screaming, crying?"

"No, I hear nothing." Emon looks to Legion and the others. They all shake their heads in response. "No one else hears this sound you speak of."

Gwen looks at him in disbelief. She opens her mouth to speak but finds the words choking in her throat as an apparition takes shape before her. Just above Bethany's thrashing, trembling body, a sphere of light appears. The light grows in intensity and size, from a small pinprick soft glow to a large, man-sized orb. Faces and half human forms protrude from the surface only to melt away.

"Dear God in Heaven, what is that?" Gwen whispers, trembling in fear. She crosses herself in the Catholic fashion, feeling that only God could disperse such an evil as this.

"Why, what is it that you see?" Emon asks anxiously, following her horrified stare but seeing nothing. The others look to each other nervously, everyone but Legion, who can barely contain his excitement.

"I think she is hearing and seeing the Spirit come to claim the child," Legion announces. "Gwenevere, you are witnessing what is called the transferring of spirits, what humans would call a demonic possession. Do not be frightened. The spirit cannot harm you," he tries to assure her. "This must be confusing to you, my love, so let me explain," Legion continues to instruct her, caring nothing for the state of the child. "The purpose of the Vampire venom is two-fold: first, to kill off the mortal body whilst making the mind incapacitated; second, to separate the human's spirit from their physical body so that the spirit of an unborn Forsaken might take their place. Drinking the Vampire's blood stops the venom from completely killing off the body and fills the child's empty veins, pumping new blood to the heart. This is what makes her immortal.

"All the Children of Cain are born without souls, like still-born babes, but within three days, a spirit will claim the empty vessel, bringing the child to life. Only Vampires are not born, for we are the only creature on Earth that cannot reproduce. This is the price of our immortality. However, in his infinite wisdom, the Father of Darkness gave the first Vampire this gift so that we, too, could create life in our own image, so that we might destroy the souls of the children of God one human at a time, taking their bodies for ourselves."

He divulges all this information with a kind of glee in his voice. Legion's words sicken Gwen as she watches the screaming, wailing orb of blinding light descend into the child's chest, absorbed into her body as if becoming one with her. Instantly, Bethany ceases to fight. Her body relaxes as if comatose and she closes her eyes. The painful screaming gone, Gwen begins to feel calm once more.

Jezebel and Lethawyn release the girl, allowing her to rest. They smile at their companions. Ryan laughs while Lucca flexes his arm, clenching and unclenching his fist, the wound at his wrist already healed.

"Now all we have to do is wait. Like I said before, it takes three days for the full transformation to be complete. During that time, the forsaken spirit and the original spirit of the body, will fight for control of the girl. In most cases, the human just gives in and their soul is lost forever in the abyss between this world and the next, never to find peace or salvation." Legion smiles ruefully at this. "When the girl awakens she will be someone else. Her former life and all her memories will still reside in the mind, but Bethany Rose, the girl from Callicoon, will no longer exist."

Emon interjects. "But, on occasion, a human soul will resist the transformation, refusing to give up their mortal frame to another. In this case, humans will simply die, their bodies wasting away. This only happens to humans, The Forsaken cannot be turned."

Curiosity compels Gwen to ask, "Why? What happens?"

"Death, of course. You're immune to the transformation, but not to the venom's poison. Even the tiniest drop of it will kill you. It's fortunate that a Vampire can control the flow of venom, or every bite would be lethal," Legion answers her with sound validity.

Gwen nods numbly that she comprehends, the strength drained out of her body.

"Take the child away," Legion commands his children. He strolls dispassionately toward his throne. Immediately, Jezebel throws the limp form of Bethany over one shoulder and follows her two female companions out of the chamber. Lucca also turns to leave.

"Lucca, I will need another guinea pig tomorrow and everyday hereafter. Understood?"

"Of course, my Lord." Lucca smiles and bows, leaving Emon and Gwen alone with Legion.

Finding her strength, Gwen turns to face her Master without needing Emon's assistance. "You can't expect me to go through with this every day. I won't do it! I can't!"

"I do, and you will. You will do whatever I ask of you. We will repeat this exercise until you successfully heal Ivan of your curse. That's a life lost for every day you disappoint me. You don't want that on your conscience, do you, my love?"

Despair swells within her chest. She knows that he will make good on his threat. Gwen shakes her head bitterly in response.

"My darling wife is weak, Emon. Please escort her to her chamber."

Emon bows respectfully to his Lord. Stepping forward, Emon offers Gwen his arm. She takes it gratefully. Legion ignores them as they leave, his attention already diverted by his daily correspondents and other official business. For the moment, the Master is pleased with the magnitude of Gwen's brutal talents.

CHAPTER FOURTEEN

Fourteen and Counting

egion is as good as his word. Failing to successfully revive Ivan the next day, or the day after that, Gwen finds herself paying the price. The second victim brought before her for Legion's daily experiments is a middle-aged man picked up during his morning run, right off the streets of Scranton in the early morning hours just before dawn.

Legion orders Gwen to duplicate the curse she put on Ivan on this poor man. Under the influence of the ring, she obeys. The curse takes the same effect on the jogger, yet despite Legion's insistence and threats, she finds that she still cannot untangle the web of her magic once it is cast. Being of no further use to them, the jogger is taken away by Lucca. What happens to him after that Gwen is never told.

The third victim, an elderly woman, is doomed to the same

fate. On the fourth day, frustrated and desperate, Gwen asks for permission to spend the whole day alone with Ivan in his chamber. Her request granted, Gwen sits and studies the Vampire for hours. Instead of attempting to remove the spell altogether, as she has in the past, Gwen decides to try a new tactic. Delving deep into his conscious, Gwen examines the individual threads of the magic spell engulfing his mind, searching for a hole, a loose end, or some kind of weakness that might help her unravel it. This exposes her own psyche to the dark curse, causing her to lose her focus and become melancholy. To dispel the effect she has to take frequent breaks, making progress slow. Finally, Gwen discovers a weakness. Pushing with all the mental force she can muster, she breaks through. The dark cloud of the curse begins to fade from Ivan's mind.

Although she is bemused from the results of the spell, Gwen has the presence of mind to leave before Ivan can fully recover. Stumbling feebly down the long corridors, Gwen finds her way to the grand chamber, searching for Legion. Slethum the Ogre informs her that it is almost dawn and thus the Master has retired to his bedchamber for rest. Reluctantly, Gwen continues to Legion's dark, oppressive room. She knows it would be safer for her to send one of her servant girls to relay her message, but she doubts that Legion would believe it unless he hears it straight from her. Gwen reluctantly raps her fist upon the dark, stone door.

Legion drags her into Ivan's bedchamber again to face the man she almost killed, an encounter she would have liked to postpone until sometime later, when the Vampire had time to work out any feelings of hostility he might harbor for her. However, upon hearing the news that his devoted servant has awoken, Legion had to see it for himself, insisting that Gwen accompany him.

They enter the room to find Ivan sitting up in his stone bed, shoulder hunched and head down as if dizzy. Gwen stays half-hidden behind Legion's tall figure, hoping to stay out of sight.

"Ivan, old friend, you've awoken! How do you feel?" An almost genuine concern in Legion's voice puzzles Gwen exceedingly.

Startled, Ivan looks up, noticing his visitors for the first time. His skin is drawn and pale, even for a light-deprived bloodsucker. His eyes are all black, the pupils lost as if swimming in a pool of black oil. His hair has grown out, hanging down around his shoulders, greasy and dirty, facial hair thick in a mountain-man-style beard and mustache upon his face.

How long has he been under this spell? Gwen wonders, mentally counting back the days since her encounter with Ivan on the balcony. Realization starts to dawn on her. *It hasn't been just days or weeks, but months. Has it really been six months? No, it can't be!* Living every day in a walking catatonic state, Gwen has to admit that time got away from her. She barely survives each day, shutting out the world and time, only doing what she must.

I must stay alert. I must stay strong, otherwise I'll lose myself in this world, and I'll never escape. I've wasted too much time already.

Ivan looks at Legion a moment as if trying to remember his face. When he finally speaks, his voice is raspy and hoarse due to the six long months of silence.

"What happened? How did I get here?"

"You mean you don't remember?" Legion asks curiously, stepping toward him, revealing Gwen in the doorway behind him.

Ivan begins to speak, but upon the sight of Gwen, his face changes. In an instant, full comprehension comes to him. She can see it in his eyes.

With a snarl in his throat, the Vampire lunges toward her, whizzes by Legion, and quickly makes the twelve foot distance that separates them. Gwen feels the air in the room as he moves, seeing him come toward her and anticipating his movements. The air electrifies her and her body shivers as she instinctively summons the powers within, ancient words she has never spoken spilling forth from her lips, a surge of energy and life welling from her gut and bursting outward from every pore to shield her from her attacker.

Ivan runs into the invisible barrier, ricocheting backward as if hitting a brick wall. He hits the ground, but like a spring he is back on his feet again, lunging for another attack. Gwen braces herself, prepared to hurt or kill if she must. Neither one of them notices Legion moves between them, taking hold of Ivan's shoulders in his strong hands, holding his fellow Vampire back from the child Witch. Ivan kicks like a rabid dog on a leash, clawing and barking at unobtainable prey.

"That's enough out of you two! What's done is done," Legion shouts at them.

"She must die for the good of the colony and your throne! If you don't want her Wiccan blood on your hands, then let me do it. I'd gladly kill her for you, my Lord!" Ivan wrestles to get free from Legion's grasp, attempting once more to get at Gwen.

"Don't be ridiculous. The girl is not a threat to anyone now, least of all me. I have made the Witch my bride and bonded her to me through the wedded serpents. I command her now, and she must obey. This also makes her your Queen, and you must honor her as such." Legion's voice is cold and commanding.

"You can't be serious! Honor that little slattern as my Queen! I'd rather stake me 'self in the heart!" He ceases to struggle in his Master's arms. Ivan spits a stream of blood in Gwen's general direction.

"Not only will you serve her, but I am counting on you to keep an eye on her when I cannot be there to protect her from the others, and from her own stupidity."

Gwen and Ivan give him identical looks of astonishment and outrage. Legion cuts them off before either can speak out in protest.

"And you are never to use your powers against Ivan again, am I understood?"

Gwen nods curtly, her jaw clenched as she attempts to stare down Ivan. He meets her gaze with a sneer, yet still nods to his liege in response to his command.

"Very well. That will be all then, Ivan. Get your rest. I need you to regain your strength quickly." Legion releases Ivan and turns to Gwen. Come, my pet, your work here is done." Gwen senses Legion's silent command through the serpent ring to retract the magic shield about her. Instantaneously, the flow of magic within her evaporates like a mist, leaving her vulnerable once more. Legion takes her by the arm, ushering her out of the room and safely away.

To her dismay, Legion leads her back to his chamber to rest with him. He orders her to get into bed. She obeys by the force of the ring, trying to hide the panic inside.

Legion's two boy servants undress their Master with practiced hands, stripping him down to his loose trousers, folding every item of clothing with care. After their task is done, Legion dismisses them. Gwen watches the boys go with apprehension, knowing that as long as someone else is in the room her husband will not touch her. Gwen hurries and closes her eyes, pretending to be asleep. Legion saunters to the bed, giving her a wicked smile. She senses rather than feels him as he lies down next to her. For a long, disconcerting moment the room is silent until Gwen feels Legion's cold breath in her ear, his presence all too near.

"You forget, my love, that I know all that you feel, and although I can't exactly read your every thought, the ring does acquaint me with the state of your consciousness. You cannot fool me," he hisses, amusement thick in his chilling voice.

The comforter suddenly ripped off of her, Gwen flinches. Her eyes spring open to see her Lord leap on top of her like a cat pouncing on a mouse. He pins her arms and legs down beneath him effortlessly.

"I am well pleased with your progress today. Your strength in the craft is improving considerably. However, your body is as weak as a human babe. This will never do. Perhaps it is time we train your body to be equal to the power of your mind."

Gwen opens her mouth to speak, but the look in his eyes stops her. He begins to laugh, a sound that turns every nerve in her body to ice. With the gleam of giddy insanity in his eyes, Legion throws back his head, releasing a growl as his fangs tear forth from his gums like twin ivory blades. He dives toward her, blood lust twisting his beautiful face into that of a demon, Legion's deadly-white fangs glisten in the candle light. In that moment, the world becomes a kaleidoscope of pain, emotions, sensations, and colors for Gwen, and then everything else fades into blackness.

* * * * *

In the months that follow, Gwen has several new challenges thrust upon her. After Ivan fully recovers from the curse, Legion makes him Gwen's personal bodyguard and his own secret spy, commanding Ivan to follow her as if he were her shadow, making a record of her every action, word, or deed. This pleases neither Ivan nor Gwen, whose general animosity for each other continues to gain in potency with each passing day. Neither dares outright refusal or defiance of their Lord's commands, so they reluctantly oblige him. Ivan takes out his rage on his servant boy Peter. Gwen is mortified when Emon tells her the news of his brutal death. She tries to tell his sister Lydia and his cousin Jessica, her servant girls, but they comprehend nothing. Peter's death weighs heavy on Gwen's heart.

The next trial in Gwen's never-ending life of tribulation is the awakening of Bethany Rose Wilson, the child with whom Gwen witnessed the changing of a mortal into an immortal for the first time. Just as her Lord said, three days from being drained and partaking of the venomous blood, the girl arose from her death-like state, forever changed. Her skin has no pigment, cold and waxy. Her eyes lost their color and their innocence, replaced by a somber gray with a dangerous gleam. Along with a new set of razor-sharp fangs, she has a whole new personality as well. The child who begged Gwen for mercy, who wanted nothing more but to go home to her family, is replaced by a much older soul. A woman with a cold indifference for life and a childlike joy in manipulation and torture now resides within the child-size frame, answering to the name Lynette instead. The child Vampire soon becomes a constant enemy.

If she thought her daily experiments with magic were exhausting, she has physical combat training heaped onto her plate. Her tutor, Lucca the Vampire, instructs her in many forms of hand to hand combat and weaponry. Gwen's opponents are the strongest and most deadly hunters, warriors, and assassins amongst the clans of the mountain—Giants, Dwarves, Ogres, Goblins, Vampires, and even Vinita the Elf woman.

In these exercises, Legion disables her by severing her ability to harness her powers, forcing her to defend herself with her physical strength alone. At first, her progress is slow and her failures numerous, resulting in bruises, broken bones, and spilled blood. Determined to prevail for her own well-being and sense of pride, Gwen takes great pains to condition her body, to withstand pain and build muscle mass through daily exercise, learning many fighting techniques and mastering numerous kinds of weaponry to enhance her skill. She acknowledges that no matter how strong she becomes, there will always be opponents that she cannot best with sheer strength alone, so eventually, she begins to use her intellect to find weaknesses in her opponents as well.

She observes that the Giant can be over taken if she hits him directly under the knee, causing him to lose his balance and tumble over, thus bringing the massive creature within her range to inflict trauma to the head.

Dwarves, to her surprise, are both fearless and relentless fighters, incredibly adept with the spear and axe. Besting them takes great determination, endurance, and a heavy shield, but eventually she learned to wear them down through patience and being fast on her feet.

Ogres throw their weight around, lugging massive clubs while throwing rocks and mallets as weapons. This leaves them vulnerable in a close range attack, especially if she can separate them from their weapons. Because they have stronger muscle mass built on the right side of their bodies, they wear thick metal armor on the left side. She can deal them a killing blow if she gets close enough to stab a blade up under the gaps of the armor, such as under the arm or at the base of the neck.

The Goblins' sporadic and undisciplined fighting style makes them incredibly dangerous and frightening. Their weakness is their ill temper and tendency to act before they think. If she goads them on, insulting and mocking them, without warning they make an awkward, foolhardy attack, thus leading to their defeat.

Two of the most deadly adversaries are the Vampire and the Elf. The Vampires rely heavily on their speed and superhuman strength, defeating their challengers by striking at them like a snake and then crushing them, or hurtling them about like a rag doll. Most often they simply tear their captive apart with their bare hands or fangs.

The Elves' fighting style is acrobatic and elegant, something between kung fu and ballet. Their bodies moved in a sequence of kicks, flips, and punches so swift and fluid she can barely distinguish one move from the next. They also fight with long swords and staffs. No matter how she tries, she can never best either foe without magic. Vinita takes great pleasure in Gwen's failure, enjoying their sparring matches, relishing every broken bone and every drop of Gwen's blood that she spills.

Every time she gets knocked to the ground, Gwen gets back

up on her feet. Even though she knows it is fruitless, determination makes her drudge on, fighting with everything that she has.

During her captivity, Gwen learns to keep track of the time, vowing to never allow herself to become accustomed to life in Bec LaNuff.

After all, she tells herself daily, *I'm only passing through.* One day she would find a way out. Until then, Gwen keeps track of the passage of time in a chart in her sketchbook, along with drawings of the things she has seen, and the important things she has learned whilst captive under the mountain. Keeping this daily record helps her maintain some semblance of sanity, in her otherwise dark existence.

* * * * *

Two years have passed after Gwen first entered Legion's realm. While she lives amongst beings that never change or grow, time has transformed her from a girl into a budding young woman. Thanks to the magic of puberty, Gwen now stands five feet seven inches tall. Along with sprouting legs, she has grown womanly curves, accented by a tiny feminine waistline. Her ample bosoms always get in the way, making her feel absolutely awkward and lumpy. She'd hate them entirely if it weren't for the fact that they seem to repulse her Lord as much as they do her.

Her husband no longer showers her with attention. He hates to watch her age. Something about it sickens him. If she were human, he would have simply turned her into a Vampire long ago. *Another upside to being a Wiccan,* Gwen reflects often.

Legion has stopped visiting her bedchamber and started taking other lovers instead. Just as he had before Gwen became his bride, he beds girls like Melody, human simpletons to worship and adore him while he plays God. Most importantly, they serve as someone to replace Gwen in bed, for which she is all too grateful. She can't help but feeling sorry for them. They think they are in love for the first time, and with such a being, it's like a fairytale to them. *Poor fools!* Gwen mourns. It doesn't take Legion long to tire of them, and then, one day, they're gone.

"Why doesn't his majesty just turn one of his lovely little girls into a Vampire like he did Bethany—I mean Lynette?" Gwen asks Emon one day, curious.

"I believe it is because he enjoys their frailty. The knowledge that he can end their lives as easily as crushing a bug thrills him," Emon replies. Gwen wishes she hadn't asked.

Sometimes Gwen feels responsible for their lost lives, but she is powerless to help them or to stop him for now. One day, she will be rid of the ring, and then nothing will protect Legion from her vengeance.

While the Lord of the mountain finds his bride repulsive, everyone else seems to find the new Gwen alluring. It's almost as if she has a hypnotic power over them, like some kind of love spell. According to Emon's historical records, some Wiccans possess a magical trait known as the glimmer. A person with the glimmer has a supernatural ability to cause sexual desire in others, to appear beautiful or charming regardless of their natural appearance. Gwen starts to believe that she has the glimmer.

It would explain why the male inhabitants of Bec LaNuff are behaving as though they've just met Gwen for the first time. When she walks into a room, everyone stops to look at her as if they can't help themselves. They just keep staring, their eyes wide with admiration and awe. Some are struck speechless. Others start babbling like idiots. Several of them approach her one at a time, trying desperately to get her attention, stumbling over themselves and each other to have the opportunity to be near her. It is really disconcerting to the humble tomboy Gwenevere. The only time they don't make fools of themselves is when His Worship escorts her about the place, opting to pine for her from a distance instead. *It is embarrassing, really. It makes my skin crawl and my insides shiver.*

Gwen finds she needs to look for the positive in all things or else she will go crazy. After all, today is her birthday and she finds herself feeling glad that she's getting older. When they were kids, Raven and Gwen had a tradition of listing all the things they were happy about on their birthday, the reasons why it was a "happy birthday." So she makes herself a list in her sketchbook.

List of things I am happy about on this birthday:

1. I am happy that I'm alive.

2. I am happy that I get to sleep alone in my own bed.

3. I am happy that I have Emon to teach me, and the library's wealth of knowledge from which to learn.

4. I am happy that I am learning more about my gifts and my own kind.

5. I am happy that Raven is out in the world, safe and far from here, and that I will get to see him again someday.

6. I am happy that I'm becoming a stronger fighter every day.

7. I am happy that I got the cook to make me chocolate cake for dessert tonight.

8. I am happy that one day I will leave this place and go on to live my own life.

Gwen finishes her list and stows the sketchbook and art kit away under her bed. Tired from another typically exhausting day, she stretches out like a cat, feeling every aching bone in her body relaxing with the movement. Changing into her night clothes, she enjoys the rare privilege of dressing herself for a change, having already dismissed her maid servants for the night.

On her vanity table sits a silver tray with a large slice of chocolate cake covered in chocolate frosting and adorned with a single wax candle. Most of the tribes of Cain don't indulge in sweets or desserts, so she was pleasantly surprised to find that, when she sent Lydia with her special request to the cook, that she actually returned with this slice of birthday cake. Where they found the candle she isn't sure, but it makes her smile to think of the little Dwarf cooks scouring the kitchen cupboards to find it.

Perhaps they remembered that I requested the same thing last year, and were prepared this time, Gwen contemplates.

Unlike her first birthday spent in Bec LaNuff, this year she celebrates it alone in her room. It doesn't bother her; after all, she never wanted to be the center of attention, and she never really got used to the idea of receiving presents. This is much more her style.

Gwen carries the birthday cake on its tray over to her bed and places it on the nightstand next to her. Murmuring a simple spell of fire, the wick of the candle suddenly lights. Gwen waits a moment to see if the ring will punish her for this unlawful use of magic, but relaxes after several minutes go by without incident. Sitting on her bed, Gwen leans toward the cake. Closing her eyes, she makes a silent wish and blows out the candle. While she is devouring her chocolate cake, the realization dawns on her that she has been stuck here for two years.

Oh, well, I better not dwell on that now. I'm trying to be positive, she tells herself. Aloud she says, "Happy Birthday, Gwen! Today, you are fourteen and counting."

CHAPTER FIFTEEN

Angelo

The world as Gwen knows it is about to change drastically. This premonition comes to her gradually, like a cloud of mist gathering and forming inside her mind until the sensation hangs heavy in the air about her. Gwen focuses her attention on the present, hoping to dispel the ominous impression of the future.

Gwen sits in front of a mirror trying to do her hair as she hurries to make herself presentable. She is late, and Ivan is waiting for her just outside the bedroom door. Because of her talent for sensing the thoughts and auras of other living beings, she could sense his presence even if he weren't there every morning to act as her guard and escort. Although she long ago became accustomed to the presence of such an ill-mannered, pig-faced, English

Vampire hovering over her, after a restless night of tortured dreams and obscure nonsensical visions, Gwen doesn't think she can stand the sight of Ivan this morning.

She can almost feel him tapping his foot impatiently as he waits for her on the other side of the stone wall that divides them. She can hear his mind buzzing with activity, but his thoughts are hidden from her behind his strong mental shield. Only humans wander about with their minds unguarded, oblivious to the reality that people like her out in the world can pluck thoughts and memories out of their heads as easily as plucking fruit from a tree. The Forsaken shield their minds from telepaths by focusing on a mental image or a memory and letting go of all else, like a person might during meditation. Only a very strong-willed and intellectual being can hold the shield and think regular thoughts at the same time. Thus, most Forsaken only shielded themselves when they know they were in the presence of a Witch. Of course, not all Witches are telepathic, but none of the citizens in Bec LaNuff are taking any chances with Gwen nearby, bound by the ring or not.

Her room is a modest little bedchamber carved out of the living stone of the mountain, located in the lower levels of the fortress, near the servant's quarters. She had, until recently, been living in a room twice as large in an upper level of the fortress in the Vampire wing near to her husband's room. A conceited twelve year-old little vixen from Wisconsin, Danielle, demanded the right to the nicest room and the most elegant wardrobe as Legion's newest love. Gwen had been evicted from her Queenly chamber and all of her expensive clothing. Her jewelry, her gifts, and even her two servant girls had been seized and awarded to her replacement.

Unlike her predecessors, all simple-minded, timid, love-sick fools, Danielle is conniving, malicious, ambitious, and besotted with herself. This, Gwen thinks, makes her a perfect match for the Lord of the Mountain. Danielle came by choice. She knew right from the start about the advantages and disadvantages of being Legion's mistress, and gave into him willingly. Legion hadn't needed to manipulate her with his Vampire charm like any of the previous girls. Danielle jumped at the opportunity to align herself with such an attractive and supernatural being.

Naturally, Danielle and Gwen despise each other. With her cool, calculating, pale blue eyes, her slim, delicate frame, and her doll-like features crowned with a head full of golden curls, Danielle is Gwen's polar opposite. Gwen has yellow-green eyes, a tall, curvy figure, and the face of a goddess with hair that hangs straight like a luxurious curtain of luminous black, against her creamy skin.

Feeling threatened by Gwen's beauty, power, and her status as Legion's wife, Danielle puffs herself up by treating Gwen like one of the servants, ordering her about or ignoring her as if Gwen should not speak without being spoken to first. This grates on Gwen's nerves. Danielle throws herself at Legion like some cheap tramp disgusting, flirting and kissing on him right in front of everyone, prancing around as though she is Cleopatra vying for the attention of Julius Caesar. As much as they aggravate her, overall Gwen is happy to see them together. After all, Danielle keeps Legion's cold hands and soulless eyes off of Gwen's anatomy.

If only she'd keep her mouth shut and didn't pal around with that Lynette creature, then everything would be peachy, Gwen thinks to herself as she goes about combing and fixing up her long silky black hair, doing it half up with braids on either side, leaving her bangs to swish across her forehead and the rest of her dark mass of hair smooth and straight to hang down her back.

Once a chubby little seven year-old girl, Lynette is now a vicious miniature Vampire with a sadistic nature, the spirit of a grown woman trapped somewhere within. Blaming Gwen for her part in the events of the night that made her a child for all eternity, Lynette is determined to discredit or destroy Gwen at every turn. Whilst Danielle is desperate to be the object of Legion's undivided attention, the child Vampire and the young Danielle have become instant companions and allies. Sharing a delight in tormenting and oppressing Gwen, the dynamic duo make it their mission to drive her out of her mind.

Hopefully neither one of them cross my path today. Gwen checks the results of her preparations in the mirror. *It would be all too easy to curse them, and then I'd have to pay the price.*

With a sigh, Gwen gets up from her stool and slips into her wicker sandals, adjusting the scoop neckline of her simple calf-length green cotton dress so that her cleavage is less exposed. Her apparel these days is much more comfortable and economic in comparison to the attire in which Legion used to dress her. However, she finds it hard to disguise the shape of her womanly figure no matter what she wears. If it were left up to her, Gwen would happily go about wearing jeans, a T-shirt, and her comfortable sneakers, but that kind of thing would never be suitable dress for Legion's kingly court. At least her current wardrobe is far less ostentatious than Danielle's, which is, after all, comprised of Gwen's old clothes.

"Are you coming out or not, girl? I 'aven't got all day to stand around while you preen in the mirror!" Ivan bellows, his cockney accent enhancing the condescending tone of his speech.

Gwen shoots the door a dirty look and grits her teeth to keep from making a snide comment in reply. Instead, she grabs her mother's locket from her small jewelry box on the nightstand and slips the golden chain around her neck. She turns and opens the door, leaving her room and entering the hall. As she steps into the main passageway of the servant's quarters, Gwen comes face to face with the pestilent visage of Ivan.

"Oh, I see precious 'as finally decided to grace us with 'er presence," Ivan sneers at her.

Gwen spares him only a sideways glance before she walks on, forcing the two hundred-year-old Vampire to follow behind her as she winds her way through the fortress toward the grand hall.

"You know 'ow 'e 'ates to be left waiting. You forget, love, Legion don't wait upon anyone, not even you." Ivan takes the first opportunity to squeeze by, coming up alongside her, taking hold of her arm in a firm, almost painful grip. They stop at the foot of a flight of stairs. Gwen glowers at him, jerking her arm free of his cold touch.

"You don't get to touch me. You're nothing but a pet to him, a little dog licking his boots." Her voice is cool with distain.

A couple of Ogres stroll down the steps. Gwen and Ivan stand there, glaring at each other, blocking the stairs. The Ogres hesitate as they approach the quarrelling pair.

"And you're nothing more than a shiny new toy. Once 'e's done playing with you, 'e'll pass you along to me, just like all the others." With a leer on his disgusting face, Ivan gives Gwen's bum a pinch. By reflex, Gwen turns on him, backhanding Ivan across the face. The force of the blow might have knocked any ordinary man down, but it has little effect on the immortal. Ivan's rage flares red hot, his eyes blaze.

Before the confrontation can escalate, the Ogres come closer to them. One of them, an old gray-bearded Ogre, coughs in an attempt to get their attention. Ivan turns, and the two Ogres bow their heads to him in respect. Ivan responds with a curt nod. Gwen seizes this opportunity to slip by the two massive creatures before her, and continues up the stairs, leaving Ivan to scurry after her.

They reach the grand chamber, walking alongside each other, ignoring each other like invisible companions. Once at the grand chamber doors, the two are ushered in by the head of the Guards, Slethum. He is, in Gwen's estimation, the ugliest Ogre in the entire fortress.

This evening there is a larger crowd assembled in the grand chamber than usual. Typically, Legion holds court first thing after sundown, dealing with all the disputes amongst the citizens of Bec LaNuff until about midnight. Thereafter he would disappear into the night along with most of the Vampire populace to hunt. They usually reappear, fully reenergized, around two in the morning to spend the rest of the dark hours of the night reveling in the company of his current mistress or entertaining guests in his court.

By Gwen's reckoning, it is only nine at night, and she would have been up and about between six and seven o'clock if she hadn't slept in. Gwen barely remembers the days when she slept during the night and lived during the day, but her strange sleeping pattern is only one of the many adjustments she'd made while living among the undead.

Gwen glances about the room, noting all the creatures in the grand hall. Legion is sprawled on the chaise lounge next to the throne. Danielle lies on her belly beside him, her head turned away from Gwen, one of her arms draped over his chest, and her bloody wrist pressed against Legion's crimson lips as he sucks dark fluid from her. As he does, Danielle emits moans of painful pleasure. Gwen cringes, darting her eyes away from this intimate exchange. Seeing that his Master is preoccupied, Ivan leaves Gwen's side to join fellow Vampires Lucca and Lethawyn by the banquet table laden with goblets and pitchers full of a deep red liquid.

Besides her and Ivan, Gwen counts twelve persons scattered about the room in various clusters, mingling. Ivan drinks with

Lucca and the eternal trio, Jezebel, Lethawyn and Ryan, who are never apart from each other. Vinita whispers in the corner with the Troll Lord, Hockrah.

Playing an ancient game of stones at the head of the banquet table sits the Dwarf Chieftain Volgoraff, the Goblin Lord Pallagore, and an Ogre with the unlikely name of Steve. The demon child Lynette is in attendance as well. The two of them exchange identical looks of loathing. Lynette starts across the room toward Gwen. Desperate to find some excuse to avoid her, Gwen casts her eyes about the room for some ally.

Suddenly her eyes alight on a peculiar object in the corner of the chamber. How she missed it before, Gwen can't fathom. Its size and color alone should have caught her attention the second she stepped into the room. Tucked into the corner of the room along the same wall as the chamber's massive doors is a large golden baby grand piano, which had never been in here before.

How on earth did a piano get this far underground? Who brought it here, and why would they go through so much trouble? Gwen puzzles, openly gaping at the ornate instrument that seems so alien in its surroundings, a bright shimmering jewel in a world of cold gray. Gwen can't help but be dazzled by it.

"You've noticed the new addition, I see. It took you long enough, Witch," Lynette scoffs in her eerie, deep voice, the kind of sound that should never come from a child. The word 'Witch' falls off of her tongue with such loathing one would swear the word was a curse.

Gwen ignores the chubby pint-sized bloodsucker, and wanders over to the golden piano, compelled to touch its shiny surface. Lynette follows, her brown head of curls hovering just about Gwen's elbow.

"Where did it come from?"

"It's a present for the Master's new guest. Some ancient acquaintance has come to stay in Bec LaNuff for a spell. Lucca says he's some kind of master musician like Mozart, only immortal and Italian." Lynette takes a sip of the deep red liquid within, looking up at Gwen with a smile, blood clinging to her gums and teeth with gruesome effect. Gwen averts her eyes.

"Then how come I've never heard of this guy? If he's such an old friend, why hasn't he come here to visit before?" Gwen addresses her inquires to the white and black piano keys, her tone indifferent.

"He didn't confide in you? How strange. But then again, I guess he wouldn't, would he? After all, you're only his Wiccan whore, not one of us. It's not like you're an equal or anyone important." Gwen didn't need to ask the "he" to which she referred. Neither did Gwen bother to reply to such a condescending comment, especially one coming from a seven year-old. Gwen fights the urge to crush Lynette under her feet. Ironically, this seven year-old could just as easily throw Gwen as she would toss a rubber ball across the room.

"When does this Italian Vampire arrive?" Gwen plays a C scale on the keyboard, smiling when she hears the clear chimes.

The piano sounds just as beautiful as it looks.

"He's already here." A deep, smooth, masculine voice like cold water bubbling in a creek speaks into Gwen's right ear. An icy, crisp breath, like the frost of morning dew tingling down her neck alerts her to the closeness of the stranger.

Shaken by the sensations that the voice invokes down to her very core, Gwen feels momentarily paralyzed. Breathlessness and an airy kind of buoyancy make her feel as light and unsubstantial as a leaf blowing in the wind. With a weary sigh, she slowly turns to face the stranger.

Her gaze is met by silvery gray eyes. An intense, penetrating stare laced with wild impulsiveness and masculine sexuality startles Gwen into a confused state of calm and expectation.

"The name's Angelo, originally from Vienna. I'm the man of the hour, it seems." As he speaks, Gwen notices the musical lilt of his Italian accent, the iridescent glow of his slightly tanned, smooth, immaculate skin, and the ivory-white gleam of his fangs in the candle light.

He smiles, flashing a mouth full of irregular pearly white teeth, adding a dash of character to his otherwise perfect appearance, making him almost human for a brief moment. *Obviously he comes from a time before dental hygiene, so he must be very old. I wonder if he's as old as Legion.* It strikes Gwen as odd that she never really bothered to ask her undead spouse his age.

The Italian's hair is almost black with beautiful lush curls. It's the kind of hair that lures feminine hands to tousle and caress, wrapping the curls around their dainty, little fingers in a manner both loving and sensual. Gwen imagines doing just that. She is so wrapped up in the stranger's beauty, so stunned by his presence, that it takes her moment to realize that he had asked her a question and is patiently waiting for her reply.

Damn Vampires! Do they all have to be so gorgeous? Shaking herself inwardly, Gwen gathers her composure and gives him a little nonchalant smile back, tilting her head slightly to look up into his face. Gwen fights the urge to openly look him up and down, to appraise his physique much like the way she had seen the girls at Scranton Junior High check out the eighth grade boys. Looking at him without staring, Gwen takes in all six feet of his lean masculine form, his broad, strong shoulders, long torso and narrow hips, his stance and mannerisms clearly defining him as a man who is comfortable in his own skin. He is dressed head to toe in black, tight-fitted, boot cut jeans, a tight muscle T-shirt, and black dress shoes.

Like a cross between a rock star and Edward Scissorhands, Gwen thinks to herself. *There's just something strange, dark, and sexy about him, a kind of wild, creative spirit underneath.*

"I beg your pardon?" After racking her brain for something intelligent and sophisticated to say, this was all she could come up with. At least she manages to keep her/voice steady and her face from blushing.

"I asked you for your name." A slow smile spreads across his lips, a smile so obscenely sexy, it makes Gwen's heart skip a beat.

"Oh, um…I'm Gwenevere," she states. She offers her hand to him. He shakes her hand, their eyes locked. His firm grip is both cold and soft. His thumb strokes her knuckles in a meaningful caress.

Gwen gives in to the urge to probe into his mind, yearning to know everything about this stranger. For one blissful moment she is in his head, immersed in the glow of his auras, hearing the hum of his thoughts, feeling how he feels. She senses something strange about his mind, something she has never encountered before. Instead of one conscious, there are two. Two different colored auras joined together, flashing in vibrant, dazzling colors—two spirits coexisting together as one.

Angelo's smile is suddenly replaced by a look of bewilderment. A wall springs up between her mind and his, locking her out as swiftly as springing a trap.

"Angelo, old friend, there you are!" Legion appears suddenly by Angelo's side, slapping him genially on the back, a gesture that seems odd to Gwen, having rarely seen Legion greet anyone in such a friendly manner. "Come, there are a few new members of the colony you have to meet." Legion ignores Gwen and leads his guest across the room to meet the other Vampires in attendance. Danielle lays lethargically on the lounge recovering from her bloodletting orgasm.

"Good day, Gwenevere."

"Good day," Gwen begins, but without another word, he's

gone. She was so distracted by the presence of the new arrival that she hadn't noticed that Emon entered with him. She smiles kindly at the Elf. "Tell me, Emon, what do you know about this Angelo guy? Is Legion his maker? Do you know how they met? And why hasn't he come to visit before?" Curious, Gwen hurries after Angelo and Legion, forcing Emon to follow alongside her.

"No, Legion is not Angelo's maker," Emon responds. "That man has long been dead from what I hear. What I do know is that they've been friends for about one hundred years. They met somewhere outside of Germany. They both served as generals in VWWIII."

Gwen gives him a quizzical look. "What's VWWIII?"

"The Third Vampire Wiccan War. We refer to it as VWWIII," Emon replies.

"There have been three wars between the Vampires and Wiccans? I didn't know that."

"Truth be told, we're up to five Vampire/Wiccan wars. Actually, there have been twelve major wars amongst the children of Cain. Naturally, the Vampires and Wiccans have always fought on opposing sides. There are several volumes written about the wars."

"Why haven't you ever mentioned them to me?" She keeps her voice low so that the others won't hear, which she knows is silly with Vampires in the room. Secretly she hopes they are too distracted to notice.

"Because the Lord didn't want you to worry yourself over the ongoing conflict between your two races."

"Are we at war now?" Emon shakes his head in the negative. "I want to see those books, Emon."

"I'll see what I can do, but if the Master finds out, you didn't get them from me." They fall silent as they approach the others. They stand behind Angelo as Legion makes his introductions.

Angelo was already acquainted with Lucca and Ivan. He greets them with a curt nod. Jezebel and Lethawyn give him identical seductive smiles. Angelo responds with disinterest.

"This is Ryan. She is the twins' child, and she is only six years old to the grave." Ryan bows her head slightly to Angelo as a symbol of respect to her elder.

"Are Jezebel and Lethawyn twins?" Gwen asks Emon under her breath, counting on the Elf's superior hearing to pick up her words. Emon nods in reply. "What else don't I know?"

"Quite a lot, little Witch, but believe me, the less you know of their kind the better. You've existed mostly by sticking to your books, your sketches, and staying out of the Vampire's affairs. I recommend you continue in this manner."

Gwen gives Emon a queer look, but she nods in understanding.

"Don't be fooled by appearances, child. He's just like the rest of them," Emon adds as an afterthought, looking rather poignantly toward Angelo, the beautiful dark stranger.

Legion introduces everyone else. They all share greetings, nods, and gestures of respect to Angelo. Legion introduces Lynette with a coy, little smile at his friend.

"You have a child spawn?" Angelo laughs incredulously.

"I know, I know. It's forbidden. Let those fools come into my kingdom and condemn me to my face. Until then I'll live by my own rule," Legion boasts arrogantly.

"But why did you do such a thing?" the Italian asks, intrigued.

"I thought my beloved wife might like a little friend. As it turns out, the two of them can't stand each other." Legion laughs ironically.

"And where is this infamous child bride? The one who has smitten you so, is she here?"

Danielle sits up as if suddenly awakening to the present. She flutters across the room to her lover's side, taking Legion's arm and addressing Angelo with her head held high like a Southern lady accepting an honored guest into her parlor. Her diminutive form looks out of place between the two pale-faced giants that surround her.

"Hello. I'm Danielle. You must be the musician. I just love music. I especially love to sing. Wouldn't it be perfect, my love? I'll sing and your friend will accompany me on the piano. We can entertain you this evening at the party." Danielle rattles away, practically bouncing up and down in her excitement, smiling. Her attempt at charm borders on desperation. Angelo is clearly unimpressed. Nevertheless, he smiles at her, bending his head over her dainty, little hand and kissing it dispassionately.

"It would be my honor to accompany you, Danielle."

She beams up at him like a fool.

"Never mind that. Danielle can't sing. She hasn't the talent for it." Legion swipes Danielle's hand from Angelo's grasp in an effortless movement, almost too fast to be witnessed by the naked eye. Danielle glowers at him, anger radiating hot beneath her skin. Oblivious, Legion holds her hand in both of his, massaging his boney fingers into the meaty flesh of her palm in a nonchalant manner, as if it's second nature. Danielle's whole body relaxes and the anger drains out of her. Gwen can tell that she is under a kind of hypnosis, a weakness that he exploits to keep her in line. Danielle all but purrs in delight.

"Gwenevere is the songbird I spoke of earlier," Emon speaks up. He gestures with his hand to Gwen beside him.

Angelo shifts smoothly. He turns to give her his full attention, a seductive smile already on his lips as he reaches for her hand. "Ah. No wonder you were admiring the piano. Do you play?"

"Not very well. I've never really had lessons," Gwen confesses.

"I'm sure you're just being modest. I could be your tutor if you like."

Legion drops Danielle's hand abruptly and steps up to Angelo's side. "What a marvelous idea. Yes, my dear, I think that would please me greatly."

"It would be my pleasure to serve one so lovely," Angelo whispers, placing a tender kiss on her delicate hand as his grayish-white eyes peer into her soul with barely hidden lustful intentions.

In a gesture as swift as thought, Legion snatches Gwen's hand from Angelo's grasp, intervening his friend's kiss. In a motion that reeks strongly of possessiveness and arrogance, Legion draws Gwen to him as though leading her in a dance, forcing her body up against his intimately.

"My love, I don't believe you've been properly introduced. Gwenevere, this is Angelo, one of my oldest and most trusted friends." He speaks inches from her face, his lips almost touching hers. Gwen feels both frightened and strangely aroused by his closeness, hating her body for betraying her with its weak, carnal needs. Legion smiles, feeling his effect on her through the bond forged between them by the ring. He turns to Angelo. "Angelo, let me introduce my devoted wife Gwen, lost daughter of Wicca."

Something like disappointment and shock flashes behind Angelo's cloudy eyes. The instant passes and he smiles broadly, making a grand bow to Gwen, his hand over his heart.

"It's a great honor, Mistress." Gwen returns this gesture with a brisk nod, feeling completely at a loss, her emotional state all a-jumble with the hormones and pheromones in the air around the three of them, choking off all reason.

Everyone returns to their respective groups to mingle. Angelo joins in a toast with Legion and little Danielle while Gwen and Emon wander off to sit on the piano bench and chat. As the evening progresses, the citizens of Bec LaNuff drift into the grand hall for the night's entertainment. Tonight's party is all for the honored guest Angelo.

Gwen drills Emon for every little tidbit of information she can glean about the stranger while feeling the Italian's eyes upon her, his gaze following her throughout the evening.

A feast of delectable food is served for the breathing, blood-pumping members of the assembly. The Vampires hang back from the dead carcasses of animals, fresh-baked bread, and vegetables with looks of distaste as though the enticing smells of food are repellant to them. They drink from their gold and crystal goblets, their lips stained red. Finally, the time for feasting is over, and the food is cleared away.

"Our guest of honor will treat us with one of his original compositions," Legion announces. Everyone stops and stares, their eyes locked on the confident form of Angelo as he crosses the room to stand near the piano.

Turning, he faces the congregation.

A boy with a blank-faced expression hurries to the Vampire's side wearing the red loincloth, marking him as a servant. He bows before Angelo, holding in his outstretched arms an ancient violin case. Angelo opens the case casually, pulling out an antique instrument varnished a stunning, deep scarlet. He removes the bow and closes the case. The servant scurries away to meld into the crowd. Angelo stands loose and at ease, positioning the blood-red violin under his chin, his bow at the ready.

He dives into his performance, wielding his instrument with an energy and mastery unlike anything Gwen has ever seen. He looks up amidst the music. Spying Gwen's face in the crowd of admirers, he gives her a wicked smile. Gwen feels her cheeks flush red hot. He must have seen something in her eyes, in her expression, that delighted him. She looks away, ducking behind the other guests.

Stop being an idiot, Gwen. He's just another Vampire. They all have that way about them. He's just teasing you. Besides, if you so much as think about smiling back, Legion will kill you. This dark thought sobers her instantly, for she knows the truth of it.

You can't hide from me, gorgeous, a voice speaks loud in her mind, interrupting her train of thought. Gwen gasps, stopping dead in her tracks.

Who are you? How did you get in my head? Gwen thinks these questions hesitantly, half-suspecting the answer.

I'm the stranger from which you're trying to hide. But you can't hide. I can feel you in the crowd. Come out where I can see you. The Italian's voice speaks to her, his words sending shivers down her spine.

Gwen hangs back, wandering in and out of the audience, listening to the sound of Angelo's brilliance, his fingers achieving their own kind of magic.

No. I'm happy where I am, thank you very much, Gwen retorts. *So you're a mind-reading, music-loving Vampire, then?*

Yes. Why? Haven't you ever met someone like yourself before?

No. I sort of thought I was one of a kind, she replies sadly.

You are one of a kind. And you're special. I can tell.

Gwen doesn't know what to say to this, so she says nothing, and a silence falls between them. She turns her attention to his music, letting it fill the void in her mind his absence leaves. It is an emptiness she has never known before.

Song after song, Angelo's genius impresses the assembly, none more than Gwen, who has always harbored a deep love for music. As a girl in St. Paul's Orphanage she found her only acceptance from the other students whilst singing in the choir. She never really believed in the words of the hymns, or the lessons in the Bible or the sermons, but she loved the rush that came over her when she sang. The music took her to new heights, her spirit soaring in the rafters of the chapel. Gwen's heart is in her throat, the nightingale inside her longing to burst forth. Her body longs to sway, to dance to the melody of his strings.

When she thinks she is unable to remain still a moment longer, the music stops. Applause erupts from her companions and she claps along, feeling lost in the moment as adrenaline dumping in her muscles.

"Bravo! Your skills continue to amaze, old man!" Legion bellows over the applause. The others quiet down to give their Lord the floor.

Angelo bows to Legion, a kind of arrogant swagger in the way he does it. Clearly he doesn't fancy himself inferior to the Lord of the Mount, but he has the good sense to show his friend a certain amount of respect in front of his subjects. "If it pleases you, grandfather, I thought I might accompany your beautiful songbird on the piano." He gives a wry smile at his old companion over the expanse of the room.

For a moment the citizens about the chamber seem to hold their collective breath, waiting for Legion's reaction. None had ever dared to insult or make a jest at the Lords' expense before, not even one as slight as this.

"Excellent notion!" Legion replies, giving a little laugh, a sense of familiarity in their exchange.

Perhaps Angelo is not so respectful after all. Gwen reassesses the relationship between the two ancient creatures. *Are they really friends? If so, just how close are they?* It seems unwise to get caught in a tug of war between two supernatural beings. Silently, she decides to steer clear of them both until the musician makes his departure.

You can't hide from me forever, Gwenevere. Yes, he's my friend, but we're not so close that I wouldn't risk his friendship for a chance to become more intimately acquainted with you. You'll find that I can be very friendly, Angelo whispers inside Gwen's head. She is stunned into silence, a strange sensation of heat radiating from her southern region all the way up into her chest. She fights to contain the feeling.

Danielle, who had been sitting at Legion's feet with her head lying upon his knee, sits up, beaming up at him expectantly. Legion ignores her, gets to his feet, and scans the assembly looking for a familiar face.

"Gwenevere? Where are you, my love?"

Reaching out through the bond of the ring, Legion senses Gwen in the crowd. One moment he is standing before his throne, and the next he appears at Gwen's side, startling Gwen half out of her skin. She barely contains an outcry of alarm. Legion takes her by the elbow, the party guests parting before them as he leads her toward the open floor. At the first sight of the two of them emerging from the audience, Angelo's eyes lock on Gwen's.

An eternity seems to pass as she walks toward him, his gaze overwhelming everything else. She feels no one and nothing else in the room but her and Angelo. Her heart drums in her ears, her palms sweat, her breath catches in her throat, and for the life of her she cannot look away. When she stands before him, his tall, masculine frame hovers over her, his smoky eyes taking up her whole field of vision. A moment of intensity lingers between them, a lifetime caught in one another's eyes.

We are the same, you and I. I promise you, the two of us shall become one, he tells her with silent lips, communicating with provocative images in her mind.

He smiles, and the world begins to spin once more. Gwen lets out the breath caught in her lungs and finally breaks eye contact. She turns to her husband and forces a genial smile up at the pale, blond Vampire Lord.

"What shall I sing?" Gwen asks in as pleasant a tone as she can muster.

"Whatever you like, my dear. Angelo is well acquainted with all music from all eras. I dare say he knows as much about the humans as yourself. He has lived many a year amongst them performing as an entertainer. He's even been in quite a few bands playing what you call rock 'n' roll." He gives his friend a smirk of amusement. They exchange a look that seems to say, "We agreed to disagree on this subject a long time ago."

"You name it, I can play it. On any instrument you like," Angelo adds, a self-satisfied smile touching his perfect lips.

"How about *Phantom of the Opera*?" Gwen asks. "'Think of Me,' perhaps?"

Angelo smirks at this and takes his place at the golden piano. Legion nods and takes his place back on his throne across the massive room leaving Gwen to stand alone.

What a befitting choice. Think of me as your angel of darkness, your Phantom, and you'll be my Christine, my angel of music. Gwen hears the laughter in Angelo's voice. She tries not to smile.

Just play the song, piano man. Stop trying to flirt with me. I know how your kind works and I won't give in to your charm.

Angelo begins to play, his fingers as deft on the piano keys as they were on the violin strings. His hands seem to dance to the very music they are creating. Letting the music take hold of her, Gwen allows herself to forget the enormous crowd of creatures before her and begins to sing. Her voice rivals that of the famous female Broadway vocalist, her performance moving all that hear her voice.

"Think of me, think of me fondly

When we've said goodbye

Remember me once in a while

Please promise me, you'll try ..."

Gwen is so caught up in the melody that she almost stumbles over her words. Then Angelo begins to sing along with her. She realizes that he is taking the male part of the song, forgetting that it is really a duet and not a solo. Trying to hide her embarrassment she looks to Angelo, who looks back at her, singing while he plays, as if he were singing the words just for her.

"Long ago, it seems so long ago

How young and innocent we were

She may not remember me

But I remember her..."

He sings as beautifully as he plays, his tone rich and warm. *Michael Crawford, eat your heart out,* she thinks, silently. She thinks she can hear Angelo laughing in response in her head.

She joins in at her cue, and together, they sing. She doesn't bother to look into the crowd, and he doesn't bother to look down at his hands as they play the hauntingly beautiful melody on the piano's enchanted keys. They sing the remainder of the song as if they are singing to each other, only breaking eye contact when the last notes are played and the last words sung.

The assembly erupts with cheers and applause.

Before Gwen knows it, dawn fast approaches. Legion dismisses her from the gathering. Gwen says her goodbyes. She turns and leaves the grand chamber, feeling the sensation of eyes upon her back as she walks down the hall. She stops and looks over her shoulder. There, standing in the doorway, is Angelo. He smiles at her, bowing his head in a playful sign of respect. Gwen gives him a little wave in farewell before heading back to her own bedroom way down below into the bowels of the mountain.

Time for all the things that go bump in the night to go to bed, she thinks to herself.

Except for me, of course. I never sleep. Maybe I should come and visit your room?" Gwen finds the sensation of Angelo in her head strangely comforting, almost as if he were her conscience.

I don't think so. I'm pretty sure my... I'm pretty sure Legion wouldn't like that.

I don't care what he thinks. He isn't my *Lord. But let's not talk about him, tell me what you think? What do* you *want?* Angelo seems genuinely interested in her by the tone of his voice, but Gwen can't trust someone she can't see. The very fact that she was carrying on a conversation with someone separated from her by miles of granite is startling.

I think you're a complete stranger, and I want to go to bed and be left alone, Gwen replies, so tired all of sudden that she doesn't have it in her to flirt. She descends a flight of stairs toward the servant level.

If you just give me a chance, I promise you'll fall in love with me. Just wait and see.

Are you always this confident? Gwen asks, laughing at his candor.

Yes. Do you always play this hard to get?

No, I'm not hard to get. I'm unobtainable. Especially for you. Now stop pestering me. You might not need sleep but I definitely do. I am a mortal, after all. In fact, it's kind of our thing.

Fine, he says, chuckling. *Until tomorrow, then. Goodnight, my angel,* he whispers.

Gwen enters her cold, little room, exhausted. *Goodnight, my stalker,* she whispers back, and cuts off the connection, throwing up mental walls around her consciousness for privacy. She undresses and gets into bed, a mischievous smile on her lips. With a sigh, Gwen lies down on the bed, her emotions a confused mess of the rational and irrational, but she doesn't care.

She closes her eyes and lets her mind get swept away with girlish fantasies of romance, danger, and a hero named Angelo.

CHAPTER SIXTEEN

Morning Dew

With Ivan hovering behind her like a pale-faced shadow, Gwen raps her fist against the cold, stone surface of the door before her. She fights the urge to reach out mentally into the room beyond to touch minds with the man within. *I won't let him in again,* Gwen reminds herself. *I acted foolishly. I must keep my mind closed off. Sooner or later he'll leave this place, and things will go back to the way they were.* The thought should comfort her but it doesn't. Conflicting emotions boil within her. *I can't get attached. After all, he's one of them.*

The door is thrown open and Gwen finds herself looking up into Angelo's handsome face and tousled, brown, curly hair. His gray and smoky eyes smolder. Along with a pair of faded blue jeans, he wears a white, collared shirt left half unbuttoned, his sculpted chest visible. His feet are bare. He flashes Gwen a crooked little smile, and she gives an inward sigh.

"I'm here for my lesson," Gwen says, a nervous note in her voice. "I'm not early, am I? We did agree to meet at eight?"

"No, I was expecting you. You're right on time. Come in." He steps aside to allow her admittance into his chamber. She steps inside, her eyes inspecting the room.

His chamber is beautifully furnished with a canopy bed, nightstand, desk, armoire, and a small table with two chairs all in a deep mahogany finish. On his bed, a black overnight bag sits open, his clothing and other personal possessions neatly laid out. His old violin case lies nearby, along with a stack of loose papers with musical scales and notes scribbled by hand. The room is otherwise neat and orderly. His servants, two young human boys, kneel in the corner, reminding Gwen of her own former maidservants.

Ivan attempts to enter the room, but is blocked by Angelo. "You won't be needed, 'ol chap. She's safe with me." He slaps Ivan good-naturedly on the shoulder. Ivan doesn't return Angelo's carefree smile. Instead he looks as if he's about to protest, but Angelo coolly turns his back on him, shutting the door in his face.

Gwen stifles a laugh. Upon her last sight of him, the look on Ivan's face is priceless. She has never seen anyone treat Ivan so nonchalantly before.

"Wow, I'm guessing you two aren't friends." Gwen laughs.

"Nope," Angelo smiles wickedly. "Shall we get started?" He doesn't bother to button up his shirt, not that she minds too much.

He takes a seat at the table and indicates the chair across from him. Gwen sits.

Angelo whistles sharply, and the two boy servants' jump to their feet to do his bidding. "Bring the violin to me, and then get lost, boys," he commands.

One of the servants rushes to the table with the requested instrument, bowing as he hands it to his Vampire master. Angelo takes the violin and places it on the table. The young men exit, bowing and scraping as they go. Angelo ignores them, turning his gaze to Gwen. They are completely alone. Gwen feels anxiety swelling in her chest.

They look at each other across the table. She senses him mentally trying to enter her thoughts, pushing at the walls surrounding her consciousness.

"Why are you shutting me out?" he says aloud.

"Look, I know you're Legion's friend and all, but that doesn't mean you and I need to be friendly. I actually really enjoy music so it doesn't bother me that I have to come here every day and learn from you. I'm here because I want to be. Not because he told me to, and not because of you." Gwen folds her arms across her chest for emphasis.

"Okay." Angelo grins. He leans forward to take Gwen's left hand in his, the fabric of his shirt sagging to reveal a toned pectoral and a perfect brown areola. The sight makes her heartbeat quicken. He smiles up at her knowingly.

"Things are to be strictly professional between us. Understand me?" she continues.

He nods. Turning her hand over palm side up, he traces the lines of her hand with his pinky finger. The feel of his cold skin on hers titillate her senses. He brings her hand to his mouth, kissing every one of her soft, delicate fingertips.

"I regret that we must damage these with calluses. Your skin is perfect," he whispers.

Gwen retracts her hand from his grasp. "All right, enough of that, Casanova. I'm not here to flirt." She picks up the violin gingerly, eyeing the instrument with interest. "If you're not going to take this seriously, then I'm leaving." She looks him square in the face, a stubborn set to her jaw.

"I apologize. You want a serious and straight-faced tutor, then I'm your man."

Gwen looks at him doubtfully. After a moment of consideration, she nods. Standing, she takes the violin and places it on her shoulder, putting her chin on the chinrest. "I hold it like this, right?"

"Right." Angelo stands and walks behind her. He adjusts her position slightly so that she stands erect, the neck of the violin tilted upward. He hands her the bow. She takes it from him silently. "First, you'll have to learn the basic chords." He steps behind her once more, wrapping his arms around her body. He places his hand over top of her left shoulder atop the neck of the violin, taking her right hand holding the bow to position it above the strings.

Gwen's heart beats violently, his body pressed firmly against her back. His embrace is almost intimate. She feels a slight pressure at the base of her spine, accompanied by a gentle throbbing. Realizations dawn on her with a click in her brain, the mental image taking shape without her volition.

"So was I in your dreams last night? Because you were in mine," Angelo whispers with his cold breath in her ear and upon her neck.

Gwen's face goes red with mortification and suppressed lust. In a huff, she wriggles out of his embrace, pivoting on her heel to flee from him. She tosses the violin on the bed, not wanting to hurt the instrument no matter how mad she might be at its owner, and races to the door. She comes up short when she finds Angelo suddenly standing before her, barring her route of escape.

"Look, I'm sorry. I got carried away." He is honestly repentant, his voice sincere. "Please don't leave. I guess being alone with you excites me." The truth of this is evident from the impressive bulge in his jeans. Gwen pretends not to notice.

"Just act your age and we won't have any problems, all right?" she retorts, exasperated.

"Of course," he smiles pleasantly.

Gwen lets out her breath. "Thank you."

"Speaking of age…how old are you, if you don't mind my asking?"

"Fourteen. Why, how old do I look?"

"With that figure? Seventeen, at least." He openly looks her up and down appraisingly, a greedy little smile spreading across his lips.

"Oh, please. Even if I were older, you'd still be a dirty old man hitting on someone far younger than you," she says with righteous indignation.

"That means you get to benefit from my wisdom and experience. I know how pedantic this place can be. Allow me to liven it up for you."

Gwen ignores this comment. "I told you my age. Aren't you going to tell me yours?" she asks, her hands on her hips.

"I'm two hundred forty-four years-old. Why? Is age important to you?" he asks curiously.

"I don't know. I've never really thought about it." She pauses, reflecting, adding, "Aren't you just a little bit ashamed to find out you are trying to seduce a minor?"

"Not at all. I'm a Vampire. That kind of thing isn't important to us. When I was mortal, you would be considered grown up at sixteen and married already. Fourteen or seventeen, it doesn't matter. I'll have you either way." Angelo raises his eyebrows at her suggestively, grabbing Gwen by the waist and pulling her toward him.

Before she knows what's happening, he has her entangled in his arms, pressed up against his chest, his lips finding hers. The kiss sends icicles shooting through her blood and heat shooting from her groin. He parts her lips with his tongue, exploring the inside of her mouth, tickling her tongue with his. Gwen feels her body giving in. She fights the urge to cling to him, to press herself firmly against him. Melding into his body will take over her powers of reason. She shoves away from him, struggling free, gasping for breath as their lips part and their bodies separate. She pushes him firmly away from the door. Flinging it open, she turns on her heels and glowers at him. "Grow up!" She slams the door behind her.

She can hear a deep rumble of laughter behind her, but she doesn't care. She ignores the laughter and Ivan's questions, not caring that she's acting like a child, and storms off to her room. With a slightly bruised ego and a heart rate through the roof, Gwen proclaims to herself, *I want nothing to do with Vampires, most of all pompous sex fiends named Angelo!*

* * * * *

Gwen sits with her back straight, her eyes focused on the sheet music before her as her fingers play across the golden piano's black and white keys. She ignores the others in the grand hall, diligently practicing the piece of music that her tutor gave as this week's homework. Over the past six weeks, Gwen has studied under Angelo's tutelage, covering the basics of the violin, the piano, and the acoustic guitar. Her progress has surpassed everyone's expectations. She hates to admit it, but Angelo's suggestion of learning through telepathy seems to be paying off. The method requires the two of them to have rather intimate mental contact. She finds it difficult to keep her thoughts from straying, especially with such an attractive distraction hanging around. *Imagine trying to convince a man you're not interested in him when he knows all the dirty fantasies you're having in your head in which he is the star.* Gwen maintains a detached attitude toward him despite it all. To his credit, Angelo has behaved himself admirably since her first lesson aside from the occasional wagging of eyebrows and sexual innuendo.

Gwen can feel everyone's eyes on her back, but she's used to having an audience by now. She plays the last measure beautifully, with the confidence of a seasoned musician. Legion applauds loudly, his two ardent admirers Danielle and Ivan showing arrogant indifference for Gwen's talent. They applaud insincerely along with their Master nonetheless. Angelo stands next to the massive golden instrument, beaming with pride over his clever pupil. Gwen bows her head in humble acceptance of their praise, rising from the piano bench to take her leave for her daily nap. Ivan steps forward, prepared to do his duty as her guard and escort Gwen to her chambers.

Abruptly, one of the large granite doors opens, admitting one of the Ogre guards inside. Everyone stops to watch as he approaches Legion's throne. The Lord looks up at his underling with mild interest. "Yes?"

"The Vampire child, Lynette, requests entrance into your court, my Lord." The guard bows his head slightly in respect, his eyes cast to the floor as he awaits Legion's decision.

Legion examines his long, manicured fingernails as if he has all the time in the world. "I haven't summoned her. What does she want?"

"She says she has a surprise for you. A 'sacrificial offering,' she called it," the Ogre speaks in his deep, rumbling voice.

"Hmm. Very well, she may be allowed to enter." Legion dismisses him with a wave of his hand. The guard hurries away.

A moment later, the doors are flung open wide to admit a chubby figure with short curly hair and gray, soulless eyes. Lynette looks uncharacteristically happy. She carries a small, brown, leather bag with a drawstring holding it shut. Something moves frantically inside it.

"My Lord! Look what I caught just now while on the hunt." She comes up to her Master's massive golden chair and holds the little brown sack out to him. Lynette's face beaming with pride, her fangs gleam in the light whilst she radiates with excitement.

Legion takes the wiggling bag from her cautiously. He quirks an eyebrow at her. "What are you up to, Lynette? This isn't another bat, is it? I've told you before that I don't share your taste for animals."

"No, no, it's nothing like that. Be careful—it's a feisty little devil," she answers gleefully, her teeth showing white in her wicked little smile.

"Gwen, come here." Immediately, Gwen feels her body obey without her volition, moving by the force of the ring upon her wedding finger to bring her next to Lynette, before Legion's throne. "Be ready to confine the creature should it try to escape," he commands. Gwen gathers the flow of magic around her, preparing a spell for controlling air and space.

The instant Legion undoes the drawstring of the pouch in his hand, something bolts out, whizzing through the air like a blue streak of light. It flies with such speed that Gwen can hardly keep her eye on it, let alone cast a spell upon it. She needs to focus her magic on the creature for the spell to work.

"Capture it, you fool!" Lynette orders. She ducks as the blue Fairy dives toward the little Vampire's head. Legion laughs uproariously, watching everyone dart away from the angry little creature buzzing above them. Gwen watches as the blue blur moves about the room like a bee, looking for a window or an exit to the outside world.

Gwen feels Angelo's warm presence outside her mental shield, gently pressing against the magic, keeping him outside as if he were mentally knocking on her front door asking to come in. Gwen glances over at the Italian Vampire, who responds with a pleading look. She sighs, nodding, and lets her guard down, allowing him admittance into her inner world.

What is it? Gwen asks silently.

It won't let me into her thoughts. It doesn't trust Vampires. Why don't you try? She'll listen to you.

Why would she trust me? Gwen asks incredulously.

Because you're a Wiccan. Fairies are the Wiccans' only true ally. Your ancestors took an oath when their alliance was forged that they would never speak a lie to one another, Angelo explains.

You mean I can't lie to her, and she can't lie to me? Seriously?

Exactly. Now, would you talk her down, please? She's starting to make me dizzy, Angelo admits.

I'll try. Gwen severs the connection, immediately shutting him out once more. Angelo gives her an exasperated look. She ignores this and turns her mind toward the Fairy, which still flies frantically about the grand chamber like a lightning bug trapped in a glass jar.

Gwen approaches the Fairies' conscious with hesitance, focusing on the creature's brilliant rainbow aura. She senses the mythical being's life force is wild, fearless, and strong—a stubborn will mixed with a childlike vitality and passion for life. The creature, alert for danger, immediately senses Gwen's mind seeking out her own. The Fairy suddenly stops mid-loop-de-loop and halts in the air, looking from face to face for the Wiccan. In her panicked state, she completely missed the presence of the two breathing, blood-pumping members of the group.

The Fairy looks first at Danielle, and then at Gwen. When her eyes alight on her, Gwen sees instant recognition upon the small, blue, feminine face. She opens her mind to Gwen without hesitation. Her demeanor relaxes at the knowledge that a Wiccan is present. Gwen notices that the Fairy's aura becomes less chaotic in its rhythm and movement until it becomes nothing more than a pulsating hum, soothing and peaceful like a hummingbird hovering over a lush petunia garden.

Don't be afraid. I am a friend. Gwen sends the message through the channel connecting her mind with the Fairy's.

"What's happening? Why is it staring at the Witch like that?" Lynette demands, glaring at Gwen.

"She's talking to it telepathically," Angelo and Ivan say simultaneously. They give each other a strange look and then go back to staring at the blue Fairy.

"It's frightening. I thought Fairies were nice, sweet little things," Danielle chirps, her tone like a whiny little girl's. Legion gives her a condescending pat on the head for reassurance.

Gwen ignores all this and focuses on the small creature's thoughts, trying to decipher the images and memories she sees in her mind. She sees far off lands, strange beasts, and hundreds of little blue faces.

Who are you? Did they catch you, too? I'm going to tear that little bloodsucker's eyes out! What do they want with me? How do I get out of here? My brother will never let me live this down for as long as I live. He'll go on and on about what a fool I am for the next hundred years! Her thoughts pour into Gwen's brain like water overflowing from a boiling pot. Gwen struggles not to drown in it, barely managing to understand her thoughts before the Fairy dives into a whole new topic in a most nonsensical manner.

Whoa! Slow down, I can't keep up with you. If you would just stop thinking for a minute, I could hear myself think and answer some of your questions, Gwen tells her mentally.

Oh, sorry, I didn't mean to confuse you. I haven't talked to a Wiccan in a while. I forgot your kind doesn't think as quickly as we do.

That's all right. I've never communicated with a Fairy before. What's your name? Gwen asks.

Morna of the Morning Dew, but my friends call me Morna. And you are?

Gwenevere. Gwen for short.

Nice to meet you, Gwen. So what do we do now? Are you their prisoner, too?

Everyone watches as the two of them converse telepathically, unblinking.

Kind of, Gwen continues. *I'm bound to the pale, blond Vampire, the one sitting on the throne. He's keeping me here against my will. He tricked me and married me without my knowledge of what was going on.* The words rush out of her just as easily as the Fairy's thoughts had. She is startled by her own candor. Here she is, telling a complete stranger about the most mortifying experience of her life as if it were common place. *Whoever cast the truth oath spell between the Fairies and Wiccans must have been a powerful Witch,* Gwen marvels.

The Fairy giggles inwardly. *You're a funny Witch.*

Look, we have to be serious now, understand? There isn't time for any chitchat.

You are right. Tell me what the pale eyes wants then, Gwen.

Gwen turns to Legion, as the others all stare at her

expectantly. "She wants to know what you want with her," Gwen tells the Vampire Lord.

"To drink her blood, of course." Lynette interrupts Legion, who was about to speak. He shoots her an angry look, and she wilts before his cold face, shutting her mouth and casting her eyes downward.

No! They can't have my blood! You have to protect me, Sister Witch. My people would risk their lives for your freedom if you help me obtain mine. Please! the little creature begs urgently.

What can I do? Legion controls me through our wedding bands. He can wield magic through me like a living magic wand. I am helpless. Believe me, I want to help you, but I can't see any way out of this. Gwen's shame radiates through their mental connection. The Fairy seems to sympathize with her plight.

Legion coughs aloud to get Gwen's attention. Gwen reluctantly looks into her Master's face, afraid of the command she knows is about to be spoken.

"Seize the Fairy and bring her to me, my beloved. It would please me greatly." He speaks in a light thoughtless manner, the Fairy's life a thing of insignificance to him.

"What will you do with her? Will you drain her? Do you honestly think I can stand by and watch you kill one of our own kind? I don't condone murder, but I understand now how our kind feels about humans. I've made my peace with the murders I've witnessed here in the past, but this I cannot allow. Aren't we brothers and sisters? Aren't we all descendants of the same mother and father? Is nothing sacred to you?" Gwen demands, staring her Master in the eyes with defiance.

The room has gone silent. Everyone stares at her in utter shock and amazement. No one has ever spoken to Legion this way. Gwen never has either, especially not in front of his subjects. Danielle and the other Vampires turn to watch Legion's reaction. Gwen waits for her punishment.

Legion's face goes still, his whole body rigid. He sits frozen, his eyes staring at Gwen. The pale white mist of his eyes grows dark gray and hazy, manifesting the rage boiling within. In a flash, Legion stands before Gwen. He strikes her across the face with bone-shattering force. A blinding light shoots behind her eyes at the pain and the room spins as the impact of the blow knocks Gwen down to the floor. Angelo appears at her side, catching her in his arms before she hits the ground.

"Don't interfere!" Legion hisses at Angelo. "She is my wife and she will do as I say!" His roaring words fill the grand hall, echoing everywhere off the stone walls.

"She's only a girl. She's ignorant of these things. I'll take her to her room. Let Ivan deal with the Fairy," Angelo says calmly. He cradles Gwen in his arms. She presses her face up against his neck to hide her tear-stained cheeks, not wanting Legion to see her cry. Gwen pretends to be unconscious even though she knows her Master can sense otherwise.

Come on, Gwen, hurt him. You could if you just tried hard enough. Maybe you can overcome the power of the ring, she tells herself. She reaches out to the magic and instantly feels darkness surround her. He has already blocked her from her power. The emptiness that fills her is overwhelming. She tries again, willing the darkness to dissipate, trying to reach past the mist that surrounds her mind to grasp the source of all creation beyond, but she can't. Instead, she feels an invisible fist clench her heart. The pain racks her body. She gasps aloud as the excruciating pain makes her numb to the world. She admits defeat and withdraws into herself, the torture of the ring vanishing as her spirit breaks. She cries silent sobs into Angelo's shoulder.

Legion lets out a strange guttural sound in frustration, sounding almost animal in nature. "Get her out of my sight!" He dismisses Angelo with a wave of his hand, turning his back on them. "Ivan, get that thing down. I'm hungry."

Gwen tries not to call out in protest. She knows it's useless. They won't listen to her, for they know nothing of compassion. They are Vampires, soulless creatures of the night, beings born of blood and death.

Angelo turns and carries Gwen toward the door. He calls out to the guards on the other side for the doors to open. Gwen hears the stone doors scrape against the granite floor as the Ogres push them open to allow them to leave. She doesn't dare look up, or to look over Angelo's shoulder, too afraid of what she might see.

I'm sorry. I tried. I'm a pathetic excuse for a Witch, Gwen moans regretfully to Morna the Fairy, feeling the creature in the room behind her as the Italian carries her from the room and down the hall.

No. You are braver than many I have met before. Don't worry about me. I've gotten out of worse situations than this. Vampires aren't as tough as they think they are, Morna says reassuringly. She senses love and warmth through their mental bond, feeling a new kinship to this being.

Good luck. Oh, and while you're tearing Lynette's eyes out, could you get rid of Ivan and Legion for me, too? That would really help me out. The fearless and optimistic energy of the Fairy is so contagious, Gwen can't help but jest. Hope begins to brew from within. *Maybe,* she thinks, *all is not lost after all.*

No problem. And when I'm done with the pale eyes, I'll come and find you, Morna tells her lightheartedly. *We'll bust out of this joint together. You'll see.* Morna severs the connection between them, leaving Gwen to her own thoughts once again.

Gwen feels laughter inside her chest. She contains it, fearing that Angelo will think she's gone mad, crying one moment and laughing the next. She hopes against hope that the little Fairy is as strong as she is fearless.

* * * * *

Angelo carries Gwen silently to the servant's level of the fortress, bringing her to her own bedroom door. The hallway is empty, save for them. Gently, he sets her on her feet. Gwen looks up into his face, tears dried upon her cheeks, her eyes red, her skin

pale from the pain she has suffered. To Angelo she couldn't be lovelier. His heart aches in a way that he's long forgotten. Emotions torment him, emotions that Angelo the immortal has never felt before. Only Angelo the mortal knew this kind of love, respect, and desire.

"Don't worry about the Fairy. I'll take care of it." He takes Gwen's chin in his hand, stroking his thumb below her lower lip. "Think of it as a gift, a token of my affection." He leans in and places the lightest of kisses upon her lips, barely brushing her lips with his. He turns and walks away, leaving Gwen staring after him in bewilderment.

* * * * *

Gwen awakens with a start. She sits up in bed, clutching her blankets to her chest in fear. All at once she is overwhelmed with the sensation of being watched, her supernatural perception alerting her to the presence of someone lurking in the pitch blackness of her bedchamber.

"Who's there? I know someone is here. I can feel your mind, even if I can't hear your thoughts," she speaks aloud into the dark. She could easily use a spell to light the lantern and illuminate the room, or form an orb of fire in the air, but Legion would feel her use magic even in the smallest degree, and he has made it perfectly clear how he feels about her casting spells without his permission.

"Don't be afraid. I brought you something." Gwen hears

Angelo's voice just inches from her ear. She jumps half out of her skin, letting out a yelp in alarm. Immediately, Angelo clamps a hand over her mouth to stifle her shout. "Shhh. You're going to wake everyone up. If anyone knew I was in here alone with you at this hour, it wouldn't be good for either of us," he warns. Gwen nods in understanding. He slowly removes his hand from her mouth.

"What are you doing here, you lunatic?" she says in a harsh whisper.

"Bringing my fair maiden a token of my love," he whispers back, his face lost in the dark room. He grabs her hand without needing to grope around in the dark. She feels him place something small into her open palm.

"What is it?" she asks as she closes her hand around the object. It feels cold, like metal. The flat object fits perfectly from one end of her palm to the other.

"It's a copy of the key to Lynette's chamber. She has the fairy caged up, hidden within," As he whispers, his lips press against her ear, his cold breath sending a shiver through her. All of a sudden, she is aware of his body's nearness, and her heartbeat quickens.

"What? I don't understand." She turns her face toward him, knowing this will bring their lips close. He doesn't move, but stays dangerously close to her, their faces so close that their noses touch.

"I convinced Lynette and the others that it might be an interesting experiment to see how long it takes a Fairy to starve to death. Her blood will taste just as potent when she's at the brink of death as it will when she's healthy, so they agreed to keep her caged up and torture her for their amusement." She feels, rather than sees, him smile at his own genius.

"That's horrible! Why would you do that and then come to tell me about it? I thought you said you'd help, not make things worse!" Gwen says, outraged, but still trying to keep her voice down.

"No, I said that to buy us time. I couldn't just walk in there and demand they release the thing. They would think I'd lost my mind or gone soft on them," he explains, taking her other hand in his. "This way we can wait for the right time to free her, and make it look like she escaped on her own. That way no one suspects either of us, and your little Fairy goes free."

"Oh. Well, I guess that's a pretty good solution. It's better than nothing," she admits. She looks down to where their hands clasp. She imagines feeling his cold skin against her warm flesh, what it would feel like to lie naked in each other's arms. She gives herself an inward shake, dispelling the image and returning to reality. "Thank you so much. It means a lot to me."

"You're welcome. I'd do anything to earn your love." He lets go of her hand and cradles her face between his two large, cold hands. This time she doesn't pull away. "Tell me what I can do to make you love me."

"I don't hate you. I just don't trust you," Gwen laughs lightly.

"I can work on that. Just as long as you don't find me completely repulsive." He chuckles, and she finds the sound

soothing to her ears.

"I just don't see why you're going through all this trouble for me."

"I know perfection when I see it. Something as beautiful and as rare as you deserves to be worshiped, not enslaved." He leans in and offers her a gentle kiss, sweet and kind. Gwen feels his arms encircle her, surprised at how easily her body fits with his. Just when she thinks of giving in and kissing him back with all the suppressed desire inside her, he pulls away, letting her go.

"Where are you going?" Gwen asks, not able to conceal the disappointment in her voice.

"Back to my own room. Ivan would just love to catch me in here with you." He kisses her forehead and then recedes into the darkness of the night. "Goodnight, my love," he whispers.

"Don't call me that. That's *his* name for me. Just call me Gwen. I don't need a pet name. It's degrading."

"Anything you ask of me, I will do." Gwen hears the door open and for a moment she sees the light of the lanterns in the hall illuminate Angelo's silhouette in the doorway. He steps into the hallway and she sees him in the light for the first time. He wears nothing but a tight pair of boxer briefs, leaving absolutely nothing to the imagination. His bare chest and arms are perfectly sculpted, with a washboard stomach, the very image of a Greek god in a Calvin Klein underwear commercial. He smiles at her as he pulls the door shut. "Goodnight, Gwenevere," he says. The door closes, shutting him out of her view and dismissing the light from the room, leaving her in the darkness once more.

Gwen can't sleep. Her mind is wide awake, buzzing with thoughts of Angelo and Morna the Fairy. At last she gives up trying to sleep and instead makes an orb of light that hovers just over her head as she gets out of bed and moves over to her desk. Pulling out her sketchbook Gwen opens to a blank page and begins to scribble out various rescue plans. As she does, she works out every possible obstacle and dilemma. If she can't save herself from this hellhole, at least she can try and save Morning Dew.

CHAPTER SEVENTEEN

The Face of Reality

A few days later, the large domed courtyard teams with the citizens of Bec LaNuff. Everyone goes about their daily lives. None of them give so much as a second glance at the red-cloaked figure that walks among them, making its way toward the upper level of the fortress. If any of them suspected that the Lady of the Mountain—the Wiccan Child Bride of the Master—was hidden within that crimson cloak, they would have immediately raised an alarm. Lord Legion made it a law that the Wiccan called Gwen must never be allowed to roam the mountain alone. She had to be accompanied at all times, guarded for her own safety and for the safety of others. For this reason, Legion made Ivan her bodyguard and constant shadow.

In her disguise, Gwen is invisible to them, just another servant off to do her Master's bidding. Not all the human servants are considered beautiful of face and body, and thus are required to wear long red robes and hoods to cover their unsightly appearances.

It's pretty hypocritical when you consider how ugly Ogres and Goblins are, and how nobody makes them hide their faces, Gwen reflects as she casually traverses the stairs and passageways up to the Vampire wing.

What did you expect? Vampires are naturally shallow. They only like beautiful things. Besides, there isn't anything in the world that could hide the ugliness of Ogres and Goblins, Angelo comments in reply, hearing Gwen's inner-most thoughts through the open mental connection between them.

Gwen laughs. She comes to the open landing just before the grand hall and the large hallways on either side, the left leading to the Dwarf's quarters and the right leading to the Vampire wing. Gwen pauses only briefly, trying to imagine Angelo and the other Vampires mingling within. She recently found out that while she is sent away for her daily "nap" Legion has all his Vampire minions congregate in the grand hall.

"This is the perfect time for us to steal the Fairy from Lynette," Angelo had explained to her earlier. "Everyone will think you're sleeping. Ivan won't be guarding your door because he'll be at the meeting as well. It's perfect."

Gwen asked Angelo what exactly went on in these "Vampire Only" meetings. He told her that it wasn't anything important, just typical Vampire politics, nothing of interest to a Wiccan.

Gwen bows her head low, letting her red hood cover her face. Not that it matters, because the Ogres guarding the Grand Hall would pay no attention to a servant anyway. Letting out a sigh of relief, she continues down the right passageway. No Vampires wander the hall and she makes it to Lynette's bedroom without incident.

I'm there. Are you sure you can keep her busy? Gwen asks through their mental bond.

Yes, I'm telling her all about VWWIII, Angelo replies.

Nice! You're telling her about killing Witches, aren't you? That's really sensitive of you, Angelo, Gwen chides him sarcastically.

In his own defense, he says, *That was before I met you. Back then I didn't know Witches could be so cute.* Gwen rolls her eyes at this, wondering if Angelo senses it. He lets her know that he does.

Gwen takes a deep breath to gather her courage and pulls the key out one of the pockets in the red cloak. She fits it into the lock. Turning the knob, Gwen pushes the door open. She slips quickly inside the room, trespassing into Lynette's personal oasis.

The room is much like the bedchamber Gwen lived in when she first came to the mountain. The large stone room has beautiful furniture and ornate décor, linens, and accessories. It's a little messy, with clothing strewn about. Gwen is surprised to find a woman's bra carelessly draped over the back of a chair.

Why on earth does Lynette need a bra? She's got the body of a child, Gwen wonders to herself. She feels guilty for the thought.

Lynette never complains about being stuck for all eternity in child form. Perhaps she hides her frustration under that cold, condescending persona. That would explain part of why she hates Gwen so much, with her long legs, budding feminine beauty, and generous curves. *She's jealous,* Gwen realizes. The thought almost makes her feel sorry for the little Vampire, but then Gwen remembers the countless cruel things she has seen the little monster do, and the feeling instantly evaporates.

Lynette's servants hadn't been in to clean yet. According to Angelo, the servants were due to clean the Vampire's rooms within fifteen minutes, so she had a small window of time in which to find the Fairy and release her.

When a Vampire drinks a Fairy's blood, they inherit its magical powers for a brief period, sometimes lasting a couple days to a couple of months depending on the strength of the Fairy. According to Emon, several thousands of years ago the Vampires discovered this, and they began hunting down the fairies, destroying their villages, effectively killing off entire colonies in one sweep. The Fairies fought back, declaring war on the blood-sucking monsters, and the outcome had been disastrous for both sides.

Emon had told her that Fairies were an endangered species. Gwen assumed this was because of humans cutting down rainforests and building strip malls everywhere they pleases, but Vampires were responsible for this depletion. Gwen learned this from Emon's book of records called *The Great Wars of the*

Children of Cain.

Stop daydreaming, Gwen, and get your head straight, she commands herself. *Find the Fairy and get the hell out of here!*

Gwen expects to find the Fairy's cage in plain view, sitting on her nightstand or on the dresser, but the cage is nowhere in sight. Gwen grunts in frustration.

Reaching out with her mind, she searches the room for the Fairy's mental brainwaves. At first she almost misses it, her aura so weak and faint, but then she finds her. The cage is tucked on its side, hidden in one of the lower drawers of the large dresser. The only other thing in the drawer is a plate of old food, rotting and decaying just out of reach of the cage, but in clear view of the weak, starving Fairy.

Gwen is sickened at the sight of Morna's thin, pale, little body. She lies on the hard wires of the cage, as limp and lifeless as a wilting leaf. *I'm too late!* When she sees Morna's chest rise and fall with shallow breaths, she gives a sigh of relief.

Gently, she removes the cage from the drawer. She lays it on the floor. Searching her mind for the proper words, Gwen utters a spell, in the true tongue, praying silently that it's a small enough bit of magic so as not to be noticed by Legion. The cage unlocks with a click, and the door pops open. Very carefully Gwen reaches her hand into the cage and retrieves the small girl, her body as light as a butterfly's in her palm. Morna doesn't wake as Gwen stashes the little Fairy into her pocket for safe keeping. Gwen wishes she had a better place to put her, somewhere she wouldn't get jostled around too much, but her pocket is the best she can do for now.

Before replacing the cage back inside the bottom drawer, Gwen bends the cage to look as if Morna had broken out on her own. She leaves the drawer open just a crack, just big enough for a Fairy to climb out. She then quickly makes her exit.

With her heart racing and her palms sweating, Gwen hurries down the hallway as an army of human servants come bounding up the hall from the opposite direction. She averts her gaze so that she doesn't make eye contact with them as they pass her. She knows they are all brainwashed, zombified remnants of their former selves, but still she expects one of them to stop her, to call out for help, or chase her down. Nothing happens, and before she knows it, she finds herself in the servants' quarters once more.

She opens her bedroom door and dashes inside, feeling safe again once the door is securely shut behind her and the lock is bolted.

Gwen crosses the room and sits on her bed. She removes the still- unconscious Morna from her cloak pocket and lays her gently on her pillow. She looks so pathetic, yet peaceful. Gwen can't help but relate to her, to feel as if she knows her and understands her, even though they are practically strangers. Maybe it is the old vows of their ancestors that draws her to the Fairy, or perhaps the fact that they are both prisoners in this dreadful place. Whatever it is, Gwen makes a silent promise to protect Morna, whatever the cost.

* * * * *

When the Fairy is found missing, Lynette, in a magnificent rage, demands that a search is made of the entire fortress, starting with Gwen's bedchamber. Gwen humbly lets Ivan and Lynette enter her quarters and stands aside as they ransack her room. They find no sign of the Fairy. Lynette gives Gwen a suspicious glare before stomping out of the room to continue her search for her lost captive. Ivan looks about Gwen's ruined room and gives a laugh. He steps over a broken chair and an overturned table on his way out the door.

Gwen waits a minute or two before slamming the bedroom door shut and hurrying to the Fairy's hiding place. She sits on her bed and opens the little jewel box on her nightstand. Lynette had removed every last piece of jewelry from the box and thrown it around the room, but thankfully had left the box itself alone. Using a fingernail, she pries up the black felt bottom of the box, which opens a lid to a smaller compartment underneath. Morna lies there, asleep on a bed made of torn bits of cloth. The Fairy is tucked inside a sock-like sleeping bag. Gwen retrieves a couple torn scraps of bread from her pocket and sets them aside where the Fairy can reach them should she get hungry. Gwen finds a thimble in her old duffle bag inside a small sewing kit. She takes it over to the picture of water sitting on her dresser and fills is with a couple drops of water, setting this inside with the Fairy as well.

She doesn't want to leave the little thing in the dark, but she also can't have the jewelry box sitting open in case someone

comes into her room unannounced. Gwen imagines Morna waking up every morning in her dark little compartment, as if in a coffin. Gwen asks Angelo mentally to find something small that would glow in the dark and give the Fairy light. Angelo agrees. This comforts Gwen a bit, and she closes the secret compartment, and closes the jewelry box completely.

This done, Gwen looks about her room. "It looks like a hurricane just passed through," Gwen remarks to herself. With a groan, she gets up and starts to clean up. A few things are broken, but it is a small price to pay for her new friend's safety. When the room is orderly again, Gwen gets ready for her daily music lesson.

She brushes her long, silky hair into a high bun on her head. She wears a long green tunic with loose, comfortable cream-colored slacks underneath. She slips on a pair of wicker sandals. Gwen stops to examine her reflection in the mirror, satisfied at how grown up and sophisticated she looks, "I'm not dressing up for him," she tells herself, knowing it's a lie.

She smiles and hurries toward the door, stopping for a book on her nightstand that needs to be returned to Emon. She grabs her guitar case from its place by her closet, and fitting the strap of the bag over her shoulder, leaves her chamber.

Ivan comes down the hall just as she exits her room, annoying and on time as always, to escort her about the fortress, as if she didn't already know every room and passageway in the place. The temporary freedom of wandering around in servants' robes is still fresh in Gwen's mind and she tries not to feel bitter about it. If she could have, she would have kept the red servants' cloak that Angelo stole, but the robe belonged to one of Lucca's servants. Eventually, it would've been missed, and suspicions raised if he hadn't returned it immediately.

Grumbling to herself about Vampires and their stupid rules, Gwen meets up with Ivan.

"Aren't you supposed to be on a search party right now?" Gwen asks.

"Lucca took over for me. Mark me word, Lynette won't stop looking for that vermin."

Gwen ignores this and continues on toward her destination. Ivan falls in step with her. From the corner of her eye she sees Ivan give her a quick once-over with his silver, metallic eyes with a taunting smile.

"What's this, Princess? Going to meditate in a temple, or are we tryin' to impress someone?"

Gwen looks down at her clothing. She has to admit the outfit does make her look just a little bit Hindu. All she needs is a sari and a red dot painted on her forehead and the look would be complete. She aimed for a look of sophistication, to make her look older than she is. *For myself, of course, not for Angelo,* she insists again mentally.

"They're just clothes, Ivan. You know how little I care for fashion. Besides, there isn't anybody worth the effort, so obviously I'm not trying to impress anyone!"

"Right, love. Of course. I'll just 'ave to tell the Master that 'e

isn't worth your consideration, won't I? You're just jealous that 'e took all your pretty things away and gave 'em to that little minx Danielle, ain't cha, sweetheart?" Ivan walks side by side with Gwen as they make their way up toward the Vampire wing, toward Angelo's bedchamber.

"Ha! Me, jealous? Of that little whore? Don't be ridiculous!" Gwen answers hotly, picking up her pace. Raising her chin in defiance she pushes onward, impatient to get to Angelo's room and away from Ivan's undesirable company.

Learning music has awakened something in Gwen, a kind of freedom and independence that lifts her spirits beyond her dismal existence. She attacks her lessons with vigor, taking on each new challenge, reveling in the feeling of accomplishment she gains. Her passion for music is only exceeded by Angelo's desire to teach, to share his knowledge with Gwen. He is always patient and understanding, never cross or condescending if she doesn't perform a piece of music just right. He seems to get great fulfillment out of watching Gwen succeed and encourages her in every way he can. She realizes what a rare gift and opportunity it is to study under a musician with over two hundred forty years' experience, one who has studied all forms of music from all over the world. He has mastered every instrument known to man and some that Gwen never even knew existed.

Today's lesson is the guitar. At the end of every lesson, Angelo plays a piece of music on the chosen instrument for Gwen. Her homework is to learn that music and play it herself as best she can from memory upon their next meeting. She feels a little nervous about yesterday's assignment, a difficult and confusing violin piece with lots of finger picking and key changes that she just couldn't get the hang of. She knows her teacher won't make fun of her if she makes a mistake or two, but still she wants to impress him and please him. Gwen feels a tangle of nerves working into her gut as she raps upon Angelo's bedroom door. Ivan takes his place aside the door, already assuming the position of sentinel.

Angelo answers the door in his usual nonchalant manner, shirtless, his hair a curly, untamed mess, and bare-footed as always. He gives Gwen a lazy smile that makes her tingle all over and then gives an uncaring glance at Ivan, who sneers back at him with distaste.

Gwen can't help but imagine what a duel between these two men would look like. She'd put her money on Angelo for sure. He might seem sloppy and reckless, but deep down she is positive Angelo is cunning and lethal. Only a fool would underestimate someone like Angelo. Gwen smiles at an image that suddenly appears in her mind, of Ivan mangled and begging for mercy. She suppresses a vengeful laugh and steps into her tutor's bedchamber.

"And what's so funny?" Angelo asks as he closes the door behind her.

"Oh, well…" Gwen opens her mind to him, showing him the image that had just passed through her thoughts. Angelo laughs ruefully and Gwen smiles.

"I've thought about tearing that idiot limb from limb before. More than once, I might add. Unfortunately, killing another Vampire is the ultimate sin. Legion wouldn't much like it," Angelo confesses aloud.

"Why do you two hate each other so much? So far I haven't seen any of the other Vampires really quarrel with each other. They seem to all get along pretty well."

"Oh, they fight. Believe me, this bunch argues and bickers more than any other nest I've ever lived with, but they are united in their belief that they are superior to all other creatures. Most Vampires don't believe in airing their dirty laundry in public."

Gwen sets the book and her guitar case down on the table in the corner. She unzips the bag, pulls out her black acoustic guitar, and she sits down to tune the instrument.

"And what about Ivan?" Gwen probes.

Angelo puts on an old black Led Zeppelin T-shirt littered with holes and tears in the fabric. He retrieves his own instrument and joins her at the table. "Oh, that. It's stupid, really. You wouldn't guess it, but Ivan fancies himself a ladies' man, a real heartbreaker. When Legion succeeded to the leadership of Bec LaNuff, I came to pay him a visit. I caused a bit of a stir among the female Vampires at the time." Gwen quirks an eyebrow at this, which Angelo notices. "Hey, I didn't do anything to deserve the attention. I was new meat and they were tired of the same old faces, that's all," he says in his defense. "As Ivan sees it, I stole away all his girlfriends, but according to Legion, no one was much interested in Ivan to begin with."

Yeah, I don't blame them. I wouldn't touch him if he were the last man on Earth, Gwen thinks to herself. Angelo laughs aloud at this.

"What, the cockney accent doesn't do it for you?" Angelo teases.

"No, it doesn't."

"How about Italian?" Angelo gives her a wink. Gwen blushes, turning her face away to adjust the tuners at the head of the guitar. "Sorry, I'm just trying to figure out what your type is."

"I'm fourteen, I don't have a type yet. All I know is that I'm not into Ogres, Goblins, Trolls, Dwarfs, Giants, Elves, or Vampires. And I'm not too keen on humans either," Gwen answers.

"That doesn't leave you with many options," Angelo observes.

It leaves me with Wiccans, Fairies, and Werewolves. Gwen mentions mentally.

"You should give me a chance. I think you'll find I'm not like the other Vampires."

"So you keep telling me," she replies, giving him a little smile. "At least you don't dress like one." Angelo looks down at his blue jeans and old worn T-shirt with a look of mock offense at her criticism.

Gwen laughs in response.

The book sitting on the table catches Angelo's eye and he picks it up. "What's this? Your homework from Emon, your other tutor?" he asks aloud.

"Yes. It's a book about the Merpeople and Atlantis."

"Is it any good?"

"It's interesting. I mean, I like studying other tribes' cultures and customs, but sometimes I wish I could get my hands on a regular novel. I miss going to the library in New York and getting a bunch of paperbacks to take home so I can stay up all night reading. I miss the wild fun of fiction." Finished tuning her guitar, she focuses her full attention on Angelo. "Don't get me wrong. I love history, but sometimes it just fries your brain with all its boring facts. I like to exercise my imagination a little." Gwen realizes she has gone off on a tangent. She gives an embarrassed little smile.

Angelo looks as though she just said the cutest thing ever. "You want to hear a secret?" he asks.

Gwen nods.

"The truth is, I've never read anything that wasn't sheet music," he confesses.

Gwen looks at him in astonishment. "You're joking! You've been around for over two hundred forty something years, and in all that time you've never read a book?" she asks incredulously, as if it is blasphemous.

"That's what I'm saying. I never felt the need. I'm not illiterate or anything. I read and write well. I've read newspapers and such, but not a whole book. The only entertainment I've ever longed for is musical. Nothing else matters," he replies.

Gwen shakes her head at him in dismay. "You just don't know what you're missing. I only wish I had some books to loan you. I guess I still have one or two books from the old days stowed away in my duffel bag. I've read them a hundred times so you can have those to start, but honestly that's the best I can do. Would you read them if I brought them to you?"

"Of course, if that would please you. I'd do anything you asked of me," he concedes. Gwen pretends not to hear this declaration of devotion, her cheeks glowing red.

"I've asked Emon for new books and things like that before, but Legion forbids that I have any luxuries. He lets me draw, just as long as I don't anger him, but he thinks human literature is a waste of paper, and unworthy for his..." Gwen pauses a moment, mentally pushing away the thought of any relationship with Legion out of her mind. She continues, "...for me to indulge in."

Angelo watches her intently but says nothing.

Gwen shrugs. "So I've been denied my favorite pastime. Maybe you could stop by a bookstore or something one of these nights when you're out... hunting." The last word tastes bad in her mouth, but she looks at Angelo with hope in her eyes, feeling like a child.

"Like I said, I'd do anything for you, Gwen. Just tell me the titles and I'll see if I can find them for you." Gwen gives him a brilliant smile that lights up her face. He can't help but smile back.

"Before we get started with the guitar, are you ready for today's quiz?" Angelo asks, setting the history of Atlantis down.

He moves to his desk, where his violin case sits open He brings the deep red violin and its bow over to the table.

"I guess so," Gwen sighs in resignation. Sitting her black guitar aside, she takes the violin from his cold hand. She looks over the beautiful antique instrument in silent awe. The workmanship of its construction is evident even to a novice such as Gwen. The varnish is a vibrant yet deep red, like red wine, the shape is curvy as a women's silhouette, and the scroll at the head has been carved into the shape of the eagle's head.

Gwen tightens the screw on the base of the bow till the hair has the right tension. She attaches the shoulder rest to the back of the red violin and sets it in place on her left shoulder, taking the proper stance. Looking down the length of the violin, she sets her chin on the chin guard. Closing her eyes, she takes a deep breath and begins to play.

Gwen lets the music flow through her in the way she embraces and wields magic, filling her consciousness with its melody, as if her bow were an extension of her own arm and the violin a part of her body. To her surprise, she performs the piece beautifully without a mistake. Smiling to herself, she opens her eyes to see Angelo smiling quietly back at her. She lowers the violin into the rest position, tucked against her body beneath her right arm, her hand holding its neck with the bow hanging in her left hand.

"That was… magnificent," Angelo praises. Gwen blushes, self-pride radiating through her skin.

"Where did you get your violin?" Gwen asks. "It seems very

old. Whenever I hold it I feel like I'm grasping onto infinity. It feels almost alive when I play it."

Angelo's face takes on a faraway look. Gwen wonders if maybe she asked an inappropriate question. He gives her a soft, sad little smile. "You know, you and I can cut through all the mystery, forget all these getting-to-know-you questions and chitchat and just show each other what the other wants to know."

Startled by this thought, Gwen puts the violin and bow down on the table.

"You mean open ourselves to each other completely? Do you expect me to just let you into my head and give you full access to every last one of my memories?" Gwen feels the apprehension building inside her chest. She tries to remain calm, but the idea of letting someone inside her that way seems far too intimate.

"And I'd let you into my head as well. I could show you what it was like to live two hundred years ago. You could walk with me down the streets of Vienna, when it was the musical and artistic capital of the world. You could meet my mentor. You could meet my maker, watch me die, witness my rebirth. I offer you everything that I am. I'm sure you're as curious of me as I am of you. Please let me in."

Overwhelmed by his sudden show of emotion and the intensity in his voice, Gwen is suddenly at a loss for words and uncertain of her feelings. Her knees feel weak. She sits to take a moment to think it all over.

All those things sound beautiful to her—wonderful,

mysterious, and tragic. She wants to know everything about him. She wants to understand him, hoping that in doing so she might understand the part of herself that is falling in love with him. On the other hand, she also wants to find fault in him, something to give her a reason to push him away so that he can't hurt her, so that she can be safe, even though she is lonely, longing for a friend, a fellow soul to find joy and understanding.

"I promised myself I wouldn't trust anyone ever again after what Legion did to me," Gwen confesses. She can feel her heart breaking all over again as the memories of her first days in Bec LaNuff come flooding back, the sense of wonder in finally finding her own kind and the acceptance for which she always longed. The awakening of womanly desires and lightheadedness of discovering love's first infatuation. The joy of being loved by one she held in such high esteem, only to have it all ripped away in one dark and miserable moment of betrayal and violence.

Angelo moves as slowly as a hunter, as if trying not to startle a doe, as he kneels before Gwen's chair. He takes her free hand in his. He looks into her eyes, a murky storm of emotions swirling in the silver-gray of his irises.

"You can't keep the world out forever, Gwen. Believe me, I've tried. Sooner or later something, or someone, will come along and change your perspective on things." He cups her cheek in his other hand, his cold flesh soothing to her nerves. "And you'll realize you weren't really alive until that moment, and you'll never be the same."

His meaning is unmistakable, his manner so tender that Gwen feels all her resistance melt into oblivion. She relaxes, realizing only now that every muscle in her body is tense. "I'm curious, but I'm also afraid. Please, don't turn my thoughts against me the way that he does. Promise me you won't hurt me." Gwen can't hide the tremor in her voice. Gwen, the stubborn, strong, proud, and indestructible young woman is gone. All that is left is the little girl she had once been, wandering alone and cold in the snow holding her little black shoe.

Angelo's eyes seem misty, but no tears fall. "I promise, Gwen, I will never hurt you." A poignant smile creases his lips. "All I want is your trust."

Gwen closes her eyes and places her hand on his cheek, her warm fingertips meeting with his soft, cool skin. And then she lets go. She opens her mind and her soul to him, letting down every magical wall she has built around herself over the years to allow this man into her inner world. Instantaneously, his consciousness flows into hers, their minds touching and melding into one another as real and powerful as a physical embrace.

The warmth that fills her is infinite and overpowering, their joined minds expanding into a vast horizon of possibilities. All at once she is one with him and he one with her, their souls entwined, their essences pouring into each other, filling a void neither one ever knew existed. Their minds are awash in one another's auras. Hers is a shimmering pearlescent pale-green light rippling like water; his is a dark maroon with flashes of bright white light like dazzling thunderbolts. Where their two souls touch, their auras bleed into one another, creating a kaleidoscope of colors. Their auras are a musical hum harmonizing perfectly, complementing each other, creating its own unique melody.

She absorbs his life through images, emotions, sounds, smells, and touch, all shifting and changing from one pivotal moment in his life history to the next. Through her eyes Angelo sees all of Gwen's childhood, her brief moments of joy appearing like bright sparks of warmth and light amongst the general gloom of her sad existence. They share a lifetime together, sending and receiving one another's memories through this open channel. Living each other's lives from their first memories to the present, they come to a complete knowledge of one another. They are now so intimately and profoundly bonded that they can no longer feel the separation of their two souls.

Tears fall and trail down her cheeks, but she is so overcome with the bond between them that she doesn't move a finger to wipe them away. It seems as though an eternity has passed since they began but only minutes have passed. At last there is nothing left to share but the present. Through his eyes, Gwen sees a vision of herself upon their first meeting. She was beautiful and fierce, radiant and alive in a world of coldness and death. She feels his love, and desire for her through their bond. She feels the hope and the joy that overcomes him every time she is near, erasing any doubt she ever had of the sincerity of his affection for her.

Simultaneously, Angelo sees himself in the images of Gwen's

mind. He is a strong, dark, and mysterious figure bringing excitement into her dull and dreary world. He is overpowered by the feeling of sweet love and acceptance she radiates through their connection. He feels humbled by the power of her newfound faith in him. She trusts him. With him, she feels completely safe, able to depend on another person absolutely for the first time in many years. He is a bright spark of light shooting through a pitch black, starless sky.

He trembles inside, afraid he might disappoint her, wanting so desperately to be the hero she believes him to be. She whispers his name, and his fear evaporates. A new resolve takes shape within him, a determination to love and protect Gwen till final death comes for him.

"I will be yours as long as you walk this earth. Nothing will keep us apart," he vows in a hushed whisper.

Gwen is crying silently, soft sobs racking her slender frame as she basks in his utter devotion. "I love you."

Reluctantly, they drift to the surface of consciousness, coming back to the present, relinquishing their hold on each other's souls and settling back into their own bodies once more. Slowly, they regain control of themselves as if waking from a deep sleep, their mental exchange leaving them both weak.

Gwen opens her eyes to see Angelo standing before her, a hand extended to help her up from her chair. She accepts it, her joints and muscles aching as she stands. The top of her head reaching his shoulder, she looks up into his silvery, shimmering eyes. He bends his head to hers, their lips meeting in a deep and tender kiss, their arms encircling one another in a loving embrace.

When they step back from each other, they still hold on as if they might lose their balance and fall. "You were an orphan, too. Your mother abandoned you. Mine died. Neither of us ever knew our fathers."

"You've been scared and alone for so long and yet you've been so strong—not just for yourself but for Raven, too. Oh, Gwen, you're so brave!"

Their words pour out, spoken on top of the other yet they still hear and understand each other as they speak.

"Your mentor gave you the red violin, because he loved you so much. I'm so sorry he died like that. How terrible it must have been for you."

"Dennis Keller deserved to die, Gwen. You shouldn't blame yourself for it. You defended yourself against a real monster. Don't forget that you saved those poor kids. Cara will be fine now. Dennis can't hurt anyone anymore, thanks to you." Blood-water tears slide down Angelo's flawless cheek. They hug one another as they cry for each other's lifetime of sorrows and injustices.

"I can't believe that your maker would trick you like that, that he lied to you for so long. You've lost so much. How can I ever begin to make it right? I want to be everything to you, to make up for the life you could've had." Gwen's voice almost breaks with the hopelessness she feels.

"It's okay, Gwen. You've already given me so much. I never

thought I would love again, and here you are in my arms." Angelo buries his face in her silky black hair. "Let's not dwell on the sad times. We're together now. That's all that matters."

"Yes, everything will be different now." Gwen smiles. "I love that you play the violin each morning at dawn to keep track of the days, so that you don't forget the passage of time. It's just poetic and beautiful. I have to admit it's kind of creepy that you varnish your violin with human blood, though."

"I'll stop that little habit, if you'd like." Angelo kisses her on the forehead, an amused smile playing across his cold lips. "Anything else you object to, my love?"

"Yeah, please don't call me any pet names, like 'my love,' or 'darling,' or 'sweetheart.' That's what Legion and Ivan call me, and it makes my skin crawl. Just call me Gwen, please."

"But in the heat of the moment, what should I call you?" Angelo asks, cocking an eyebrow at her suggestively.

"Even then, Gwen will do just fine." Thoughtfully she adds, "I read somewhere that no word is more beautiful to a person than the sound of their own name. It's like a special way of saying 'I love you.' It's more intimate, I think," Gwen says, shyly.

"I agree. I can't think of a more beautiful sound than Gwenevere." Angelo kisses her passionately. Gwen melts in his arms, her body seeming to fit with his, like two parts of one whole.

Eventually, they release one another, remembering that Ivan's is just outside the bedroom door. They return to Gwen's musical training, picking up their instruments. Throughout the lesson, their eyes linger on one another, their faces alight with identical lovesick grins. Their giddiness is thick in the air, mingled with the music of the violin and guitar.

They take turns playing their favorite loves songs. Angelo plays "Fallen" by the Beatles, "Love Song" by The Cure, and "Every Time I Look at You" by Kiss, serenading her with his beautiful tenor voice. Gwen plays "Naked" by Avril Lavine, "Killing Me Softly" by The Fugees, and "I've Got a Crush on You" by Frank Sinatra. By the time their hour is up they are laughing at their own corniness and the new bond they have forged. Gwen reluctantly leaves Angelo's bedchamber, turning to run back into his arms twice to kiss him again before she finally forces herself out the door.

Fully aware that she is glowing from head to toe and can't stop smiling to save her life, Gwen heads back toward her room, ignoring Ivan as he falls in step beside her.

"What are you so 'appy about?" Ivan asks, suspicion thickly mingled in his cockney accent.

"Oh, I just love playing music, that's all," Gwen sighs, trying to repress the euphoria within.

"Uh-huh. Sure you do." They walk along together for a long while in silence.

"If I didn't know better I'd say you had yourself a little crush on the musician."

"Don't be an idiot. I'm not that stupid. One Vampire is the same as the next. You should know by now that I hate you all."

The afterglow of her mental connection with Angelo seems to have slowly faded away in Ivan's presence, leaving Gwen cold with fear.

"Ha, 'bout time you learned the way of things. Now you're really a Witch. You hate us, and we hate you. Just you make sure you remember that Angelo's been wooing and killing young lasses like yourself for more than two centuries. He may seem romantic and charming but he's a blood-thirsty killer like the rest of us. Besides, if you so much as touch him, the Master will tear you limb from limb for your betrayal." He pauses for dramatic effect. "Your death would be no loss to him or to your Italian. You can be easily replaced," he adds ruthlessly.

They walk until they reach the grand entry. The Ogre guards open the double doors to allow them entrance into Legion's court.

"I'll be watching you." Ivan smiles maliciously before he turns his back on Gwen and enters the great hall. He leaves Gwen to stare after him, rooted to the spot by a sickening feeling of dread, all her warm and fuzzy feelings gone in the face of reality.

CHAPTER EIGHTEEN

Hope of Escape

*T*hat evening Gwen wakes from her usual dreams of the far away kingdom, and the handsome boy of blue eyes and golden hair, to the sound of a voice whispering her name in her ear. At first she thinks the voice too is part of her dreams. She dismisses it, gathering her blankets around her and turning on her side to go back to sleep. Accidentally, Gwen knocks something large and solid off the edge of the bed. A feminine cry of alarm disturbs the silence of her darkened room, accompanied by the sound of something hitting the ground with a soft thud.

Gwen sits up, wide awake. She utters a spell of illumination. An orb of light appearing in the air above her head, which throws the room instantly into full light.

"Who's in here? Angelo, is that you?" Gwen looks about the room, frantic.

"No, do I look like a blood drainer to you?" a feminine little voice chirps nearby. Gwen follows the voice to see someone peering over the side of her stone bed.

Sitting on the granite floor, sprawled out in a most unladylike manner, is a blue-skinned girl in garments the same color as her flesh. Her attire appears to be made out of some kind of pearlescent, cobwebby material which clings to her figure in a way that leaves nothing to the imagination. The young woman looks about seventeen, slight of build, with delicate features, small pointed ears, extremely sharp, high cheekbones and golden eyes. She has soft baby-doll lips, a sharp, and pointy nose complemented by a very pronounced clef chin. All this is set against a long, wavy, golden river of hair reaching down her back to her knees. The girl gets to her feet, rubbing her tender behind, and Gwen sees that she stand barely over five feet tall. She also notices that the girl isn't wearing any shoes or socks, and that her toenails on her little dainty feet, and fingernails on her child-sized hands are glittery blue.

"Who on Earth are you and why are you in my room?" Gwen asks, half annoyed yet intrigued by the beautiful little stranger scowling at her from the foot of her bed.

"Morna of the Morning Dew, you fool! Remember? You locked me up in your jewelry box! Is this any way to treat a fellow sister in magic?" the girl asks, trying to seem intimidating and fearsome. With her sweet little voice and her sprite-like face, she fails miserably.

Gwen can hardly believe her eyes. "Morna the Fairy! But you were no bigger than my hand before, now you're… almost human size."

"You really are ignorant for a Witch child. Don't you teach anything to your young anymore? Everyone knows that Fairies can alter their size for their own protection. Sometimes it's safer to be the size of a butterfly and to fly around as we please. Other times it's easier to walk around like the rest of you." Morna climbs up onto the bed and settles into a cross-legged position. She pulls her hair over one shoulder and begins to meticulously braid her long golden locks, her fingers moving purposely as she speaks.

"No, I didn't know that," Gwen says, "but I wasn't raised amongst my own tribe. The Wiccans don't even know I exist, I guess. I met a few a while ago but they tried to hurt me. Other than that, I have never encountered anyone of my own kind."

"That explains why you've been allowed to be kept prisoner in this place for so long. I wouldn't have believed that Wiccans abandoned their children like this, letting them wander into Vampire hands." The Fairy clicks her tongue on the roof of her mouth in disapproval. "Someone should have come for you long ago. This is no place for magic folk. It's too dangerous. This mountain is made of a special kind of stone that weakens our kind, makes it very difficult to feel magic in the world around us. It is a poison, the minerals of these rocks. The deeper in the ground you go, the stronger the power of the stone becomes, and the weaker your strength will be."

Gwen listens to her new blue Fairy friend with growing horror. *No wonder Legion had me put down in the servants' quarters. The only place lower in the mountain is the dungeon and the store rooms. That explains why he won't let me go outside even for a moment. He's afraid I'll regain my strength if I'm away from the mountain, that I might be able to break free from the bond of the ring.*

"I didn't know that either," she admits aloud, feeling like the perfect simpleton. *I could fill the world twice over with all the things I don't know,* Gwen thinks bitterly.

"No matter, Witch child. You know it now. So you call yourself Gwenevere?"

"Yes," Gwen answers uncertainly, "but please call me Gwen."

When she finishes braiding her hair, Morna tosses the long thick lock over her shoulder. In the reflection of the mirror on the opposite wall Gwen can see Morna's back clearly. With her hair out of the way, Gwen can see the Fairy's wings folded up against her back as if coming out of her shoulder blades—two large, beautiful, blue, pearlescent wings, the bones visible through the transparent sparkly blue skin. Morna changes her position and kneels, her eyes intently searching Gwen's face.

"Gwen." Morna repeats the name as if trying to memorize it. "And you do not know your family name or what branch of Wicca from which your parents were born? Not even the name of your family's coven?"

"Nope, I don't know any of that. I'm an orphan. I grew up amongst the humans." Gwen tries to keep the sorrow out of her voice, not wanting Morna to pity her.

"The Wiccans are like an ancient strong tree in the woods. They have old, sturdy roots in magic and the natural world, and their families are old, most dating back to the first Wicca, the thirteenth son of Cain. The branches of those families can be traced by the color of a Witch's eyes." With this Morna leans forward to get a closer look at Gwen's face, more specifically her yellow-green eyes. Gwen is a bit taken back by this intrusion into her personal space, yet she remains still, letting the Fairy's fierce golden eyes scan over her.

"I don't know all the family names of the first, second, or third circles of Wicca, but yours looks to be important eyes. There is much wisdom and strength in them. You seem as if made of old magic. True magic flows around you in your energy. That means you could be a First Circle Wiccan," Morna observes seriously.

"What's that?" Gwen perks up, curious now.

"First Circle Wiccans are pure blood. Second Circle are half breeds with other tribes, like an Elf, or Fairies. And Third Circle Wiccans are half human and thus considered lesser Wiccans," Morna informs Gwen of this enthusiastically, clearly enjoying the opportunity to teach someone less knowledgeable than she.

"Wow. I'm learning all sorts of new things today," Gwen remarks.

"Your people will want to know about you," Morna says, nodding to herself.

"Do you know where the Wiccans are? Is there a coven nearby?" Gwen asks eagerly, pushing back the bed covers.

"Yes, a coven is two days flight from the Mount of Blood." Morna informs Gwen excitedly.

"Mount of Blood? What's that?"

"It's what the name of this place means. Bec LaNuff is 'Mount of Blood,' or 'Blood Mountain.'"

Gwen shivers involuntarily. She pushes the feeling aside, focusing on the matter at hand. "Morna, are you better now? Do you think you can get out of here? Is there some way I can help?" Gwen asks eagerly, inwardly reminding herself not to get her hopes up.

"Yes. I feel well enough to fly, yet it's still too dangerous to try it. Vampires have a great sense of smell, especially when it comes to Fairy blood and flesh. My people believe that the Pale Eyes can smell us from over a hundred stone throws away." Morna's eyes examine Gwen as she speaks, traveling over her face and body and then lingering on her luminous black hair.

"If that's true, then why didn't Lynette find you when she was searching my room earlier? She even looked in the jewelry box where you were hiding." Gwen self-consciously starts to run her fingers through her hair, wondering if it looks like a terrible mess, because Morna's gaze keeps returning to it.

"Oh, this Lynette. Is she the little demon Vampire child that captured me?"

"Yes, the one whose eyes you wanted to tear out, remember?" Gwen confirms.

"Yes, that is still my plan, but it will have to wait." She pauses to reflect, biting her plump purple-bluish bottom lip as one hand reaches up involuntarily to idly play with the pointed tip of her left ear. "It could be that your scent masked my own. Witches have a very distinct smell that can be very alluring to the pale-eyed night children, but your blood tastes strange to them." Morna pauses a moment, her attention caught once again by Gwen's hair. Reaching out she takes some of Gwen's hair between her little fingers and rubs the fine stands between her fingertips. "Your hair is wonderful, smooth, and dark."

"Thank you," Gwen answers, not quite sure what else to say. *Why is she so interested in my hair?* Gwen wonders.

"May I have some of it for my nest?" Morna asks hopefully, a bright little smile a lighting her sweet face.

"You want some of my hair for your nest?" Gwen asks incredulously.

"Oh, yes, very much. We fairies like to build our nest of animal and human hair, and yours is very soft, which would be nice to sleep in. And the color would disappear in the dark of night, blending in and making it hard for predators to seek. Also, your Witch scent would throw off Vampires and other blood drinkers, so… yes, your hair would make a most ideal Fairy nest," Morna informs her excitedly.

Gwen smiles. "Sure, you can have some of my hair. Unless we can think of a way to get you out of here, I don't know what good it'll do," she adds bitterly.

"Is there no opening, an entrance, or a breach in the stone wall that leads out into the open air? If you could carry me in your pocket, we could walk right past the pale-eyed blood fiends without them smelling me. I could fly once I am out of range," Morna suggests happily, her face animated with the prospect. "But then I guess you don't know of any such place or you would've escaped already." Morna's face falls into disappointment.

"No, I do know of such a place. It's high up the mountain and I cannot fly like you. Even if I could, my wedding bond wouldn't allow me to leave the mountain. It's physically impossible for me to leave without the ring killing me." Gwen explains this as the Fairy listens intently.

"That is regrettable. However, if you could take me to this place I could get away. I could fly to the coven in my miniature state and send help for you. Surely your sisters would come for you, orphan or not. You're still a Witch," Morna reassures her with a friendly smile.

Gwen smiles back. She can't help but like the little blue girl, with her honest forthcoming way and her infectious smile. "But wait a minute. Aren't Fairies magic wielders, too? Isn't there something you could do to break the bonds of the ring? I was hoping maybe you knew some sort of magic spell we could cast, or you could teach me one that might release me from my curse."

"I'm afraid that would be impossible, and deadly. The four races of magic all have their own kind of power, each completely unique to them. A Fairy could no sooner teach a Witch to do Fairy magic than a Witch could teach an Elf or a Mermaid for that matter. We're simply too different. We think differently." Morna changes positions, crossing her legs once more in front of Gwen. She raises both of her hands, her palms held outward. Morna gives her a meaningful look indicating with a nod that Gwen is to press her hands in the same manner against hers. Gwen does, looking into Morna's golden eyes with curiosity.

"You think like a human, with reason and logic, feelings, memories, and life experience influencing your every thought and action. Elves think only in logic with barely any trace of emotions. The Mermaids use magic almost purely by emotions, thus making them unpredictable and unsteady in craft, almost unable to focus or harness it to do their will. While my kind is fierce and free of boundaries, we think as the Earth thinks. We feel and move as she does, living and dying with her constant sway. We embrace and use magic as pure energy, not as spells or potions. We don't wield or channel its power as your kind does as if taming a wild beast. The Fairy lets the magic live through us. It uses us to gain Mother Earth's grand design."

As she speaks, Gwen feels a strange energy pulsing between their palms. A tiny, brilliant blue lightning bolts shooting between their fingertips, a jolt of electricity shooting through her veins. A static charge spreads over Gwen's flesh, reaching all the way up into her scalp. A deep feeling of calm washes over Gwen immediately after, leaving her feeling giddy and carefree for the first time in almost two years.

Morna continues. "In the past, our ancestors tried to link their energy together to fight against our joint enemy the Vampire in the wars of old. Most who attempted this magical bond were burnt up. The fierce power fried them in a flash of light, killing both Fairy and Wiccan alike. Some just burnt out their magical fuse, losing the ability to wield magic forever. Rarely has anyone succeeded." Morna retracts her hands from Gwen's, the little magical surge between them instantly ceasing. "For this reason, I cannot help you escape on my own. I'm sorry, my Gwen, my new Wiccan friend, but your best hope is your own kind. They will surely make your captor pay for his crimes against their sister."

"I like the sound of that!" Gwen confesses, giving Morna a rueful smile. She rubs her fingers against her palms, her skin still tingling from Morna's electrifying touch.

Morna laughs, smile lines creasing at the corners of her almond-shaped golden eyes.

"If we can't link, then what on Earth was that you just did to me?" Gwen asks openly.

"Just a sample of my kind of magic. I was cleansing your spirit," Morna explains, shrugging her shoulders in a way that seems more like an ordinary teenage human.

"Oh, well, thanks. I do feel good. I think I may not be your best bet as far as escapes go. Legion watches me like a hawk. He even has his little guard dog Ivan follow me around whenever I leave my room," Gwen explains, resentment clear in her voice.

"Can't we just go now? I believe it is daylight outside, most of the Vampires are asleep, and aren't you supposed to be sleeping, too? As the Vampire Lord's companion he must have you living on a schedule, correct?" Morna asks hopefully.

"Well, yes, but the ring will alert him if I leave my room during the day. He'll know that I'm up to something if he detects that I'm awake and wandering around the place unguarded." Gwen sighs, shrugging her shoulders in helplessness.

"Can you show me where to go? In our thoughts, I mean?"

"Yes, I can do that." Gwen reaches out telepathically to Morna's buzzing torrent of thoughts, finding her mind open and welcoming to her intrusion. Gwen inserts her memories of the passageway up to the stone balcony into the Fairy's head, making sure to remind her that she must go through the Vampire wing to reach it. Morna acknowledges this warning, grave yet determined.

"We shall wait till evening. I will hide in your pocket as you go about your day. When we're close to the way out, you will let me know when no one is looking. I will slip out and fly off as fast as my wings will carry me," Morna says with a determined set to her pointed little chin.

"We'll probably get caught, but still, it's worth a try," Gwen concedes, stifling a yawn. "We should really get some sleep, then. Fairies do sleep, don't they?"

"Yes, quite a lot. We prefer to sleep twelve to sixteen hours a day."

"Wow. No wonder you need a comfortable nest." Suddenly an image of Morna curled up in a bird's nest amongst its eggs pops into her mind, immediately followed by the image of Morna fighting with a bird over a slimy tasty worm for breakfast. Gwen suppresses a wave of nausea at the idea of eating such things.

She probably doesn't eat worms. I'll have to ask her what Fairies eat tomorrow. Gwen smiles at her guest. "All right then, let's get to sleep. We'll put your great escape plan into effect tonight."

"Okay." Morna sits for a moment, a nervous look on her pale blue face.

"What is it?" Gwen asks, concerned.

"Well, I was wondering if I could sleep in your hair?" the Fairy asks shyly, a slight rosy tint coloring in her high-boned cheeks, making her skin look almost purple.

"You want to sleep in my hair?" Gwen chuckles a bit at this. "Wouldn't you be more comfortable sharing the bed?"

"No, I find being full size much too awkward. Too many limbs get in the way. It's easier to find a comfortable position when you're small." Gwen can't argue with her reasoning. Often she herself wishes she could be shorter again. Long legs, however appealing to one's figure, had an awful habit of getting in the way.

"Okay, why not? You can test drive my hair before you add it to your nest," Gwen adds, giggling. Morna gives her a mock scowl in response.

"You might want to cover your eyes. Transformation can be a bit blinding," Morna warns. Gwen looks at her, not fully comprehending. The prospect of seeing Morna change is too fascinating to miss, so Gwen keeps her eyes focused on the girl in anticipation as she moves to stand next to the bed.

Morna closes her eyes and relaxes her whole body as if falling into a trance-like sleep. Her skin begins to shimmer, illuminated by a light from within. The illumination grows in intensity, causing her to appear sparkling pearl-white instead of blue. Suddenly, Morna's entire body disappears into a brilliant flash of light, accompanied by the sound of rushing wind, like a miniature tornado. Gwen turns away instinctively, shielding her eyes from the blinding light, seeing black spots in her vision and Morna's outline burned temporarily on her retina. The light disappears with a popping sound that makes Gwen's ears ring.

She turns to look at the spot where Morna had been and sees nothing but white chalky dust in a ring on the floor. The hum of tiny wings flapping at high speed comes up on Gwen's right. She turns to see Morna in her original state, as big as her hand—blue, and as perfect as a little porcelain doll. Once, Gwen thought that Fairies were the stuff of children's fantasies, and yet here she is, with a real life Fairy flying around her head. Morna does a loop-de-loop above Gwen for her entertainment.

Gwen laughs. "All right, enough showing off. It's bed time, Tinkerbell." She stretches, and lying back down, she pulls her covers over her body, arranging her hair so that it fans out on the pillowcase before she settles into the bed.

Who's Tinkerbell? Morna asks telepathically.

Oh, just another Fairy I know, Gwen laughs.

Morna buzzes toward her, resting on her black luminous hair. Gwen turns her head slightly to watch. The Fairy walks around in a circle and then lays down on her side, scooting around on her little rump and arranging herself just right until she is in a comfortable sleeping position. She curls up into a ball, covering herself with her wings. With a peaceful and grateful smile, Morna closes her eyes and goes instantly to sleep.

Gwen smiles, tired. As she closes her eyes she extinguishes the ball of light hovering near the ceiling, sending the room back into absolute darkness. Gwen sighs inwardly, a feeling of renewed hope and peace settling in her breast. She falls asleep to the sound of her new friend and possible savior purring in her ear, and to the hope of escape.

CHAPTER NINETEEN

In a Blaze of Light

*T*wo days have passed and still no sign of Morna or her Witch friends, Gwen thinks fretfully as she taps her foot on the stone floor. Legion, who sits on his throne beside her, gives her a quizzical look.

"Whatever is the matter with you, my love?" Legion takes her warm hand in his dead one in an affectionate gesture that earns Gwen a scowl from Danielle from the chaise lounge. Gwen ignores her. "These past days you've been wound up so tight. Come, tell me what's troubling you," Legion commands, the barest hint of real concern in his voice.

Gwen stops her nervous twitching, looking away from her Master's colorless eyes toward Angelo who sits at the opposite end of the room, playing chess with the Troll Chieftain. He looks up, sensing her gaze and smiles at her. Gwen sighs.

"Nothing, it's nothing. I'm just restless, that's all."

"You're not getting much sleep recently, I've noticed. You have frequent mood swings, and you're behaving oddly as well. Something is definitely wrong, Gwenevere, and I demand to know what." Legion pulls her around to stand before him on his throne still keeping a firm cold grip on her hand.

"I… it's just that I…" Gwen struggles desperately to think of something, any kind of excuse for her behavior, anything but the truth.

The large chamber doors are flung open to admit Lucca and Ryan. They burst into the room. Ryan looks almost frantic while Lucca looks as hard as a warrior charging into battle. Gwen takes this opportunity to slip out of Legion's grasp and retreat behind the throne as the two anxious Vampires approach their Master.

"Wiccans are at the outer post. They are demanding admittance." Lucca's dark voice rolls forth from his lips like thunder in a dark night. "They say they want to speak with the Lord of the Mount."

"They're here for the girl, I just know it! If we don't let them in they'll force their way in," Ryan adds nervously, her voice almost giddy with fear. "If they find her, it'll be war, won't it?" She looks between Lucca and Legion for an answer.

"Yes, full out war. It doesn't take much to set off a Witch!" Lucca confirms.

Angelo and Ivan suddenly appear before the throne next to the others, their faces showing opposite emotions. Ivan radiates with bloodlust, smiling smugly with a crooked grin. Angelo looks grave, a troubled air about him, determination in his shoulders and jaw.

Legion sits stone-still. He then moves with a silent, deadly grace, his face calm while his eyes blaze white with suppressed rage. He stands from his regal throne, looking down on his underlings.

"Lucca, go and tell the guards at the outpost to grant the Wiccans admittance. Personally escort them, and bring them straight to me." Lucca bows briskly and stalks out of the chamber. Ryan goes to follow after him.

"No, Ryan. I have a task for you as well. Take Danielle with you and go to Gwen's bedroom. Hide any personal items you can find and have Danielle lay on her bed and touch her things to hide her scent." Ryan bows deeply, grateful to have a task to keep her occupied.

"Wait, why should I help hide the Witch? Why can't we just get rid of her? If they want her so badly, then they can have her back! Send her back where she belongs. Nobody wants her here! She is not one of us." Letting her jealousy and irritation get the best of her, Danielle babbles on in a high-pitched squeal, stomping her foot at the end of her sentences for emphasis.

"You're the one who doesn't belong. You're human, you little twit, or did you forget?" The words burst out of Gwen's mouth before she can suppress them, her anger and fear making her voice dark with rage.

"I don't have time for this childish squabbling." Legion advances on the diminutive Danielle, looming over her, his penetrating stare bearing down on her, white hot, his barely-contained wrath boiling just beneath his pale skin.

"You will go and do as I tell you to! Now!" He speaks calmly, enunciating every word as if speaking to an idiot. He grabs Danielle by her slender arm and shoves her toward the door, turning his back to her with cool indifference. Danielle struggles to suppress her whimpered sobs as she hurries quickly to catch up with Ryan, who also leaves to do the Master's bidding.

Gwen and Legion's eyes meet. He holds her captive in his colorless, cold gaze. All at once he moves like a blur, suddenly appearing just in front of Gwen. Her breath catches in her throat. She stumbles backward in fearful shock, backing up against the stone wall behind her, its cold, hard surface giving her some sense of mild comfort.

"Might I ask, my darling wife, how Wiccans happen to be on my doorstep? Why on Earth would our mortal enemies suddenly stop by for a visit this way, unannounced?" Legion moves slowly toward her, like a snake slithering toward a mouse trapped in a corner, knowing full well it'll have a new meal in its jaws at any moment. "You wouldn't have anything to do with this would you, my love?"

He reaches out and touches her face with the back of his cold, bony hand. Gwen holds her breath, but does not flinch, cower, or tremble before him. She keeps her head high and her eyes meeting his willfully. Slowly caressing her neck, Legion's hand moves downward, his hand circling about her throat in a quick, graceful movement, which startles her.

"We need to get her out of sight, old friend," Angelo whispers in Legion's ear, appearing as if out of a mist at the Lord's side. "There isn't time for this now. The Witches may come in at any moment. If they find her here, it could be the end of us." His voice is urgent yet strong, betraying none of his feelings buried within. To Legion he speaks only logic and reason, but Gwen can hear his thoughts in her head. She feels apprehension tearing him apart.

Legion slowly lets go of Gwen's neck. He sighs calmly, his entire demeanor changing to his usual aristocratic loftiness. "You're right. I'll deal with her later." Legion turns away from Gwen and Angelo, and walks over to Ivan. The two Vampires immediately fall into a hushed conversation of their own.

Gwen, what were you thinking, sending for Witches? Didn't you think for a moment what the consequences would be? If they find you here, it's death to anyone who abated your imprisonment, Angelo scolds Gwen mentally, his frustration barely masking his deep love and concern for her. *If any of us are attacked by the Witches or defend ourselves against them, and the Witches live to tell the High Council what went on here, it would be outright civil war amongst all the tribes once more! It's taken a long time for everyone to recover from the last great war. I wouldn't be so eager to start another. You know not what war is like.*

Gwen shouts back through their telepathic connection. *What did you expect me to do? You think I like living here as his slave? Don't you know that I would do anything to escape? What do I care if some Vampires die in the process? I hate them all, and I want to see them pay for what they've taken from me!*

I know how you've suffered, Gwen. I've seen it, and now that I know you inside and out. I understand your hatred. But did you ever think that you might be leading your own kind into a death trap? Yes, they come here willingly, because they can't abide one of their own captive to a Vampire. But they are greatly outnumbered here. Even with magic they cannot beat us all, not inside the mountain where their powers are weak. They'll be slaughtered, and their deaths will be on your conscience. I know you don't want that.

What do you want me to do? They're already here, Gwen replies defensively.

Before Angelo can reply, Legion and Ivan appear at his side.

"Come along with me, princess," Ivan sneers as he roughly takes hold of Gwen's arm. Angelo bars Ivan's path, a threatening gleam in his silver eyes.

"Where are you taking her?" Ice seems to drip from Angelo's words.

"Some place where she can't cause any more trouble," Ivan answers smugly. "What's it to you, pretty boy?"

"Come now, you two, this is no time for your rivalry. Ivan,

away with you," Legion says irritably. He paces the room for a moment before he takes a seat on his throne, arranging his robes to give his best impression of regal status.

Ivan smiles brightly at Angelo before he steps around him, dragging Gwen. She looks back to Angelo, pleading with her eyes for his intervention.

"Angelo, I need you to help me receive our guests. Let's show these peasants what true power and nobility look like." Reluctantly, Angelo tears his gaze from Gwen and joins Legion by his throne.

Don't worry, Gwen, I'll come find you as soon as it's safe. I promise.

Gwen loses sight of Angelo as they walk out the grand doorway onto the landing, the Ogre guards watching them curiously. Suddenly, Ivan scoops Gwen into his arms. "'Old on tight, love," he leers through crooked teeth. In a whoosh, he propels them forward, moving as if rushing through water.

Everything around them blurs as he speeds through the halls and passageways of the fortress, the citizens scattering before them. Ivan weaves through the crowd in the domed courtyard, heading downward toward the lower levels. Gwen barely has time to register that they've passed the servants' quarters before they enter into a dark stairway. All of a sudden, Ivan stops with a gust of wind. He sets Gwen down on her feet. She stumbles, trying to regain her equilibrium as the room spins around her in a haze. Bile threatens to gag her, but Gwen gets control of herself and forces it down. Ivan laughs at her unapologetically. Once the world is stable, Gwen takes a look at her surroundings.

Only one small lantern lights the room, casting haunting light. It's a bare rock cave, damp, cold, and confined. Gwen notices the gaping hole in the floor on the other side of the cave. A sick, sweet smell like mold and rotting garbage wafts toward her from within. She looks at Ivan apprehensively. He points toward the hole. Gwen slowly walks toward it, a sinking feeling in the pit of her stomach. She peers over the edge, looking into a pit in absolute darkness. The smell is overpowering, almost reaching out to grab her and pull her in.

"What is this place?" Gwen asks, but deep down she already knows.

I'm in the dungeon. I'm in the deepest part of Bec LaNuff. Gwen shudders. *They'll never find me down here. No, this can't be! I've waited too long for a chance to escape. Finally someone's come to rescue me and I won't let them lock me away.* Gwen makes a mad dash toward the dark entry and the stairway.

Ivan moves faster than she does, appearing in front of her, blocking her only route of escape. Gwen stops short, her chest heaving and her eyes wild with panic. The two of them stare at each other, both waiting for the other to make the first move. Staring into his pale eyes, Gwen utters a spell, sending out her evil power toward him even before he can react and move out of her way. But the spell is weak, the ring and the effect of being so far under the poisonous rock of Bec LaNuff renders her powers all but nonexistent. Ivan is hit by a weak surge of burning energy, which fades as quickly as it touches him. He shakes it off and turns to Gwen, laughing, his eyes gleaming in triumph.

Suddenly, the ring restricts her veins and her body instantly loses strength. Gwen crumples and falls backward as if boneless. Ivan snatches her up before she can hit the floor.

"Stupid, arrogant, little Witch!" Ivan scoffs, carrying her over to the dark pit.

"I will kill you someday. Just remember that, you ugly dog," she says in response. Smiling down at Gwen so helpless and paralyzed, Ivan unceremoniously releases her, dropping her into the empty space.

She screams into the darkness as she falls straight down into nothingness, the feeling of being completely detached from the world disorientating to her. A moment later she hits a mass of water, sending a painful shock through her entire body. The rush of water fills her ears, her eyes, her mouth, and her lungs, dragging her downward.

She sputters and fights toward the surface, bursting forth, gasping for life. She gags up cold, dirty liquid from her lungs as she wades blindly though the water. Finally, she feels the solid mass of a large stone and a rock wall and she pulls herself onto it. She huddles up against the wall, shivering as her wet clothes cling to her, the air cold as ice upon her naked skin. She looks around her at the pitch-black chamber. The only thing she can distinguish is the dark surface of the water, the reflection of the light from high above making the ripple of the water visible as they move.

Gwen looks heavenward at the pit's opening, which appears as a pale circle above her. The sound of distant laughter reaches Gwen.

Something inside her snaps.

Everything is lost. I'm never going to get out of this place. I'll die here, deep in the ground. Silent tears streak down her cold cheeks as she sinks into despair. *It's no use. The Witches won't find me. They'll leave me behind, trapped.* She hides her face in her hands and sobs.

She loses track of time and space in the triple darkness of her surroundings, her spirit, and her dismal future. Hours pass, but Gwen doesn't notice. She's lost in a sea of her own misery. Several times she tries to reach out for the comfort of magic, that unseen force of knowledge, beauty and power which flows through all living things. Nothing is there but a dead, empty silence and a devastating sense of isolation.

A white streak appears above her and then a man hovers there, his pale lifeless skin glowing pearlescent in the dim light from above. His supernatural inner light burns outward in the darkness.

"Had enough?" His cold voice asks as he approaches Gwen, his white eyes boring into her soul with their restrained anger. Before Gwen can even answer, Legion sweeps her into his arms. She shoots upward, the pit's opening above becoming ever larger as they approach the top.

Gwen squints her eyes to readjust to the light in the cave,

noticing that Ivan still stands sentinel at the entrance to the chamber. Legion dumps her on the cold floor. The jolt shoots pain through her tail bone up her spinal cord, but still she doesn't cry out.

Dread overtakes her. Her mental warning bells go off in full alarm as she takes in Legion's demeanor. She realizes for the first time that the Lord of the Mount is stripped of his usual finery. He wears only a plain, white-collared shirt and a pair of black slacks with bare feet.

He paces round the small confined room, keeping his eyes upon her. As he moves, he unbuttons his shirt cuffs and ceremoniously rolls up his sleeves to his elbow.

"You have caused me quite a lot of trouble today, girl. Oh, don't worry, I fooled those simpletons. I put on quite a show if I do say so myself. They claimed that a Fairy came to them with a story about a poor abused Witch forced into slavery and matrimony to a Vampire." Legion laughs sardonically, his beautiful white fangs catching in the light. At the sight of them, Gwen slowly begins to edge backward away from her Master.

"Of course, I told them I had no wife, let alone a Wiccan one, but they weren't convinced. So, naturally they had to search the entire fortress just to make sure. You might have guessed by now that this rock pit specifically blocks all magic. Even if they happened to stumble down here and find you, you would have looked and felt like a human to them, just as long as they didn't get a good look at those eyes of yours. You have very Witchy eyes, my dear. Have I ever told you that?" Legion pauses, asking in an almost pleasant voice.

"No, you haven't," Gwen replies quietly. "I had to find that out from the Fairy," Gwen admits with a dark tone.

"No matter. Your little group of friends has already left, and is likely half way back to their coven by now. It's a pity, really. I feel sorry for you, Gwenevere. You came so close to freedom, didn't you? You thought you were so clever, sending the Fairy to do your dirty work. I don't know how you stole the Fairy, and I don't care. I hope it was worth it, child, for it is to be your last act of insolence against me." With that, Legion rushes upon her, fangs bared and blood lust in his ghostly eyes.

* * * * *

Frantically, Angelo runs down the halls of Bec LaNuff, the citizens stopping to watch him curiously as he passes. He pays them no heed, for his only thought is of Gwen, his only desire to find her before it is too late.

Why can't I feel her or sense her at all? She still has to be here in the fortress. He'd never let her outside, not even to keep her hidden away to save his own hide. She's so powerful, he'd never let her go. He passes down the stairs leading into the servants' quarters, quickly making his way to Gwen's room.

He thrusts open the door without knocking, knowing already that the room is empty. He looks frantically about for some sign of his love, some clue to where he might have taken her. He leaves the room with a sick feeling in his heart, the heart that only recently learned to beat again, all for Gwen. If she is lost to him forever, his heart will die all over again. He will have no reason to keep on living, undead or otherwise.

No, she isn't dead. She can't be! Even Legion isn't that crazy. To kill Gwen would be to sign his own death warrant. He knows that! Angelo reasons with himself, resisting the dark thoughts that threaten to destroy him. *She's asleep, that's all. He must have had Vinita put her to sleep so that she wouldn't try to escape and get to the Wiccans,* one part of him concludes. *Then why isn't she dreaming? Even in her sleep I can sense her thoughts and know where she is.*

Angelo wanders deeper and farther into the belly of the fortress, down past the corridors and rooms to the crude tunnels and caves which look nothing like the opulent upper levels. Down here is the main entrance into Bec LaNuff, nothing more than a small crack in the outer rock wall leading through a tight canal into a regular dark cave with no way out but a hole in the ceiling. To anyone but the inhabitants of the mountain, it would seem innocent, just a cave.

Angelo heads toward the main entrance, stopping short when he comes to an intersection in the passageway. Three tunnels lead off of this. The one to his right leads to the store rooms, where all the extra supplies and provisions are held. The one straight ahead goes on to the drop off that leads straight down into the cave and on to the main entrance. The left tunnel leads down into the dungeon.

His instincts tell him to go left, down the stairs. He obeys, hurrying down the dark stairway with ease as his supernatural night vision leads him where mortals would stumble. At the bottom of the long, winding steps, Angelo sees a figure standing in the doorway.

Ivan! Angelo grits his teeth and charges with his full force toward his enemy. Hitting Ivan square in the back, Angelo sends him reeling forward, clearing the doorway. Angelo stumbles into the room with the full momentum of his charge, almost falling on top of Ivan, who spins around to defend himself from his unseen attacker. Angelo spares no time for Ivan, his eyes full of the horror before him, a white-hot rage boiling within.

Legion, blood stains all over his crisp white shirt, crouches over, clutching a lifeless and bloody figure of a girl to his chest, his head bent over her neck, feeding.

Gwen's head hangs limply to one side, her ebony hair touching the floor. Her face is as pale as death and her eyes closed tight as her body shudders in pain. Her clothing is torn to pieces, her lovely skin beneath it covered in welts, bruises, scratches, and bite marks. Legion looks up at Angelo, his mouth red with her blood clinging between his white teeth and fangs, dripping off of his chin and down his chest. The man he once called friend looks at Angelo with a careless curiosity, no pity or remorse in his soulless eyes.

"This better be important," Legion warns, still holding Gwen in his grasp as if he might return to his meal at any moment.

Angelo steadies himself, fighting the urge to step forward and tear the bastard limb from limb. He is nearly as old as the Frenchman. Surely he might to beat him, but Ivan is there as well. Between the two of them, he might not survive. Trying to kill either would be fruitless. Gwen would likely get killed in the process.

If she isn't already dead, his dark thoughts remind him. *No, she's barely alive. I can see her aura flickering around her head and hear her heart beating faintly in her chest.*

"It wasn't her fault. I was the one who let the Fairy go," Angelo announces, getting amazed looks from the other two Vampires.

"I knew it!" Ivan shouts. "He's on her side! He helped her! They've been sneaking behind your back the whole time. I told you so, but you wouldn't believe me."

Legion shoots Ivan an annoyed look. "Don't be stupid, you twit. Angelo would sooner stand in the sun than fall in love with a Wiccan. He's not a fool," Legion scolds. Ivan opens his mouth to protest but quickly shuts it as Legion's icy glare cuts him short. Legion straightens, letting Gwen fall limply to the floor at his feet, never sparing a glance for his so called bride. "Go on, then, tell me why you let the Fairy go, Angelo."

"I wanted her to myself," Angelo admits, crossing his arms over his chest. "I only convinced Lynette to keep it captive so that

I might find an opportunity to steal her away. Also I wanted to hear it sing. They have the most beautiful singing voices of all the creatures on earth. I was curious." He speaks nonchalantly, with his usual arrogant swagger and a touch of embarrassment for good measure. Ivan looks at him suspiciously, but Legion just stares back, incredulous.

Suddenly, Legion bursts into a high peel of laughter, shaking his head in derision. "So typical! You always were greedy and impulsive. So how did she slip away from you then, old man? Can't you keep a hold of a tiny little Sprite? You're slipping in your old age."

"Who are you calling an old man? You're the one who's ancient," Angelo fires back, forcing a sly smile on his face, concealing the loathing deep within. "I showed her to the Witch child, boasting about what I had done. The damn thing bolted. She was just too fast for me. And before I could catch up she flew up the staircase to the upper balcony and disappeared into the early morning sky. I couldn't very well chase after her now, could I?"

Ivan chirps in, "If that's true, then why didn't you just tell someone what had happened?"

"Well, it's a bit embarrassing to admit," Angelo answers coolly. "I am truly sorry about the bloody Witches showing up. I figured the Fairy would have gone home instead of wasting its time trying to help a Witch." He shrugs his shoulders, dismissing the whole incident as mere folly.

Legion laughs. "I guess there's no accounting for taste." He carefully unrolls his shirt sleeves, redoing the cuffs of his complete ruined shirt. "Don't worry about it. No real was harm done. I thoroughly enjoyed seeing the look on their faces after they all ran around the place like little mice just to come up empty handed. They're not likely to bother us again." Legion pats Angelo on the back and heads toward the stairs.

"Wait. What about the Witch?" Ivan asks sourly, feeling rather annoyed at being overlooked once again.

Legion pauses on the stair to look over his shoulder at his handy work. He looks thoughtful for a moment.

"I'll take her back to her room," Angelo intercedes, moving quickly toward Gwen's side.

"There's not much left of her, I'm afraid," Legion says. "If she lives, it will serve as a lesson to her. If she dies, well, then I guess I'll miss her troublesome willful spirit. She does liven things up a bit around this old place." Legion waves his hand imperially, dismissing them both before he turns and leaves. "Very well, take her away."

Ivan waits a moment, staring Angelo down with an ugly sneer. "You don't fool me none, pretty boy. I have my eye on you." He stomps out of the dungeon after his Master, leaving Angelo alone with what remains of Gwenevere.

Gingerly, Angelo scoops her wilted figure into his arms, forcing himself to hold in the angry sobs that beat at his chest. He carries her carefully up to her room while battling with his own wretched emotions.

I had promised she would be safe. I promised to protect her. I make a pathetic hero, Angelo chides himself. A single blood-water tear escapes down his cheek as he lays his beloved down on her bed, but he doesn't wipe it away. Lying down beside her, he cradles Gwen in his arms. Closing his eyes, he prays for the very first time in over two and a half centuries.

* * * * *

It takes Gwen two weeks to recover, and in that time Angelo never leaves her side. Emon and Vinita came in to check in on her on occasion, but they were forbidden to use magic to heal her. Legion likewise wouldn't allow Gwen to heal herself, and since he controlled her will by the ring, she had to obey.

During her convalescence, the lovers planned their escape. After countless hours scheming, they finally decided that the only way to get Gwen out of the mountain is to call on a little help from Morna the Fairy.

Gwen tells Angelo all about her late night conversation with the Fairy about Witches and Fairies joining together to do magic, explaining the dangerous risks involved.

"You'll get yourself killed, Gwen. It's not worth it."

"If I stay, he'll kill me anyway. It's inevitable. I can't wait around for that day. It might work and if it doesn't, I'll die trying," she tells him with conviction. He doesn't like it, but Angelo agrees to follow Gwen's plan.

Several days later, everything is in place for Gwen's departure. Angelo himself had gone to Morna with a message from Gwen explaining everything, and to his relief and agitation the Fairy agreed to help.

Even now she waits just outside the mountain, Angelo thinks for the hundredth time today. *Everything has to go just right. Gwen has to be at the right place at the right time, saying the same spell at the exact moment that Morna casts her own magic without the fortress walls for their scheme to work. Failure to do so could mean death for Gwen.* Angelo shudders at the thought.

Though his part in the whole thing is over, he still got Gwen the long red servant cloak to disguise herself, and now all he had to do was act normal and wait. He couldn't go anywhere near her, he couldn't help her, couldn't say goodbye. He had to have an alibi, had to look completely uninvolved in her escape. Anxiety gets the best of him, and he finds himself wandering the halls of Bec LaNuff toward the upper balcony instead of going to mingle with his fellow Vampires in the Grand Hall as usual.

He knows that he's risking everything, but he can't help himself. He needs to see her safely gone with his own eyes. He passes by the grand chamber and heads down the hall, ascending the stairs up to the stone balcony above. As he approaches the top of the stairs, Angelo hears voices arguing. He quietly emerges into the hallway keeping his back against the wall as he makes his way toward the archway leading to the balcony.

Set against the night sky, he sees Gwen cloaked in red,

struggling to free herself from Ivan's grasp.

"Thought you could sneak way, eh? We'll see 'bout that." Ivan grabs Gwen, throwing her over his shoulder to carry her back inside. Gwen screams and struggles to break free, kicking and hitting the much stronger Ivan.

Oh, no! What is he doing here? He's going to ruin everything. If she doesn't cast her spell soon it'll be too late. Angelo breaks free of the wall and hurries to Gwen's aid.

Gwen elbows Ivan hard in the jaw, causing the Vampire to stumble in pain, losing his grip on her. Gwen slides to the ground while Ivan spins around and lunges at her.

She opens her mouth and chants the spell, saying the words as clearly and as quickly as possible, hoping to finish before Ivan can get hold of her again.

"*Annunae, Calabrae Suna, Tossa Illuminate,*" Gwen chants over and over again, as Ivan moves toward her.

Time seems to slow down before Angelo's eyes. Before he can reach Ivan, before Ivan can reach Gwen, the air electrifies around them. All at once, a bright light burns out of Gwen's chest, growing exponentially as it consumes her.

Blinded by the light, Ivan stumbles and falls before Gwen, his leg touching her as the light spreads onto her limbs. Ivan screams in horror as the white light burns him, his leg set ablaze with pure white flames. He scrambles backward to get away from her, rolling on the ground to put out the flame that eats at his immortal flesh.

Angelo is deaf to Ivan's screams. He is stunned by the marvel of Gwen ablaze in white light before him. He stands rooted to the spot, watching Gwen disappear into the light. Her face is the last thing to go. She looks up and sees him there, their eyes meeting for just a moment. The the wind whirls around her and then her face is lost in the light, her figure shrinking until she is little more than a streak of light. With a banshee-like scream in the wind, Gwen winks out of existence, gone in a blaze of light.

CHAPTER TWENTY

The Last Embrace

Her world is made of a shrieking mass of blinding white light, infinite and shapeless. She has no form. She can't feel a single bone in her body or a breath of wind on her skin. She is nothing and everything simultaneously, free of all connection to the world and universe, yet somehow remains a part of every living thing, knowing and feeling everything around her.

Suddenly, she is physically torn from the light into a physical being once more, regaining her sense of flesh and bone as she comes back to the real world. Everything hurts, as if passing through the birth canal, like a baby ripped from a place of comfort and security into a world of pain and uncertainty.

One by one her senses kick back in. The sense of touch, smell, taste, and sound shock her with their sudden intensity after the emptiness she knew well. Her sight is the last thing to return, the world dissolving from perfect brightness devoid of color or shape into a multi-layered, multi-colored world of dimension and chaos. Her head rings with dizziness, and, unable to control her balance on her flimsy legs, Gwen collapses, finding herself lying on a hard dirt floor.

She squeezes her eyes tight to stop the world from spinning. She takes deep, steadying breaths, enjoying the soothing darkness behind her eyelids. She silently listens to the room around her. The sense of enclosure is obvious by the muffled sounds outside. Birds chirp, wind blows and rustles through the trees, nature surrounding her little world. She smells old pine, dirt, and ash from a long-cold fire.

Gwen realizes that she is shivering from head to toe, and that she is completely naked. Her girlish modesty balks at this, but her sensible side tells her that her nakedness is the least of her troubles.

"I'm lucky to be alive right now," Gwen speaks to herself.

Slowly she opens her eyes, allowing herself a few moments for her vision to adjust to the light. She finds herself in an old log cabin, the kind of modest, one-room wooden structure that the early settlers stuffed whole families into.

Gwen pushes herself up on the palms on her hands, peering around the small room. An old fire place and chimney rest on one wall, a few tree trunks set on their sides, with a pile of firewood against the wall next to the fireplace. In the other corner holds a large pile of fresh hay with blankets thrown over top, looking soft and inviting. Not yet trusting her own strength, Gwen raises herself to her hands and knees and crawls to the makeshift bed. Random strands of hay stick through the blankets and poke at her bare flesh, tickling and itchy. She tries to readjust her body to find a comfortable position, but finally gives up.

"I guess it's impossible to lie naked comfortably in a haystack," Gwen says to the empty room, staring blankly at the wooden beams on the ceiling above her.

A deep rumbling accompanied by a hollow emptiness in the pit of her stomach tells her she is starving. Not a moment later, she realizes that her bladder is full to the bursting point. With an unladylike grunt Gwen sits up, every joint and muscle screaming in protest at the movement. She scans the room for some kind of nourishment and possible covering for her exposed body. She spots a familiar red duffle bag lying at the foot of her hay bed. With the effort of an old woman, she manages to scramble over to the bag. It seems to weigh a hundred pounds as she pulls it onto her lap. Unzipping it, she sighs with relief when she sees her old familiar clothes and personal belongings within. Gingerly, she manages to dress herself in a loose yellow striped shirt and blue jeans, not bothering to put on a bra or panties, because the effort is too much for her feeble limbs to accomplish.

Besides, no one's here, so no one will mind if I go commando just this once. She chuckles to herself at the thought. Somewhere in the back of her befuddled brain, she realizes she must be in a state of shock. She ought to be more frightened at being all alone in this unknown place, so weak and so vulnerable. She ought to be elated at achieving her long-sought goal of freedom, yet all she can feel is numbness. She can only handle one thought, one emotion at a time, tentatively avoiding any chance at overwhelming herself, afraid she might send herself into a panic.

Her stomach grumbles again. Gwen sighs, rummaging through her bag, finding the cloth bundle of left-over scraps of food she prepared the night before. Gwen takes this time to think as she treats her famished body to a meager meal of bread, cheese, and water, enjoying the satisfying feeling of doing such an ordinary task in such an extraordinary situation.

The sunlight glints off of her gold serpent ring. Gwen stops eating for a moment, staring at her left hand. Disappointment rushes up to her and she makes a desperate attempt to stifle a sob in her throat. Then hope arises out of her fear. Gwen sets her food aside. She reaches her hand towards one of the logs lying near the hearth.

"*Gainien Raisa,*" Gwen chants apprehensively. Instantly the log rises from the ground toward the rafters. Gwen waits for the pain, for the cold to squeeze the blood out of her heart. She holds on to the magic for several moments, the log just floating in the air. Nothing happens.

Gwen gasps, releasing the power to let the log fall to the ground with a thumb. Suddenly she bursts into giddy laughter. Still laughing, Gwen clamps her right thumb and index finger onto the ring and tugs. Her laughter stops. She tugs, yanks, pulls, and wrestles with the gold serpent encircling her wedding ring finger, but it doesn't budge, not even the tiniest bit. It's as if it's become part of her hand. The snake's emerald eyes smile up at her mockingly. With a frustrated sigh Gwen tears her gaze away from the twisted unwelcomed memento.

"At least I made it. I'm actually free! It's been two and a half years, but I'm finally out of Bec LaNuff. I'm finally free of Legion. If I never see his face again, I will die happy." Some dark part of her soul laughs at this thought. *No, you won't be happy until he's dead. You won't be happy until you rip his head off with your own two hands.* A twisted sense of satisfaction comes over her at the thought of bringing such a violent end to her own personal terrorist.

Her meal finished, Gwen awkwardly gets to her feet, determined to solve her other bodily need. She makes a quick scan of the cabin and sees nothing that will serve as a chamber pot. Grumbling to herself about Vampires and Fairies and their insensitivities, Gwen makes her way slowly toward the cabin's door.

With a little effort, Gwen manages to push it open. Cautiously, she peers out, half expecting an attack from some unknown spy hiding in the trees. She finds a typical wooded clearing, the sun high in the blue sky. Birds chirp cheerily in the summer greenery of the forest, the mountains somewhere in the distant horizon. She senses no mental presence near, only wild animals. She carefully walks over rocks, dirt, and twigs in her bare feet to the cover of the trees, finding a suitable cluster of bushes in which to take care of her business. Several minutes later, Gwen emerges from the woods feeling more at peace with her body and the world around her. Still, she hurries back to the safety of her modest hut.

Having spent all the energy her wasted little body had stored, she collapses on the bed of hay and drifts off into a deep, fulfilling sleep to recharge her inner batteries. *When I wake, Angelo or Morna will be here, and everything will be okay,* Gwen promises herself, barely able to complete the thought before she falls fast asleep fearful of her uncertain future.

* * * * *

Two large golden eyes peer down on Gwen as she awakes. At first, she feels a twinge of panic in her gut, as if a wild beast somehow wandered into the hut while she slept.

"Ha! You're alive and in one piece! You did well for a first try. Just you wait, after some practice we'll get really good at spell-joining. You'll see." Morna's hummingbird voice dispels Gwen's feelings of panic.

Gwen sits up awkwardly, her joints and ligaments still trying to recall their regular functions. Morna leans over Gwen's bed of hay in her full human form, her beautiful wings tucked delicately behind her back. Her face is just a touch too close to Gwen's. Her long golden hair hangs down, tickling Gwen's forehead and cheeks. Gwen makes a shooing gesture at the blue-skinned Fairy.

"No offense, Morna, but you're making me claustrophobic. Give me some room to breathe, please."

At this, Morna instantly plops down on the floor, legs crossed and hands folded in her lap, looking quite demure except for the look of excitement on her ethereal blue face.

Since the room doesn't spin as she looks about, Gwen assumes that her sickness from earlier has subsided. She hears the crackling pop of a fire and turns to see a good blaze alive in the old fireplace, providing a yellow glow of light to the dark hut. Through the open window, Gwen sees the starry night sky outside.

"Night has fallen," she tells herself. "Angelo should be here soon." A swell of anticipation gives her the strength to rise from the hay. She looks down at Morna. "You sure he knows how to find us?"

"Yes, I showed him the way in my thoughts. He should be able to find this place without any trouble." Morna bobs her head on her dainty little neck.

The Fairy produces a small pouch made of several large leaves and twine from her belt. She gestures for Gwen to hold out her hand. Out of the bag falls a strange mixture of twisted black roots, dried berries, and various leaves and herbs. "Here, eat this. It'll help your body and spirit regroup from the transformation. We Fairies always eat black root and elderberries after the summoning of magic. It's good for you."

Hesitantly, Gwen tosses the Fairy remedy into her mouth,

chewing the tough root with effort, and then swallowing the whole concoction. It tastes bitter, dirty, and sweet all at the same time.

"Taste good?" Morna smiles expectantly at Gwen, who nods in affirmation, forcing a smile to hide her distaste.

"Where are we? I mean, when was this cabin built, the American Revolution?" The heat from the hearth beckons Gwen, and her cold, weak body wanders over to the fire of its own volition. Moving as the wind, Morna appears at Gwen's side. She bends down and blows into the fire. Suddenly the flames blaze brighter, reaching higher, sparks flying.

"This is the old hermit's cottage. Every coven has one, a place where the banished and shamed go to be punished for their transgressions," Morna says seriously.

Gwen hears the night sounds of the forest around them, of wild creatures roaming, owls hooting, crickets chirping, and wind rustling in the treetops. The one sound she waits for is the sound of Angelo's footsteps. Her ears perk up at the slightest change in the rhythm of the night even though she knows that her love moves with the stealth of a predator, a creature at one with the night. So wrapped up is she in these contemplations, Gwen barely hears Morna's reply to her question.

"I'm sorry, did you say we're near a coven?" Gwen asks, her full attention brought to the present. She turns to look at the Fairy, her golden eyes catching in the fire light.

"Aye, this is the territory of the Monroe Coven, or the Malhonna Clan, as is their ancient name," Morna replies. "They control all the Witches living in the boundaries of what the humans define as Monroe County." She stretches herself out on the dirt floor before the fire.

"Wait, do they know that we're here? How far are we from the Coven?" Gwen thinks of sitting with her friend on the floor for a moment, but her nerves force her to remain on her feet. The anticipation of seeing Angelo again for the first time as two free individuals builds inside her.

"No one knows we're here. The choice to join your own kind is yours. I feared to tell them about our plan. They might have tried to stop us. I was afraid they might get you killed by trying to barge into Bec LaNuff, or worse that they would come here and take you away, and that I might never see you again." Morna and Gwen share a look of profound understanding, one that communicates all the new feelings of kinship between them that neither can express.

Gwen breaks eye contact first. Seeing that the fire is starting to die down, she retrieves a log from the woodpile and places it on the fire, nursing the flames until they roar to life again. An awkward silence magnified by the darkness around them and the cacophony of sounds from the forest surrounds them.

Gwen can sense something bothering Morna, yet she patiently waits for her to speak first.

"I thought there might be a confrontation if they were here when your Vampire arrives," Morna says to Gwen's back. Slowly, Gwen turns to face her.

"We could simply explain that he's a friend. Surely they can't hate *all* Vampires."

Morna looks Gwen square in the face. "Oh, but they do, and with good reason. You are of two different tribes, completely different races, so naturally they would disapprove."

"They wouldn't approve of our relationship, you mean. I don't care what anyone thinks, Morna. I love him." Gwen moves quickly to the window and looks out into the dark night, avoiding Morna's disapproving gaze.

"I don't approve either, Gwen. I know we barely know each other, but our races' oaths of loyalty make me bound to protect you. I say this as a friend, Gwen: Please leave, before he comes. Forget him. Go to the Coven and learn to be one with your own kind. I think you'll be happier there." Morna lays her hand lightly on Gwen's shoulder.

Gwen turns to look into the Fairy's gold eyes, seeing a great love and tenderness that leaves her speechless.

"Here, take this." Morna places a white, glimmering rock into Gwen's palm. "Whatever you choose to do, take this to protect yourself."

"What is it?" Gwen asks, peering at its pearlescent surface with fascination.

"It's a guardian stone—a special rock that can absorb magic. Witches often use it to store spells. Some use it like a magic grenade," the Fairy explains, looking up at Gwen.

Gwen looks at her, one eyebrow arched incredulously.

"Only the Witch or Warlock who casts the spells on the rock

can handle it without being harmed. If anyone else were to touch it, all the power within is released, destroying everything near. If ever you are too weak or unable to use magic, this will protect you."

"I see. Morna, I—"

"Gwen!" Angelo's voice cuts through the tension between the unlikely friends, breaking their private little moment in time. Startled, they turn their heads toward the door. Angelo's dark silhouette blocks out the moonlight, his face partially lit by the golden firelight, a creature both terrifying and beautiful.

"Angelo!" Gwen's heart rises out of her chest and into that one word. She pushes past Morna and moves into his arms. He holds her to his chest, burying his face into her black mass of hair, all of their suppressed and unrealized emotions spilling over and overflowing into their embrace.

"I thought I might have lost you. You went up in flames and you were just gone. I've been going crazy, staying there and acting calm, pretending I knew nothing, while fearing that you perished in the escape. I can't believe you're here!" He pulls back to look at her, and takes her face in his large, cold hands. "You're all right, then?" Their eyes meet and lock in on each other's souls, knit together in an unbreakable bond .

"Yes. Thanks to Morna." Gwen turns and finds the hut empty behind her, the space before the open window vacant.

"She must have flown out the window," Angelo says, placing his hands on her shoulders and turning her to face him again. "She'll return in the morning to say goodbye, I'm certain of it." He tucks a stray lock of hair away from her face, his cold finger tips caressing her skin, giving her a delightful shiver.

"Angelo, I lo—" He takes her mouth passionately, his kiss stopping her words. Breathless, Gwen kisses back, clinging to him with all her strength.

With the effortless strength of immortality, Angelo sweeps Gwen up into his arms and whisks her across the room, gently lying her down on the bed of hay like a delicate doll. He looks down upon her, half her countenance touched with the golden glint of the fire, the yellow of her eyes burning with their own flame. She reaches out to him, yet he hesitates. He takes her hand in his and kisses it tenderly.

"Gwen, I love you. You know I would never hurt you, right?"

"Yes, I know. We've been inside each other's minds, we've touched souls. I know you as well as I know myself. I trust you, Angelo." Gwen touches his cheek with her free hand.

"It won't be the same as it was with—"

Gwen cuts him off by reaching behind his head, pulling him toward her, and kissing him. They kneel in the hay as their warm lips converge, stopping the loathsome name from being spoken.

She kisses him with a slow, deliberate intensity, drawing Angelo into a dizzy, maddening desire. She pulls back just before he loses his all restraint and looks with misty eyes into his face.

"He doesn't have anything to do with us. Let's never speak of him again. Promise me." Gwen's voice comes out as a hushed whisper.

"I promise. From now on we will leave him behind us. It's just the two of us from now on." He pulls her closer to him, pressing her against him. "I want nothing to get between us. I want you for my own."

Angelo takes her lips, and with deep passionate kisses, slips his tongue into her mouth. She responds welcomingly, moving with him to meet his desire. He begins to kiss across her cheek, and then nibbles her ear. Gwen closes her eyes and moans with pleasure, her heart beating like a drum. The sound of her heart and the pulsing of her blood is hypnotic to him. With anticipation and hunger, he moves his cold lips down the sensitive skin of her pale neck.

Gwen gasps and withdraws from his embrace, looking at him with muted fear. His needlepoint fangs gleam in the fire light. Angelo looks at her, startled. He reaches for her but Gwen puts a hand up to his mouth to stop him.

"No blood. You can have my heart, and my soul, but... my blood I can't give. It's too much like what he... I'm sorry, I'm so sorry, I just can't." The years of abuse still seem so fresh in her mind, every violent and sexual act committed against her crushing her under its weight. She closes her eyes, tears slipping out from under her eyelids and down her soft cheeks. Gwen shakes with wretched sobs, with years of unshed tears, the denied agony and hatred breaking forth from the depths of her soul.

She feels Angelo's cold, soothing embrace as he encircles her in his strong arms. Gwen nestles her head under his chin, burying her face into his shirt, willing the memories to stop, wanting the world to fade away and leave her alone with the man she loves.

"Gwen, don't cry. Listen to me. I can wait for that. I can wait forever if I have to, and if that day never comes, then I'll understand. I have never loved like this. Now I understand all of those feelings and memories my mortal self once had of love, the kind he was willing to die for. I would die for you, Gwen. I want you to know that."

Gwen's tears subside. She sniffles as she pulls back to look up into his pale face, his eyes shining like polished silver, mingled with hope, fear, and love.

"There's only one problem, Angelo. You're already dead." She tries to maintain a straight face as she speaks. He looks at her, a slow smile spreading across his beautiful face. Simultaneously, they burst into laughter, breaking the silence of the night and the tension that surrounds them.

"I forget sometimes that you're only fourteen," Angelo comments, smiling down at her.

"Almost fifteen. My birthday's in six months."

"Okay, fifteen then, That means only three more years until you're legal." Angelo nonchalantly slips his dark gray shirt over his head in a slow, sensual manner, showing every muscle of his chest and arms in one single, deliberate motion. Tossing the shirt aside, he's left bare-chested, his skin beckoning for Gwen's touch.

"Not like my age really matters, does it?" Gwen asks.

"Not to me," Angelo replies. With a wicked smile, he leans in to kiss her. Gwen takes in a breath to steady her racing heart, and then he brings her mouth with his, their lips and tongues doing their own kind of mating. Angelo slowly leans closer, placing his knees on either side of her, forcing Gwen to lie down on the hay as he presses his body down upon hers.

His full weight upon her sends a pleasant little shiver of excitement through her body. She reacts by running both of her hands down the smooth, icy skin of his back, shivering.

Angelo pulls back. "Are you cold?"

Gwen nods.

"Hmmm." Angelo raises his eyebrows at her suggestively. "Let's get you warmed up, then." Swiftly, he sweeps her up in his arms. They move across the room to the hearth like a gust of wind. He lies her down on the floor, at least a foot or two away from the dwindling fire.

Gwen reaches a hand toward the fire. "*Flare Mes Roara*," she chants, a small ball of fire shooting from her hand into the fireplace. The fire bursts into a sudden roaring flame. Lying back on the ground, Gwen looks at Angelo who kneels at her feet. "Impressed?"

"I am. I haven't gotten to see you in action much before. I guess I'll have to get used to your witchy ways."

"Of course you will. And I'll have to accept you and all your vampy ways."

Crawling over Gwen's slender frame, Angelo lifts the hem of Gwen's shirt and bends his head to kiss her sweetly all around the bellybutton and along the top of her pelvis just above the waistline of her jeans. He dips his tongue into the sensitive skin of her navel and Gwen convulses with ticklish pleasure, suppressing a giggle.

They look at each other a moment, both a little nervous.

Gwen gulps and shyly averts her gaze to the fire.

"Gwen? What's wrong?"

She turns her head and finds Angelo lying on the floor beside her. She looks into his eyes and her fears melt away, leaving her with nothing but a deep longing to be loved, understood, wanted, needed, and held close. Her need propels her toward him.

Her lips crash into his, meeting in a long, emotional kiss. Gwen rolls on top of Angelo, their skin ice and fire intertwined. His kisses become more urgent, the pounding of her heart and the rush of her blood loud in his supernatural ears. He rolls her onto her back. "I love you, Gwenevere," he whispers breathlessly in her ear.

"Angelo, I need you. Make love to me." Gwen lets one hand slide down the pale skin of his abdomen to playfully caress the sensitive skin just above his pubic bone. He gives a shudder and a little groan from the back of his throat.

Angelo pushes himself off of her to look into her face, her golden green eyes blazing with passion. "Gwen, are you sure? We can wait. It doesn't have to be tonight."

"I know. Think of this as me exercising my independence. For the first time in years I'm free to do what I want. And I want you." She reaches up to him, grasping him by the back of his hair she brings his mouth to hers and kisses him with all the intensity she has left in her. One of Gwen's hands trails down his chest towards the fly of his jeans. Slowly, she unzips his pants.

Angelo stops kissing her and gently pulls away, removing her hand from his waist. Gwen looks at him, confused.

"What, you don't want to?" she asks uncertainly.

"Yes, very much."

"Then what's wrong?" Gwen thinks for a moment. "I thought you said age didn't matter to you."

"It didn't until now, but… Gwen, what do you want? I know there's a Coven nearby…" Gwen senses Angelo's hesitation, the fear and sadness beneath his thoughts, "If you want to be with your own kind, I'll understand. I want only what's best for you. I—"

"I want to be with *you*. I've met some Wiccans before and it wasn't such a pleasant meeting. I also gather from all of Emon's lessons that true Witches don't approve of wild ones like me." Mentally, she shows him flashes of images and feelings from the incident in the ally in New York several years ago. He absorbs this memory, understanding everything she experienced. "Apparently I'm considered dangerous, or crazy, or something," she continues.

Angelo laughs, the sound echoed by his inner mirth. It has quite the pleasant effect on Gwen. "You're not crazy, Gwen, but I have no doubt that you're absolutely deadly to your enemies. I'll do my best to stay on your good side." He smiles at her.

"You better. I'm not only a feral Witch but a teenage girl. You don't want to mess with me."

Angelo suddenly grabs her, rolling on top of her and pinning her beneath him in a playful attempt at wrestling. Gwen shrieks with laughter as she struggles to squirm out from under him. Finding her physical strength inferior to his, she makes a show of giving up and accepting defeat.

"Get off of me!" Gwen uses her voice in the strange tone that commands people's wills, staring Angelo dead in the eyes.

For the briefest moment his smile disappears from his face and a blank, mindless expression replaces it, his eyes glazing over. His thoughts become muted and empty, his emotions calm and still as if he feels nothing at all. Immediately he moves off of her, scrambling to his feet. He then fights the control of the entrancing spell. He shakes his head visibly, closing his eyes to break eye contact with Gwen's haunting eyes. Inwardly, Gwen feels his thought patterns return to normal as he regains control of his own will.

Astonished, Gwen laughs aloud. Angelo glares back at her.

"What on Earth was that? What did you just do to me?" He tries to sound angry, but their mental connection betrays his true feelings. He's impressed, fascinated, perhaps a little uneasy, but he's not afraid of her.

"I entranced you. It's my version of your Vampire mind control trick. It only lasts as long as I'm in eyesight, and only if I'm very specific about my commands." She smiles up at him sweetly. "Are you angry with me?" she asks as she sits up and wraps her arms around her knees.

"I'm not angry, but don't ever do that to me again!" Mentally, he shows her a vision of the kind of punishment she'll receive if she dares entrance him again. Gwen laughs aloud. Giving her a false scowl, Angelo walks over to her. Gwen gives him her hand and he helps her up to her feet. They stand there a moment, suddenly lost in each other's eyes. Gwen steps closer and wraps her arms around him, resting her head on his shoulder. They fall silent as they share all their inner feelings, both loving the peaceful noises of the forest outside their little hut.

"So we're not going to have sex tonight?" Gwen asks, her face still pressed against his shoulder.

"No, Gwen. I know you don't think of yourself as a child, but really you are." Angelo feels Gwen's mental annoyance at this statement and hurries on. "You've experienced things that have aged you beyond your years, but you haven't really had time to live a normal life. You're not emotionally ready for that kind of relationship, not after what's been done to you."

Gwen looks into his eyes. "But I want this with you. I want to move on from all of that. I'm… well, I guess I'm used to it now," she reasons.

"Well, you shouldn't be." He bends his head to kiss her forehead. "I don't want to be like him. Don't you see it would be like I was taking advantage of you, just like he did?"

"No, it wouldn't…"

"No, Gwen." Angelo takes her by the shoulders and looks into her eyes. "You need time to heal. I want to have that with you someday. In fact, I look forward to it." He laughs ruefully. "I want to make love to you when you're well over this. I don't mean that for you, but also for me. I have no desire to be a means of revenge or denial for you. We'll make love when you're ready, when you're emotionally and mentally fit. Not a moment before."

Suddenly he feels Gwen mentally withdraw from him, shutting him out.

"I'm tired and cold," she says as she casts her eyes downward. Angelo can hear her teeth chattering.

"Let's go to bed, then. You've had a long day, and you need your rest." Without another word he lifts her into his arms and carries her over to the bed of hay. Kneeling, he lays her down and crawls over to rest beside her.

Gwen turns on her side to look at him, trying her best to ignore the itchy sensation of the hay.

Silently, he watches her. "What are you thinking?"

"It wouldn't be revenge." Gwen whispers. "You're not a rebound kind of thing. You're..." She averts her gaze to the ceiling, unsure what to say next.

He reaches out and takes her hand in his, intertwining his fingers with hers. She looks down at their joined hands, and then up at his face.

"I know. I love you enough to wait for you."

Gwen swallows hard, her eyes becoming misty.

"Please don't shut me out." He reaches for her and she curls up into his arms, melting with him. After a moment she releases her mental guard, and her thoughts and feelings pour into his mind. Angelo and Gwen lay there a long while, sharing a multitude of thoughts, ideas, and emotions without ever saying a word. Mentally they agree that Gwen will not seek shelter with her own kind; instead, they will travel the world together.

"You know he'll never leave us be," Angelo speaks aloud.

"I know. That means I'll have to run. I'll have to hide for the rest of my life." A cold breeze blows through the window into the room. Gwen shivers in response to the cold and the fear of such a hopeless future.

"And I will be with you every day from now until then." His cold flesh does nothing to dispel her chill.

"Won't he give up eventually, maybe someday when I'm old and gray? Won't he forgive you then for stealing me away? Can he really hold a grudge that long?"

"If ever there were someone who could hold a grudge for an eternity, believe me it is Le—" Angelo stops himself from saying his name at the last moment, silently cursing himself for being so insensitive. Gwen feels him chastise himself and sends a message of forgiveness through their bond.

"Oh, I believe it. I've been at his mercy for a couple years. I know what he's capable of."

Flashes of memories of her nights spent alone with Legion come unbidden to her mind. Those nights when he beat her, when he bled her and drank from her, when he let her think he was about to kill her, only to have his way with her instead. Gwen tries to shut these images out as soon as they arise in her mind's eye, and she instantly feels Angelo's anger and despair at these thoughts. She feels his inner struggle to fight his own rage, impressed by his mastery of his own.

"You don't even want to know the terrible things he did to his own father when he was still human. Becoming a Vampire has only magnified his evil and vindictive nature."

"So we have no choice. We have to go into hiding," Gwen concedes sadly.

All she had ever wanted in her life was a home of her own, a safe place to stay and live in peace forever, and someone with which to share it. Once she thought she might find that home with her dear friend Raven. It had been too long since she saw him and he seems all but lost to her forever. Now in her dreams she sees only Angelo sitting beside her. Sadly, she realizes that she will age while he will not. She would die and he would live to love another. The thought makes her desperate, jealous, and lonely.

Angelo pulls away from her and looks into her magnificently strange eyes.

Aloud he says, "Gwen. Hear me now, and know this: I will love you as long as I live no matter how long you are on this Earth. I will protect you from him with my immortal life. I will stay by you no matter how old you are, for you will always be my Gwenevere. You will always be beautiful. My love will be yours until our last kiss, until the last embrace."

CHAPTER TWENTY-ONE

Prey

High above him, the full moon casts its silvery light over the forest. The winter breeze blows through his fur, but he doesn't feel the bite of the cold. Over the years he has become accustomed to the elements of nature on his monthly hunts, when his civilized human nature is overcome by the animal inside, transforming him from man into wolf. Now long past puberty and into manhood at the age of nineteen, Raven can at last control his transformation, except during the full moon.

He'll never understand why a big hunk of floating rock 238,857 miles away has such a strong effect on him. All he knows is that no werewolf can resist the beast under the full light of that celestial sphere. Raven, like the rest of his kind, must take the wolf's shape and hunt for living flesh, compelled by the monster inside.

In his animalistic form, Raven runs wild through the woods, his paws barely noticing the chill of the snow beneath them. He sniffs the air for the scent of his prey on the wind. A familiar smell reaches his nostrils. He bolts to the right, charging through the trees. He smells the fresh mountain spring at the same moment he hears it, long before he sees it with his golden eyes. Breaking into the clearing, he finds the doe, his prey. She dashes away from the spring to escape him, but it's already too late. Raven leaps and lands on top of her, pinning her beneath him. Instinctively he bites down on her neck and tears out her throat with his massive teeth, her blood tangy sweet on his tongue. His prey goes limp beneath him. The light in her eyes extinguishes at her moment of death. He spits out the remnants of the animal's throat and digs into the meatiest part of the carcass. The hunt is over and the feasting begins.

"I've always wanted to see that," a young woman says.

Startled, Raven scurries back from his meal to look into the trees around him, but his wolf eyes cannot detect the voice's origin.

"Sorry to disturb you, Wolf." A sudden movement alerts him to the presence of a man to his left. To anyone else, the man might have blended into the forest, his skin as black as night. "I am Lucca, and this"—A teenage girl drops from the trees and lands effortlessly on the ground—"is Ryan. We are Vampire."

Raven looks at the two of them through the eyes of the beast but understands their speech with his human mind. They speak the true tongue. He is not surprised at this, for his new pack told him that all the Forsaken did. Still, he can't help but be taken aback. He remembers a time not too long ago when he thought there were only two people in the world who knew the true tongue, but that seemed a lifetime ago.

Somewhere nearby, another wolf howls into the night. Ryan moves as if to hide behind her companion but stops herself. She reeks of fear to Raven. A second howl pierces through the night just behind the two Vampires, followed by more, and then more, until the forest is full of the cries of his pack. Only when the wolves emerge into view does Lucca seem to finally take notice, giving a sardonic smile to the lot of them.

"Come now, we aren't here to pick a fight. We are looking for a wolf who answers to the name Raven." The black man's voice is darker than the bleakest night. Raven does not care for the smell of him either.

None of the wolves reply. How could they? As far as Raven knows, only Gwen could converse with their kind while under the influence of the Beast. A kind of electrified silence fills the clearing, until the anxious teenage vampire can hold her tongue no longer.

"Are you sure these are Werewolves? Maybe they're just plain old wolves. Could the Master have been wrong?" Ryan eyes the pack suspiciously, her fear wafting all around them, her scent overpowering. Through the shared link between him and the pack, he knows that all of them are a little agitated by these unwanted visitors.

"Yes, they're Werewolves, and the one we seek is among them. Unfortunately, it is a full moon," Lucca replies to his young companion. She gives him a confused look, so Lucca continues, "They cannot change their shapes until dawn. They cannot speak to us but they do understand us."

"Then why isn't anyone doing anything? They're just staring at us," Ryan asks in a low whisper.

"Let me handle this. Stop talking and calm down. They can sense your fear and it upsets them." At this, Ryan seems to grow even more fearful. Lucca shakes his head in frustration, turning to look at the wolves in turn.

"Forgive my companion. She is still young, She knows nothing about anything." Ryan glares at him, but Lucca ignores her. "We have a message for Raven. We seek the girl Gwenevere. She was living amongst us as our guest, but now she has been taken by an enemy vampire named Angelo."

Raven's ears twitch at this. Lucca notices the response and takes a step closer to him. A large silver wolf growls in response, making Lucca stops in his tracks.

"Raven, our Lord is very distressed about her abduction and has sent several of his followers out to find her. We believe that if Gwenevere were to escape her Vampire captor, she might come to you for help."

Gwen has been living with vampires! The last I heard she ran away from her foster family, and her foster father died mysteriously. Why would she live with these creatures instead of coming here to be with me? And now she's been kidnapped by one of them!

"Our Lord anxiously awaits her return, and has sent me here to give you a message. Tell Gwenevere that we can protect her from this villain Angelo. Tell her she needs not hide out with you wolves. She is not to blame and the Master will forgive all if she just comes home."

His mind reeling, Raven thinks, *Just who is this Master and why would Gwen need to be forgiven for anything? What the hell is going on?*

Brother Raven, what do you make of this? The voice of his pack master Keefe interrupts Raven's inner musings. He speaks to his fellow wolves via a psychic thread.

I don't know what to think about all this. Last I knew my friend Gwen was living with the humans until she disappeared. I haven't heard from her since they separated us.

Is there any reason to believe these soul drinkers? Would she align herself with their kind?

Maybe she was desperate.

Should we trust them? Or should we run them out of our territory? the pack Master asks.

Something is wrong here. My instincts tell me not to trust them. This might be a trap for Gwen. They might be her enemies for all we know, Raven replies.

I agree. Vampires have always been deceitful.

Another pack wolf, Jason, joins in on the conversation. *What should we do, then? Can we kill them? Can we? Can we?*

Raven looks at Lucca, who waits patiently for any reply from the wolves.

Maybe we should kill the man and take the girl captive to question her about Gwen, Raven thinks. *I'd like to know what happened to her.*

They don't know where she is. If they did, they wouldn't come around here looking for her, Jason points out. *I say we slaughter them both!*

Your blood lust will get you into a lot of trouble someday, Jason, the pack Master warns. *My command is to kill the man and keep the girl alive.*

Fine. Maybe she'll be fun to play with later, Jason adds. The other members of the pack laugh inwardly at this.

The wolves howl in unison, startling Ryan. Lucca, on the other hand, changes his casual stance into one of a warrior, poised to attack.

"I have no quarrel with you, wolves. The girl isn't worth getting yourselves killed for. There may be several of you, but I have never lost a fight."

"They must have her," Ryan hisses. "I told you! They're hiding her and that filthy Italian traitor!"

Raven growls at Ryan, baring his sharp teeth. His fellow wolves, eager for action, wait for him to make the first move.

"Know this before I kill you," Lucca says, all attempts at

civility gone, his voice even more dark and formidable. "Our Master made your little bitch his whore. She may have escaped for now, but once she is caught he will make her suffer till she begs for death!"

The Beast taking over entirely, Raven snaps, snarling at Lucca. The rest of the pack flanks them on all sides. Ryan whirls around to cover Lucca's back.

A new scent wafts on the wind, and then suddenly two more Vampires emerge from the trees behind his pack mates. Both are women with the same honey-colored hair. One is very tall, the other about five foot five. They smile wickedly as they begin to circle the pack. The younger Vampire, Ryan, seems to regain her confidence.

It's a trap! Jason yells through the bonds.

Do not fear, Pack Master Keefe proclaims. *We still outnumber them. Their lives will end tonight.*

"Your hide will make a beautiful gift for my master. You'll look well before his hearth," taunts Lucca, letting out a dark laugh as he stares Raven down.

Raven leaps into the air as Lucca lets out a guttural yell and charges him. Animal and Immortal collide midair and then crash to the ground, Lucca struggling to keep Raven's jaws from clamping down on his head. Snarling and yowling, the rest of the wolf pack attacks.

Although the sound of battle rages around them, Raven ignores the others. All he can see is red, literally and figuratively.

Lucca's arms and chest are covered in bloody gouges, his clothes torn. His every muscle strains to keep Raven at bay.

Suddenly Lucca gets his feet up under Raven, using his full force to throw the wolf off. Raven sails through the cold night air, landing with a bone-cracking thud in the stream ten feet away. He tries to get up but collapses. Several bones are broken, including his ribs. The fight gone out of him, Raven lets out a pained whine, calling for help from his pack mates.

Lucca appears instantly, standing in the stream beside him. He gives a self-satisfied smile to the wounded beast. Groaning, he cocks back his head as his fangs extend. They gleam white in the moonlight, twin blades of bone. With a laugh, Lucca falls upon his prey.

Chapter Twenty-Two

Appearing Human

A soft nibbling awakes her. A cold, metallic breath tickles her inner ear, startling Gwenevere out of her dream-like state. Frantically pushing the unknown person away, she scrambles out of bed. Panicked, she stumbles across the pitch black room, away from her unseen attacker.

"Don't bite me, don't bite me!" she cries out.

"Gwen! Wake up, it's just me!" A concerned male voice with a slight Italian accent speaks to her in the darkness. Suddenly, a light pierces her eyes, momentarily blinding her. When her vision adjusts, she looks about the room.

She stands in the middle of a small Chicago apartment—a combination of bedroom, living room, and dining room. All the windows are covered with black, opaque drapes, blocking out the sunlight. The only light comes from a lamp on the end table next to the bed, giving the place a moody atmosphere.

"You were having another nightmare."

Gwen turns to look at Angelo sitting on a mattress amongst disheveled bedding in the middle of the room. His striking silver-gray eyes contrast with his dark, curly hair. His look of shock and concern reminds Gwen all at once of the here and now. She straightens from her defensive crouch and breathes deeply, trying to soothe the frantic beating of her heart.

"Oh, Angelo," she sighs. Walking towards him, Gwen notices that her left ring finger burns and itches terribly. Instinctively, her right hand scratches around the heavy metal ring whose icy cold weight forever burdens her, trying to sooth the pain in her flesh. As always, she keeps her eyes averted from the sight of it. She doesn't bother trying to remove the ring anymore. She has accepted its presence as a part of her, just as its Master would always be a part of her haunted dreams. His face still haunts her, his visage always waiting behind her eyelids in the dead, dark abyss of her tortured memories.

At least last night's dream was about Raven instead. But why? It felt so real, like I was there, like it was really happening. Did I just see a vision? Gwen fears it was, and can't help but wonder at the outcome of the battle. *It was just a dream,* she tells herself before shaking off the thought.

Feeling like an absolute fool, she climbs back into bed next to Angelo, pulling the covers up. He props himself up on an elbow to look at her.

"Are you all right?" Angelo asks, concern visible on his handsome face as he tucks a strand of her long black hair behind her ear.

"I'm fine, it was just…" Gwen shudders and closes her yellow-green eyes tight.

"You don't have to talk about it if you don't want to." Angelo leans in and kisses her closed eyelids gently with his velvety, cold lips.

A soothing sensation washes over Gwen, causing her tensed muscles to relax. Letting out a moan, she peeks out from under her eyelashes at him and smiles. Suddenly, she reaches up and pulls Angelo on top of her, kissing him passionately. His cold breath and skin sends a chill through her as he lovingly embraces her. After a moment, he tries to pull away but Gwen puts her hand behind his head, holding him in place, his lips pressed to hers. She kisses him greedily. Angelo finally manages to free himself.

"That's enough. Don't you have a bus to catch?" He rolls off of Gwen and out of bed, strolling over to the kitchen to check the clock on the stove. "Yep, it's six. Time for lazy teenagers to get up and dress. You'll miss the seven o' clock bus if you don't hurry," he mocks.

With an annoyed groan, Gwen rolls over, turning her back to him and pulling the blankets up around her to go back to sleep.

Chuckling, Angelo walks over and playfully kicks her blanketed form in the behind.

"Ouch! Leave me alone," Gwen yelps. She remains snuggly bundled in bed.

"You sleep too much." Angelo jumps onto the bed and stands over her, placing his feet on either side of her, jostling her about.

"To you, everyone sleeps too much. You don't sleep at all," Gwen replies, her voice muffled beneath the covers.

Angelo laughs, and stepping over her, falls onto the bed beside her. This time, his attempt to jostle her out of bed causes the mattress to buckle beneath his weight and sends Gwen rolling toward him. She shouts in protest.

"I'll never understand the appeal of sleeping. Why would anyone want to be unconscious, completely vulnerable, and unaware of the world around them for hours on end? Even your dreams seem superfluous to me. After all, you already have daydreams where you can imagine anything. Instead, you should change the world to suit *you*. Dreams are almost impossible to control, and they often turn into nightmares."

Angelo turns, pulling the covers back, and looks at Gwen. Gently he strokes her cheek with his fingertips.

"I think it'd be better if you never slept at all," he says in a hushed whisper. "Your nightmares are far too vivid."

"I wish I knew how to control them. I've tried for years but it almost feels as though they aren't my own."

"What do you mean?"

"I don't know." Gwen pushes the covers back, turning her gaze on Angelo.

The two of them had been living in this small studio apartment for about a month now. The entire apartment consists of a tiny kitchen along one wall, a main living area, and a door on one side leading into the bathroom with a midget-sized bath tub. Angelo thinks the bathroom has character. Every surface, from the floor tiles to the tub, has a layer of filth caked upon it that no amount of disinfectant could possibly obliterate.

They aren't penniless but since they are on the run, they can't afford to draw attention to themselves. So they have spent the last six months on the lamb, living in hovels like this. The furnished apartment came with a soiled twin-size mattress, a fold-up card table with a set of two folding chairs, an ancient twelve-inch television with rabbit ear antennae, and a beat-up old dresser minus a leg. They found the nightstand and lamp from the dumpster out back; sadly these two items are their finest possessions. The black drapes are the only household item they brought with them, the only permanent fixture in their gypsy lives for the past six months.

Although a veritable dump, within its walls she has been happier than anywhere else in her entire life While she is still very young, in her short time she suffered in ways that she can never forget, not in a hundred lifetimes. Without Angelo, her life would still be a dark and dismal existence.

"What's for breakfast?" Gwen asks, stretching her aching back before rolling onto Angelo's chest, snuggling in under his chin.

"Why are you asking me? I'm not your cook," Angelo answers dryly, running his fingers through the strands of Gwen's long, silky hair, gently working out the tangles put there by a restless night's sleep.

"It would be nice if just once you woke me up with breakfast in bed, and we lived in a clean, beautiful apartment with real furniture and sunshine coming in through the windows. Don't you think that'd be nice, to start the day like other people, getting up with the sun?" Gwen whispers, her face pressed against the cold skin of his neck.

He tenses beneath her, gently pushing her away and gets out of bed in one smooth and fluid movement. Gwen groans at being moved from her comfortable resting place and rolls back onto her elbows to observe Angelo with wistful eyes as he moves restlessly about the room.

"No, that doesn't sound nice. Sometimes I think you forget who you're talking to. We're all out of food anyway," Angelo replies.

"Well, so much for romantic gestures involving food, then. Why don't you come back to bed?" Gwen says in her most seductive voice.

Angelo laughs, hauling her out of bed without any preamble. Sleepily, Gwen lets him lead her over to the card table where he pushes her down into a chair. Immediately, he goes to the kitchen and returns with a glass of water, handing it to her. He sits in the chair opposite her.

"*Bon appétit!*" He smiles wryly.

Gwen looks at the filmy water in her glass and back at him

with a look of revulsion. "You've got to be kidding me. This is it? What are you trying to turn me into, an anorexic?"

"You'll have to get yourself some groceries while you're out." With that, he leans back in his chair. "Luckily for you, food is easily acquired in this modern day to satisfy your adolescent appetite. When I was your age, when we had to grow our crops and slaughter animals with our own two hands."

"Yeah, yeah, Grandpa. I bet you walked to school barefooted, too. In the snow. And uphill both ways," Gwen mocks.

Angelo shakes his head at her. "That line's older than I am. And I'm definitely not your grandfather," he says with a laugh.

"Good thing too, 'cuz this would be a little awkward otherwise." Gwen smiles wickedly as she walks around the table to sit on his lap. She wraps her arms around his neck. Angelo takes her into his arms and leans his head down for a kiss.

"What about you? Should I get you a little something from the pet store?" Gwen asks absently just before their lips touch.

Angelo grimaces. The moment ruined, Angelo gently pushes Gwen away from him and remains quiet for a moment.

"I'd still rather feed the natural way, thank you very much, but you insist on treating me like your pet snake. Unless... you've changed your mind about...?"

"No biting! It's my blood. Get your own!" Gwen replies too quickly. She tries to hide her nervousness by running her hand through her hair and avoiding his eyes.

"I would, but as you've pointed out before, we need to lay

low." She hears the displeasure in his voice, but doesn't know what to say.

Walking past her, Angelo goes about the apartment straightening up, a thick silence hanging in the air with all the things left unsaid. When the bed is made, Angelo walks over to the dresser and rifles through the drawers. He places their clothes for the day on the bed. Although strange and unfamiliar to him, he seems to revel in the simplicity and irony of behaving like ordinary mortals. He finds great pleasure in taking care of Gwen, like a husband dotes upon his beloved wife.

Sometimes it is difficult to remember who they really are, tempting as it is to forget all that happened. They almost feel like any other couple living together, in love with a future bright and endless in its possibilities. With a deep sigh of sadness, she forces herself back to reality.

Gwen finds a great deal of pleasure in roaming the streets of Chicago alone. Something about the constant noisy hum that vibrates through the streets and bounces off the buildings of a big city is like music to Gwen. She feels surrounded by a pulsating vibrant life force. The multitudes of people she passes on the street carry it with them with every step they take, renewing her faith in humanity. Although the world around her moves at a bustling speed, she feels calm and comforted knowing that there are ordinary people living perfectly contented, simple lives. It puts a smile on her face to watch them scurry about to their jobs, or to school, or wherever, and know that they have a home and people to love them when they return at the end of every day.

Not many years ago, Gwen would have felt envious of the humans. Back then she was no one and had nothing. She was a gypsy, sleeping on park benches, under trees, beneath freeway overpasses. She was an orphan who stole her food or swindled the innocent passersby into giving her their money. Gwen didn't miss those days. The guilt of those necessary crimes still plagues her from time to time. Since those debts can't be repaid, she has no choice but to leave that all behind her. Now she was with someone who truly loved her. Now she has a home of her own where she finds refuge. Gwen smiles to herself, comforted by the thought.

Quickly, Gwen drinks her glass of water, and puts the empty glass in the sink. Grabbing a sponge and some dish soap, she cleans her glass. Angelo has great wealth that he's accumulated over his long lifetime, hidden away in various secret places. Legion knows the location of some of these secret hoards, but not all of them. Angelo retrieved some money for them to live on, although he fears it might be too risky to collect anymore of his store. They take great caution, living sparingly. Some days they make extra cash performing in parks and street corners, singing and playing the many instruments they have mastered. With a sigh, Gwen rinses out the glass and puts it on the counter to dry.

Just as Gwen turns around, she sees Angelo walk past her on his way to the bathroom, a towel in one arm. He pulls his shirt off over his head with his other hand, exposing his perfect muscular form.

"Is there room in the shower for one more?" Gwen asks with an exaggerated wink.

Shirtless Angelo chuckles, his chest and shoulders shaking as he beams a boyish smile at her. "Perhaps next time."

"That's what you always say!" Gwen grumbles. "I bet that the shower would be a lot hotter with me in it."

He stops at the door and looks back at her. "You, Gwen, are a brazen flirt."

"And you, sir, are a hot tease," Gwen fires back.

"How do you figure that?" Angelo winks and closes the bathroom door behind him, smirking. A moment later she hears the water turn on.

Gwen smiles broadly following after Angelo. She tries to open the bathroom door but it's locked. Gwen glares at the doorknob and, grumbling to herself, she walks to the dresser and grabs her own towel. She sits on the bed, waiting for her turn. While she sits, Gwen converses mentally with her now-naked boyfriend.

Well, you were *quite the scoundrel when I met you. With your suggestive remarks, your shirt always unbuttoned, your random passionate kisses and your wandering hands. Not to mention you did show up in my bedroom in the middle of the night one time in nothing but your underwear. And a very tight pair of underwear, might I add.* Gwen hears his mental chuckles. *Then, the second you win me over and we're out on our own you start playing hard to get whenever I throw myself at you. I'd say that makes you a tease,* Gwen adds good-naturedly.

The shower shuts off, and a few moments later Angelo exits the bathroom clad only in his towel. Gwen raises an eyebrow at this. Angelo saunters across the room and dumps his dirty night clothes into the laundry basket.

"Even now you insist on wandering around half naked in front of me." Gwen taps her foot on the floor, impatient. "Angelo, I'm only fifteen. You can't expect me to keep my hands to myself."

Smiling, Angelo walks over to the foot of the bed where he laid their clothes earlier. Giving her a suggestive look, he lets his towel fall to the ground.

Gwen is shocked for only an instant until her eyes alight on a very tight pair of black boxer briefs covering his body. Gwen's face is priceless. Angelo erupts into laughter. Glaring at him, she hops off the bed with her towel in hand. "You enjoy tormenting me, don't you?"

"I love it," Angelo proclaims, dimples creasing his cheeks.

Gwen reluctantly turns away from his magnificent physique. Shaking her head, she walks into the bathroom and turns on the shower, purposely leaving the door wide open, just in case. Even though she knows Angelo is not quite ready to walk through that door, she wants him to know that she welcomes it.

Gwen quickly strips out of her night clothes and hops into the shower. Ten minutes later the shower shuts off and Gwen steps out, shivering. Retrieving her towel from the grungy counter top, she quickly rubs the moisture off her body.

She finds her clothes in a pile just inside the bathroom door. Gwen considers walking into the other room in her birthday suit just to see Angelo's reaction, but decides against it.

It would serve him right, the prude!

Gwen tosses her towel on the counter and gets dressed. After donning her underwear and bra, she slips on an old faded-black t-shirt over her head and puts on her loose-fitted gray jeans. She dries and combs out her long black hair, brushes her teeth, washes her face, and returns to the living room. Angelo, already dressed in a tight blue t-shirt and blue jeans, sits on the bed cross-legged, reading. Gwen got the book for him from the library only the day previous, knowing he waits for Gwen to return from her daily errands by reading and playing his violin.

After putting her socks on, Gwen finds only one of her shoes lying next to the bed. She turns to Angelo. "Have you seen my other shoe?" She bends down to peek under the bed but finds nothing.

Immediately, Angelo puts down his book and goes to the nightstand next to the bed retrieving Gwen's errant shoe out from under it. "Here." He tosses the shoe at Gwen. She catches it and sits down to slip on her sneakers. "You sure have the messy teenager thing down. It's just lucky for you I'm here to pick up after you," Angelo teases.

"Hey, I thought you liked being the maid." She finishes tying her shoes, flashing Angelo a mischievous smile.

He shakes his head at her, settles back onto the bed, and

continues reading. Gwen smiles from ear to ear. Feeling her stomach growl, she turns towards the kitchen for another glass of water.

While filling her glass from the faucet, Gwen remembers the many hours they spent in heated debate over books and music. While Gwen instructed Angelo on the great literary works of humanity, Angelo tutored her in music. They spent a couple hours every day in this fashion, the two of them taking turns being teacher and pupil. Falling in love in the process had been an accident.

She often wonders if her former Master had ever suspected what was happening between his oldest friend and his "little woman," before they ran away together, fleeing from his tyrannical control and leaving their own world behind to live as fugitives in the human's society.

"Boy, I must be in a dark mood today," Gwen says under her breath. She didn't want to think of her former life as Legion's slave. She wished she could forget everything about him, his face, his touch. Even his name causes her to shiver with revulsion and dread. Just thinking of that monster makes her skin crawl—the touch of his phantom hands, his unseen lips kissing in the most intimate places, the sting of his razor sharp fangs as they pierced her flesh. In her mind she sees the blood, so much blood. White satin sheets drenched in it. Something cold pressing down on her, hissing in her ear as he…

The cold metal ring on her hand sears with cold, sending a

wave of ice-laced pain through her veins straight to her heart. Gwen gasps, dropping the glass in her hand to the floor.

A sudden surge of panic overtakes her, engulfing her in its terrible embrace. She begins to hyperventilate, her heart racing like a metronome at top speed, beating faster and faster until her chest feels as if it's about to cave in and puncture her over-worked heart.

Closing her eyes tightly as she can, she forces the memories out of her mind and into the darkest recesses of her mind, pushing them as far from her consciousness as sanity will allow. When she feels her heart beat slower, her breaths come in more regular intervals. As the panic subsides, she realizes that she has collapsed onto the kitchen floor. She opens her eyes and looks into Angelo's frightened face.

Alarmed, he collects her into his arms. As she buries her face into his shoulder, she fights back the tears that have sprung unnoticed from her eyes during her panic attack.

Angelo strokes her hair and rubs her back in a soothing, loving motion. Feeling herself again, she pulls away from him, using his arm for support as she climbs to her feet.

"I'm sorry," Gwen says apologetically.

"What are you sorry about?" he replies, frustrated.

"I'm sorry you have to see me like this. I don't want to upset you," Gwen answers weakly. Holding onto his arm, they walk together to the table and Gwen takes a seat in a chair, her strength weakening. Instantly, she crosses her arms and lays her head on them to stop the spinning room.

Kneeling beside her, Angelo rubs her back. "Gwen…" he starts.

"Don't worry about me. I'm fine," Gwen says unconvincingly.

"I'm thinking that maybe you ought to stay home after all. Come on, let me carry you to the bed. You should lie down."

"No, I'm all right." Gwen lifts her head from the table and looks up at him, flashing a forced smile. "Please stop fussing. I just need a moment to collect myself."

It was just a stupid flashback. Just a memory, Gwen, that's all. You're never going back there. He'll never touch you again, she promises herself. Her words seem to calm her shattered nerves and strengthen her resolve.

Meanwhile, Angelo steps into the kitchen and begins cleaning up the shards of Gwen's water glass. Once finished, he brings her a second glass of water and places it by her head on the table. He paces the room, waiting for her to show some sign of improvement. He resists the impulse to hover over her.

Angelo hopes that he can heal her, to show her she has nothing to fear from him. *But how long will it take for the nightmares to stop and the panic attacks to cease?* He has an eternity to devote to her, and though he would gladly wait as long as she needed, Gwen's life would pass by, changing and aging her until death, in what will seem like a blink of an eye in his never-ending timeline. Sensing their time together is fleeting, he hates to waste a single moment in misery or woe. He wants her to be happy, but for whatever reason he couldn't do it for her. Gwen must save herself.

All he can do is wait.

Gwen stands, her legs a little wobbly at first, but quickly she steadies herself. When she looks at Angelo, she finds him standing next to her, ready to catch her if her strength should fail.

"I'm fine. Now please stop. I've got to go. I've probably missed the bus already."

"No, I would have heard it downstairs. I think it's running late." Angelo tilts his head to one side and listens with his natural superior hearing to the sounds of the people in their apartment building and on the streets below.

Stepping around him, Gwen slips on her black leather jacket and grabs her bag from where it hangs on a hook by the front door, slinging it over her shoulder. She turns and reaches for the doorknob. An instant later, Angelo's hand places itself on hers. Taking her hand, he turns her to face him.

"Gwen, you can't keep pushing me away. You don't need to put on an act for me. I love you. I wouldn't mind a few tears on my shoulder every once and a while." Angelo strokes her cheek with his cold finger tips. "He has nothing more to do with us. Remember that," he whispers intently.

"You're making too big a deal out of this. I'm fine." She smiles in an attempt to lighten the mood between them, but still Angelo holds onto her hand. One look tells her he isn't convinced. She continues, "If you insist on making this into a big drama, then we can talk about it this afternoon when I get back. I really have to go now."

Gwen turns to leave, but his captive hand holds her back. Sighing in resignation, Gwen turns around, closing the gap between their bodies and laying her other hand on his chest. She reaches up to kiss him, his lips meeting hers half way. He wraps her in his arms as their kiss deepens. Gwen breaks away first. Walking backward toward the door, she maintains eye contact with Angelo until the very last moment. Before she opens the door and walks out, she pauses. "I love you... always," she says, then, as if afraid he's about to follow after her, Gwen hurries out the door. She shuts it behind her and quickly heads down the hall, feeling the distance between them widen with each step.

A strange foreboding creeps into her thoughts. *Why does it feel like I'll never see him again?* The thought makes her shiver. *Nonsense, you're just paranoid, Gwen. No one knows we're here. And even if they did, Chicago is a big place. The chances that one of Legion's spies would find us here is slim to none.* She finds a bit of comfort in the thought.

The airy sound of a violin drifts down the hall to her ears. She turns to look at their apartment door and imagines Angelo somewhere within, his blood red violin tucked beneath his chin, his bow stroking the stings in its own kind of dance to the music its master creates. This was Angelo's tribute to the dawning of a new day, a sight he will never see.

Shaking off her strange mood, Gwen steps into the elevator and pushes the lobby button on the control panel. The doors close, and, as the elevator plummets downward, Gwen begins to feel at ease again. Thinking of window shopping and wandering the busy streets of the hectic concrete city, she makes a list of the food she will buy at the grocery store, the pet store, and the books she will borrow from the library.

She quickly forgets the nightmares and the panic attack that a moment ago threatened her. Humming along to the tune that Angelo plays above, she shifts mental gears, falling back into the routine that has now become her everyday life. Today, like every other day, she will keep up the pretense of appearing human.

CHAPTER TWENTY-THREE

Not Alone

Gwen rides the city bus, headed downtown toward the local library—her last stop of the day before returning home to Angelo. She sits alone, her large tote sitting on the seat next to her and the grocery bags on the floor by her feet. She contemplates what she will eat when she gets home, oblivious to the two teenage boys sitting across the aisle, staring at her. They whisper amongst themselves.

"Hey, you," one of the young men, a large broad-shouldered blond, says as he leans toward Gwen. "Hey. Girl with the long black hair. I'm talking to you."

It takes Gwen a moment to return from her reverie to the present. She turns a quizzical gaze on the two young men.

"Yes?" Gwen replies, barely concealing her impatience.

"What's your name?" the boy asks, trying to smile in a charming manner.

Gwen grimaces in response. "It's none of your business." She turns away from them and returns her gaze out the window. She hears the two young men react in surprise but doesn't turn back. A moment later, Gwen feels a tug at her bag and looks up to see the blond boy remove her bag from the seat. He drops it in her lap and takes the seat next to her. Immediately, his skinny little friend climbs into the he seat in front of her. Leaning over the back of the seat, he looks at her and his friend.

"Now that wasn't very nice," the other man remarks. "All my boy wanted was to know your name. Isn't that right, Nick?" The skinny one addresses Gwen but nods with his head in the direction of his muscular friend next to her.

"Yeah, that's all, baby." Nick takes the opportunity to scoot closer to Gwen, letting one arm rest on the back of the seat. "Like he says, I'm Nick. He's Jeremy."

Jeremy smiles and winks at Gwen, who returns his gaze with a blank stare. "I don't really care what your names are. I just want you to go away. Understand?" She says this in a condescending tone, addressing skinny Jeremy first and then Nick.

Outrage flashes in Nick's eyes, but he forces his lips to smile congenially anyway. Casually, he moves his arm from the seat behind her and wraps it around her back, gripping her arm with his hand and pulling her closer to him.

"You know, for a pretty girl, you're kind of a bitch," emaciated Jeremy replies, grinning smugly with a wicked gleam in his eyes. Jeremy starts to laugh. Nick immediately joins him.

Gwen sits in silence until their mirth subsides. She turns to Nick without looking him in the face. She removes his hand and slips the arm out from behind her, scooting away from him as if discarding a piece of garbage.

"I'm giving you until the count of ten to stand up and go back to your seats. And you are not to talk to me, look at me, or think about me as long as I'm on this bus. Do you two idiots understand me?"

Gwen can barely contain her amusement at the sight of their stunned faces. Apparently, no woman ever talked to them like that before. *Well, it's about time.* She waits for the two boys to react. They looked at each other, bewildered for a moment.

"Someone needs to teach this little whore some respect," Jeremy comments to Nick.

Nick nods in agreement. "Girl, I think you'd better be nice to us. You wouldn't want anything to happen to your pretty little face now, would you?" Discreetly, he pulls a butterfly knife from his coat pocket. He brandishes it dangerously close to Gwen's face.

The other passengers on the bus ignore them. No one even thinks of coming to the young girl's aid.

Gwen sighs. *It figures,* she thinks to herself. *That's the problem with humans. They're all cowards.* Not that she needs their help, but still it would have been nice if, just once, someone would bother to show a little backbone. For all they know she could be an ordinary, helpless, teenage girl, and still they sit, staring straight ahead as if nothing is happening. "Humans," she grumbles out loud. Gwen doesn't respond to the blade, or to Nick's threats. She just sits there, completely calm and collected.

"One," Gwen says loudly, her voice even and commanding. The boys break into a peel of laughter, mocking her.

"Two." Gwen counts on, her face implacable as stone.

Smiling broadly, Nick scoots closer, pushing her right up against the window, trapping her. He raises the blade of his knife and moves it along the contours of her jaw and cheekbone as if tracing her face in the air, the blade only inches from her flesh.

"Three." Narrowing her eyes at Nick, she continues to chime at a regular pace, "Four."

"Can you believe her? Man, you're either stupid or you've got a death wish, princess." Jeremy, kneeling on the seat in front of her, leans in, getting right up into her face.

Gwen doesn't bat an eyelash. "Or maybe I've just got bigger balls than you," she retaliates, the corners of her lips curving in a slight smile. "Five."

Jeremy's face goes red in anger, but Nick bursts out laughing. Jeremy shoots him a look of irritation.

"Six," she goes on, ignoring them completely.

"What are you going to do if we don't leave you alone?" Nick asks as he places his free hand on her thigh and squeezes. He smiles at her smugly.

"You two have got to be the unluckiest morons in all of Chicago. Out of all the women in this city, I'm the last one you want to mess with." This time Gwen lets a deadly sneer cross her face. "Seven." She smiles mockingly at them.

"I get it. You think you're a tough little bitch," Nick practically growls. "I'm impressed. I really am. But you don't seem to understand, sweetheart. You don't want to mess with us." He presses the knife against her throat.

"Eight." Gwen raises an eyebrow at Nick, as if daring him.

"You know what? I'm tired of this bullshit," Jeremy shouts in Gwen's face. He turns to Nick. "I say we take her in the back and have a little fun with her."

"Nine." Gwen almost laughs with wicked glee at Jeremy's agitation. *He's scared.* She smiles inwardly at the thought. *Good. But his blockhead friend doesn't seem to get it.*

"I like the sound of that," Nick replies. Turning his slimy gaze upon Gwen, he looks her up and down as if undressing her with his eyes. "I want see what you look like under these clothes." He runs the dull side of the blade down her neck to the collar of her shirt, slipping the tip of it into her blouse as if he is going to cut open the fabric. "I bet you look real good," he whispers in her ear.

The gesture makes her skin crawl in such disgust that her face contorts with rage. Holding in the urge to bash his head into the window, her body tenses, and through clenched teeth she hisses, "Ten!"

In a flash of arms, Gwen seizes both of Nick's hands. She

moves with inhuman speed. Jeremy watches in shock as Gwen disarms with complete and total ease a man twice her size.

She twists Nick's wrist in a quick forceful motion, causing him to drop the weapon. The blade pricks Gwen's skin, slicing her briefly before it falls onto the floor at their feet.

Nick yells out in pain and surprise. The sound of his breaking bones muffles the river of profanity that spews from his lips. In the same instant, she pries his other hand from her thigh, crushing it with as little effort as she would crumble up a piece of paper. With a light thrust of her arms, she shoves Nick away from her, sending him flying across the aisle, hitting the opposite wall of the bus with a loud metallic thud. Out of the corner of her eye, she notices Jeremy pick up the knife from the floor. She stands from her seat to confront him as Jeremy lunges in a pathetic attempt to stab her. Gwen doesn't move. She stands and looks into his brown eyes as if boring a hole into his soul.

"Stop." Gwen's voice makes a deep, hollow noise which penetrates into Jeremy's skull, reverberating all around him as if everywhere at once. Her command engulfs his every thought in an overpowering net of confusion and bewilderment. Stopping short, he stumbles forward a few steps before regaining his balance. He looks up at her, his face going blank, and then stands up straight, his body stiffening as if standing at attention before a drill sergeant. His eyes lock on hers, enraptured by her gaze.

"Give me the knife," Gwen commands, bringing him out of his stupor. Jeremy obediently hands over the knife, as complacent as a little child. He looks at her, awaiting her next command as a dog would look upon his master.

"Sit down."

Immediately he obeys, sitting next to his unconscious friend with a big, happy grin upon his face, as if all were right in the world.

Only then does Gwen turn her attention to the other passengers on the bus. Every single face has turned toward her, their eyes transfixed on her, their bodies rigid as if hypnotized. Gwen glances to make sure the bus driver is still driving and sees him sitting just as erect as everyone else. He gazes upon her through the rear-view mirror, his eyes wide and fixed upon her face.

Gwen gasps as she looks through the windshield and sees the cars ahead of them coming to a stop at a red light. In the blink of an eye she is standing next to the driver. He turns his head to look at her.

While holding his gaze, she commands in an urgent voice. "Stop the bus!"

Instantly, the driver springs to life, as if Gwen pushed the 'play' button on his remote. Gwen braces herself as he stomps heavily on the brakes, causing the bus to lurch to a stop inches from the car in front of them. Gwen and the rest of the passengers jerk forward and then backward with the bus's momentum.

After regaining her balance, Gwen heaves a heavy sigh of relief. She takes a moment to let the jittery excitement of fear melt away from her body. She is brought back to the present by a blaring car horn. Looking up, she sees that the traffic light ahead of them has turned green and the line of vehicles has already started ahead of them. Several of the drivers behind them honk their horns impatiently.

"Keep driving," she commands the bus driver in a soothing voice. "Now pull over at the next bus stop and let me out," she instructs. The driver obeys, a ridiculously wide grin on his face. As he drives down the road and approaches the next stop, Gwen notices, to her dismay, that a large group of people waits for them there.

She quickly turns to face the other passengers who are still sitting in their seats at attention, awaiting her next command.

She clears her throat. "Nothing strange happened on this bus. You saw nothing unusual. When the others come onto this bus you will act and behave as you normally do. You will go about your business doing what you always do and will remember nothing. You will forget that you ever saw me as soon as I step onto the curb." When she finishes speaking, she breaks eye contact. Instantly everyone around her relaxes. As the bus pulls up to the curb, Gwen turns to the driver and whispers similar commands to him, holding his gaze until the last word is uttered.

Outside, waiting pedestrians begin to shout impatiently for the doors to open. Quickly, Gwen turns and goes to the doors. Looking over her shoulder to the driver she barks, "Open the doors." The doors open inward in front of her. A moment later, a crowd of bodies rush aboard, forcing Gwen to push and shove her way down the steps to get past them and off the bus. Without pausing or looking back, Gwen hurries down the street, mentally following the bus and the minds of the people within until it passes far from her and the reaches of her mental boundaries.

Only then does she release the air in her lungs. She continues to walk as fast as she can, never relenting in her breakneck pace. She forces her way through the busy streets, shoving people out of her way as she goes. Ignoring the shouts of angry pedestrians, she continues walking, completely oblivious to the world around her, tormented by her own thoughts and emotions.

I seriously could have killed us all, she thinks to herself. *Had I not stopped the bus driver, he would've rammed right into traffic, maiming us and the people in the other cars as well.*

She swore to herself that she would never entrance other people unless absolutely necessary. She could have easily disarmed the two thugs on the bus without resorting to magic, yet without a thought in her head, she'd acted on instinct.

And I almost killed dozens of people because of it! she yells at herself. *What will Angelo say when I tell him?* In her mind, Gwen sees Angelo in front of her and hears his voice in her head.

Gwen, you just can't keep going around letting your emotions rule over you. You could have exposed us. Our enemies will be on our heels, and then we would have to flee again. Can't I let you out of my sight for even an hour without you trying to destroy half of Chicago?

Okay, so maybe he wouldn't say that last part, she corrects herself. *But I'm sure he'll be angry when I tell him what an idiot I've been today.* She lets out a frustrated sigh. *I wouldn't have to resort to violence or magic if only my boyfriend weren't afraid of the sun,* Gwen grumbles.

As much as she loves Angelo, a part of her resents that he doesn't live and behave as an ordinary man. She longs to walk down the street hand in hand with him on a sunny day instead of having to skulk about at night as if they had something to hide.

Well, we do have something to hide, she reminds herself.

Suddenly, she remembers her old friend. Nothing would have happened on the bus today if Raven had been with her. With his impressive bulky form and the dark brooding demeanor, he could've easily frightened off the two morons on the bus. She remembers last night's dream. A river of memories floods her mind with visions of the boy who was her first and only friend.

She reminisces of her first days at St. Paul's orphanage and the first time she ever saw him. Nine-year-old Raven, sitting alone in a tree, looking down at the other children as they played in the yard around him. Everyone teased him for being so different and slow, and everyone was afraid of her because of the strange things that happened whenever she was near. So they had naturally been drawn to each other.

Although big and strong for his age, Raven was painfully shy and timid, like a frightened little animal, while Gwen was the fearless one, taking on anyone who dared to make fun of her friend, regardless of how much older or bigger they were. After a while, the other orphans learned to stay away from them.

A dozen other memories dance nimbly in her mind as she walks through the city. If only she knew of a way to reach out and find Raven again.

Taking a deep breath to steady herself, Gwen stops and looks around for a place to sit down. She spies a bench goes to it, weaving her way through the throng of pedestrians. With a sigh of relief, she plops onto the bench. Leaning forward, she cradles her face in her hands and rests her elbows on her knees to collect her thoughts.

Everything's all right. I fixed my mistake. Now no one will remember. I can just go on as though nothing happened, she reassures herself, but a terrible realization dawns on her.

I forgot about Nick! She gasps, sitting bolt upright and stares dumbfounded into space. *He was unconscious. He didn't get entranced. When he wakes up he's going to remember everything, and he'll be all the more suspicious because his friend and everyone else on the bus will say they saw nothing.* She groans aloud, shaking her head in disbelief. *Oh, Gwen, you're such an idiot! Now calm down. There's no way he can find me, right? I mean, it's not like he knows my name or anything.* Just as the thought begins to comfort her, another terrible realization occurs to her.

I left my bag and the groceries on the bus! She quickly thinks of the contents of her bag, searching mentally for something that might lead back to them and their apartment. There are no bills, they pay everything in cash. She didn't have an I.D. Her library card had a fake name on it. All he had to do is go to the library and look her up in the database to find out where she lives. They had her real address on file.

Gwen curses aloud. There's nothing to be done now, she supposes. She can't track him down on her own, and by the time the sun sets, Nick's scent will be too faint for Angelo to pick up.

There's nothing to do about it but pick up and move again. She groans inside. She hates moving from place to place. All she ever wanted was a home, a place where she could be safe and never have to leave, a place she shared with loved ones, a sanctuary from the world's judging eyes. Where she could use her gifts and not feel afraid of being caught doing magic. It's a lovely dream but a dream is all it will ever be. Other people have happy lives full of simple pleasures. Not Gwen.

I suppose I better go home and tell Angelo. With a sigh of resignation, she gets up and starts walking back the way she came. It's a long walk back to their apartment and though she has just enough money to ride the bus back, after the incident earlier she had no desire to ever ride the bus again. Besides, the long walk home gives her plenty of time to think and clear her head before she must confront Angelo. She doesn't look forward to the lecture in store for her, but she'll feel safe and protected as soon as she is in his arms again.

I knew I should've just stayed home today. She laughs

inwardly at the irony. *And I still haven't eaten anything.* Her stomach growls at her in affirmation. Gwen walks on, deep in thought, wondering what kind of breakfast she can buy with the couple of dollars she has left after buying groceries, where they might run next, and how much money they could make performing on the streets to pay for their escape. She makes her way through the city streets and on toward her tiny, little apartment and her immortal Italian beau. She thinks of Angelo, knowing everything will be okay as long as they're together.

Meanwhile, behind her, someone follows. Gwen continues onward, completely oblivious to the fact that she is not alone.

CHAPTER TWENTY-FOUR

Possession

As Gwen makes the long trek home, she finds herself thinking about all the things she's going to miss about living in a big city. She'll miss the crowded streets, Hayward's grocery store, and the little coffee shop down the street from their apartment where Gwen drags Angelo every other night. Most of all, she will miss the feeling of being anonymous. Living in such a large city makes her feel safe, as though she can blend into the crowd, just another freak among the multitude of diverse and strange cultures that make up Chicago.

Her thoughts find their way back to the time when she lived in New York, three years ago with Raven. She was eleven, and he only fifteen.

She misses him more than she'll ever admit to Angelo. Raven was like a brother: strong, dependable, kind-hearted, and long-suffering. He put up with Gwen's many antics, her talent for getting into trouble, without ever complaining. She misses the sense of belonging to a family. She belongs to Angelo now, but she fills the role of a lover, part of a coupled pair. It isn't better or worse than what she had with Raven, just different. Suddenly, Gwen is torn from her reminiscence by a strange sensation.

The hairs on her neck stand on end as a shiver runs down her spine. She has the strangest feeling that she's being watched. She tries to shake it off, but still the feeling persists. When Gwen cuts through the park a couple of blocks from home, she knows with a certainty that someone is following her.

Outwardly she remains calm. She keeps walking at the same dispassionate pace that she has for the past hour, keeping the expression on her face unreadable. She nonchalantly deviates from her course. She heads toward a rarely-used archway in the fence that leads from the park into an isolated alleyway near several abandoned warehouses. If anyone follows, it would be all too apparent that they are stalking her. She chooses the alleyway because it's the perfect place for her to confront an attacker. No one but the occasional squatter lives in this part of town, leaving her free to defend herself, using any method necessary without fear of onlookers witnessing anything unusual.

The alley is narrow with two high-walled factories jutting up into the sky on either side, casting it into shadows even midday. The alleyway itself is cluttered with liquor bottles, car parts, and rusty, old machinery from the surrounding factories. A large tarnished dumpster, a torn, beat-up, green couch, and an ancient television rest in the corner near the far end of the alley. Beyond the archway and the alley, there is only one other way out, leading to a deserted road.

Gwen turns at the end of the alley to face the archway, blocking off the other exit, awaiting her victims to wander into her trap. Mentally she prepares herself, thinking of all the possible assailants that might walk out of the park.

Could Nick have woken up as I was leaving and followed me all this time, waiting for an opportunity to strike? It seems unlikely, but no other alternative presents itself to her. She can't think of any reason why some random stranger would follow her, so she dismisses the idea immediately.

Whether it was their inherent disgusting nature, or because of the overwhelming hypnotic sexual power of her presence that enticed Nick and Jeremy to attempt to sexually assault her, she'd never know. Certainly they were creeps to begin with, so her unusually strong brand of pheromones probably only aggravated their filthy intentions. In that case she feels just a little bit sorry for them, but not that sorry. *They deserved what they got.*

Suddenly Gwen feels the presence of three beings approaching the gateway, their minds somewhat muddled, making it hard for her to detect whether they're human or Forsaken. She finds no entrance into their minds to identify them. Although this is somewhat suspicious, it isn't anything too alarming. Often when humans are sick, insane, senile, intoxicated, or infant, their thoughts are an incoherent jumble, making them very difficult to decipher.

Gathering her mind into a shield of protection against a magical attack, she takes a defensive stance and awaits their appearance in the alley. To her astonishment, a mother and child walking their large Saint Bernard on a leash exit from the park and walk into her alley, seemingly unaware of her presence.

The woman is young, perhaps thirty years old, wearing a raincoat with a hood that covers the upper half of her face, which is downturned towards her son, whispering to him in a low voice. The little boy's age is harder to determine because of the strange clothes he wears. The sleeves of his shirt and the cuff of his pants are several inches too long for his stumpy little limbs. *It looks almost as if he were wearing his older brother's clothes,* Gwen observes. She can barely see his face because of the large baseball cap on his head which casts his face into shadows. As for the large, slobbering dog, he looks like a normal dog, so Gwen gives it no further notice. She is just about to turn and walk away, dismissing her earlier premonition as simple paranoia, when a thought suddenly occurs to her.

The dog! she thinks to herself. *His mind hadn't felt like an animal's.* Without any outward change in her appearance, Gwen continues to walk as if nothing is wrong. Mentally, she reaches out to the dog's mind, trying to probe into his consciousness without being detected. If it were really a dog, her presence in his thoughts would only confuse it, otherwise…

Gwen hasn't time to finish the thought, before she finds

herself barred by a mental block. Behind this wall, she senses a pulsating, violent intelligence, which is most certainly not human. There is no time to react to this revelation however, for in the instant she touches his mind, she senses the prickling sensation of magic being drawn, causing the hairs on her arms and neck to stand on end.

Throwing herself to one side of the alley, Gwen barely manages to dodge the ball of energy that comes hurling to the spot where she stood. Missing its target, the energy ball bursts into a million sparks of light as it hits the wall.

Cursing under her breath, Gwen springs to her feet, gathering the energy around her into the core of her body, the words of the pure tongue on her lips, preparing to cast her spell to repel her enemies.

Facing her foe, she finally sees them for what they truly are. What she had thought was a mother and child is in fact a female Elf and a Dwarf. The woman flings off her raincoat, revealing herself to be Vinita, the Elf-mate of her former tutor Emon, and loyalist to Legion. The Dwarf she doesn't recognize. Obviously he shaved his beard to appear young and childlike. He could be any number of the many Dwarfs she met while living at Bec LaNuff. To her horror, she notices that the dog is shifting, his body mutating its shape.

Gwen curses her luck. *Of course. I should have known he was a changeling.*

"*Du-Day Windah!*" She utters the spell, the words pulling

from her energy. Instantly a gust of supernaturally strong wind forms from her core, blowing with unstoppable force towards her assailants.

The blast sends the Dwarf flying backward, his feet going over his head as he blows over like a tumbleweed. Vinita fights back against the wind, trying with all her strength to press forward and get to Gwen. With determination, she sends another ball of light toward Gwen, shooting the deadly sphere from her out-stretched palms. The wind conversely pushes against the dangerous orb of light, forcing it to slow. It dwindles until it vanishes from existence.

Meanwhile, the changeling has been completely unaffected by the magic wind, and transforms from a hairy, slobbery, mangy dog into a tall, grotesque Giant with an enormous misshapen head, a large nose and mouth, and one large eye. Back to his original form, he stands several stories tall. He slowly moves toward Gwen, a menacing smile upon his broad, hideous face.

Gwen utters another spell. Behind her the dumpster rattles and begins to move, hovering several feet above the ground before it hurtles through the air, striking the Giant in the chest and knocking the monstrous beast off his feet. He groans in pain as he hits the pavement. Moments later, he attempts to get back up on his feet again, but due to his bulky, awkward shape he stumbles and falls onto his back.

Gwen uses the larger items lying about the alley as projectiles against the Giant as he struggles to regain his footing. He is unable to defend himself as the objects fly at him.

Something pulls Gwen's feet out from under her. She instantly collapses to the ground, hitting her rear end hard on the pavement below. She yelps in pain. Her focus broken, the wind spell dissipates and the atmosphere in the alleyway becomes calm, the wind gone as quickly as it came. She loses her focus to control her magical assault on the Giant as well. The television that had been floating in the air aimed at the Giant's head suddenly falls to the ground, landing on the pavement and breaking into pieces with a thunderous crash.

With a snarl on her face and a sharp short blade in hand, Vinita pounces, knocking Gwen flat onto the ground. Gwen takes hold of the woman's hands, trying to fend off the blade aimed at her throat. The two of them grapple with each other, Gwen trying desperately to fight against the Elf's superior strength, and Vinita trying to crush Gwen with her weight, eagerly attempting to lodge the blade into Gwen's flesh. Gwen manages to get her knee between their bodies and uses it to shove off her attacker. With a loud exclamation, Vinita rolls off of Gwen. Wasting no time, Gwen reaches for the hand holding the knife and twists Vinita's wrist sharply, forcing the Elf to scream in pain and drop the weapon. Gwen swipes the blade quickly off the ground before Vinita can seize it and brandishes it in the Elf's direction.

The two women are now back on their feet, facing each other. Vinita gives her an icy glare, her piercing, pale green eyes menacing. Gwen returns the gesture with a mischievous, leering smile, mocking and taunting her opponent.

Just as Gwen is about to lung forward and attack the Elfin woman, she finds herself clutched in one of the Giant's enormous fists. His grip grows tighter and tighter as he lifts her off of the ground and into the air. Gwen shouts angrily as he brings her up close to his disgusting deformed face.

She smells foul breath coming from his open mouth, his lips crusted and cracked as he gives Gwen a toothy smile, revealing that he has very few of his teeth left. Gwen fights the urge to empty her stomach as the stench from his mouth and the rest of his body waft in her direction.

How could I forget about the Giant? Gwen stabs Vinita's knife deep under one of the Giant's massive fingernails. He howls in agony, losing his iron-clad grip on Gwen, and lets her slip between his fingers. With a painful thump, Gwen falls to the ground below.

Her knees ache from the impact, her feet stinging with pain. Quickly, she pushes the sensation from her body, redirecting her attention to her surroundings. She has to keep her wits about her. Gwen forces herself to stand.

A guttural female yell comes from behind her. Gwen spins around as Vinita rushes toward her, another palm outstretched as she yet again attempts to hit Gwen with magic. As the ball of energy begins to glow within Vinita's palms, Gwen utters another counter spell. Gwen braces herself for the impact of the ball of light.

At the same time, Gwen reaches out and forces herself into the mind of the Giant as he stoops down to sweep her up in his hand once again. She focuses all her might into penetrating his mental barrier, probing until she finds a weakness.

While she is occupied, Vinita's magical projectile crashes into Gwen's chest, throwing her backward. The energy transfers into her body, sending a surge of adrenaline through her limbs, her strength replenished and magnified. Outwardly, she pretends she is weak and drained, lying on the ground as if unconscious.

Letting her body relax, Gwen listens to her surroundings. She detects the loud, haggard breathing of the Giant Light feminine footsteps click on the pavement toward her. Gwen allows her breathing to slow, willing her heartbeat to slow to an even pace. Knowing that Elves have extraordinary senses and can see long distances and hear even the smallest of sounds from miles away, Gwen feels Vinita approaching. *It's imperative that they believe I'm down for the count,* Gwen reasons. *What I'm about to do will only work if I can catch them completely off guard.* Vinita stands over her. Gwen waits for the moment that Vinita will reach into her mind, trying to enter through the hole in her mental defenses that her orb of energy should have been able to break through.

Then it happens. Gwen springs to her feet, coming face to face with Vinita. Instantly, Gwen shoots out her own orb, formed of energy, light, fire, darkness, and all the hatred she feels for her enemy. Appearing instantaneously it strikes Vinita at point-blank range. The Elf's eyes widen in shock and horror as she's hit, the impact hurtling her backward. Gwen doesn't even watch her fall knowing that by the time Vinita hits the ground she'll be unconscious. Gwen's spell traps the Elf's mind in a comatose state, unable to regain consciousness until she fights off the darkness that engulfs her or Gwen releases her from her mental prison. It is the same spell she accidently unleashed on Ivan.

Gwen turns to look at the giant looming over her, his countenance glazed over. He seems asleep on his feet. Gwen smiles to herself. When she attacked the Elf, Gwen also waged a mental assault on the protective barrier surrounding the Giant's consciousness. Breaking through, she completely overwhelmed the creature's every thought. He is now her puppet. With a simple thought from Gwen, he lifts one leg in the air. Gwen lets out a triumphant laugh. Amused by her newest toy, Gwen forces the Giant to dance around her before forcing him into his dog form once more.

Gwen stands, amazed by her own power, when a sharp, piercing pain bursts from below her left ear. Reaching up to touch the spot, her fingers brush against a dart protruding from her flesh. She yanks the dart out, tossing it to the floor before spinning around in the direction it had originated. The abrupt motion of her body causes her to become dizzy, the world blurring before her eyes. The energy drains out of her body and she collapses to the ground. Gwen lands on her back, her head hitting the pavement hard with a loud clunk, although Gwen is already beyond the capacity to feel the pain it causes. Her power over the Giant slips from her grasp as she begins to lose control of her own thoughts.

Where did that dart come from? she thinks as her mind fades. Using all of her strength and concentration she cranes her neck in the general direction the dart had been shot. After a moment, her vision clears and Gwen sees the Dwarf standing on a branch of a tree along the edge of the fence-line bordering the park. In one hand he holds a long tube. From her position, the Dwarf seemed to be standing on his head. It takes her muddled mind several seconds to realize that he isn't upside down, she is.

Everything goes dark around her as the Giant steps forward, his shadow blocking out the sun. The last thing she sees before she completely blacks out is the Giant reaching down, his hand outstretched to take her into his grasp.

In the blackness that follows, she can neither feel nor hear anything of the outside world, consumed by her own thoughts. She chastises herself, cursing her own stupidity and arrogance. Had she kept her wits about her, she would have remembered the Dwarf. She should have sensed any attack thrown at her. Instead she let her hatred blind her.

Suddenly she remembers the Guardian Stone tucked away in the pocket of her leather jacket. Ever since Morna gave it to her, she kept it just in case. Gwen wonders at her own stupidity. *You had an emergency bit of magic and forgot to use just when you needed it most? Way to go, Gwen. That was a stupid mistake.* She feels her consciousness slip into the darkness of sleep. She struggles to hold on to her thoughts. But slowly, one by one, those thoughts and memories vanish. The last thing to cross her mind is Angelo.

* * * * *

The Italian sits on a folding chair, staring at the door before him. Resting his elbows on his knees, he cradles his head in his hands. His red blood-varnished violin and bow sit on his lap. His focus is fastened on the door. His eyes bore into the wood, willing the door to open and for Gwen to stand in the doorway. Angelo lets out a long frustrated growl, letting the fantasy fade.

Gwen was supposed to be home hours ago. Luckily it's the late December and the sun will set soon. With the protection of night, he will set out to search for her. The thought of Gwen in danger makes him feel cold and hollow. If anything happened to her, he'd never forgive himself. He would spend the rest of his eternity hunting down the source of Gwen's misery.

Looking around dispassionately, he observes the appalling state of their studio apartment. The room around him is ransacked. The chest of drawers, which had held their clothes, has been thrown against the opposite wall, the wood splintering, the drawers spilling out onto the floor. The mattress that served as their bed is up against the wall, standing on end, the bedding scattered about the room. The fold-up table and the other chair are bent and twisted, no longer resembling their original forms. The television has a massive hole in the screen. The nightstand lies on its side in the kitchen. The ceramic lamp, shattered into pieces, lay at the foot of the refrigerator. One of its shards lies next to his foot. He bends down and picks it up. Looking at it with a deadly stare, Angelo crushes the shard in his fist until nothing's left but dust. Coolly he shakes the remnants away, the dust falling to the floor.

His eyes drift to the clock on the stove. *Only 6:00 p.m.,* he thinks to himself. *Still at least a half hour until full dark.* For a creature who hadn't paid any mind to the passage of time in centuries, he suddenly finds waiting even a minute longer unbearable. The longer he's delayed, the more anxious he becomes. Some part of him hopes that she simply lost track of time, but Gwen wasn't like that. She wasn't flighty or irresponsible. She was a very capable, mature young woman. She wouldn't make him worry like this needlessly, would she? Unless something terrible had happened to her…

The thought sends a wave of fear and absolute rage through his silent heart. He can't sit idle another second. Angelo knows that Gwen is a very talented Witch. She can defend herself from just about anything. She'd been trained to fight against any number of opponents. He also knows that only another magic wielder could defeat Gwen. He lets the realization sink in. *They've found her. That has to be it. There's no other explanation.*

His anger has been building up over the last several hours, and now that he finally admits this horrible truth to himself, his self-control slips as he overflows with rage.

He knows what he must do. When the light of the day finally

fades into the blackness of night, he will find her. He made the mistake a long time ago that Legion would only send his Vampire minion to hunt for him and his stolen bride. Angelo wonders now at his own mindless assumption. It makes sense that Legion would want to separate them from each other, because together they could have easily thwarted any attack.

He will return to Bec LaNuff and face his old companion and former friend. It would be him against Legion and all of his followers. He won't stand a chance against so many, and Angelo knows it. Legion will not give up Gwen without a fight, and he will not fight fair.

A thought occurs to Angelo that gives him hope as well as hesitation. Gwen once made him promise that if he ever found himself in this very situation, that he would solicit the help of her childhood friend Raven. The idea of asking a Werewolf for help does not appeal to Angelo. However, he gave his word. If this Raven were as devoted a friend as Gwen believes, he would undoubtedly come to their aid. Angelo always had a knack for tracking. He could even find those who didn't want to be found. Ironically, if Gwen had been absconded by anyone other than himself, Legion would have asked him to track her down. Angelo has no doubt that he'd be able to locate Gwen's long lost friend. Sneaking into the mountain fortress, together they would attempt to rescue his beloved.

Angelo slips his bow and violin into their case, gathers up all their belongings into Gwen's duffel bag, and dons his leather jacket. On his way to the door, he checks the time once more. The clock reads 6:15. Yes, he'd waited long enough. He leaves the apartment behind him in tatters.

Then and there Angelo resolves that he will save Gwen. He will go with or without Raven's help. One way or another, he will free her. If he had to give his own life to do it, it's a sacrifice he would gladly make. He will fight Legion for her, and with his life, he will claim once and for all that she is his. *Gwen is my life, my world, my heart's most prized possession.*

CHAPTER TWENTY-FIVE

Captive from Daylight

*T*he darkness slowly fades from her vision. Gwen hears a young girl's mumbling voice, and short, fast footsteps pacing back and forth on a stone floor nearby.

Lamp light penetrates through Gwen's closed eyelids. She is hesitant to open them. Confusion fills her mind, afraid that the light might aggravate her splitting headache. Irresolutely she lies there a few minutes, listening to various peculiar sounds until her curiosity gets the best of her. Peeking out from under her eyelids, she sees a gray, curved stone ceiling above her. Signs of the strokes the Dwarves' chisels and hammers made centuries ago are still evident in the rock surface. Gwen lets out a groan.

I'm back in Bec LaNuff, the very place I promised myself I

would never set foot in again. The harsh reality sinks in.

"Oh. You're awake?" Gwen bolts up, having completely forgotten the voice she heard a moment ago, startled to find herself not alone. A small blonde stranger stands before her at the foot of the bed.

With a shocked cry, the shapeless young girl jumps back, crashing into a bookshelf behind her. Several leather-bound books tumble to the floor. She covers her mouth to silence herself, her eyes darting toward the closed door of the small chamber. The sound of shuffling footsteps continues from down the hall. Gwen goes rigid as she stares at the door apprehensively.

"What's going on in there? Is she awake?" says an awkward voice through the wooden door, obviously unaccustomed to speaking in English.

"No, no, I just saw a spider. It scared me, that's all," the blonde girl stammers out, her body quaking with fear.

This seems to amuse the guard outside, for he lets out a loud, brusque guffaw and walks on down the hall.

Gwen listens to his fading footsteps with increased relief. She takes a quick look around at what had once been her bed chamber. It isn't so much a bedroom as a cave with a door.

Gwen sits on a small mattress atop a rock platform bed. The rest of the furnishings are exactly as she left them the day she escaped Bec LaNuff. Gwen notices absently that someone has taken off her black leather coat and hung it on a peg by the bookshelf.

Gwen reaches over and peers inside the jewel case beside her bed, seeing familiar trinkets and ostentatious jeweled tokens of Legion's affections. She has to touch them, to convince herself they are real, that this isn't all a nightmare too.

Gwen fights the wave of panic that threatens to engulf her. She has to keep a firm grip on herself. She can't afford to lose it now. Not here. She refuses to show any weakness, knowing full well that Legion would be privy to her humiliation. Once upon a time, she had friends here even in this godforsaken place, but that was a long time ago, and she couldn't be certain if their loyalty still lay with her. Gwen vows that she will appear strong and undaunted no matter what kind of punishment Legion has in store for her. She must keep her wits about her to find a way out of this mess. *And I will, one way or another.*

Determined, Gwen lets out an anguished sigh, and then turns her attention to the small girl standing before her.

Short, blonde, and young, the girl appears to be eleven or twelve years old. She looks innocent with blue doe-like eyes, a button nose, and a thin mouth, all set in a little heart-shaped face. Her skin fresh and pure, her yellow hair hangs in gentle waves around her face, flowing down to the middle of her back. She is attired in an elegant long white dress covered in pearls along the bodice. The straight-cut dress shows off the girl's lack of curves or bosom. Gwen imagines that she is as skinny as a reed beneath all that white fabric.

"You're his type, all right," Gwen announces after her head to foot inspection of the child.

The girl stares back at Gwen, her face drained of color, her lips trembling. Gwen's scrutinizing gaze must intimidate the little thing. Gwen forces herself to make a friendly smile.

"What's your name?" Gwen asks in the most pleasant tone she can manage.

The girl's face goes ashen. She puts a finger up to her thin lips to signal that Gwen should be silent.

"Don't be afraid. I've sealed the room with magic. No one will be able to hear a word we say." Gwen crosses her legs nonchalantly, leaning back comfortably on her palms.

"I'm... ma-ma... Ju-ju... I'm Julie," the girl stammers. "So you are a Witch? Everyone's talking about you like you're some kind of villain. They call you traitor and a Witch. But I didn't believe them."

Gwen listens to the fear in her voice and smiles. "Don't you know what kind of place you're in, girl? Surely you've noticed that most of us aren't human here?"

Julie nods, visibly trembling.

"You must be very brave then, to sit alone in the same room with such a dangerous person." Finally, Gwen asks, "Why are you here?"

"I was curious. He said I could sit with you. He said he would make an example out of you and that I would do well to be nothing like you. You must have done something terrible to make him so angry."

"And who is 'he'?" Gwen can't help asking the question even though she already knows the answer.

"Why, the Master. He's called Legion. I thought you knew him. He sure knows you." Julie seems baffled that anyone wouldn't know her Master.

"So you already call him Master, then? That's good. You'll do much better than I did. Your life here won't be nearly as trying as mine was." Gwen tries to sound comforting, but she can't help feeling sorry for the stupid little girl.

Julie seems taken aback by this sudden revelation. "You lived here? How long did you live here?"

"I was here for two and half years," Gwen replies in a dispassionate tone. "But I escaped."

"Escaped?" Julie looks quizzically at her. "Why would anyone ever want to leave this place?" The awe is thick in her voice.

Ignoring Julie's question, Gwen reaches out with her mind to touch the girl's consciousness. She finds no resistance, proving that the girl is in fact human. Their race is so trusting without any suspicion that people with Gwen's gift could even exist. Telepathy is the stuff of fantasy to them.

She makes quick order of the girl's recent memories, including the night she met the Vampire Lucca. To Gwen's disgust, the girl was not taken against her will as so many human slaves are.

Instead, Julie was a runaway looking for something better than the life she'd been living. Dreaming of excitement and adventure, she snuck off only to run into Lucca, who made Bec LaNuff sound like a paradise compared to her sheltered existence. She went with him willingly, believing she would be a princess in a stone castle fairytale.

Retreating from the girl's mind, Gwen returns to the present once more. "How long have you been here?" Gwen asks Julie in an attempt at idle conversation.

A perplexed expression upon her face, Julie shakes herself to dispel the bizarre thoughts that came unsummoned, the effects of Gwen's mental intrusion.

"Oh, I've been here three months, I think. I can't really tell. They won't let me go outside yet. They said I had to stay low until my family stopped looking for me. Master says that will be very soon!" Julie smiles enthusiastically.

"Did he tell you what happened to the last girl?" Gwen knows it's cruel to mess with the simple-minded fool, but she can't help herself.

"What other girl?" Julies face goes still, her blood running cold.

"Danielle. She was his favorite when I left. Before her, there was Stacey, then Laura. I guess I've seen six girls, including you, come and go since I first came here."

Gwen has her total attention now. "Where did they go?" Julie stammers.

"They died," Gwen responds in a cold, hollow voice.

Julie trembles, her body convulsing with terror. She tries to speak but a sound at the door stops her. They both turn toward it as the sound of a key turns in the lock.

Gwen flattens herself on the bed, arranging her limbs in the same position they were when she awoke, closing her eyes and pretending to sleep. A moment later, the door is flung open and someone enters the room, the chill of death entering with him.

Gwen listens closely to the approaching footsteps, a kind of dragging, shuffling sound. *Ivan*, Gwen confirms to herself, knowing his foul, dreadful smell so well. Even if she hadn't already known him, his thick Cockney accent would have given him away.

"What's going on in here?" He addresses Julie in English.

"Nothing, I was just watching her sleep." Julie replies in a small, frightened voice.

"Don't lie to me, love!" Ivan slurs. "The Master said he felt her make magic not a moment ago."

Gwen peeks out from under her eyelids and sees Ivan, the ugliest man she has ever met, lifting his arm as if he is about to backhand the girl. Julie cowers before him, trying to squeeze herself as far into the corner of the room as possible.

Gwen opens her eyes and sits up, clicking her tongue in disapproval at Ivan. At the sound, he quickly turns to face her, Julie no more than a memory.

"Aren't you the big man, picking on a little girl?" Gwen taunts him.

"He told me you'd awakened. You should know better than

anyone, no one pulls the wool over the Master's eyes." He gives her a crocked, toothy smile, showing off his razor-sharp fangs, gleaming white and deadly. "I said you'd be back. Now here you are. Oh, I'm going to enjoy watching you beg for mercy when you get what's coming to you."

"I've never begged for mercy before. What makes you think I'll do it now?" Gwen inquires, a steely tone in her voice.

"Ah, but the Master was never this angry before. He was always willing to forgive your minor indiscretions in the past, but not this time, love. You've crossed the line this time." A satisfied sneer spreads a crossed his ugly countenance.

Gwen ignores him, changing the subject. "I don't suppose you know how Vinita found me, do you?"

"Oh, yes, that was a bit of good luck, that was all right. You see, Vinita, Ruinan, and Owarth were out on a scouting party. The Master offered a very generous reward to anyone who could capture you, he did. Anyway, there they were, following a lead they got that you were in Chicago, wandering the streets without a clue where to look, when all of a sudden the Elf felt someone using a terribly large amount of magic nearby. They were waiting at the bus stop, they say, when who should step off of the blooming bus but you! The very one they've been looking for!" He bursts into loud, obnoxious laughter, fully enjoying the moment.

Gwen isn't amused. She waits several moments for Ivan's mirth to subside, her anger and annoyance building, her rage smoldering like hot coals about to catch fire again until she cannot hold it at bay any longer.

"How's your leg?" Gwen smiles smugly at him before looking down at the disfigured limb. His left leg is twisted, blackened as if charred and deformed. She is surprised he can stand on it, or even walk at all. The deplorable sight does nothing to squelch her satisfaction in having been the cause of his pain. She'd wondered all this time if her spell left a mark. Gwen smiles haughtily when she looks back up at him.

The backside of his hand strikes her across the face, delivering a skull-shattering blow. Gwen's body lurches sideways. Gwen puts her fingertips up to her mouth as she brushes away the blood. Besides her bleeding lip, the side of her face stings and her headache from the drugs is now ten times more intense. Her catlike green eyes blaze at Ivan with an unadulterated rage as she fixes him in her stare.

Without a thought, Gwen reaches out with magic and takes a hold of Ivan. He lets out a surprised yelp, the sound cutting off as she begins to squeeze the life out of him. She lifts him off the ground, his mangled leg dangling lifelessly as his good one kicks violently. He makes a choking noise as his throat constricts. His eyes cry tears of blood. Instead of saliva, a trickle of blood dribbles down his chin.

Behind him, Julie screams and bolts from the room. Gwen ignores her. Her only concern is to finish what she has already begun. A demented smile crosses her face as she prepares to squeeze every last drop of blood out of the Vampire's body and crush every last bone.

A cold shiver shoots from the ring, coursing through her body and a sudden shudder causes her heart to constrict. The pain is unbearable, causing Gwen to release her victim. Ivan falls to the floor, sputtering and squirming on the ground.

Gwen clutches at her chest, her left arm going numb, her heart beating faster and faster in its attempt to pump blood to the lifeless limb. Her vision begins to blacken. Her chest feels as if it's collapsing into itself.

Then she feels the Master's presence in the doorway. He steps forward, a cold smile on his pale marble face. She refuses to look up at him. Instead she allows her body to go limp as she falls back onto the bed. Gwen feels her entire body slip into paralysis. She doesn't faint, but chooses to close her eyes and fake it. He would undoubtedly do something terrible to her for striking out at Ivan, his favorite. Her punishment is inevitable, and because of the ring on her finger, constricting her every move, she is powerless to stop him.

Someone takes her by the feet, while someone else takes her under the armpits. They heft her off the bed and carry her from the room. As uncomfortable as she is, Gwen forces herself to keep up her charade. They continue on down the tunnel and onward toward an unknown destination. Their footsteps echo off the stone walls as they proceed further into the depth of the mountain fortress. She can feel Legion's presence at the head of the procession, leading them on. She tries to rifle through her memories of the place, to recall her location and where they might possibly be headed, but it is no use. She feels disoriented but refuses to open her eyes. *I will put off looking into Legion's face as long as I can.* His face, more than anything else, will bring on the panic and the fear she suppressed deep inside of her.

They enter what feels like a large chamber. She hears the loud bang of the door as it is closes behind them, and hears the sound of several personages chattering excitedly as they enter.

Her two escorts release her, dropping her abruptly to the ground. Sharp pain shoots through her tailbone as she hits the floor. Gwen can't help gritting her teeth and letting out a groan.

"I thought you were conscious. It is rather silly of you, dearest. First, you use magic to talk privately with my darling Julie, and then you try to kill poor Ivan." She hears Legion's musical lilting voice. His footsteps echo as he walks in a circle around her. "Why you hate the poor man so I'll never understand. After all, he did save your life. He's harmless once you get to know him, but you were always prone to delusions about your own superiority. I remember being quite surprised at just how arrogant you were when you first joined our little community. You were so young, and so terribly naive, yet so damn sure of yourself."

With a frustrated sigh, she opens her eyes. The feeling in her limbs slowly returns. Her head is still splitting in two, but at least the room isn't spinning. She slowly pushes herself up into a sitting position and looks at her nemesis.

They are in the Master of Bec LaNuff's bedchamber, and they

are not alone. Besides herself, Legion, and the two male human servants who escorted her, together there are at least thirty other people in the room, all of them Vampires. The entire nest is present except Ivan, who's probably somewhere licking his wounds. She recognizes them all from the eldest to the infant Lynette.

Legion appears before her just as he had in her nightmares. The dreams were a warning. She knows that now. For here she sits, only a feet away from the source of her nightmares. He is as immaculate as ever and opulently dressed. Once, she looked upon him with awe. She thought he was beautiful, even noble. Now her eyes were open and she sees the ugliness beneath.

The lantern light catches the glint of gold and shine of gems from his ring upon his left ring finger. Gwen longs to tear that ring right off of his hand and destroy it. But that would be pointless, for his ring is as indestructible as its mate. Even now her own ring burns with cold pain upon her wedding finger. She'd fought against the evil of the rings with all of her might, but now that she is near him again the ring took possession of her once more. And she could do nothing to stop it. If only he weren't wearing his ring. Then she could finally kill him.

Generally she avoided looking upon the ring, but she casts a glance down at it. When Legion gave her the ring as a present for her twelfth birthday she had been entranced by its mystical beauty, blinding her to its evil. The ancient rings were fashioned after the first set of magical binding rings that first enslaved a mortal woman to a life of pain and degradation.

"You're thinking of our bond, I see," Legion sneers, interrupting her thoughts. "I'll admit I hoped your time away from this paradise and my loving benevolence, living as a pauper with that peasant minstrel, might have changed your attitude. Perhaps you might have learned a little gratitude?" He doesn't give her time to answer, the hatred in his voice too apparent to miss.

"No, I'm sure you haven't improved. You're already lying, using magic without permission and trying to kill my children. I fear your manners are worse than ever."

As Legion rambles on, loving the sound of his own voice as he always did, Gwen notices the childlike Lynette giving her a very smug expression, clearly enjoying the moment. Gwen gives the little monster a smile laced with hatred in return. She hates them all. And the feeling is mutual. Suddenly Gwen realizes that the vampire Ryan is missing.

Wasn't she the one in my dream the other night? The one who tried to attack Raven?" Gwen looks for Lucca, Jezebel and Lethawyn's faces but they are absent from the crowd. Suddenly she is sickened by the thought that the dream was not really a dream but a vision of something that really happened. Gwen fights back the panic, remembering Raven had been wounded, about to be torn apart by Lucca, as the last thing she saw before waking. Gwen bites down hard on her lower lip, forcing herself not to burst into tears at the very thought that her long lost friend might actually be dead.

If he were dead, I'd know wouldn't I? I'd feel it. Like part of me was missing. Gwen searches her soul for some indication, hoping that her intuition is strong enough to answer her fears. She feels nothing but uncertainty. She forces back the doubt and the heart-wrenching sadness. *I'll find out the truth soon enough. If he is dead, then I will avenge him.*

Moving slowly, she rises off of her knees and stands before Legion, ignoring the others with her head held high. Her demeanor is as arrogant and commanding as the man before her.

"You have no respect, child. I can see now that I underestimated your foolishness. You must be taught a lesson. And when I am done, you will beg for mercy and kiss the ring upon my hand." He says the words with a cool aristocratic distain. His children laugh.

"Now where have I heard that before?" Gwen taunts. "I have never bowed to you and I will never beg. After all you've put me through, don't you know me at all?" Gwen spares a fleeting disinterested glance at their audience. "Have you finally decided to kill me, then? Or are you going to feed on me, and simply have your minions tear me apart?" She questions him in a dispassionate tone.

"No. I haven't yet decided if you shall live or die, but either way, you will suffer for the insult you caused me by running off with that… that…" He doesn't finish.

"Traitor!" several of the Vampires shout. Others hiss, "Witch Lover!" They supply other colorful insulting names for the one that had overstepped his bounds by stealing the Master's bride.

"I haven't betrayed anyone. I was never yours to possess. And as far as I see it, Angelo did nothing wrong. I wasn't actually spoken for, and I did choose him. I never loved y—"

Legion cuts her off with a roar. "Enough! Silence her." He turns to his loyal children, signaling for them to proceed. He turns his back on her, stalking towards the elaborate bed.

The minions descend upon her, snickering as they come toward her, slowly encircling her, surrounding her on all sides with evil smiles and taunts upon their lips. Their fangs now razor-sharp, every muscle in their bodies seeming to be tense as if they are preparing to pounce at any moment. Gwen feels she will drown in this sea of faces, each one different, yet they all share the same sinister smile, the same evil intent.

Gwen tenses, she breathes slowly to help herself remain calm. As they draw nearer, she takes a defensive stance, readying herself for their attack.

Legion stops and turns back to them. "Gwen." The commanding tone in his voice causes Gwen and her would-be-attackers to pause and turn their attention to him.

"You will stand there and you will not defend yourself. I know in the past I encouraged your training in self-defense, but I fear I was too over-indulgent. Perhaps I gave you too many freedoms. I feel somewhat responsible for your predicament, so I have decided to re-educate you. You have a very stubborn streak, along with many other faults that you must unlearn. Remember, I do this with your best interests at heart, my darling. From now on, things will be very different. I promise you that." He smiles maliciously, obviously pleased with her reaction.

Gwen is horrified. For a moment, her face betrays all her emotions, but quickly she regains her composure. *I will not show fear. I will not beg. I will not cry. I can get through this*, she chants to herself. Then, she looks into the hostile faces surrounding her, and she feels the panic threaten to overtake her.

She doesn't have time to let her fear get the best of her, for suddenly one of the Vampires steps forward and hits her hard in the gut, the impact like a battering ram to her soft flesh. Instantly, all the wind rushes out of her lungs. She gasps for air as a jolt of pain shoots through her body. After that everything becomes a blur as they all converge on her at once. Punches fall upon her like hail in a storm, coming from all directions. She tries to fight back but instantly feels the ring resist her, her arms and legs pined to her side, her body unable to obey her commands.

Gwen falls to the floor, her body bloody and battered, as the abuse goes on. The Vampires take turns, letting those in front have their fun. Then one line steps back, allowing the next group to begin the next round of assaults. Kicked, scratched, bitten, clawed, punched, wrenched this way and that. Someone tries to tear her hair out. Through it all Gwen protects herself in the only way she can, by retreating back into her subconscious, letting her surroundings fade from her mind and severing her connection with her body. She still feels the pain in the distance, like a sharp blinding light out of the corner of her eyes, but she ignores it. She chooses instead to transport her mind to a higher plain of consciousness, finding peace in her inner-sanctuary.

In this trance-like state, it takes her a long time to realize that her assailants have fallen back, and even longer for her to force herself to return back to her body, and her consciousness back to the present. Immediately upon fully rejoining her mind to her flesh, she feels the immeasurable damage done to her frail, mortal form. The pain sends blinding waves through her body, causing her to moan involuntarily as she tries to move into a sitting position. Instantly, she can tell that she has several broken ribs, a busted lip, two soon to be black eyes and possibly a concussion. She feels dazed and disorientated.

She ties to look up at Legion but the room begins to spin. Instinctively, she doubles over and spills the contents of her stomach on the floor, which is nothing more than bile since she hasn't eaten. The act seems to clear her mind, helping her to regain a little composure. Wiping the remnants of the spittle from her mouth with her shirtsleeve, Gwen turns her attention back to the monsters surrounding her. Without thinking, she reaches out to magic, making the puddle of her bodily fluid vanish and instantaneously chanting the healing song her mother had song over her cradle.

"*Dah-Day-Wente, Curea-Longa, Babeta-Lovota...*" All over her body a warmth penetrates down into her bones, healing her aches, cuts, and contusions as it sweeps through her body. When the song is finished applying its healing balm, she springs to her feet in a quick motion, not caring if they see how little their attack affected her. She ignores the hisses and words of disapproval from Legion's minions, and instead turns her attention to the man himself. Several Vampires approach, ready to attack again, but Legion signals for them to fall back with a disinterested wave of his hand.

"I can see that you're trying to make a point, my love. That there is no point beating you within an inch of your life if you can just chant a few words and heal yourself. I applaud you for that." Legion strolls toward her, the smooth exotic motion of his body sensual and lethal.

Gwen steps back to keep a distance between them, but instantly she feels the invisible bonds of the ring restrict around her like a strait jacket, holding her in place.

"You haven't learned a thing, have you?" Legion continues. He reaches out and gently strokes the side of her face with one long, manicured fingernail, tracing the contours of her chin.

Gwen turns her face away from him and spits on the floor.

Legion smiles wickedly. "Don't worry. I know exactly what to do to bring you in line. Although, if you ask me, it's more of a privilege, a reward rather than a punishment, which for some reason you never appreciated at all."

He takes Gwen's face in his hand. She tries to resist, but the magic of the ring makes her body go rigid. He leans in, forcing his lips to hers. She squirms but is unable to pull away or stop him. He steps forward and takes Gwen into his cold embrace, forcing his tongue into her mouth and kissing her in a rough, violent manner. Her muffled cries of protest have no effect on the violence of his affection. When Legion pulls back, releasing her from his embrace, she stumbles backward as the invisible bonds fall away and she is given full control over her body once more.

Horror and panic seize her in their cold grasp. She knows exactly what he has in mind for her ultimate punishment. He did it to her a hundred times before in this very room. He hates watching her age, that she knows, and she has no doubt that her womanly form is repulsive to him even now. Nonetheless, he will still take her, just to prove that she is his to possess and to have whenever and however he desires. She feels the compulsion to scream, but represses it, deep down. Resisting him is futile. She knows it, but still a wave of nausea rises from her stomach. It takes everything in her to swallow the bile and keep her composure.

Legion snaps his fingers. Instantly one of his human servants hurries to his side. Without taking his eyes off of Gwen, Legion removes his blue embroidered robe and hands it to the boy. Legion slowly undresses himself, handing over every garment with great care to the servant, who takes his time folding each article of clothing.

"What are you doing?" Gwen all but screams at him, pointing to the audience of Vampires still lingering across the room, watching them. "We're not alone!" She can't hide the tremor that finds its way into her voice.

"My apologies, dearest. I must have failed to mention that we will be performing in front of an audience tonight." A dangerously smug smile spreads across his face.

Gwen is stunned by this revelation. Things are most certainly worse than ever before. To begin with, he'd never let any of his Vampire children so much as a touch a hair upon her head, unless he himself was amusing himself by having Gwen spar with them. Even then she had always been allowed to defend herself in some way. He had beaten her on numerous occasions and had taken his liberties with her body more times than she cares to admit, but at least he always did so in privacy. What he does now is unprecedented. She had once thought he was capable of every kind of evil, but this? No, not this.

Legion stands before her, stripped down to his trousers, his pale alabaster chest magnificent in its chiseled perfection. He has removed all of his fine jewelry as well, save for his wedding band. The ring was his only protection.

He waves his servant away. "Come to me," he commands Gwen, using his control of the ring to force her body to comply against her mind's fervent will.

Gwen feels revulsion, fear, and panic surge through her as her body moves on its own accord toward the man she loathes above all else. Fighting with all her strength, her body moves on, carrying her unwillingly across the room right to Legion's outstretched hand.

There's nothing you can do to stop him, Gwen, she tells

herself as he whisks her off the floor and carries her over to the bed.

He can have my body, but he cannot have me. He cannot hurt me. I will not cry. I will not scream. I will not let him see how much I suffer. I will show nothing. I will feel nothing, she chants to herself, drawing comfort and strength from the words. She can endure it. She has to.

He sets her down on her feet next to the bed. Gwen refuses to look into his face, staring at his bare chest with an emotionless expression.

"Take off your clothes," he commands.

He leans over and takes off his trousers. Gwen turns her face away and closes her eyes. She feels her will struggle and thrash against the command as her body hurries to obey her Master's order. Her hands shake and jerk violently as they slowly remove her shirt, her pants, her shoes, her socks. Behind her closed eyelids she hears and feels the people present in the room. Her body shivers, standing there in her underwear, feeling the cold stone room closing in on her. Surrounded by darkness, Gwen dreads what's coming next.

Sensing Legion's move toward her. Gwen instinctively moves back, but stops as he reaches out and takes her by the arm, pulling her to him. She stumbles forward as he shoves her onto the bed. She falls on her back onto the silken covers. She hears the others in the room whispering, snickering, feeling their eyes upon her. Her skin crawls with the knowledge that they're here, watching her every expression and reaction.

Fighting the urge to scream at them, she delves into her subconscious, shutting out the world around her, her body distant, numb, and lifeless. She pulls away from her body, burying herself in pleasant thoughts and memories that will drown out the things being done to her.

She finds herself floating out of her body, her soul leaving its physical prison behind to soar out of herself and beyond. In the distance she is aware of Legion's hands upon her body, removing her underwear, touching her, groping her. She pushes the sensations away, fleeing from it further into her personal haven within her mind.

At the moment of penetration, it is difficult to stay detached from her body. He treats her without consideration, using violent swift movements to fulfill his own lust. Gwen knows his routine all too well. Legion always took great pleasure in inflecting pain upon her during sex, the excitement heightened by sensing her pain flowing through their rings. In the end he always left her with bruises, cuts, and broken bones, with head to toe aches and pains.

Then, he bites her. Her body lurches, his sharp fangs dig into her flesh, puncturing the skin as her blood gushes forth from the wound in her neck. Gwen reaches for the blanket under her, taking a wad of the fabric and forcing it into her mouth, biting down to prevent herself from screaming aloud.

A moment later, Legion breaks though the protective walls around her mind, penetrating her every thought. The drinking of blood gives a Vampire access to their prey's mind, the victim's thoughts flowing with the current of blood as they drain them. Legion ravages her through this mental world, forcing vile images into her brain, driving her within an inch insanity. She uses all her mental powers to shut him out, to alter the horrific fantasies that he inflicts upon her into images of her own making. He resists her, delving deeper inside her consciousness, all the while ruthlessly assaulting her body with his violent mating.

He turns her memories against her, taking happy moments with Angelo and inserting himself into Angelo's place. She fights against him to no avail. Instead, she lays back and rides the tide of pain, anguish, and misery, holding onto the last shred of her sanity, willing herself to endure until Legion is satisfied. *It can't last forever. It'll be over soon.* She just has to hold on. She can't lose it, and she won't surrender. She will not submit her will to him, no matter how he tortures her.

Finding strength from her determination, she fights back with her mind and body, releasing a violent defensive against Legion and his magical hold of her. She pushes into his thoughts, violently raping his mind the way he has done to hers. She forces him to imagine himself standing in the sun, the light blinding him, his skin burning, flames licking his limbs. She makes him feel the pain of burning alive, his body turning to ash. She hears his mental scream and feels his agony. He cowers inside, withering in pain.

Then the ring takes hold of her heart. The pain is unbearable, all her sensations saturated in agony. Reluctantly she releases

Legion from her mental stranglehold. Shuddering, she gasps for air, her lungs aching. She can't breathe, she can't think, all she can do is suffer in silence. Her heart is restricted, slowing down, her world growing dark and then… all is still.

* * * * *

Gwen finally returns to consciousness, dimly aware of being dragged along a hard surface, the stone scraping her back. Someone mutters to himself in the pure tongue, speaking profanities. The stranger hefts her off the ground and tosses her limp form over his large shoulder. Her body still unresponsive to her commands, Gwen resigns to wait till her strength returns, to see where she is being taken. It seems as though they are going down a flight of stairs as the man carrying her jostles her up and down with every step. As she becomes more coherent of her surroundings, the numbness of her body recedes. The searing pain throughout her entire form is staggering. Every inch of her feels as if it is on fire, swollen and throbbing.

Her escort comes to the bottom of the stairs. She can sense a torch being lit, the glow seeping through her eyelids. Instinctively, she continues her charade of unconsciousness. The man walks forward, his feet echoing off the walls around them. He shifts her weight, and then throws her off his shoulder.

Gwen expects to hit the stone floor beneath her and braces for the impact. To her surprise, she continues to fall. In a panic, she opens her eyes and sees the man standing above her looking down into a hole, becoming smaller as she falls further downward. Seeing the round opening of the pit with shocking clarity tells her where she is. Gwen lets out a scream of terror, desperately reaching out her arms and legs trying to find something to cling to. All she finds is empty space all around her. Gwen plummets, helpless to save herself, knowing full well what awaits her below.

Finally, she crashes through the water at the pit's bottom. The impact of hitting the water stings, aggravating her already battered body. Her lungs fill with liquid. Frantically, she thrashes her arms and legs, willing herself toward the light and the surface. Bursting forth, Gwen sputters out old dirty water and gasps for air simultaneously, completely revived by the icy water. Looking around she sees that along the edges of the water, a few rocks jut out above the surface. Swimming over to one of these piles of rocks, Gwen pulls herself out. Climbing to the highest rock, she huddles against the wall. Her clothes cling to her skin as she shivers. Her long, black hair hangs down her back, a few strands dripping in her face. Gwen brushes them back behind her ears. Her vision now unobstructed, she surveys her surroundings.

She is in the underground well, thirty feet down from the chamber above. The smell of mold is in the air. A slimy residue lines the walls and the rocks, making them slippery. The only light in the pit shines down from the far distant glow of the torch above.

Gwen looks upward at the pit's mouth. An Ogre looks down at her. He holds the torch high in one hand, illuminating his gross, misshapen face. His nose large, bulbous takes up half of his face. His eyes are two different sizes, one as large as his nose and the other small one resting much lower on his face. His mouth, crooked and large, smiles, one half of his mouth turns up while the other turns down, making him appear as if he's had a stroke. She doesn't know him, so she assumes he must have joined the commune after she had escaped.

"Can you see where you're at?" the Ogre calls down to Gwen, his voice deep and slurred like a drunkard.

"Yes, I know where I am. Am I to wait here until I'm put to death?"

The Ogre shakes his head. "I don't really know. I'm new here. They told me that you're down there because you're too high and mighty." His kind voice speaks to her in a conversational tone. "I'm sorry I dropped you, but there was no other way to get you down there. I didn't hurt you none, did I?" His tone suggests that he is genuinely concerned for her health.

"Not any more than I already was," Gwen replies, surprised that she is trying to comfort the stranger who by his allegiance to Legion is naturally her enemy. She even tries to smile at him in reassurance, though he probably can barely see her.

"I'm to leave now. I'd leave the torch for you but I was told not to. The next guard will be here in a couple of hours." He waves goodbye to her and leaves, the glow of the torch dwindling away with him, leaving Gwen alone in the darkness.

Absolute blackness surrounds her. There are no shadows, no

difference from one shade of darkness to the next, just pitch black. Feeling vulnerable and exposed, Gwen shivers in her soaking wet clothes.

"Very clever," Gwen concedes. "He tossed me down here so I can't heal myself." Even so, Gwen attempts to sing the healing song, but the rock around her drains the words of their magic just like she knew it would.

One of her eyes is beginning to swell, probably already blackening. Besides her numerous other injuries, her greatest pains are in her throbbing feminine parts. She doesn't want to think about it, still quivering in disgust at the thought. Her headache has returned and her temples throb. Her stomach growls, and with a hollow pang of hunger as she realizes she hasn't eaten in more than a day.

The thought of food makes her think of the grapes along with the other groceries she left on the bus the day before. Or at least she thinks it was yesterday. She can't be certain how long it has been since Vinita and her companions attacked her in the alley. Gwen replays the events of that day over in her head, trying to keep herself from feeling alone in this dark, watery pit, trying to keep herself from breaking down and crying. She can't help thinking of Angelo and what he might be going through. She finds it is simply too much to bear.

Trusting that no one is near, that no one will hear her, Gwen lets out an anguished sob. Then she screams at the top of her lungs, letting out all her bottled up frustration, hate, and agony. It feels so good to let it out, so she keeps on screaming, feeling comforted by the sound of her own voice in the darkness. Suddenly she doesn't feel so alone. Just as she starts to feel safe, she becomes aware of a nearby presence. Halting her angry shouts, Gwen becomes still.

A voice echoes off the walls, starting as a whisper but growing louder, until it seems to come from everywhere at once, surrounding her. It comes from the darkness itself. Gwen pushes herself back against the wall, afraid.

Don't cry, my child. You're not alone. The voice is clear and beautifully masculine, neither baritone nor tenor, perfect and rich in its smooth, even tone.

Gwen looks about nervously. The voice, both unsettling and enchanting, sends a chill through her body.

Am I imagining this? Am I going crazy? She wills her eyes to see through the darkness covering her, trying to find the source of the sound, needing to see if it's real—to convince herself that her mind hadn't completely snapped. Her eyes are as useless as ever. She wishes she could probe with her psyche for the presence, to enter its mind and inspect it herself, but the pit prevents her from using magic. The mental wall separates her from the source of all the creation and she wishes vehemently to tear it down.

"Who's there?" she whispers, fearing an answer.

You know me. I have always been with you, watching over you, guiding you along your path, the omnipotent voice replies. The presence wants to placate her, but she refuses to accept this stranger as a friend or even as a reality.

"I don't know you, and I have always been alone. I am no one's child!" she shouts into the black void. A long, eerie silence follows.

I am your God, your Creator, the creator of all things. You have suffered so much, but I will save you from your suffering. All you need to do is submit yourself to me, my child. I will make everything better. I will destroy your enemies and give you everything your heart desires, the voice promises, the sound growing stronger, echoing off the walls, making them shake with the might of his words.

"God has forsaken me. I am not His, and you are not the Creator. You are a fake! I will be no man's servant. You make promises you cannot keep. I don't need you or anyone else! I'll save myself!" she screams, hatred and passion spewing forth from her lips as she shakes in violent anger.

Foolish girl, you are here because you are too weak. I can make you strong. From whence do you think your power came? It is my power and majesty that you draw from, my glory that you bask in when you control the forces of the universe. You are nothing without my favor.

"Enough. Leave me. Go away!" She feels like a fool for talking to herself but does not care. She doesn't trust the evil voice, and will not listen to him anymore. Yet he keeps talking, promising her power and riches, trying to flatter her, and, at the same time, belittling her as if she were insignificant.

In an attempt to shut out the voice, Gwen uses her old

defenses learned long ago when she first been forced into Legion's bed. She closes her eyes and buries herself in her memories, searching for a place and a time better than the present. She tries to focus on a memory, any memory, until she sees every detail, remembers every sound, every touch, every taste and sight, immersing herself in it. She transports herself to that time, shutting off the here and now.

Digging into her mind's storehouse of memories, she tries to find something distant, something completely unrelated to the mess she's in, something long ago. She finds a vague memory of her childhood, one of her very first memories, if not the very first. She wraps her mind around the vision like a blanket, drawing it in around her. For anything is better, any place safer than here, trapped underneath the ground, trying to keep from going mad, cut off from the world and those who love her, and the power that has protected her from harm. She would gladly trade places with the little lost girl she had once been, rather than be stuck in the bowels of the earth as a captive from daylight.

CHAPTER TWENTY-SIX

Prisoner

"Gwenevere!" Raven shouts into the darkness as he sits up abruptly. His hand reaches out for something or someone. Panting, Raven looks about the room. He sees his bedroom window is open, the curtains rustling in the cold night breeze.

Shirtless, Raven sleepily stumbles out of bed and makes his way to the window. He firmly shuts it and gazes out into the night a moment before turning back to get into bed. When he finally turns around, something stops him dead in his tracks. A man stands in the corner of his room, still as a statue. His silver eyes stare at Raven without blinking. Raven realizes that the man does not breathe, neither does he hear the man's heart beat. A scent hits him now that the night air is not disguising it. A combination of copper, death, and frost. Raven recognizes that scent instantly. *Vampire.*

This sudden encounter brings to mind the run in he had with four Vampires a few days ago. His pack had dispatched all but the youngest of Vampire women while suffering a few casualties of their own. The young, impetuous Jason was with them no more. Raven automatically switches to fight mode and growls at the intruder, preparing to leap at him.

"Be still, Wolf," speaks the Vampire, vacant of emotion. "We don't have time for this. I see that you have, rather unfortunately, met with some of my kind recently. Vampires from a place called Bec LaNuff." He says the last as a statement, not a question.

"You're the one they spoke of, aren't you? The one who took Gwen?" Raven asks the motionless, lifeless man, his chest heaving, barely able to contain his rage.

"I am Angelo, yes, but what you were told was only a half truth. Gwen escaped on her own. I helped her find the opportunity," the Vampire confesses as he looks down at his feet, misery in his lightly accented voice.

"So, then where is she?" Raven demands, still on guard.

"They caught her. They took her back to… him." The Vampire's voice seems to strain at the word *him.*

"Do you mean the Master that the black Vampire mentioned?"

"Yes," Angelo answers.

"That Lucca fellow said she needed to ask forgiveness for something. He said this Master would make her suffer for her betrayal."

"Yes." The Vampire pauses for a moment. "Look, it's a long story and there is no time to get to know each other or for you to learn to trust me. I came here for help. I cannot storm a fortress by myself, and every moment we delay is a moment that may bring her closer to death," Angelo adds, pleading in his voice.

Raven struggles to know what to say or how to react. *This could be another trap, a ploy to lure me away from the pack just to kill me.*

It is not. You must trust me, speaks the Vampire inside Raven's head. Raven jumps back in shock, finding his back pressed against the cold glass window.

Yes, Gwen and I share that particular talent. The Vampire answers the thought that barely began to form in his mind. *I can show you everything that happened. I can make you understand in a couple minutes what I ask of you. All you have to do is let me into your mind completely.*

Still a bit hesitant, Raven nods. He feels the Vampire enter his mind, and then something like a home video begins to play within his head, starting with the moment Angelo first laid eyes on Gwen.

* * * * *

Angelo stares down at the chunk of wood in his left hand, watching it transform by the knife whittling away at it in his right. He knows he is only indulging in this useless exercise to keep his hands busy and his mind distracted. He also knows that it is failing

miserably. All too soon his masterpiece is complete. With a dissatisfied sigh, Angelo looks down at the wooden object in his hand and wipes the wood chips off his blade, swiping it on his pant leg.

The elegant and ferocious panther is sleek of body and beautifully crafted. He looks into its eyes and imagines for a moment that they flash yellow-green back at him. Closing his eyes, Angelo allows the piece of wood to fall to the dirt at his feet.

"How much longer must we wait?" Dwayne asks. Angelo looks up at the young, brunette Werewolf across the campfire and shrugs.

"You don't know?" Quincy, another member of the pack barely out of his teens with blond spikey hair that complements his golden eyes, speaks up. "I thought you Vampires are all-knowing and all-powerful?" The young Wolf mocks.

Angelo ignores his tone and looks to Raven, who stares into the fire as if entranced by the dancing flames. "I'll know the moment they're within a few miles of us, no sooner. You may even smell them before I do. If they choose to be, the fair folk can be very stealthy," Angelo adds as he folds up and pockets his knife.

Quincy grumbles. Dwayne nods and throws a stick into the fire absentmindedly.

"I don't suppose we'll know for sure when the other pack might be joining us?" Angelo asks no one in particular. This earns him a few grumbles but no reply, not even from the pack master.

Raven's pack consists of seven men. Their leader, Keefe, is a fit middle-aged, dark-haired, Caucasian man with streaks of silver at his temples. He leans against a tree trunk at the edge of their little camp, waiting for the Native American brothers Heluska and Nawkaw to return from patrolling the woods. The last is Amani, a teenage African-American boy who paces back and forth through the little clearing of the camp. His grief-stricken face shows evidence of the turmoil he suffers within. The recently departed Jason was his best friend and first link to the pack. He, as well as all the others, is anxious to be here. They feel in some way that Jason's death has already been avenged with the slaughter of Lucca and his three female Vampire children. Their allegiance to Raven has brought them here to the valley below Bec LaNuff mountain, although in their hearts they feel this is not their fight.

Angelo takes a large breath, sampling the smells in the forest around them. Dirt, foliage, water, pine needles, animal fur, sweat, Wolf, burnt wood, and smoke. His ears only pick up the sounds of crickets and the wild life nearby, barely masked by the crackle and pop of the camp fire. *No Fairies, not yet anyhow.*

That morning Angelo tracked down Gwen's Fairy friend Morna. Her family nest rests on the other side of the Poconos mountains. They met a good distance from her home so as to not alarm the other Fairies, who might have panicked at the sight or smell of Vampire.

Morna readily agreed to help in Gwen's rescue. She promised to bring her family and to enlist the help of the local Witch coven as well. She said she would bring whoever would join them and meet him at the base of the mountain, and then together they would all plan the attack on Bec LaNuff.

The hour grows late with no sign of their reinforcements. Angelo glances at Raven.

"We don't have to wait for the others before we come up with a plan, do we?" The others, including Raven, perk up at this. Raven's gaze meets Angelo's for the first time since the Vampire woke him in his bedroom. Raven hadn't handled the revelation of Gwen's enslavement well. Angelo senses his mental turmoil as Raven struggles with his own guilt, believing that somehow all this is his fault.

"Fine. How well do you know this place?" Raven asks. The pack, including Amani and Keefe, gather near the fire to join the conversation.

"Very well. I lived here for a few years a while back."

"All right, so where's the best place to attack? Is there a secret entrance we can exploit?" Pack master Keefe questions.

"There are only two ways into Bec LaNuff: one at the base of the mountain and one near the peak. The bottom entrance is unguarded and easy to access from the outside if you know where to find it. However, only a Vampire is capable of entering through that route."

"Why's that?" asks Amani, his black skin glowing golden brown in the fire light.

"Because it is a crack in the mountain wall barely big enough for a man to force his way into, and from there it leads to a cave.

The only way out of this cave is an opening in the ceiling, which is a vertical two mile shaft without hand holds or footing. Believe me when I say that you would have to have wings to get into the fortress that way."

The pack takes in this information with disappointment. Raven asks, "So how do we get up to the peak, then? Is there some kind of trail up the mountain that leads to it?"

"No. No path will take you there. You might find one to take you part of the way but the place I speak of is near the apex. There is no way to climb up to it," Angelo answers with solemnity.

"Then what are we doing here? It's impossible to get in." Quincy's young voice takes on a nervous tone. Raven shoots him an annoyed look but his younger pack mate ignores him.

"That's why we need the assistance of Fairies or Witches. I can leap to the mountain top and enter the fortress from above, but once there I am just one man against many."

"Could you carry one of us with you to the top when you leap?" Keefe inquires, arms folded across his chest.

"Possibly." Angelo runs a hand through his curly locks. "Only one at a time though, and it would take several trips up and down the mountain."

"And we'd have to hope no one discovers us," Amani adds, shaking his head in frustration.

"Am I the only one who sees that we are totally outnumbered? It's eight of us against thirty Vampires. Not to mention the Ogre guards, the Trolls, Giants, Dwarves, and the Elves." Dwayne curses under his breath and turns away, walking toward the trees.

"So if the Fairies and the Wiccans don't show, what are we going to do?" Raven asks, desperation clear on his tan face.

Angelo meets Raven's gold eyes with a determined look, his jaw firm and clenched. Before Angelo can reply, Keefe speaks up.

"You have to decide, brother," The pack master address Raven. "Is it worth risking your own life to save this girl? If you walk away and leave her to her fate, will you be able to live with yourself?" Although his elder asks these things respectfully, Angelo sees outrage within Raven's eyes. There is no question of if he'll attempt to rescue Gwen. It is a matter of when and how.

"No matter what you all choose to do, I'm going in. Alone if I must," Angelo announces firmly.

"You won't go alone. Even if it's a suicide mission, I'm going with you." In that moment Raven and Angelo understand each other. Angelo feels Raven's jealousy and mistrust of him evaporate.

Angelo suddenly senses someone besides the pack members nearby. Heluska and Nawkaw emerge from the forest into the camp from opposite directions wearing identical expressions of alarm.

Immediately everyone jumps to their feet.

"Vampires are near!" Heluska, the older Indian brother, proclaims.

"I smelled some to the east and north of us, too. We might be surrounded," his little brother adds.

"Then it's time to fight," Keefe declares.

"No," Angelo protests. "We split up, and regroup by the creek. Separately we can out run them. If we take a stand now, we won't be able to surprise them when we attack the fortress tomorrow. If they see us, they'll send word back to Bec LaNuff that we're here. Next thing you know the whole army of the mountain will converge on us."

"All right, there's wisdom in this. Where do we meet?" the pack master asks Angelo.

Mentally Angelo shows them all the creek's location fifteen miles away.

"Agreed. Everyone move out," Keefe orders. Instantly, everyone disperses. Raven puts out the fire while the others disappear into the woods. The pack master waits for Raven at the edge of the clearing.

"We will get her out." Angelo quickly takes Raven by the hand. "Thank you for being here. The fault of this whole mess is mine alone."

"It doesn't matter now. I promise no matter what happens, I will set Gwen free!"

"If I don't make it out of this alive, I need you to give this to Gwen." Angelo slips an old gold key into Raven's palm. Raven looks down at it quizzically. Before he can ask what it's for, Angelo adds "Gwen will know what it is. She's been there before." Raven nods his assent.

The two unlikely allies pat each other on the back before they step back from one another and move toward the trees. Angelo watches Raven follow his pack master into the woods. Then, he, too, turns and flees into the dark of the forest.

* * * * *

Ivan hurries down the long stone hallway toward the grand chamber as best he can with one limp leg, shuffling along with excitement in his eyes.

That little Witch will pay dearly for what she did to me! He smiles wickedly to himself, imagining Gwen's reaction when she hears the news.

The two Ogre guards aside the chamber doors abruptly stop talking as Ivan approaches. With hands on their sword hilts they turn their misshapen faces to look at him, bearing identical looks of expectation.

"Open the doors!" Ivan barks at the guards.

"You know the rules, Ivan. I have to announce you first, and you don't have an appointment." Nimgraw, the senior of the two guards, addresses him while adjusting the armor about his thick torso for emphasis.

"I don't need an appointment to see my Lord!" Ivan hisses.

"Lord Legion likes his privacy. If he says you need an appointment, then you need an appointment, and I have to announce you before he'll let you enter the grand hall," Nimgraw informs the Vampire in an even tone.

"Then announce me already, you twit!" Ivan huffs.

Nimgraw scowls before nodding to his second in command, Winnew, to start the tedious process of opening the massive stone doors behind them.

"State your purpose in seeing the Master." Nimgraw demands formally.

"My purpose is revenge." Ivan almost giggles in demented glee. Nimgraw gives him an incredulous look, but before he can speak a word, Ivan continues. "Tell our Lord that the valley patrol has stumbled upon a group of trespassers. Tell him to expect company. They're bringing in a prisoner!"

CHAPTER TWENTY-SEVEN

Terrible Dawn

Days have passed since they dumped Gwen into the pit, and even longer since she had the sun on her face or fresh air in her lungs. The air she breathes is old, musky, and rancid. The longer she stays in this dark prison the more her lungs struggle to work properly. She can breathe, but not well, and she can feel the effects of hypothermia gripping her body.

Gwen's still soaked t-shirt and jeans cling to her chilled flesh, weighing her down. She knows she needs to get out of her damp clothes, but she figures no clothing at all would be worse in this dank, dark place. Her bare feet are painfully numb and as cold as blocks of ice. Her hands shake violently. Gwen finds it harder to touch her fingers to her thumb as time goes on.

"That's a bad sign Gwen," she whispers to herself, the sound surprisingly loud in the silence that engulfs her. "He left you to die down here. Either that or he wants you to go mad."

In utter hopelessness she holds up her left hand before her eyes, even though she cannot see the ring on her finger. With a fierce guttural cry Gwen suddenly punches her fist into the wall with all her might, the ring hitting the stone with a loud metallic clang. A painful jolt shoots up her arm at the impact, causing Gwen to stumble backwards, slipping on the rocks beneath her feet. She almost loses her balance and crashes into the water.

Her knuckles are cracked and bleeding. She can feel the deep imprints in the flesh of her palm from her nails. Gwen brushes her right hand over her left hand. The ring is completely unharmed.

The world of myth has not been kind to Gwen. Even from her childhood, she found no place in this world or the human one—except with Raven. He is the closest thing to family she has ever known, loving her as he did like a protective older brother. And now trapped as she is, she finds her greatest regret is that she might not ever see him again.

"But Angelo would have gone to see Raven, right?" she asks the darkness. The image of Raven and Angelo propelling down into her dungeon and rescuing her comes into her fantasy. Quickly she shakes the image from her mind.

"If they come here, they will both die." She knows this with a certainty that clutches a cold fist around her heart and squeezes it tight. The thought is too painful. As much as she wishes with all her heart to see either her best friend or her lover again, she'd give her own life to keep them both as far from Legion as possible.

No, she couldn't hope to be rescued. She only prays that Legion will put her out of her misery at last, letting her die in peace. She hopes that Legion never finds Angelo. Only the most painful of deaths awaits him if he ever crosses Legion's path again.

Gwen closes her eyes tight and slaps her hands over her ears to banish the sudden thought of Angelo's beautiful voice crying out in absolute pain. She can almost hear him calling out her name.

When Gwen finally opens her eyes and drops her hands into the water, she hears a faint sound above. She freezes. Straining her ears, she struggles to identify the noise. She can hear it coming closer. In a frenzy of arms and legs Gwen dives into the water and swims to the other side of the well, scrambling onto the highest rock to get closer to the sound.

Yes, she knows that sound. It is the slow shuffling footsteps of Ivan. The footsteps echo loud in her ears until they stop right above her head. Looking up, she sees the light of the torch in his hand. It casts a pale glow on Ivan's ugly grimace of a face.

"Hello, your highness!" Ivan calls down, mocking her in his thick Cockney accent. "Are you ready to beg for forgiveness yet? Or would you like to stay down there and stew in your own filth a little longer? What do you say?"

Gwen hears him clearing his throat. He spits down into the pit, his projectile missing its mark by a foot. He laughs and sneers down at her.

"What, you ain't gonna talk to me today either? Still think your too good for me, right?"

Gwen stares up at him, her face cold and unfeeling as marble. She ignores the bitterness in his voice as she says, "You are nothing but Legion's mangy dog. You may lick his feet, but I will not."

Ivan spits again, and this time it hits Gwen on the shoulder. Ivan laughs triumphantly as Gwen wipes the spit off her sleeve, disgusted. She narrows her eyes at him with a look of true hatred.

"Say what your Master sent you to tell me, dog."

The smile on Ivan's face vanishes instantly. "If you weren't so proud, little Witch, and gone along with whatever Legion asked, you wouldn't be in this mess right and about to face your doom."

Ivan spits the words at her with such venom and violence that he practically shakes with his rage.

"So he is going to put me to death then? Good. It's about time," Gwen responds dispassionately.

"Oh, he's not gonna kill you, love. He has something far more interesting planned to repay your betrayal." He sneers again, baring his fangs. They gleam white and deadly in the torchlight above.

Inwardly Gwen cringes, but doesn't show her horror to Ivan. Ivan laughs as he swings over the edge of the pit and plummets toward her. Instead of dropping like a rock into the water, he swoops down and grabs Gwen by the waist, holding her against his body tightly, and flies up to the mouth of the pit once again in an instant.

Once their feet touch the ground again, Gwen shoves with all her strength against him. Ivan holds her firmly, his disgusting face inches from hers. He smiles maliciously, baring his fangs again, licking his lips in a threatening way. He wheels her around, twisting her arm painfully behind her back, pinning it in place, and shoves her in front of him.

"Remember, Witch, no matter how pretty your little face is, it ain't half as pretty as your blood is splattered on the floor. You just try and escape, and I'll have no regret whatsoever in spilling every last drop of it. Got me?" He twists her arm even tighter.

Gwen bites into her lower lip to keep from shouting in pain, but says nothing as he pushes her out of the small dungeon chamber. They continue through the corridors and passageways of the mountain fortress. She holds her head up high and walks on as though Ivan weren't there, as though she were merely going for a stroll instead of being led to a meeting with fate.

* * * * *

Ivan pushes Gwen into the grand chamber, forcing the crowd before them to part. He leads her to the massive throne on the far wall of the room and roughly throws her down upon her knees before it.

Legion sits upon the throne, like a king looking down upon his subjects. He is surrounded on both sides of his throne by his Vampire underlings. The chamber is full of Legion's loyal followers and slaves, made up of a myriad of different mythical creatures.

She immediately rises to her feet and looks at Legion, her face revealing nothing of the turmoil and fear she feels within. She stands as erect as a queen despite the shiver down her spine and her wet dripping clothes. At her feet a puddle of water forms, mixing with the blood from her bare, torn-up feet.

I will deny the hunger, the fear, the cold and the humiliation he wants me to feel. I will never give him the satisfaction of seeing me weak. I will never be broken! Gwen chants to herself over and over again, drawing strength, as if the words alone can nourish her depraved, battered body.

Legion notices none of this. Ignoring Gwen's presence entirely, he gives his full attention to the little twit of a human standing next to him. Simple-minded Julie stands on his right, in the position of honor, the place where Gwen once stood. Upon the sight of Gwen entering the room, Julie's smile vanishes as her face goes white with fear. Without thought she releases Legion's right hand and takes a few steps back, lowering her eyes to the floor.

A frantic chattering sweeps through the chamber. All eyes turn to Gwen. Some look with respect, others with the intent of boring holes into her flesh. Only then does Legion turn his attention to the assembly. He raises his hand and immediately a silence falls like a blanket upon everyone. At last Legion looks at the dark, proud girl before him.

Gwen meets his pale, silver-white eyes. Once she had been made a fool by those very eyes. Now with great ease she resists the hypnotic power of his gaze and faces him as though he were nothing but a snake to be crushed beneath her heel.

He might have everyone else fooled, but she no longer sees the beauty in his pale, lifeless face. She did not have the same illusions of him which she once had, once upon a time when she was Julie's age.

She couldn't really blame the girl. After all, Gwen was once that naive. Only now she sees all the little cracks in his stony countenance. He is nothing more than a vulture, a parasite that feeds on the innocence of others, the weakest of all predators. And deep down she knows that he is afraid of her, even more than the sun in the sky.

A dark, malicious smile spreads slowly over Legion's face as he looks upon her. The sinister gleam in his eyes sends a jolt through her body. She never knows how far he will go. While all Vampires have ancient traditions and laws that they live by, and even judges and a king that they obey. Legion believes himself above those laws, answering to no one. The only thing that has ever frightened him is Gwen, and the knowledge that she could destroy him.

Something in his eyes tells her that the humiliation and degradation is not over yet. He will not simply let her die. He will torture her until his own vile appetite for suffering is satisfied, his wounded pride appeased. Only then will he allow her the release of death.

With a gesture of Legion's hand, Ivan steps forward, eager to follow his Master's command.

"Bring him," Legion orders.

Ivan hurries across the room with as much speed as his lame mangled leg will allow. The crowd parts before him as he exits the great chamber.

"I have a gift for you. A little entertainment, so to speak." Legion says. Nonchalantly he snaps his finger. One of his human pets steps forward, holding a large bowl of fruit. He holds the bowl beneath Legion's outstretched hand and waits patiently for his Master to choose from its contents. Legion pulls out a sprig of grapes and waves the young servant away indifferently.

Holding out the grapes, he turns to Julie, who still stands timidly against the wall, not looking at Legion. Clicking his tongue and holding out his hand to her as if she were a dog, he beckons her forward. Reluctantly, Julie steps up to his side and takes the grapes, quickly eating a few to appease her Master. She averts her eyes, as if looking upon Gwen would turn her into ash. Legion reaches out his hand and pats her on the head affectionately.

Legion wants Gwen to feel how far she has fallen by comparing her depraved, sickly form to Julie and her rosy cheeks, her full stomach, and beautiful attire. Gwen ignores this. Inside she is panicking, yet outwardly she struggles to maintain control. *Who is this "he" that Ivan was sent to bring forth? Could he mean Angelo, or even Raven?* She can't bear the thought of either of them being in this place, not now. *But who else can it be?*

"Aren't you curious what I have in store for you?" Legion

smiles smugly.

"We could do without the theatrics. This is between you and me. We don't need an audience."

"Oh, yes we do. It's much more exciting this way. Besides, I have to make an example for the others." Legion looks down his nose at her with his usual aristocratic air. He smiles condescendingly at the whole room.

"Then kill me already. There's no need to drag it out," Gwen replies coolly, as casually as if talking about the weather.

Legion laughs. On either side of him, the Vampires laugh amongst themselves, baring their fangs as they smile at her maliciously. When Legion's laughter subsides, he stands to address the entire chamber.

"You must choose: Shall I be merciful and grant a quick death to our unfaithful Queen, or should we punish he who tempted her? She is only a child. She was beguiled, led away by one of our own, one who has centuries of wisdom. One who should have known better." Legion's booming voice fills the chamber, the audience enraptured by his every word.

All around her the room erupts, Vampires shouting in agreement, others in outrage. Several chant, "Kill the Witch!" Others call out, "Death to the traitor!" Many stay silent, afraid to speak out against Legion, afraid to show that their allegiance lies with the condemned and not with their Lord. Legion smiles broadly at the assembly, enjoying the tumult and noise, thriving on the hostility and anger he's created in his subjects.

Ivan enters the room again. Legion holds up both of his arms in a gesture that causes all of the assembly to fall silent. A cold shudder shakes Gwen to her very core. Every head turns. Only Gwen refuses to follow Legion's gaze. She refuses to move, refuses even to turn her head and look over her shoulder. If Legion's words had not confirmed her fears, the sensation of Angelo's presence nearby is the final nail in the coffin of her hope.

The room erupts with shouting and name-calling. The assembly is enraged and impassioned by the prisoner Ivan leads before him. He brings the bruised and battered man inside and sits him beside Gwen at the base of Legion's stony throne.

It takes everything in her power not to throw herself into Angelo's arms and weep, to hold him close and beg Legion to spare his life. Instead she stays in her place, erect and emotionless, trying to keep her heart from bursting and her eyes from overflowing with fresh tears.

She doesn't turn to look at him, afraid to see what they've done to him. If she were to look at Angelo, all her strength and fortitude would fail her. She can't let that happen. She will obtain no pity from Legion. Her pain will only entice him to hurt Angelo more, just to watch her heart break before his very eyes. If she and Angelo have any chance of surviving this ordeal, she will have to hold everything in. Angelo needs her to be strong enough for both of them.

"What will it be then? The Witch?" Legion pauses, holding out his hand towards Gwen. He looks to the audience expectantly.

A great many roar in approval, shouting all manner of obscenities at her.

Legion looks down at Gwen, a self-satisfied grin on his face. Addressing the audience, he goes on. "Or shall it be the traitor? He who takes what does not belong to him?" Legion hisses the words through his teeth. He gestures in Angelo's direction and waits for his followers to answer.

The reply is a tremendous cry of voices, many chanting again, "Death to the traitor! Death to the traitor!" The number of the voices shouting for Angelo's death doubles that which spoke against Gwen.

There has to be something I can do, some way I could save him. There has to be hope. This can't be the end. Not like this. I've been through too much and loved Angelo too dearly to watch it all disappear now.

"Bec LaNuff has spoken." Legion smiles with sadistic glee while the assembly erupts in shouts and jeers of approval.

Two human servants seize Gwen and turn her towards the door. Finally she sets her eyes on Angelo, or what is left of him. For the briefest moment their eyes meet. His face, now paler than ever, is sunken in, his eyes set in dark chasms. His once lush brown hair falls out in strands, cuts and gouges all over his bare arms and chest. His entire body is covered with dried blood. Angelo's once-perfect muscular build is now emaciated and sickly. The jeans he wears hang loosely about his too-visible hip bones. Despite all this, he tries to flash her a smile, his dimples barely visible in his hollow checks.

Gwen can't stop the sob that catches in her throat or the tears that drip hopelessly from her eyes. They stare at one another until Ivan and a few Ogre guards take hold of Angelo. They lead him out of the grand chamber, Gwen and the rest of the assembly following in a procession. She can only see little glimpses of Angelo through the Ogres around him as they lead him down the hall and up towards the stone balcony above.

Realization dawns then, and Gwen is full of apprehension as they come near the steps to the balcony. *What time of day is it? Is it light out?* Gwen doesn't know until they reach the top of the stairs and sees the early morning sky beyond the archway. It is still dark, though dawn is not far off. Crippling horror fills her. She stumbles against her human escort, barely able to keep moving. A sudden surge of anger forces her to act. She shoves herself hard against one of her guards, knocking him against the wall of the tunnel. He loses his grip on her and she slips away from the other guard, making a mad dash towards Angelo and his death troupe as they march through the stone archway onto the balcony.

All at once Gwen's body constricts, the air around her confining her, rooting her to the spot. With a feral growl she tries desperately to break the invisible bonds. Legion's cold laugh comes from behind her. She watches as he walks slowly around her. Gwen pants, her nostrils flaring in her rage. Legion turns to face her and smiles smugly, as the procession waits behind her in the tunnel and the stairway beyond.

"Obviously his death sentence will be carried out as he fries in the morning sun, but I wouldn't want you to miss your last moments together. It gives me pleasure to tell you that you'll have a front row seat to his demise." Legion's smile is beyond triumphant, his eyes manic with twisted joy.

Suddenly the bonds of air around her carry her forward, her feet moving without her control, walking her out on the balcony. Legion follows. Only now does Gwen notice the two wooden posts standing opposite each other in the center, anchored to the ground by large rocks holding them erect in place.

Her body is compelled towards the one on the right and she finds herself turning towards it, her back against the post. Legion snaps his fingers and the two human guards, now recovered from Gwen's attack, spring on her, one grabbing her wrist and the other forcing her roughly against the wooden post. She feels the pain and cold steel on her flesh as her hands are bound tightly together in strong iron manacles.

Across from her, weak and lethargic, Angelo is bound more securely to his own post by the Ogre guards. Ivan stands nearby, instructing them. The hideous Vampire looks up when he feels Gwen's gaze and, smiling, bows his head toward her in a mocking salute. Gwen ignores him, emotionless, and averts her gaze toward Angelo. After he is bound by several chains, his hands manacled behind his back, the Ogres and Ivan step away and return to the archway. Legion is left alone with them, out in the open, dressed like a king and arrogant as ever as he smirks at them both. He looks up into the brightening sky and closes his eyes, taking in a deep breath of the fresh mountain air.

He turns to Gwen, his face somber. "Gwen, I wanted you to know… I never really wanted to harm you. However, this should be a reminder that you are mine and belong to no other. As long as you live none may touch you but me." His voice is dark in its sincerity.

Legion turns his gaze on Angelo. "You, I trusted above all others. You, to whom I owe my life, I have loved more than a brother." Legion's voice cracks and he takes a moment before he continues. "Your betrayal breaks my heart more than you shall ever know. It pains me to do this, but it must be done. I forgive you, Angelo. Go into darkness in peace."

The pain in his voice shocks Gwen, but she is not able to see his face as he leaves them. Gwen watches the chief Vampire slowly recede back into the safety of his fortress, the rest of the citizens of Bec LaNuff following behind, back down the stairs and out of sight. Only Ivan, a few Vampires, and the Ogre guards are left behind, watching them from the safety of the stone archway.

"Gwenevere." She turns to look at Angelo, his voice hoarse and dry. "I'm sorry, Gwenevere, this is all my—"

"Don't, Angelo. It's okay. I..." Gwen struggles a moment to find the right words. "I have no regrets. I love you." A tear streaks down her cheek, her voice trembling with emotion.

Still Angelo continues. "Gwen, there's something I have to say. I can't leave you like this..."

His words break off as the sky brightens above them. Gwen can feel the heat of the sun as it begins to crest the mountain's peak. Terrified, she looks back to her love, not wanting to watch his death but unable to tear her eyes away from him. As he begins to speak she tries to forget the world around them, tries to will the sun to stay hidden, and wishes it were in her power to keep at bay the terrible dawn.

CHAPTER TWENTY-EIGHT

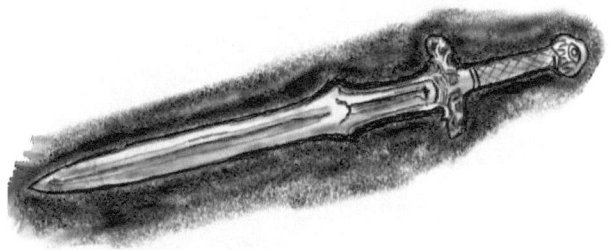

The Offspring

A chorus of howls fills the early morning, echoing off of the valley below. Startled Angelo and Gwen both turn. A torrent of wind along with a great tumult of shouting and chanting rise up towards them, growing louder. All at once men and women and massive wolves float up and land on the balcony before them. More and more follow after them, strangers crowding the stone platform.

The Ogre guards charge forward to attack the intruders. Ivan, suddenly terrified, orders them back. "We're outnumbered, you fools! Fall back to the grand chamber. Hurry!" he orders as he turns and flees inside along with the other vampires.

The Ogres are not so lucky. Men and women descend upon them, some chanting spells, others hurtling balls of fire and light towards them as the Ogres attempt to hew them down with their swords. Blood and the scent of burnt flesh are carried on the early morning breeze.

A large gray wolf howls at the sky and charges after the Vampires, his pack following close behind on his heels. The animals' howls echo off of the tunnel as they scurry down the stairs and out of sight.

A dark-skinned woman hurries toward Gwen with an entourage of women behind her.

"Who are you?" Gwen asks. She can't hide the relief in her voice.

"I am Juniper Jefferson, leader of the Monroe Coven," the woman replies as her fellow Witches start to unbind Gwen.

"No, help Angelo, not me! The sun is rising and we have to get him inside!" she shouts at them urgently.

Juniper looks at her, shocked. "Why should we save the life of a Vampire?" she asks, her voice laced with disgust.

"Gwen!" When she hears his voice, Gwen turns away from Juniper to see Raven running toward her.

"Raven! How did you find me?"

"Angelo tracked me down. The whole pack wanted to help when we heard you were in trouble." Gwen smiles, overjoyed at the very sight of him. "Where is he?" Before Gwen can respond, an unnatural scream is heard above the tumult of the battle around them. Gwen gasps as she realizes that the sun has risen.

"Angelo! Someone help him! Please, Raven, get him inside now!" Raven hurries towards Angelo. Gwen is unable to see either of them through the group of Witches surrounding her. His tortured screams pierce her ears.

The Wiccans free her from her bonds and Gwen rushes to aid Raven. When she catches sight of them, her heart stops. Angelo writhes in pain, still bound to the wooden post, flames engulfing him, his skin charred black beneath, his cries relentless as the sun continues to rise above him. The fire's heat makes it difficult for Raven to get the manacles off of him.

Gwen turns on the Wiccans around her. "Save him! Please, I beg of you. Do something!" she pleads, desperate. When no one moves or says a word, she turns back to Angelo, preparing to save him herself.

Gwen reaches out to her power, tries chanting a spell to put out the flames. Nothing happens. The words are as useless, as if she spoke in gibberish. The power is not there. Pain shoots through the ring, up her fingers, in the veins to her chest, and Gwen collapses to her knees with an anguished shout of defeat.

"Gwen! You're alive!" Morna lands on the balcony and rushes towards her, smiling with tears in her eyes. Then Morna sees Gwen's face and her anguish, and her smile disappears. Angelo's screams catch the fairy's attention and she looks upon him in horror. Recognition dawning, she hurries to Gwen's side.

"Angelo!" she cries in stunned horror.

"Can't you help him?" Gwen asks her friend as tears stream down her face.

Morna nods curtly and hurries over to Raven.

"Stand back!" she shouts at him, and he makes room for her. "*Na-cu wae, no-cu wae, em-ba sae, na-cu wae,*" the Fairy chants with her palms outstretched towards Angelo.

Gwen watches as the flames move toward Morna, as if sucked into a vacuum disappearing into her palms. Her hands and her arms turn bright red as the heat is consumed within her, the little fairy's body quaking under the strain. With a shout, Morna stumbles back, the heat unbearable, breaking her spell. The fire, however, is momentarily extinguished.

Raven moves quickly, breaking the steel manacles around Angelo's wrists. He carries the Vampire's limp and blackened body from out of the sun and into the dim archway.

Gwen finds the strength to stumble towards them, falling to her knees at Angelo's side.

"Angelo? Angelo, speak to me, please," she pleads. He lies motionless, no remnants of his striking beauty left. He is nothing more than a charred mass of flesh. The smell of him makes her choke as she begins to sob. "What did you have to tell me? Say it! Speak, damn you! Please!" Gwen pushes Raven aside and gathers Angelo into her arms, not caring as the heat of his corpse burns her, her clothing beginning to spark wherever it's touched.

"Gwen, he's gone," Raven whispers urgently in her ear. "I'm sorry, but you have to let him go. You'll catch on fire if you don't."

"He needs blood," Gwen half whispers. Wild-eyed, she looks about for something sharp. Her eyes alight on a pointed rock nearby and she scrambles to it. Hurrying back to Angelo's side, Gwen takes the sharp edge of the rock and presses it to her wrist, swiping it away with a quick gesture. Gwen gasps at the pain but bites down on her lip to control it..

"Gwen, no! What are you doing?" Raven demands in terror, grabbing the bloody rock from her grasp.

Gwen ignores him, placing her bleeding wrist above Angelo's burnt, flaking lips, cradling him with her other arm. The red fluid drips through his slightly parted lips into his mouth. Desperately, Gwen tries to squeeze more blood out of her veins into her lover.

Behind her, Gwen hears the battle between the Ogres dissipating, the Wiccans starting to gather around her. Gwen ignores them, her eyes fixed on Angelo's burnt, mutilated face, willing him to move, to show any sign of life. Gwen starts to panic. "He needs more blood. It's not enough." Gwen lunges at the rock in Raven's hand, intending to open every artery in her body if needs be.

Raven leans back, turning quickly to hurtle the rock against the side of the mountain where it breaks into several pieces with a loud crack. Gwen stares at the place the rock hit with a bewildered glare.

"Morna, please can you try to heal him?" Gwen asks in a shaky voice.

"I can try." Morna whispers. Still holding Gwen against her, Morna reaches out one hand toward Angelo's singed body. "*Mae, Mae cura fi ry, cura betta wae.*" The fairy chants, rocking with the rhythm of the words.

Gwen watches Angelo intently for any sign of change,

willing him to open his eyes, to move even a finger. After ten minutes Morna slowly stops chanting and goes silent. Gwen stares at her lover numb, unable to speak.

"Gwen? Are you okay?" Morna kneels beside her, gently prying Gwen's arms free from Angelo's smoldering corpse. Numb, Gwen lets Morna gather her into an embrace, her gaze drawn to the remains of the love of her life. Tears blur him from her vision as her body shakes with wrenching sobs, blinding out the throbbing pain from her wounded wrist.

"I'm sorry, Gwen," she hears Raven say. "I swear I will get the bastard who did this. I have to join my pack now. Where can I find this Legion?"

Gwen looks up at Raven standing above her, her face changing from stunned sadness to deadly rage. "No, I'll be the one who kills him. Nothing would make me happier." Gwen's voice is acid steel.

"You're too weak child, and untrained," Juniper Jefferson speaks up. "You should not be wielding any magic at all."

"You worry too much, Sister Juniper," a younger woman with bright yellow hair chimes in, addressing the dark-skinned Wiccan. "She is bound to him by the rings. She can harm no one."

"Yes. Leave the Vampires to the Wolves, child, and come home with us. You are in great need of healing," an elderly woman with all-gray hair and purple eyes adds. She reaches out to Gwen as if to tear her from Morna's arms.

"Come with us. We can protect you." Now a tall man in his

thirties with green eyes and brown hair steps forward, one of the few male Wiccans present.

"I'll find him, Gwen. Please go with them now. Get away from this place," Raven pleads. The howls of the wolves echo up the stairs. Without another word, Raven turns and runs to their aid.

Gwen watches him go with a jealous need to follow and join the fight. "You wouldn't help him," Gwen accuses the Wiccans. "You stay up here while the Wolves fight this battle alone, outnumbered! You are all cowards. I do not belong with you." She looks at the Wiccans who surround her, these strangers who think they can swoop in and take her away. She hisses at them like a demented stray cat. She startles the lot of them, a few falling back, apprehensive. Gwen stands, and taking Morna by the hand, races into the tunnel and back into the hell that is Bec LaNuff.

* * * * *

Gwen leads Morna down the stairs towards the great chamber. The ornate doors stand agape. The Ogre guards lie dead in bloody heaps in front of it. The sounds of fighting emanate from within. Men shout and beasts bark and growl as they struggle to kill one another. Vampires throw Wolves against the stone walls, while the Werewolves bite off the heads of the Vampires, or tear them limb from limb. Their bloodcurdling screams reverberate off the walls of the cavern. Not many of The Forsaken have joined the Vampires in this fight. A piece of metal catches Gwen's eye. Without hesitation she swoops down to pick up an abandoned bloody dagger which she can use as a weapon.

Gwen looks into the grand chamber, looking for some sign of Raven or Legion. She spots Raven in wolf form sparring with Ivan, the scene almost a reflection of the one she saw in her nightmare not long ago. Raven leaps towards Ivan, who quickly sidesteps the wolf. Catching the animal in midair, Ivan throws Raven to the hard granite floor. Raven yelps in pain, stumbling back on his paws. The two encircle each other, Raven trying to gather his strength for another attack. Raven suddenly dives at Ivan with snapping jaws, catching the Vampire's right ankle in a sharp bite. The vampire roars in pain, falling to the ground, as Raven begins to gnaw at the already mangled limb.

Gwen points in Raven's direction and Morna follows as they make their way through the throng. Ivan scans the floor for a weapon, something, anything he can use to defend himself and finds a large blade. Raven, however, doesn't see it. He releases the Vampire's leg and makes a move, as if to pounce upon his captive.

"Raven, no!" Gwen calls out, but it is too late. Just as the Wolf leaps toward him, Ivan swings the blade, slicing the animal across the belly. Gwen hears the mental scream of the man simultaneously with the wretched howl of the animal. Raven falls limply besides Ivan, lying on his side, the rise and fall of his chest labored. The Vampire smiles wickedly at the defeated creature and rises to his feet, blade raised, preparing to cut the beast's head off.

Gwen's banshee cry comes only an instant before her dagger

meets flesh. Ivan stops abruptly with his blade above his head, his eyes wide in shock. He looks down at the blade wedged in his chest and laughs ruefully. A screeching wail, reminiscent of a thousand banshee cries, erupts. The sound sends blinding pain into Ivan's cranium. With a scream, he drops the sword, the metal clanging as it hits the marble floor. The Vampire clamps his hands over his ears in a feeble attempt to block the excruciating racket out. He hears the scrape of metal on the floor and only has a moment to register Gwen's face before him, holding the sword in both of her hands. With a warrior's battle cry and all the strength she possesses, Gwen swings the blade. In a gush of blood and gore, Ivan's head and hands separate from his body. The rest of Ivan the Trusted finally falls to the ground, forever dead.

Morna ceases her screeching. Gwen spares only a moment to pull her dagger from the Vampire's heart before turning to Raven. Her eyes fix on Raven's naked form, lying injured near the ostentatious gold piano, blood gushing from his abdomen. Exactly when he changed back into his human form she doesn't know, but the mere sight of him makes the severity of his wounds all the more real.

"Raven!" Gwen cries out. The Witch and the Fairy run to his side as the others continue to battle about them.

"Gwen," Raven gasps, blood gurgling from his mouth and down his chin as he gags. He reaches towards her. She takes his hand and presses it against her cheek.

"You'll be okay," she tells him. "You hear me? Morna is

going to heal you. She's going to stay with you." Gwen looks down at the bloody dagger in her shaking hand, whispering to herself, "They all have to die." She gives Raven's hand a squeeze. "I'll kill him. His reign ends today!" Gwen promises, her voice stealthy and cold as she turns to leave.

"Wait, Gwen. This is foolish. Please don't!" Morna begs, her large golden eyes frantic.

"I'd heal him myself but I can't. I'm useless as long as I wear the ring." Gwen explains to her friend, taking Morna's hand and placing Raven's hand in hers. "I will return when I have spilled every drop of his blood." Gwen turns and rushes into the fray, leaving Morna to stare after her in bewilderment.

Raven gasps for air. Morna turns her golden eyes to him, his likewise-colored eyes gazing up at her, frightened. All at once Morna feels a deep spiritual connection with this man.

Overcome by emotion, Morna gulps. "She'll come back. I swear, you and I will see her again," she promises. Closing her eyes, Morna chants a healing spell.

* * * * *

A small girl stands before the open doors of Bec LaNuff's grand chamber, seeing before her hell itself run rampant. The smell of so much blood entices her Vampire hunger, while the sight of so many of her dismembered comrades strewn about sickens her. She gulps, numbness seeping into every pore of her miniature Vampire body. Her maker, Lucca, never returned from his hunt for the Witch, and neither had her blood siblings Jezebel, Lethawyn, and Ryan. She's felt alone and adrift since she felt their final death through their blood bonds. The other Vampires are still family, but not her blood. Across the room through the carnage she sees Lord Legion, the Master of all Bec LaNuff and Ruler of her kind. It is her duty to rush to his side and fight for him, to put her life on the line to protect her liege, yet she is rooted to the spot. The immortal blood in her veins is liquid ice as she watches a Werewolf tear a Vampire's head right off its shoulders with its massive jaws. All allegiance forgotten, Lynette turns and rockets down the hall.

* * * * *

Gwen shoves her way through Vampires and Beasts, ignoring them all as she searches out her prey.

She finds Legion grappling with an oversized gray wolf. He manages to get a hold of the beast's jaws as they try to clamp onto his throat. With a guttural yell, Legion wrenches the animal's jaw apart, tearing the top of the animal's head clean off of its body. Blood splatters across Legion's torn and kingly attire. He wipes the blood from his face and licks his fingers casually, staring dispassionately at his victim.

"Legion!" Gwen shouts. Startled, the Lord of the Mountain turns a wild eyed stare toward her.

"So the Coven came back for you, did they? And they brought

their mangy pets with them, it appears." He gestures arrogantly at the Werewolves around them as if they were pups. "I don't see any of your comrades with you. Could it be they don't want to risk their lives for you? Wiccans may pretend to be noble but they are not fools. They know a lost cause when they see one." He steps over the body of a fallen Vampire, hesitating only a moment to recognize one of his lost children before turning his icy glare back to Gwen. "Werewolves are not very bright and will charge headlong to their deaths, even for one as insignificant as you, darling."

"He's dead." Gwen replies, ignoring his insults. "Not that you care. And now you will join him." Gwen's voice is dark and empty, her eyes wild. She raises the dagger in her right hand, staring him in the eye.

Legion laughs. "You've lost your mind, my dear, if you think a puny piece of metal like that can protect you from me." He sneers at her as he saunters closer.

"It dispatched Ivan with little effort." Gwen says, smiling coldly. "However, this blade isn't for you. Even if I were quick enough to cut off your head, I wouldn't grant you such a merciful death." Gwen holds out her left hand palm down, curling all but her ring finger into a fist. The gems of her awful wedding ring gleaming in the lantern light, on her only protruding finger.

Legion stops dead in his tracks. With a half-crazed yell, Gwen brings the blade down. Blinding pain shoots through her arm as the weapon severs her finger from her hand, just above the first knuckle. Her finger falls to the ground in a spray of blood. Free of its anchor now, the serpent ring clatters to the floor, rolling away across the stone tiles.

Gwen drops the blade, clutching her injured hand with her able one, her knees buckling beneath her. As she falls, she chants, *"Da-day winda, cura longa, babeta lavota,"* over and over again until the pain fades away, and her body is restored. The bleeding stops as her hand heals over, leaving a fleshy stump just above the knuckle where her ring finger used to be.

Gwen looks up for Legion. He is nowhere in sight. She mentally searches for him amongst the fighting forms in the chamber, but he is no longer in the room. She senses him, lower in the fortress.

Feeling the magic serge through her, untamed and unshackled by the ring, makes her feel euphoric. Gwen collects all the energy she can muster, filling herself to the brim. In her rage she absorbs more and more energy until it threatens to overtake her completely. Bec LaNuff begins to shudder and vibrate, as if attacked by some monstrous earthquake. With her rage at the boiling point, Gwen releases it all at once. The surge of power spreads forth, an explosion of light from Gwen targeting all her enemies in a fatal strike. In an instant every Vampire and Ogre that fights in the grand chamber is extinguished, their cries of alarm cut short as they burn out of existence.

Overcome with the power of the magic, Gwen laughs like a lunatic and bolts for the door. *Legion, unlike his spawn, is still very much alive,* she reminds herself.

Like a wild animal Gwen bursts from the grand chamber. She charges down the corridor that leads to the lower levels. Her mind searches for her prey amongst the many living things within the mountain.

She screams wildly as she enters the stained glass courtyard, many of the citizens of Bec LaNuff fleeing before her. The mountain trembles as the stained glass dome shatters above her, colored shards raining down. The wails of pain from the injured fall on her ears as the rest of the inhabitants flee like roaches scattering.

Using all the power in her mental voice, Gwen shouts out a warning to all the citizens of the mountain. *Get out! Get out now or you will all die under the mountain!* she warns, feeling even as she sends the message that her control over the force around her is beyond her reach. She cannot stop it now. *Emon, get Vinita and get out now!* Gwen sends the private message to the proper source, feeling the mind of the Elf in his quarters with his comatose mate. With that, Gwen continues downward, heading for the servant levels.

There is only one place on Earth that coward would go to escape me. One place he would hide to keep himself safe. She skids to a stop as she almost passes by her old room and hurries inside.

"Where is it?" she shouts. "I need it!" She tears the room apart, power surging through her as her mind goes into a frenzy, causing the mountain to shake more violently. Suddenly she spies the white gleam of the Guardian Stone on the floor in front of the bookshelf, lying next to her fallen leather jacket. Gwen smiles triumphantly, a mad gleam in her eyes.

* * * * *

Legion drops out of the sky into the black abyss below, splashing down into the water as he hits the pit bottom. He momentarily submerges in the water before he shoots out again, leaping through the air and landing atop a crop of rocks along the edge of the wall.

Above him the mountain trembles. *She's gone mad,* he realizes. *If she plans to kill me by pulling the mountain down on top of us, then she's a greater fool than I thought.* He knows he could count on Gwen's arrogant headstrong nature, sending her straight to the place where her powers are useless. He doesn't have to wait long before the naive little mouse lands right into his trap.

With a lunatic yell, Gwen drops like a stone into the water. Legion waits for her to emerge but she doesn't. Legion dives in, disappearing below the surface.

A moment later, the two of them burst forth from the water's surface. Gwen struggles to stab Legion in the heart with her dagger while he holds her hands captive and tries to bite her. With a wild rage, Gwen suddenly rams her skull into Legion's forehead. The sound of the impact echoes against the stone walls, as Gwen's vision blurs and the room spins. She hears Legion cry out in pain as he releases her hands.

Still disorientated, Gwen slashes the air with her blade, hoping she might catch the Vampire while he's momentarily incapacitated. When her vision clears, she realizes that Legion is no longer there. She grabs for the Guardian stone in the pocket of her now-wet leather jacket. She tries to pull from the magic stored within. She can feel the magical source writhing within the very molecules of the stone, but she can't pull the energy from it to form a spell. Gwen chants a few favorite magic words anyway as she frantically turns in place looking for any sign of him. The seconds drag on in eerie silence. while the mountain trembles. Rocks dislodge from above and fall into the water around her, as the spell she unleashed tears the mountain apart. Gwen stops, steadying her breath as she scans the dark water. She can see very little in the dim light cast from the torchlight in the cave above.

What if there's a way out of the pit under the water? Legion has lived here a long time. He knows every route of escape. The thought troubles her. *I can't lose him now. I can't walk away without knowing once and for all that he is dead. I can't spend the rest of my life looking over my shoulder, watching the shadows,* she tells herself.

As she prepares to dive headfirst into the water, something grabs her ankles and drags her below. Gwen lets out a yelp of surprise, managing one deep breath of air before she's pulled under. Once below the surface she sees that her legs are in Legion's steel grip. He floats beneath her without straining, needing no air to survive. Gwen thrashes, desperately trying to free herself. It is useless. Her opponent is much stronger than she. Changing her tactic, Gwen dives down towards him, causing him to lose his grip on her as she bends and twists her body to attack him, the dagger still in her hand. He smiles at her through the murky water, his brilliant white teeth and pale, unearthly eyes glowing in the dim light. Gwen crashes into him, and makes a try for his heart, but Legion catches the blade in his hand, forcing it from her grip. Gwen kicks him in the gut, sending Legion somersaulting through the water, away from her. She seizes the moment and makes for the surface.

Gwen gasps for air as she quickly swims towards a cluster of rocks. She scrambles to get out of the water and as far from the edge as possible. She crouches on the rocks, watching the pool around her desperately. Legion does not resurface.

Above her, Gwen can sense the mountain tearing itself apart. She knows she has very little time to kill her target and still escape. Then a realization hits her. *Without magic I cannot hope to get out of this pit. I can't fly or leap high enough to reach the opening.* She tries to shrug it off. *That doesn't matter now. All that matters is that I see Legion dead... finally.*

Still she sees nothing in the water. "Come out, you coward! Only the spineless rape a child. Only the gutless hide when judgment comes. For once, act like a man and face me!" Gwen's frenzied screams echo and bounce off the crumbling cavern around her.

From her peripheral Gwen sees something move, but she reacts too late. Legion grabs her by the leg and tries to drag her back under the water. Gwen clings to the rock as she fumbles for the Guardian Stone in her pocket. Her hand wraps around it and she turns onto her back, twisting her leg in Legion's grasp. He laughs at her in his usual mocking tone and moans in painful pleasure as his fangs break forth from his gums. Before he can bite down on her bare ankle, Gwen retrieves the rock from her pocket.

"Burn in hell!" With a triumphant yell she flings the Guardian Stone directly at his chest.

A blinding light bursts forth when it hits him, engulfing him in it. Brain-shattering cries reverberate off the cavern walls as the mountain falls about them. Gwen cringes backwards, barely rescuing her leg from being consumed by the deadly light.

Just before the light extinguishes, Gwen hears a tremendous rumbling from above. She looks up to watch the mountain fall down upon her. Closing her eyes, she braces herself, ready to be crushed and buried alive.

* * * * *

Morna surveys the devastation around her. Bec LaNuff, this mountain fortress once proud and tall amongst the majestic Poconos, is now sunken in upon itself, nothing more than a heap of dirt, plants, and rubble. She watches as the Wiccans search through the debris for survivors, using magic to aid them. The moans of the wounded and the wailing of the disheartened emanates from the impromptu shelter the Wiccans built for the survivors. Under a crop of trees lay the dead of Bec LaNuff in several rows.

Morna stands at the foot of the nonexistent mountain. Nearby, what's left of the wolf pack huddles together, naked. Some receive healing incantations from the Wiccans.

Perched on top of a boulder one man sits alone, staring into the wreckage of Bec LaNuff as if all the life has gone out of him, his bare back turned away from his pack. He hunches over, seeming not to care that he's naked and sitting on a hard lump of rock.

Even from afar, Morna can tell that Raven is crying silent tears. Her heightened Fairy senses can smell their distinct saltiness, hear the gasping breaths of the sobs he holds within. and feel the anguish that he struggles to bear. Her heart aches all on its own, but somehow, seeing Gwen's childhood friend suffer like this only multiplies her pain tenfold.

Moments after healing him, the mountain began to fall apart. Morna warned the other Wolves to get out before she managed to prop Raven up onto her back. She flew out of the chamber and up to the balcony with great effort, trying desperately to keep the unconscious Raven from falling to his death. Not long after, the rest of mountain came down, an enormous dust cloud rising into the air. When the dust settled, the Wiccans showed up to save what was left of the inhabitants of the fortress. None of the survivors are Vampire.

As the hours pass with no sign of Gwen, Morna fights the anger and resentment that builds within. Morna pleaded with her family to come with her to help save her Wiccan friend. Some of her nest were willing to aid her, but most were not. This left the decision to the Fairy Queen. The woman Morna had admired all her life forbade any of the Fairies to assist in the rescue of the Witch called Gwenevere. "Had she noble blood or any claim of importance, then it would be our duty to help, but where she is an unwanted orphan and imprisoned by our mortal enemy, I cannot permit it." Morna tried to argue but the Queen silenced her with a cold disdain. "The tribe of Fae Ree has much dwindled. Our numbers are too few. I will not risk the life of one of ours to the hands of the Vampire, not even for a Witch." Despite this decree, Morna slipped away from the nest in the early morning hours, leaving behind her home and her own kind forever.

Bringing herself back to the present, Morna tries to focus on the positive. Even if she failed to save her friend, there are others Gwen loves who have survived. The Elf scholar, Emon, the one that Gwen told her about, was found half dead in the grand library with his unconsciousness elfin mate. Instead of fleeing the disintegrating mountain, he went to the library to save as many documents and books as he could. His last minute decision to hide under his large, indestructible desk saved both their lives.

Anyone in the lower levels of the fortress, such as the servant quarters, is most likely dead. If any survived the destruction, their chance of rescue is hopeless, buried too far beneath ground to ever be located, even with magic. Few of the human servants are alive.

Morna remembers the names of Gwen's former serving girls, and hopes at least to learn their fate. Gwen always wanted to free them from their imprisonment. She felt she owed it to their dead brother and cousin, Peter.

But I don't know what Lydia and Jessica look like, Morna realizes. She glances over to where Raven still sits. *Perhaps I can ask Raven to help me search for them. A useful task such as that might help him keep his mind off of Gwen. At least till they find her.*

The Fairy tries to convince herself that her friend is not dead, yet part of her fears the worst. Morna slowly flies to Raven, her heart heavy yet strengthened with new resolve. From this day forth she will stay by his side, her oath of friendship to Gwen transferring to her fellow orphan.

At least he won't be alone, Morna thinks. *If Gwen is found, dead or alive, I will stay with him throughout the days of his life and watch over him for Gwen's sake.* Although comforted by this thought, Morna still gives a silent prayer.

Lord of Darkness or God of Light, whoever is listening, I beg thee to spare the life of Gwenevere if she be not already dead. She deserves a better death than to be buried alive with her enemies, The Forsaken and their lost offspring.

A sneak peek at

THE THIRTEEN TRIBES OF CAIN SERIES

Book Three

The Decree

*T*he pain is all she knows. It is everywhere and nowhere as if her body is made of it instead of flesh and bone. Gwen has no sense of space or time. The only thing more real than the pain is the weight of the mountain crushing her. She wills her body to move, nothing. Her eyelids are lead, taking effort to force them open. There is nothing but darkness. The smell of blood overpowers the scent of dirt, rock, and water in the air. She opens her lips to take in a breath and tastes blood, the only moisture in her otherwise dry mouth. She coughs and blood spurts out onto the dark stone surface before her. Instinctively, Gwen moves as if to wipe the blood away from her mouth. She finds she can't feel her limbs at all.

I wouldn't be surprised if every bone in my body is broken. The realization should cause her to panic but she's much too befuddled to think or feel just yet.

With effort Gwen tries to remember where she is or how she got here. Her memory is a fog, her head throbbing fiercely.

It feels as though I've got a concussion, she muses trying to collect herself.

Flashes of images pass through her befuddled mind as everything begins to click back into place. Being attacked by Vinita in the park, waking up in Bec LaNuff in her old room, trying to kill Ivan, and then…

Gwen closes her eyes tight not wanting to recall the events that happened afterward. Nonetheless, Angelo's visage comes to her mind. She'll never forget the look on his face before… the sun rose and burned him out of existence.

Choking on the sobs that come unbidden, she can't keep his screams out of her head. She can't un-see his charred, blackened body. Her arms still remember the feel of his stiff and lifeless corpse. She groans in pain both physical and emotional, not sure which hurts worse. She lets the tears come now, letting all her agony pour out of her.

The rage that sent her after Legion to avenge Angelo still pumps through her veins. She recalls the crazed state of mind she had been in when she decided to cut off her own finger. The goal was to sever the ring that bonded her to Legion. Maiming herself hadn't been of any importance in the heat of the moment. Oddly, Gwen feels the sensation of that missing finger as if it is still there. In some ways it feels more real than the digits she has left.

Everything that happened afterward: Raven being injured, Morna staying behind to heal him as she chased Legion though the fortress seems a bit fuzzy. However, her struggle with Legion in the pit is crystal clear now.

I'm buried under the mountain, Gwen realizes. *Or, at least what's left of it.*

She recalls releasing the power that tore Bec LaNuff apart. At the time she hadn't cared about anything other than killing the monster that had enslaved her and murdered her love.

How am I still alive? She asks herself, not completely certain she wants to be living at all.

"You're alive because I'm not finished with you yet," a voice answers her unspoken question. It is in her mind just as much as it reverberates off of the rocks around her.

Gwen stiffens, knowing instantly the person behind that disembodied voice.

No, not you again!

"Of course, it's me. I have always been with you," the voice replies as the image of the dark stranger takes shape in her mind. The first person the lost orphan had encountered after coming to, wandering in the snow ten years ago. "After all, who else would look after you as I have?" She tries to push his image away but he refuses to let her mind go onto other thoughts. He is everything, there is nothing else.

"Why can't you just leave me alone?" she yells. Her voice echoes, and then disappears as if she never spoke.

"What an absurd thing to say." He smiles in her mind, his pitch black eyes devoid of soul or light. "You are mine, child. You see, I'm very heavily invested in the outcome of your little life."

"What are you rambling about?" Gwen's not sure if his words are confusing because the man speaks nonsense or because she's had a few knocks to the skull. "You're nothing more than a figment of my imagination brought on by delirium and depression. The only thing you're *invested* in is seeing me lose my mind!"

"Nonsense," he chuckles. "Everything you have endured, everything you have suffered, I have made possible so that you might become that Witch you were destined to be!"

"Say I believe you, and you're not imaginary. How exactly does making me suffer make me into anything other than a mostly dead freak who no one can love? What kind of destiny is it you're preparing me for?" Gwen coughs up more blood, her throat aching from the overuse. "Besides, what's the point of going on without Angelo?"

Gwen was too busy letting out her rage at the dark stranger to realize that his image has finally left her mind. She waits for some kind of response from the man but she feels as though his presence has left.

She hates to admit it but she's not relieved to have him go. Without him she is just a trapped thing waiting to die, alone and un-remembered.

Writers depend on their readers

Thank you for taking the time to read my book! The Forsaken is book one in a the six part Children of Cain series, to keep up to date on the releases of future volumes in this series you can follow me at any of the following:

www.rjcraddock.com

http://rjcraddockauthor.blogspot.com/

https://www.goodreads.com/RJCraddock

www.facebook.com/RJCraddockAuthor

https://twitter.com/RJCraddockwrite

Your feedback is appreciated

A story not read is a story not realized. You the reader give my words life; your imagination brings them one step closer to reality. If you enjoyed getting to know Gwenevere and reading about her world, please leave a review on the following sites:

https://www.goodreads.com/RJCraddock

http://www.amazon.com/dp/B00DQA9OZI

http://www.barnesandnoble.com/w/the-forsaken-r-j-craddock/1115287679

ACKNOWLEDGMENTS

Credit goes to my husband for watching the
kids so I could get away to writer's retreats to finish
this book. Also, to Rebecca Rode for having a fantastic
cabin and being willing to let us all retreat there to write.
To D.W. Lundberg and Juli Caldwell for being my editors/
proof readers. To my beta readers for their excellent
feedback, especially Ron Millett. I wouldn't be able to do
this without the help of my wonderful critique group:
Adrienne Monson, Karen Pellet, Rebecca Rode,
Mary King and Karyn Patterson. Thanks also
goes to my publisher and design team at
Transcendent Books.

R. J. CRADDOCK

Born Ruth Jerraisetti Harris in Oka Tamuning, Guam, Ruth is the youngest of eight children. As a young child she began telling stories, developing unique characters, and conjuring fantastical worlds in her mind. As she grew older, a thirst for reading overcame her and she devoured all kinds of books, finding kindred spirits in classic novelists such as Dickens, Bronte, and Fitzgerald. She started writing her first novel at age eleven. After high school she attended the Art Institute of Phoenix to pursue her other great passion: Art. Ruth now lives with her husband and four sons in Springville, Utah.

www.ingramcontent.com/pod-product-compliance
Lightning Source LLC
Chambersburg PA
CBHW022234020726
47496CB00004B/903